Gathered Waters

Gathered Waters

CARA LUECHT

WhiteFire
Publishing

This is a work of fiction. All characters and events portrayed in this novel are either fictitious or used fictitiously.

GATHERED WATERS

All Scriptures quoted are from the King James Version of the Bible.

WhiteFire Publishing
13607 Bedford Rd NE
Cumberland, MD 21502

ISBN: 978-1-939023-30-8 (print)
       978-1-939023-31-5 (digital)

To my mother, Linda Edwards,
for her patient reading of every version of this story,
and to my grandmother, Sally Ricker,
for making sure we all knew the stories
of her grandfather, Hjalmer Blomberg.

Chapter One

January 1880 – Karlskrona, Sweden

It was not by my plan, nor was it a mistake. My husband would say the change in our path was by design. It didn't matter. Our path, divine or not, began in our home in Karlskrona. That night, like so many others, I waited. I haunted the window, drawing the edge of the parlor curtain over to feel the chilled air seep off the glass. I hoped for my husband but scanned the long shadows for the dreaded bishop and his men. I dropped the lace, only to return minutes later to repeat the ritual.

But that night a stranger accompanied my husband. A bitter wind flattened their coats to their bodies. Afternoon had weakened the sun, and frost gathered in the shade, on the lowest branches of trees and on the eastern sides of rocks and fence posts. I pressed my hand against the glass, and when I removed it an iced print remained.

They walked side by side with coats buttoned to the top and scarves wound around their necks. With each gust of wind, they lowered their faces farther into the fabric until their mouths and noses were covered. I watched the strange man pull gloveless hands from his pockets and bring them to his mouth, blowing warmth into the hollow of his palms. He rubbed them together before searching for relief in the deep recesses of his coat. His tense posture spoke of one who had been cold for too long.

I let the lace slide back into place and crossed to the hearth where the carved mantle stood well over my head; a gift of timber from my husband's family land to the north. Dark, solid, and ancient with almost no hint of a grain—one glance at the flawless carvings and glassy finish and there was no doubt why furniture with his family's Modig name was prized. I jabbed at the logs with the poker, stoking the already roaring fire.

Not only was Anders late, but it seemed he'd brought a guest. I remembered the last time we had guests at our table, when I was still a prominent hostess. Had I known, I would have put on a fresh collar.

I gave the fire one more poke, watched the sparks rise and fall, and placed the heavy iron on the hearth before moving back to the window to check their slow progress.

The children and I had waited for dinner. We had waited for more than an hour, but when the hour had passed and Anders still was not home, I instructed our housekeeper to keep the food warm in the oven. I knew the kind of response my request would garner; Elsa's warm red lips pursed out slightly and turned down at the corners. Of course, never enough to argue with, never enough to raise questions, but sufficient to communicate her distain for the way I managed the household. I had informed our nanny, Liona, that the children should be fed in the kitchen.

I turned back to the room and checked my reflection in the parlor mirror. Elsa was not a beautiful woman. I ran my fingers over my collar and down my waistline, smoothing the white shirt and tucking it farther into the black waistband of my skirt. The sewn pleats laid flat against my hips and fell in even gathers to the floor. Soon, I would have to let the waistband out again. I checked a stray strand of hair and tucked it behind my ear. Elsa had skin like a sausage, and a body to match.

The dining room table was set for two. We had not had dinner guests in some time. All had been quiet after that last, abbreviated dinner with my parents. We were advised to reconsider our questionable business decision. My face stayed flushed for hours after we walked them to the door, my sister's furtive, apologetic expression the only comfort. Our church friends disbursed soon after, as the investigations at the hand of the bishop intensified. But that evening the setting looked safe, the china modest and solid, and the room comfortable. I had become accustomed to the sparse two-person service.

"Elsa, we'll have a guest for dinner tonight." I entered the kitchen through the heavy, swinging door. "Anders and another man are on their way up from the stables."

Elsa made a grunting hum and nodded her understanding. I knew I should have asked her to respond more appropriately—certainly Anders would have been unhappy if he knew—but I didn't want to. I was tired, and she did her job well enough that I had no real complaints. I turned back to the parlor and prepared to meet our guest.

With a flurry of cold air, Anders opened the door. He followed the stranger in, stooping his six-foot-five frame just a bit to avoid the top of the doorway. In tandem, they removed their hats and shook off the cold. Shards of icy snow fell from their shoulders and disappeared into the rug.

"Brianna, I would like for you to meet Johan. He'll begin work at the base next week. Johan, my wife, Mrs. Brianna Modig."

I hadn't thought we were hiring any more laborers to blast stone for the troublesome Navy barracks project. Business was steady, but until it warmed up we didn't plan to push production any further. I sent Anders a questioning glance that went unnoticed.

"It's nice to meet you." Johan bent slightly with his greeting and continued on with the standard complimentary language of a guest.

His accent was clipped and business-like, unlike the typical workers at the base whose speech tended toward softness around the edges of the syllables, lacking in the crispness that spoke of a formal education beyond the primary years.

I thanked him and gestured toward the parlor.

His clothes hung loosely and were worn in the typical places—elbows, knees—and when he had removed his hat I'd noticed the threadbare fabric under his arms.

Once in the room, Anders motioned to one of the upholstered chairs near the fire. Johan entered, knees and shoulders prominent under his ill-fitting clothes. At some point in the past it was likely his finely tailored suit had fit his more robust form. The fabric was heavy and expensive, and the stitching looked professional. On a healthier body, the suit would have been impressive.

Johan sat in the proffered chair, relaxing against the fire-warmed cushions. His hands at rest, his fingers lax against the arms, they attested to his accustomed comfort in a room like this one; one filled with the luxuries of upholstered furniture and polished floors.

Anders and I took the sofa opposite Johan. I couldn't read Anders's expressions, but the fire warmed and lit the area, and the soft crackle of wood succumbing to flames filled the room. Had I known how this man would change our lives, I might not have been so lulled by the mundane pleasure.

"Johan came to my office today," Anders said. "He's from Varmland but traveled to the base in search of work." I smiled in welcome, wondering why a man of his obvious education and apparent family money would look for work as a stonecutter, or worse, a blaster.

I had been to the base when the work first began. I watched the dust-covered men labor like ants on a hill. I shouted questions to Anders over the hammering and drilling. He pointed out the foremen and the laborers, and told me when to anticipate the shrill call that warned the men of the coming explosion that stretched mere seconds into hours. How I held my breath waiting for the tremor and held further for the plume of dust and dirt expelled from the cavern. Johan was not a stone blaster. He was not one of those men.

"There were no open beds in the bunkhouse, so I said he could stay in the carriage house until a bunk opens up."

"And I truly appreciate that." Johan smiled. "I am looking forward to a good night's sleep."

So many men were looking for work. Families were hungry. Children subsisted on herring heads and bread made from anything that could be foraged out of the snow and ice. We had plates full of food. Johan and Anders continued to speak of work. Even the cuffs on Johan's shirt hung too large for his wrists.

At one time, years ago, the farms surrounding our home in Karlskrona were filled with thriving families. But generations of too many sons meant one hundred fifty acre farms were fenced off into parcels of less than ten acres—plots not big enough to support even a modest family. Animals grazed in the woods because every inch of tillable land that could be forced to grow rye for the family's bread was turned over year after year in hopes of a better winter than the last.

People, their family names recorded for centuries in the parish books, were moving away from inherited farms—their childhood homes—in order to scrape out a living in the soot-paved cities; rocky soil exchanged for cobbled streets. Neighboring farmers, who used to support their wives and children by their skill and hard work, grew dependent on their wives' abilities with a needle and their children's backs as hired-out farmhands. The interest had to be paid, even when shrunken parcels of land could not support the weight of the mortgages.

Johan, though, was not one of those men. His speech was trained, his vocabulary eloquent, sprinkled with cultural references and current political events. He had my attention, maybe even admiration.

The expensive mantle clock ticked while he sat with perfect posture under my scrutiny.

"Excuse me." We all turned to see Elsa standing in the doorway of the dining room. "Dinner is ready." She bowed slightly and turned, but not before Anders gave an appreciative nod. She smiled back with closed lips; just a wet slit set deep in ruddy cheeks. I would never understand Anders's loyalty to the woman.

"Well, I'm famished." Anders slapped his hands on his knees. We stood, and he motioned for Johan to join us. I fell into step, behind the two men. My husband hadn't consulted me about opening our home to a stranger. I prayed we wouldn't regret his decision.

Dinner that night was typical and unimpressive: sausages, potatoes, and bread with jam. Anders sat across from me, Johan to his right. Our guest looked hungry and was losing the battle to appear indifferent. Anders bowed his head.

We were both raised to give thanks at each meal, and we raised our children to do the same, even though our unfortunate tension with the bishop meant we were not presently attending church. But as Anders prayed a sincere prayer with Johan as our guest, thanking God for life and family, food and friends, his words rang archaic, and I wondered what the guest thought of Anders's devotion.

The chair under me had grown uncomfortable, reminding me that I had wanted to make new cushions for the dining room. I decided to go to town to look for suitable fabrics; possibly something in red, with flowers.

I cracked my eyes while Anders continued and allowed myself a surreptitious glance in Johan's direction. His eyes were closed. I noted the beginnings of lines forming in the corners, and they gave his face an aged look I suspected he hadn't earned. His high cheekbones and strong jaw line appeared severe and were at odds with his unfashionably long, dark blond hair. What I did not see, however, was any vestige of uneasiness. He appeared to pray as sincerely as we did, or as sincerely as I would have if I had not been so oafishly staring at our guest.

I bowed my head and tried to concentrate in time for the final "Amen."

Anders picked up his fork and speared a potato. "Johan will begin work in the office distributing the workers' pay."

Johan nodded in agreement, already chewing a piece of sausage. "There are simply too many for me to process anymore."

The base work was now in full swing, although Anders had bid for the project when we were still living near his parents in Varmland. After he was awarded the contract, we moved to Karlskrona in order to be near the base. There were over one hundred men employed to blast and cut stone. When the work on the structures began, there would be more than three hundred.

Johan cut another bite of sausage, picked up his glass, and took a long drink of water. Thankfully, we were blessed with a good well. His Adam's apple bobbed with each swallow. He set the glass back down on the white table cloth. "How long do you expect the project to take?"

"Most of the blasting will be done in the next couple of months. Some of the cutters are already working now, and their numbers will increase as more rock is hauled to where it needs to be on the base. Maybe another month before the first crew of bricklayers begins their work. After that, approximately a year and a half until our contract is complete. We should be done and off the base by August of next year."

I moved the potatoes around my plate. The cooling grease from the sausages turned my stomach over. I watched Elsa as she darted in and out of the room, trying to discern if she had chosen sausages specifically to vex me. The ceramic fireplace to my back radiated warmth from its painted tiles, and I wanted to escape to my room.

"A year and a half worth of work," Johan mused, bringing me back to the room and our guest. "How many men have you had to turn away?"

Anders's lips turned down and his eyes fell to the humble chunks of meat and root vegetables on his plate. Jobs were few, and seldom was there a day when he was not greeted at his office by a line of barely shod men who had left hungry families tucked away in peasant cottages while they searched for work.

"I turn away a few." Anders shifted in his chair. "I prefer to hire men who have experience working around stone. Especially this time of year, when it's so cold and the stone can break in unpredictable patterns." He sat back and addressed Johan directly. "I also will not hire anyone who doesn't appear to be strong enough for work, and I won't consider anyone who appears drunk. We do not need injuries." Anders continued to stare at Johan to gauge his reaction.

Johan nodded his understanding.

"I've already told Johan…" Anders began.

I looked up from my fork with its coagulating grease as Anders glanced at me.

"We provide no beer during working hours, and if the workers come from the midday meal appearing to be under the influence of it, they are sent back to the bunkhouse and will lose that day's wages."

Anders turned back to his guest. "Sometimes this causes men to decide they should search elsewhere for employment, but with blasting and cutting stone, I won't have them risk their lives more than the job already demands. I don't want this project to be one where the time to completion is punctuated by the crushed bodies of the laborers."

There was no beer at our dinner table. There had not been for some time. I was sure Johan noticed but was polite enough not to inquire. It made me fidget, knowing we did not offer Anders's guest—our guest—the smallest of comforts, available at even the most humble of dwellings.

Johan took an intense interest in his remaining potatoes. "I never drink beer of any kind," he confessed to his plate.

Anders's gaze darted to me, and a precarious silence filled the room. I wondered if Johan was one of those men who drank until they had destroyed their own lives; it would have explained his obvious turn of luck.

"Undoubtedly." Anders looked to Johan. "Undoubtedly, you have noticed there is none at this table."

Or, I thought, maybe he was part of some religious sect eschewing any drink that affects the mind. That would have explained his seemingly sincere prayer. He watched us with what I imagined to be the same questions in his mind.

The last time we entertained guests without the courtesy of the drink was that final dinner with my family. They visited because my father wanted to see the project at the base. Dinner after the tour did not go well. The bishop stopped by, and our food was abandoned. It cooled on our plates while my mother berated me in the kitchen and my father and the Lutheran bishop conversed like old friends.

There was no secret, no mistaking how they felt. Their evaluation of our decisions was not a mystery. Thinking he had won, the bishop left that evening with a smile. My parents delivered their warnings and left in silence.

Anders and I stayed firm in our resolve. If we hadn't before been convinced that the church intruded where it was not welcome, if we hadn't already known how presumptuous and prying our families could be, if we hadn't experienced firsthand the consequences of stepping out of our expected roles, we might have never have questioned our place there.

But it was too late. We'd already scrutinized our lives and found them wanting. Something had to change.

I looked to Anders and Johan, who in turn watched me, and each other, and the silence gave way to the clinking sounds of forks and knives against plates as we found our way to an uncertain kinship.

Chapter Two

Anna's coffee, laced with cream and sugar, was a rich brown that made me think I should like to be swallowed by it, rather than the other way around. I wrapped my fingers around her colorful pottery, welcoming the comfort after the cold—even if relatively short—ride.

"I'm sorry I haven't made the trip to see you, Brianna," my sister said to the bright cup in her hands. "You know how it is. Father and Mother seem to find ways to dictate my days even from across the way."

Anna was resigned far too early to her post as spinster. I watched as she picked up her spoon and swirled it around, the designs on the surface of the liquid changing with each small movement. Though not beautiful, she was strong with broad shoulders and large, almost masculine wrists and hands. The bread she baked with its hard crust and tender middle was infused with security.

"Don't concern yourself with it," I said. "I wouldn't expect you to visit in the dead of winter anyway."

She lifted one corner of her mouth in a half-ironic smile, knowing my daughter Hulda and I did exactly that.

Hulda played in the front room, out of sight from where I sat, but close enough so I could hear the motherly words of a seven-year-old to her baby doll.

That morning, I'd risen early and dressed quickly. After the previous night and the strange dinner with Johan, I wanted to talk to someone.

"How angry is Father?" I asked Anna, not really wanting an answer. She continued to stir.

When our parents had visited our home, they'd come to be impressed. For my mother, it was the quality of the food, the polish on the silver, and the cleanliness of Hulda and Hjalmer. For my father, it was the business.

That day, he and Anders left me to sit with my mother and discuss who had fallen on hard times, whose children did not obey, and who were the latest of the poor in the parish to relinquish their tiny farm to the bank and emigrate to America.

Anna's kitchen with its dried herbs hanging from a timber-beamed ceiling was the antithesis of anything my mother would consider civilized.

"Has mother been here?"

Anna placed the spoon on the saucer, ran her hands over the worn wood of the ancient table and looked at me with a vacant expression that harkened back to the days when, disciplined, we were sent to bed early to hide under the sheets and giggle at our formal stone of a mother.

"I didn't think so."

Facing her twenties without prospects, Anna had made the decision the previous year not to subject herself to our parents' plans for her. She was determined not to be the daughter to live with and take care of our aging parents only because she was disinclined to marry.

After too much family discussion and Anna's resolve remaining rod straight, they all agreed that she would move to the gardener's cottage. Nestled tightly in the woods, its stone façade could not be seen from the main house. Anna filled the little home to the brim with warm furniture gathered from here and there, and the cellar with vegetables and bulbs ready for planting. The house even smelled like her, earthy and solid.

I knew I couldn't live alone. I liked waking to the noise of a household full of people. "Anders brought someone home with him last night," I interrupted the silence. Outside the kitchen window, a pine branch weighted down with snow scratched against the pane of glass.

"You weren't expecting company? It wasn't the constable again, was it?"

Anna knew of the tension brewing at the base. "No, Anders was late. His name is Johan, and Anders introduced him as someone he recently hired to work in the office."

"Does he live nearby?" I could see Anna trying to calculate who we knew from the town that would take a position like that.

"He will now. Anders allowed him to bunk in the carriage house."

Anna's eyebrows lifted, and she focused her wandering, conversational glance on my eyes.

"He left family near Stockholm, but he's not married. Anders brought him home to bunk in the carriage house because there were no open beds available at the base."

"There are many men traveling for work now." Anna's magnanimous outlook intruded on my more guarded nature.

"I don't think it was work that brought him to us."

Anna sat back in her chair and crossed her arms over her chest. "What did bring him then?"

I explained the discrepancies between his appearance and his manners. "He left Stockholm because of a falling out with the church."

"What kind of falling out?" Anna scraped her chair across the wide plank floor, edging closer to the table. She placed her elbows on the surface and leaned in. "What did he do?"

"He told the bishop it was a sin for the church to distill and sell beer."

"Oh, dear."

Although we'd had our own challenges, punctuated by our voluntary removal from the parish congregation, we were never so bold as to question the clergy's authority outright. Bishop Peterson, unhappy because we wouldn't purchase beer for the workers, expressed his disappointment in more ways than one. For a time we were spied on and under suspicion of distilling our own, but later we seemed to settle on a working unease between us and the bishop.

Because we didn't seek to purchase beer from anyone else, nor did we distill it ourselves, no laws had been broken, no permits neglected, and there was little to argue about. We were proud of our tenuous middle way. We would never have seen a rebellion like Johan's as something that could be part of our future. Besides, I wasn't sure if it even was a sin for the church to sell and distill beer. I knew there must be more to the story I had yet to learn.

A Bible that matched my own sat on the kitchen table. They were childhood gifts from our teacher. Sometimes I missed the Sunday service. I ran my palm across the embossed leather. It always amazed me how the memorized words stayed alive in my mind even without the bishop's sermons. The longer we were gone from the church, the less I felt the loss, and that made me uneasy. The New Testament spoke of fellowship with like believers, but it didn't say what to do if we no longer believed as our church did.

Anna picked up our cups and carried them over to the sink, as seemingly lost in her thoughts as I was in mine.

The low evening sun and lengthening days teased a longing for warmer weather from my winter-frosted mind. But it was only a tease, and although we were encased in the carriage, the frozen air fell off the inner side of the glass to pool on the floor.

We drove past the crooked wooden gate, and I could see just a corner of the main house where my parents still lived. Its huge stone walls and heavy oak entrance looked like they should be surrounded by a moat rather than the gently rolling, snow-covered hills that dominated the landscape.

There was a time when I'd wished my parents were people I could converse with. But my childhood evenings had been spent sitting at my mother's feet emulating her darting fingers, only to have the stitches pulled and reworked. My sister, born six years after the last of us, was too young to remember those years. She only recalled the silence and the rooms filled with sheet-covered furniture. Alone, and in the time after my parents had stopped pretending, her childhood had been spent in the laps of tutors, or more favorably, in the crook of the tree that hung over the small pond in the garden.

But my days of searching for their approval were over.

My parents had left my home after that dinner and never come back. I didn't know why I'd expected differently, but they left, and I turned to Anders, and he said it didn't matter. I had Anders, I had Hulda and Hjalmer, and I had the babe growing inside. What I didn't have was any idea of what to do with tomorrow.

Shades of deep purple clung to the horizon behind the black brushstrokes of trees. It all slipped by with the whispering crunch of metal sleigh runners on ice and the occasional soft whinny from the horses. I pulled Hulda closer and leaned my head back to watch the night and wonder if Johan was the last of the strangers Anders would bring in.

Blue and yellow squares rested in bound stacks at the bottom of my quilting basket.

They bothered me there. They nagged at me every time I reached in for the tiny scraps of white that would make my baby's quilt.

It was my winter assignment to cut the fabric into squares and half-moons for a quilt to be presented in June to a newly married couple. The fabric of impeccable quality had been donated by a woman who made sure everyone in the circle knew exactly how nice it was. But as I no longer attended the church, and by default would not be welcomed by most of the quilting circle, I could not decide what to do with the stacks of squares as they slipped farther and farther into the recesses of my basket.

I gathered them up and made my way to the kitchen, where Elsa was kneading dough with red-blotched ferocity. Grey ringlets of hair escaped her loose bun and were pasted on her mottled cheeks and forehead.

"Elsa? Do you know Mrs. Olsen at church?" I opened the conversation and quickly chastised myself for asking the obvious. Everyone knew Mrs. Olsen, and my exchanges with Elsa always seemed to turn out to make me feel foolish, even when I planned ahead of time what I would say.

"Yes, ma'am." She flipped the large glob of dough over on the wooden surface and dusted it with more flour. The neglected other half of her sentence, the half where she should have followed social protocol and asked why I inquired, hung heavy in the routine silence.

"If I give you some quilting squares, would you return them to her for me?" I dropped the pile into the basket near the fireplace and turned to escape the kitchen.

"I'll get Samuel to drive me over after the bread is in the oven."

I turned back to see the corners of her mouth dip down and her dusted hands rest on her hips. "I should have time before I start dinner."

She took another, harder punch at the dough; the top of her arms offering the exclamation with their responding jounce in her tight sleeves.

I took a breath and turned back to fully face her, reminding myself for the hundredth time that Elsa had been with Anders's family since his childhood. If the choice were mine, she would have been sent back to his parents' home.

"I didn't mean now. I meant would you mind taking them with you when you go to church on Sunday. I no longer have the opportunity to see Mrs. Olsen." I finished the statement with a little waver in my voice and a growing flush to my face. Elsa knew exactly why I could not take them myself, and I did not appreciate her making me explain.

"Mama." Hulda ran into the kitchen and stopped in front of the table where Elsa worked. "Liona says Hjalmer is in his nap now."

Hulda gave Elsa the pleading look that echoed her father's eyes, and a softer Elsa handed her a small biscuit and glanced back to me.

"Ma'am, I don't have the opportunity to see Mrs. Olsen anymore either."

"Come on, Mama." Hulda yanked softly at my skirt. Grains of sugar were stuck to her fingers and the corners of her mouth. She left a few crystals on my black skirt, and I brushed them away.

"Just a minute, Hulda. Elsa, what do you mean?"

Elsa looked at me as if she were explaining to a child, but unlike her glance at Hulda, this one showed no hints of kindness. "Samuel and I don't go to that church."

"Mama." Hulda tugged again.

I turned her in the direction of the doorway. "Hulda, please go upstairs and tell Liona that I will be there in a bit."

Hulda scampered up the kitchen stairs while Elsa resumed her kneading.

The kitchen was warm, and with the oven heating in preparation for the bread, my face continued to flush and the fabric under my arms grew damp. I shifted my weight from one foot to the other and faced Elsa.

"I was not aware. I am sorry." I didn't know why I apologized.

Elsa continued to knead. She punched the dough down, dusted it with flour, folded it over, and then turned it to begin again, all the while ignoring my comment. I wondered if, like us, she did not attend church at all, and I stood shifting my weight back and forth, foot to foot. Where she went to church should have been no concern of mine. I had no right to ask her personal questions, and by the looks of it, she had no intention of answering them.

She finished kneading, covered the dough, and wiped her hands on her yellowed apron and looked up, apparently abandoning the hope I would vacate the kitchen. I reached for the flour container to pick it up and put it away.

"You don't need to do that, ma'am." Elsa had the flour in hand before I could get it. "Why don't you have a seat in the parlor? I'll bring you some tea."

Now Elsa stood looking at me. I had planned to go through the trunk of infant things with Liona while Hjalmer slept. Time was slipping away, but I had to know why they left the church. It was disturbingly close to the timing of our decision.

"Will you go back?" I asked Elsa, not moving in the direction of the parlor. "When did you stop attending Bishop Peterson's services?"

Elsa placed her hands on the work surface and lowered her body onto a nearby stool.

I signaled for her to stay there, and I scraped the pile of flour, with its dried, rolled bits of dough, into the scrap bucket. For once, she complied with a sigh.

"We left when Mr. Modig left. He talked to Samuel, and Samuel thought he was right, that the church is involved where it ought not to be, and we would support his decision."

I paused my scraping. Leaving the church was one thing, taking others along was entirely another. The half-full scrap bucket thumped against the wood floor as I set it in place near the garden door. I couldn't think of an appropriate response for a loyalty that had taken me off-guard. Anders's discussion with Samuel was dangerous. The decision was ours alone. I turned to see Elsa's frank assessment of my silence. It made me feel too young, again.

She pushed up to stand at the counter. "I'll take the squares to Mrs. Olsen this afternoon." She began to shuffle through a stack of stained papers, presumably in search for a recipe.

Dismissed, I made my way up the kitchen stairs to check on Hjalmer with my cool hands pressed to my cheeks.

I found Liona seated on the floor in the middle of the children's sitting room. She watched Hulda cradle the porcelain-faced doll Anders had given her. Sunlight cascaded in through the windowpanes and glinted off the doll's blue glass eyes.

Liona glanced in my direction as I entered the room but didn't move to get up. Instead, she motioned to the chair next to her and smiled a greeting. She was accustomed to my presence in this room, and unlike the kitchen, the nursery made me feel at home with its sitting room filled with diminutive furniture and its plush rugs covering every inch of the floor. My mother didn't like the rugs. Most of the walls in the house were white, but the children's rooms were decorated with garden-like paintings complete with dancing fairies and mischievous gnomes peeking from behind various pieces of furniture.

Liona was very close to my age, maybe a few years younger, and she had been referred to us by my neighbor, Mrs. Olsen. That woman had her hands in everything, but in this instance I was grateful due to Liona's uncommon upbringing and exceptional education. I spoke Swedish, with a smattering of English, words taught to me by Anders when we were first married, before our evenings were filled with children and entertaining business associates. But Liona spoke English first, and Swedish, both with almost no hint of an accent. Mrs. Olsen had told me that Liona spoke Italian as well, although I had not heard her myself.

Anders received English newspapers in bundles at his office and brought them home for Liona to pore over. Sometimes they would talk about the happenings. My bits of English were largely useless when it came to reading a newspaper, but sometimes, given enough effort, I could make out the major events. On those days, they would converse in Swedish so I could be involved. I especially liked to try to make out any of the articles about America and the people who traveled there. It seemed those who chose to emigrate found either fortune or tragedy, and I wondered if there were any people who lived just average lives.

Liona sat with her legs stretched out and both hands flat on the floor behind her. I compared her tiny feet to my own, and then tucked mine under my skirt.

The dainty, dark-haired woman who sat next to me had a mind alight with mathematics, science, and literature. Liona filled the position of nanny because although she was raised with privilege, she had no privilege of her own, and she had been with us for years.

"She loves that doll," Liona said without taking her eyes off Hulda. We watched as she straightened the doll's blue dress and checked the tiny buttons on the shiny black shoes. A child's tea service spread across the table in front of the window. Hulda set her doll in the chair adjacent to hers and poured imaginary tea.

I stood and walked over to the ruffle-filled crate full of baby items awaiting my attention. White linens, embroidered with red and yellow flowers, brightened the room as I pulled them from the wooden box and handed them to Liona.

I could feel the flutter of life; I had been able to for some time. When Liona had her back turned to me, I reached down to trace the expanding circle below the rising waistline of my skirt. I didn't like how my dresses all appeared shorter in the front, but there was little that could be done about that. At least I was not living in the city anymore. The requirements in the country were more relaxed, and now that I no longer had to be concerned with impressing neighbors like Mrs. Olsen, I would be relatively free for most of my pregnancy. One benefit of alienating oneself from one's friends and family was a certain loosening of the tethers.

The room grew dark while we sorted, and eventually the fire in the hearth lit it more than the sun coming through the windows. Dinnertime approached. With Anders at the base almost every day, and the cold keeping us inside, the days dragged by. I missed the times I would go into town, to the dressmakers or the lending library, and stop to see him. However, as I assessed the piles surrounding Liona and me, I knew keeping busy over the next couple of months would not be a problem. The ladies at church always said a spring baby was perfect because it gave the mother something to do with her time in the dead of winter. In that, they were right.

I didn't even know if the ladies knew I was expecting another child.

As I reached to the bottom of the crate, tissue crinkled. Hulda's and Hjalmer's baptismal outfits rested there. I pulled one out. It was wrapped in tissue with the lightest blue pattern of dancing bears and secured with a blue ribbon. I sat down with the package resting on my knees, took one strand of satin between my fingers, and pulled.

The folded edges of tissue fell away and Hulda's baptismal dress fell onto my lap. I had forgotten how small she was. Delicate glass beads on lace sprinkled across the front of the dress. I picked it up out of the nest of tissue and brought the fabric to my face. It still retained the faint fragrance of baby. As I held the doll-sized shoulders in my hands, the skirt almost reached the floor. In truth, it contained enough of the filmy white fabric to make a real dress for her.

"Do not touch it, Hulda." Liona's voice came from behind me. I hadn't realized Hulda stood at my side admiring the dress as I did.

"Was it mine?" she whispered.

I folded the bottom up and fitted it back into the same square of tissue.

"Yes, it was." I took one of Hulda's long braids in my hands. "You are a bit big for it now, I am afraid."

"Will the baby wear it?"

"No, the baby will have its own outfit to be baptized in." I smiled at Hulda and ran my fingers down the length of her hair. It almost reached her waist and was tied with red ribbons at the end of her braids.

I dropped my hands to secure the package in my lap. Liona held the edges of the tissue together as I tied the bow.

My parents had attended Hulda's baptism, and Hjalmer's. I paused with the package in my hands. My stomach knotted and Liona's eyes met mine as we both came to the same realization. I had no church to baptize this new life. I couldn't believe I hadn't thought of that before. A wave of sadness washed over me.

A gnome, carved into the fireplace, laughed at my predicament.

I placed the tissue-wrapped keepsakes back into the crate, made a pile for mending, instructed Liona as to what the children should wear to dinner, and with shaking hands, made my way down the hallway.

Anders met me outside of my sitting room as I juggled the pile of baby clothes in my arms.

"How did today go?" He smiled down at me and reached to touch my cheek. Ever since the project at the base began, he came home with a bounce in his step.

I moved to the side to step around him. He must have thought I was playing coy, because he stepped in front of me to block my way.

"Did you realize that we will have no place to baptize the new baby?" I met his gaze, making sure he understood the severity of the situation.

He took a step back and reached out to take my shoulders. "Yes."

"What are we going to do?"

I didn't wait for the answer I knew he didn't have. He let me go, and I stepped around him.

My sitting room was small, with only two upholstered chairs and a lady's writing desk in one corner. Paneled in dark wood from floor to ceiling, it exuded warmth. There was a ceramic stove in the corner of the room that was kept stocked with coal during the day. The glass doors on the outside wall led to a hedge-bordered garden. I glanced out the windows and tried to remember where I had planted the tulip bulbs last fall.

The mending found a home in the basket with the rest, and I sat behind the desk to pen a letter to my sister Anna. There was still enough time in the day to have Samuel or one of the stable lads take it to her and get back before it was completely dark.

Pen to paper, I invited her to come and stay for a while.

Chapter Three

"Ma'am?" The young girl who helped Elsa in the kitchen stood at my bedroom door. I wondered how long she'd watched me dig through the ribbon box in search of my cameo.

Her faded dress was too short for her lanky frame. The waist buttoned at least five centimeters above where it should rest. She scratched the back of her right ankle with the worn toe of her left shoe.

"Yes?" I wished I could remember her name, but nevertheless, I would speak to Elsa about finding suitable clothing for her. She was probably one of a number of siblings, possibly the oldest. At least old enough to work and probably growing faster than her mother could clothe her, or more likely, growing beyond the notice of her mother.

She scratched the top of her thigh through her dress, bunching the fabric up to reveal her ill-fitting stockings. When she had satisfied the itch, or my stare had relieved her mind of it, she let her dress fall and linked her fingers in front of her.

"Elsa says that your guests are coming up the drive and that dinner will be ready at half past six."

Our servant, Samuel, had left about an hour prior with my note to my sister Anna. We expected five for dinner, six if Anna decided to ride back with Samuel, which was not my intention when I sent the letter. But knowing how efficient and curious Anna was, I half expected her to saddle her horse and accompany Samuel back to the house.

"Thank you." I nodded and dismissed the scratching girl without the benefit of her name. I needed to speak with Elsa.

I found the cameo and pinned it to the center of my collar. The cloudy white picture that rose from the blue background did not depict a typical cameo face; instead it was a tree bursting with snowy spring blossoms. The edges of the tiny petals had the barest hint of pink. I looked in the mirror and fingered the countless petals. Their white echoed my crisp shirt, and the blue was the exact shade of my eyes. I pinched my cheeks to bring up some color, tucked my shirt into the waistband of my skirt, and turned sideways to examine the roundness I could no longer hide. My house slippers peeked from underneath the hem of my skirt, and I experimented by bending my knees to see if I could hide them and walk at the same time. It was futile.

"You are beautiful." Anders leaned on the doorframe. He filled the opening.

I turned as he kicked up from his leaning position and walked over to where I stood. His posture looked serious and purposeful, but only due to his size, and I knew by his eyes that he was entirely too playful.

"You scared me. You shouldn't do that with the baby."

He circled around me and placed his hand on my hard stomach.

I backed up a little. Underneath his mustache the corners of his mouth rose. His familiarity with my body always skittered my nerves and struck me as inappropriate, especially when we were expecting guests.

I sidestepped and avoided his other hand. "Who, again, are we expecting tonight?"

He checked his tie in my mirror, and then sat in the chair next to the bed. As usual, he appeared relaxed, as if he were born without worries, and sitting there, with his legs stretched out in front and his ankles crossed, he was very handsome—handsome enough that none of my friends questioned my decision to marry someone more than a decade my senior. When our eyes met, he smiled at me as if he could read my mind and was happy about what he saw there. I pursed my lips at having been discovered and turned back to my image in the mirror to pretend to check for loose strands of hair.

"Johan will be here, along with a couple he said he would like for us to meet."

"Who are they?"

"I'm not sure. Johan knows them from a church service they held in their home."

I had heard of this happening, but not in our parish.

"Who is the minister of the church?"

"The husband of the couple coming to dinner."

I looked at Anders through the mirror. "How many attend his services?"

He sighed at the line of questioning. "Right now, seven families have joined his for the Sunday services."

I turned to assess his slouched frame. Seven was a specific number, and I suspected lengthy discussions had already taken place with Johan.

"Johan attends?" It came out as more of a statement than a question.

Anders nodded and met my eyes.

"And the minister? How long have the people been meeting?"

"He is a farmer."

"What?"

"The minister, he is not really a minister, he is a farmer."

A farmer. I sat down on the bed facing Anders and wondered where to start, and wondered why the conversation was happening then, when at any minute we expected our dinner guests, including a member of a church that was not a church, led by a minster who was not a minister.

We were aligning ourselves with the wrong people. These were not business owners or educated professionals; they were of another circle entirely. Although we had purposely severed contact with our previous group of friends, people we were proud to stand next to, I was not sure it was wise in our current position to befriend people who moved outside the circles of what was commonly accepted.

I picked at a string hanging from the cuff of my sleeve. "Who are the other families involved?"

Anders examined his closely trimmed fingernails and tapped a finger with each name. "Johan, who just moved here, Jakob Dahlberg and his wife, the Johanssons, and the Wellmans." He smiled at me and motioned for us to move toward the door. "I can't remember the rest right now. Oh, Samuel and Elsa also attend."

I almost tripped on the rug.

"Are you feeling well?"

"Do you mean Samuel and Elsa? Our Samuel and Elsa?"

"Yes."

I responded with a dark look intended to communicate that we had much more to talk about, especially if he thought I was going to sit through a church service with Elsa to my side, a farmer for a minister, and sing hymns. *Did they even sing hymns?* We had more—much more—to discuss, but the scratching girl was back at our door.

"Mr. and Mrs. Modig." She ran her toe across the edge of the hall carpet. "Miss Lindgren is here."

It was Anders's turn to raise his eyebrows in question. "You invited your sister?"

I relished my brief moment. "Yes, I wrote her this afternoon." And with that, I pushed past him and started down the wide hall.

In two steps he caught up to me and took my elbow. "How nice," he said, "she will have the opportunity to meet Johan, and Jakob and his wife."

I paused at the staircase with my hand on the carved banister and my toes hanging over the top stair. Anders paused with me, smiled down, and held his arm out for me to take. We descended together.

The typical noise of introductions and coats and hats and exclamations about weather greeted us as we entered the front room. Samuel stood in the middle of the crowd, having returned with Anna in tow; the substitute butler under a pile of coats and hats. Johan, the minister—who I assumed was Jakob—and his wife all arrived at the same time.

Anna had taken over the role of hostess and was busy introducing Samuel to the group while Jakob added another coat to the pile that had grown to humorous proportions. Samuel, always the entertainer, put on his best haughty face over the giant pile and turned to exit the room. His round nose and unusually long eyebrows made any true haughtiness nearly impossible as he mock-stumbled under the weight of the winter coats.

"Just ask if you need help, Samuel," Anna called to his arched back, her falsely formal voice covered by her smile.

Unnoticed by the group, Anders and I descended the stairs behind them. The other woman in the group had slight, sloping shoulders and yellow hair piled high on her head. It strained at the pins attempting to tame the wiry mass. The fashionable full sleeves of her white shirt were cuffed and secured with tiny, round black buttons.

She was the first to turn and notice us, and when she did, she touched her husband's arm, earning his immediate attention. I liked her already.

"You must be Mrs. Dahlberg." Anders took a step and nodded toward the couple. "I am Anders, and this is my wife, Brianna."

All eyes were on me. They slowly dropped from my face to my waistline, and I could feel the blush crawl up to my neck and ears.

"Elin," Mrs. Dahlberg corrected and took a step forward. "You must call me Elin."

Anna squeezed from between the men to join our small group of women, effectively cutting me off from Anders, who in turn took the opportunity to maneuver into the men's growing conversation as it moved to the other side of the room. Anna's hand brushed my arm.

"Oh," I said, remembering our guests. "Please call me Brianna, and this is my sister, Anna."

Elin turned to Anna, clearly admiring her colorful quilted skirt. It was made in a style that hadn't been popular since I was a child, but Anna preferred the heavy warm fabric to the flimsy textiles so in demand.

Elin was pretty, in a mousy way, with fierce green eyes nestled in a round, but not plump face. Her nose was straight except where it turned up a bit at the end, and it seemed odd that standing next to Anna, she looked like a child; except for her eyes. They calculated things I suspected the rest of us did not see. Strangely, it did not feel as if she measured us against some standard; her intensity felt more like a gauge, tapping into who we were. It was a comfortable scrutiny.

Our group of six made the organic move toward the parlor while the rest of the introductions were made. I settled at the rear of the crowd to watch as the men clapped one another on the back and laughed like long-lost friends. I resolved to make another trip to the offices at the base before I grew too large. I was missing something.

"Jakob tells me you have two children." Elin tipped her freckled nose as she looked up at me. "A boy and a girl?"

"Yes. Hulda is seven, and Hjalmer, two."

"We have not yet been blessed with children." Elin deftly avoided any impolite conversation about my impending delivery.

She looked up to Anna. "Do you live near here?"

"It's about a twenty-minute ride if you make the trip by horseback."

"Dinner is ready," Elsa announced from the doorway of the dining room. The lamplight from the chandelier above the table illuminated her hair from behind and surrounded her features in a smooth halo. She smiled in recognition at Jakob and Elin and took a step forward to greet them. Elin hurried to meet her with a hug, wrapping her thin arms around Elsa's thick back.

They released each other and entered the dining room, followed by Anders and Jakob, who seemed to take no notice of the breach in protocol.

From the back of the group I heard Elsa explain to Elin how she and Samuel had traveled to Varmland to retrieve Elsa's niece to come and work here. At least then I knew where the scratchy girl came from.

To my dismay, my feet poked out from underneath my too short skirt. Anna and Johan walked ahead of me into the dining room, the jovial mood of the small group evident in their relaxed shoulders and casual gait. I lowered my shoulders and tried to echo the carefree posture of the others as I followed them into the bright room.

Elsa, for once, outdid herself.

The red and white china settings, surrounded by silver with no hint of a tarnish, and glassware that glimmered under the lamps made me proud.

"Oh, this is beautiful." Elin's sincerity moved with her fingers along the edge of the china. "Elsa, you have arranged this wonderfully."

I shot a quick glance to Anders, then to Anna, and neither of them paid any heed to the conversation.

"Thank you." Elsa met my eyes, the strained etiquette bouncing between the two of us.

Anders found his place at the head of the table. Everyone responded as a family would, with no interruption in the conversation as they bumped and scraped into their chairs. Somehow, I expected dinner to be a more formal affair, but Anders's seemingly established friendships lent a blithe spirit to the gathering. I met Anna's searching gaze and focused on unclenching my teeth.

"As Jakob is with us tonight," Anders said, "I wonder if he would lead us in prayer."

The head of the household is to offer the blessing at dinner, and I wondered why Anders would choose to honor the farmer-minister in this manner. I tried to make eye contact, but he was too busy nodding at Jakob, so I bowed my head with the others at the table.

With my eyes closed, the kitchen aromas reached my conscious mind, and for the first time in months, I grew hungry. I heard Anna next to me shift in her chair, and I opened my eyes to study and twirl the ring on my finger.

"In Jesus's name, we give thanks…" Jakob's voice took on an authoritative tone, and I found I waited for his next words.

"…for the food we receive. Bless those who prepared the meal, bless this household…"

A sideways glance at my sister revealed her open eyes trained on Johan. She watched his lips as they moved in his own silent prayer of agreement. Her fingers worried a bright square of fabric stitched into her skirt.

The square could have been from any number of places. Anna was secretive in the things she kept and her reasons for keeping them. It could have been a piece of a favorite dress or something older and more sentimental. If I would have asked her, she would have laughed and said it was just a pretty scrap. I would know better, but I would pretend to believe her.

"How is the work at the base progressing?" Jakob asked.

Somehow, I'd missed the end of the prayer. The switch from Jakob's prayer voice to that of his conversational voice was seamless, unlike our Bishop Peterson, who, during prayer, lowered his tone until it resonated off the peaks of the cathedral. As a child sitting in church, I would fight the urge to hide when Bishop Peterson's usually shrill timber would grow roots and fill the church to its beamed ceiling with soul-squelching authority.

"Work is going well." Anders responded to Jakob's questions with details that failed to interest me, or the women to my left and right.

"Hjalmer has gotten so big." Anna looked up from the bowl from which the scratching girl ladled her soup. The large spoon rested on the edge and threatened to tip out, but no one else seemed concerned about their close brush with the sticky substance.

"Oh." I noticed Anna waited for my response. "Yes, he is growing fast."

Elin smiled at both of us and raised her spoon to her pale lips.

"Liona can't keep him from climbing on things. Just yesterday, she walked into the nursery to get him from his nap, and he was sitting on top of his clothes chest. We still don't know for sure how he got up there."

I sipped the soup from the edge of my spoon. It was hot and smooth and just salty enough to make me want more. I blew on it to cool it and brought the spoon to my mouth again.

The men's conversation droned on at the other end of the table while I was being warmed from the inside out. Elin's bowl was almost empty and Anna's bowl looked as if she'd licked it clean. Both of their heads were turned toward the men as they took in the discussion about blasting rock and the base. Anders sat back in his chair, comfortable with his temporary position as entertainer for the group during the hiatus between courses. Even sitting, he was half a head taller than the other men at the table.

I hadn't been to the base very often, but when I visited, the blasting that took place was by far my favorite sight to witness.

At the quarry, the workers moved over the walls of rock like bees on a hive. They each had their own task, and they emerged from their work at the wall covered in fine white powder. It caked in the wrinkles around their eyes and settled on the back of their sweaty necks. You could tell a brick worker by the way his fingernails were worn down and the nail bed was artificially shortened. Anders told me the fine lines on the workers' fingers eventually wore permanently smooth. Those were the men who filled the carts with the pieces of rock that couldn't be used for anything as large scale as foundation building.

Elsa's niece removed the empty bowls. She made her way around the table, reaching in from the wrong side. When she shuffled to Anna's side of the table, she elbowed in between Anna and Johan and grabbed both their bowls, almost tipping one on Johan's lap. It teetered, the last drips of soup sloshing to the edge of the bowl and dripping down the side. I fought the urge to stand and help, but the girl worked so earnestly in her new duties, with her brow furrowed and her top lip sucked in. Instead, I tried to remain passive.

Johan and Anna, on the other hand, reached out in case it would be necessary to catch the china, but they did so with smiles.

"Karin." Johan moved his hand to support the bottom of the bowl. "If you stack them like this they won't risk falling." He rearranged the small pile in her arms.

I made urgent eye contact with Elsa, who moved to intercept the table-side training session courtesy of one of our guests. Elsa took the dishes from the fumbling girl—Karin, as I had just learned—and prepared to bring the next course.

"Elsa," Elin said as the plate was placed in front of her. "Have you spoken with the Friebergs recently?"

Elsa looked at me and answered that she had not. She and I seemed to be the only ones in the room who had any sense of how awkward the meal had become.

I turned to Elin. "How long have you lived here?"

The last time we'd had multiple guests for dinner, they had left angry. This time, the servants were holding conversations with the guests and the guests were clearing their own places. There was a shift somewhere I'd failed to place, but as Anna smiled at Johan, Anders joked with Jakob, and Elin navigated her attention from me to Elsa and back, the room grew brighter and louder and warmer. I sat back and took in the odd turn of unacceptable, yet somehow comforting, events. From the end of the table, I caught Anders's grinning glance, and I wondered what socially ambiguous circumstance we would next embrace.

Chapter Four

After dinner, Anders answered an insistent rapping at the door. The constable stood on the other side with his hat in his hand. His coat was miss-buttoned and the tails of his shirt hung out from underneath. He wore a sheepish expression and the unmistakable look of a man who had been roused from the depths of slumber and sent out in the cold.

Our guests halted their preparations to leave and peered around Anders.

"Come in, Constable." Anders motioned for the man to come in out of the cold.

Before he stepped in, the constable glanced back outside toward another who waited in the shadows. I backed out of the crowd and over to the window for a better view of the still mounted man. He sat on a restless horse, holding the reins of the constable's. His face was dark under the brim of his hat, but his fine coat with well-padded shoulders identified him as Bishop Peterson's assistant.

My mind filled in the details my eyes failed to supply in the dark—the sharp nose and sharper teeth set in a fleshy mouth and underlined by a deep double chin. All of this on top of a thin body, but not a typically thin body. His was the kind that tended toward roundness, but had grown bony due to illness, or some other reason, leaving him with a soft, angular shape.

"I'm sorry for intruding, Mr. Modig." The constable's voice reached me from the middle of the group congregated around him. I let the curtain fall and found my place at Anders's side.

"Nonsense," he said to the man who stood twisting the brim of his hat while examining his shoes. "To what do we owe this visit?"

"There has been a question…or rather, it has been reported…"

His sentence died off and, in exasperation, he slapped his hat against his thigh. "Anders, I'm going to put it to you straight." The constable used his first name and finally met our eyes. The rest of the group stood silent. "I am here because we have some questions."

"About what?" Anders ignored the "we" that captured my interest.

The uneasy man glanced from left to right, assessing the crowd. "Maybe we should speak in your study."

Anders motioned toward the other end of the hall. We all slid aside, clearing a path. "I shouldn't be gone long," Anders excused himself as he and the constable made their way to the study.

We watched until the study door clicked shut, and then all eyes were on me.

"Well." I moved to the center. "This is certainly odd." I attempted to make light of the situation.

Anna laughed a nervous laugh. "I am sure it's nothing." The words fell flat.

"We must be going anyway." Jakob helped Elin with her coat.

"Thank you for a lovely evening," Elin offered, her words dying off as she glanced back down the hall.

I opened the door for them, and they made their way out. The man on the horse still sat in the shadows under the trees. His horse's breath glimmered silver when the light from our open door reflected off the snow.

"I must be going as well."

I turned to extend a farewell to Johan, but found his back toward me as he addressed Anna.

"It was nice to meet you." He offered a hand that Anna accepted in an awkward, business-like manner, pumping his arm up and down.

Johan released her hand and turned toward me. "Thank you for opening your home. The dinner was excellent." He glanced in the direction of the office door. Muffled conversation leaked from the room. "I do hope everything is fine." He looked at me, pausing for me to ask him to stay.

"Thank you, Johan. I'm sure all is well."

I closed the door behind him and breathed in a moment of quiet.

"How long are you prepared to stay?" I crossed over to where Anna stood at the window. We pulled the curtain back in time to watch Johan mount his horse and ride past the waiting man. When he reached the tree, he tipped his hat to the unresponsive man and glanced back in our direction. Anna waved slightly and smiled.

I turned away and leaned on the window sill. "How long do you think the constable will be talking to Anders, and why do you suppose the other man stays out in the cold?"

Anna just shook her head.

"So, how long are you staying?"

"A few days, I suppose. Do you think you will go to their church service tomorrow?"

"I'm not sure. It was nice for them to invite us, and I like them, but I'm not sure. I have to see about Anders's plans," I responded weakly, knowing full well he had thought of this all along.

"If you decide to go, I'd like to see it for myself."

We walked together to the base of the stairs. "Your usual room is ready for you," I said.

Anna nodded and stifled a yawn.

"Elsa freshened the linens, and she's waiting for instructions if you need anything."

Anna gave me the look that always made me feel spoiled and ridiculous, and then turned to make her way up to her room. "You know I won't need anything," she said as her feet hit the first stair.

The front room was still ablaze with light. I turned down a couple of lamps and listened to the tired sounds of clinking dishes and sliding drawers from behind the kitchen door. The sounds died off as I headed down the hallway to Anders's study.

The hall was dark except for the light seeping from underneath his door. It reflected off the varnished wood. I whispered past Anders's study to stand in front of my morning room. The chambers were adjoining, and I knew the muffled noises from behind the hall door might be more intelligible from the door between our rooms. I usually left it cracked open.

The fire in my room had died down and taken any ambient light with it. Voices droned from the study. Instead of lighting a lamp I moved toward the heavily draped windows. Pictures hung high on the wall. A shadow-cloaked portrait of Hulda filled the space between the two windows at the far end of the room. I tried to make out the shape of her face on the dark background, but I was unsure if the round child's features floating out of the darkness were hers, or if they were cultivated by my memory.

The silence here rested on my shoulders, which began to tingle with the humid sense of another presence in the room.

The soft hairs that ran down my spine rose damp against the starched linen of my shirt. I saw nothing save the details provided by my familiarity with the space. Pieces of furniture placed in the path to the windows offered no hindrance, and when I reached the deep velvet curtains, I pulled until the rings scraped across the high wooden pole. The glistening light of an almost full moon poured in.

A sharp intake of breath pulled my attention to the connecting door where a small shadow stood, trapped, pressed hard against a wall.

The girl Karin stared, unblinking, her eyes shining like glass marbles.

"I…I…" Her hands lifted in a protective pose, and I halted the progression I had unwittingly made halfway across the room.

"I was looking for you." Her sentence rose in pitch at the end. It was a statement in search of a believer.

Her eyes hunted for mine in a face I knew was shadowed by the moonlight behind me.

I offered no comfort. I let her fidget as the seconds stretched on. She had been discovered neglecting her duties and listening to conversations that did not involve her. In my mother's house, termination would have been swift. I was not my mother.

"I think Elsa could use your help in the kitchen."

She exhaled a shaky breath and curtsied on a half turn, almost stumbling in her attempt to round the heavy wooden door without touching it.

I stepped around the chair that separated us. The bench sitting next to the door of Anders's study still held the girl's warmth. I ran my hand across the heated fabric and wondered how long she had sat there. I lowered myself to her place and pressed my ear against the door.

"I understand your concern, but you have nothing to worry about," I heard Anders's voice clearly through the semi-hidden passageway. "In the past month we have been investigated for distilling our own beer, and found innocent. The bishop's men have slipped in and out of the base, spying for what I do not know, and now the bishop is concerned that we will pull people from his congregation to a heathen one. I can't help but link all of these. If we decide to join a different congregation, and even if it is one the church does not recognize, it's not against the law."

"I'll pass on what you've said, and again, I am sorry for the interruption to your evening." The constable's words were flat, emotionless, and I had the sinking feeling the conversation was not finished. It would just be continued without us.

I leaned back against the bookcase next to the bench and rested my head on the cool wood. Their steps retreated down the hall toward the front door. It opened and closed, and I heard Anders make his way back toward me, passing his study and entering mine.

He pushed the door open, took in the natural light falling into the room, and looked in my direction.

"Did you hear our conversation?" He shut the door behind him, taking time to lift the latch so it moved silently into place.

"Not much, just the end." I considered telling him who probably did overhear, but decided to deal with that situation later. An overly curious maid was not a concern for my husband. "I saw our company out and Anna settled in the guest room. Did you know that the bishop's man sat out in the cold the entire time you and the constable spoke?"

"I suspected as much." Anders found the chair across from me.

For a moment I allowed myself to drop the practiced ruse of the indifferent wife. My mother would have been horrified. She was the portrait of restraint and discipline, considered the ultimate hostess—she had maintained a spotless house, an exacting schedule, and severely behaved children. But my father rarely spoke to her, and when he did, he was rewarded with her barely repressed sneer.

My mother taught me to fulfill the role of wife, to manage the household and not to disturb my husband with the details. Everything I'd learned screamed at me to mind my own business, to tend the children, to ignore the questions burning in my head. In my mother's world, asking meant I didn't trust my husband. But not asking, not being involved, felt like I didn't care. I took a deep breath and looked up. "What do you think is going on?"

For the same moment, Anders put his elbows on his knees and shed the detached façade of a husband who was secure in all of his decisions. Long dark lashes shadowed his gaze, but somehow I still felt rewarded.

"They are using the question of where we are buying our beer to warrant further intrusion, especially now that they have noted the Dahlbergs' presence. The church doesn't look kindly on someone who preaches against infant baptism."

"They're those people?"

Anders watched me closely. "There is no place in the Bible that speaks of infant baptism."

I thought through my childhood Sunday lessons and tried to recall a place.

"And, now that I am feeling a bit more pressed by the intrusion, I question the propriety of the church as the only legal distiller and seller of beer in this town."

"What does the constable say?" Despite my efforts, my voice rose in pitch to mimic my mother's intense tones.

"Of course, he says he understands—that he is just doing his job."

The moonlight played on the right side of Anders's face and exaggerated the tiny lines that had begun to form in the corners of his eyes. He was silhouetted in front of the shining snow, allowing me to see meaningless details—stray hairs, the stubble on his jaw, and the curve of his ear.

"I fired someone today." He reached for the hem of my skirt. "He came to work drunk, again, and I told him to pack his things from the bunkhouse and leave."

His tone was hesitant, and I sat listening to the tiny shards of ice on glass.

"He has a wife and a number of children tucked away on a couple of acres not far from here. He rarely visits them."

I knew that the men who worked all week were tired. They counted on Sundays off to visit their families. Some workers—men without wives, men who had no place to go, or men who had spent their wages at the public houses and didn't wish to return to disappointed wives and hungry children—they chose to stay.

I imagined him as one of the latter, and his home as a place with no grass and the brown sticks of last year's dead crops poking up through the snow.

"I would contact the bishop to have someone look in on his family, but the bishop has already been alerted. It was the man I fired, Lars Ankerburg, who turned the bishop's concern toward us."

"You mean he's responsible for the constable showing up tonight?"

Anders nodded. "We'll have to be careful. The bishop must be waiting for any excuse to investigate us more closely."

"That explains the bishop's man sitting out in the cold. We don't have anything to worry about, do we?" I leaned back and rested my hands on the top of my stomach, on the place of comfort all expecting women seem to find.

Anders found my ankle and raised it to his knee. He began to knead the pliable joints through my slippers. Eventually, one slipper fell to the floor, and I raised my other foot to be attended to. I closed my eyes and tipped my head back.

"You'd like to try Jakob's church tomorrow," I stated. There was no need for a question.

His fingers halted their ministrations for a second, and then continued. "Yes, I would."

"If you think the bishop is knocking on the door now..."

"I know, but there has got to be something more. I never questioned the church's interest in things of commerce, but the extent they can go to protect what they see as their right, involving the law..."

"You're questioning more than that, or you wouldn't be seeking out another church."

He looked up toward the ceiling before continuing, "If I think one part of the church is wrong, if there is a problem with the institution or its leadership in general, then how can I have faith in the rest?"

"But nothing is ever perfect."

"Imperfection isn't dangerous, though, until it's enforced and we are impelled to abide by the wrong. That's exactly what the church is doing. They're punishing us for questioning their authority."

"If you throw out the teachings of the church, what do you keep?"

"We keep what the Bible tells us to keep."

The sentence was too easy. He found my dropped slippers and slid them back on my feet, then held his hand out to help me to a standing position.

The English papers scattered throughout Anders's study spoke of people who had emigrated solely for the purpose of finding a release from intrusive churches backed by coerced law enforcement. For the most part, they discussed the hardships befallen the citizens of Europe who had expected vast riches: poverty, death, loved ones lost in the recesses of debauched cities, never again to be seen. There were some scattered success stories, spread primarily by traveling Bible salesmen and the occasional Swede who returned with riches in tow.

I envied their spirit. Not that I could ever leave my home, but oh, I prayed that God would make me so bold as to stand in the face of what was not right, and take a step forward rather than back.

Anders was always so reserved. We were proud of our ability to compromise, but compromise took two sides, and giving way to ever more intrusive rules felt less like a breath of reason and more like slow suffocation. One look at Anders, and I knew where we would be the next day, who we would worship with, and I didn't care what the bishop or the constable thought.

I stopped Anders from closing the drapes. The swirling dreams I would have while sleeping over the shimmering winter-lit room were worth the coolness of the next morning. My soul softened in this quiet place, and prayers of childhood and the hymns my grandmother hummed and danced around my head in this room. *God who holds the children dear, watch over little me.* I used to pray it every night, and I left my room knowing I would do exactly that tonight. Anders was right. I laced my fingers through his. Our security should not be at the mercy of an ill-tempered church leader.

We made our way together through the rest of the dark house and up to our room where we found a soft fire in the hearth. We undressed and shivered until we found the heat of each other in the crisp sheets, and for the first time since childhood, I found comfort again in that simple prayer, even with the changes I knew the next day would bring.

Chapter Five

Jakob and Elin's house was large, and as the horses pulled up the drive, I realized I had expected it to be smaller. Maybe a family cottage, maybe an old farm with sagging stairs that had known generations of farmer's boots, but not the rather new looking, rather foreign looking, almost estate.

Railings lined the expansive porch, which ran the full length of the house. Solidly crafted benches greeted us from both sides of the front door. They promised easy summer evening conversations, and I was charmed. I lifted my skirts over the first stair, glad I was wearing my new cape with the satin lining, and made my way to the door.

Before we could knock, the heavy wood whispered on its hinges, and Jakob grasped Anders's proffered hand. He pumped up and down enthusiastically, clapping him on the shoulder with his free hand. Elin looked from behind. As we were pulled into the front room, I found I shared Elin's effortless smile.

The room brimmed with people. They sat on benches, chairs, and half barrels I assumed had been brought up from the barn. I spied Elsa's round back. She spoke to a woman I didn't recognize. They were surrounded by children, all appearing to be about the same age. One small boy, his cheeks scrubbed clean, buried his face in Elsa's ample skirt, rubbing his forehead against the soft fabric. Winter dirt dulled his hair, and his shoes were far too big, but heavy, farm-grade cord secured them in place.

41

His sister, older or younger I couldn't tell, rested her head against Elsa's thigh and gazed in my direction.

I smiled at her, the kind of nothing smile adults offer strange children. "May I take your cape?" Elin asked from behind me.

Turning, I unfastened the wide satin ribbon tied at my neck. The fabric slid off my shoulders as I pulled my arms from the slits. The shiny scarlet lining caught the attention of the sober child who still watched, and she lifted her head. Absentmindedly, she reached for the damaged end of one of her braids and rubbed it under her nose in a ritualistic motion that had probably followed her for years.

Elsa dropped her hand to the top of the girl's head where a part should have been visible, but instead it was obscured by the snarled wisps of slept-in braids. She brushed the girl's cheek, and I regretted that I had been thinking only of dirt and the possibility of lice finding a way back to our home via Elsa's skirt.

"This is beautiful." Elin ran her thin fingers along the edge of the satin lining. "So heavy." Almost with reverence, she studied the stitching and nap of my cape that draped across her arm.

The bright interior flashed from her elbow to her knee and the woman in front of Elsa, catching the display, took a step to her left in order to better examine it.

I moved into her line of vision and blocked the spectacle that draped from Elin's forearm. "Anders gave it to me at Christmastime." I folded the velvety fabric over so the lining wasn't visible, wishing then I had not worn the cape. I tried to calculate how many pairs of children's shoes it could have purchased.

Elin smiled. Just in appreciation for something beautiful, and I liked her even more.

"If everyone could please find a seat, then we will know if we need to find more chairs." Jakob's voice easily rose over the din. He stood at the far end of the dining room, grinning.

"Follow me." Elin handed my cape off to another person. "There are empty places next to me."

Her enthusiasm pulled me toward the front where Jakob stood. We picked our way through a maze of chairs and children who had found seats at their parents' feet. Two girls, about Hulda's age, played the same game I'd taught Anna one afternoon while sitting with sun-warmed hair in a yellow-green field. The younger of the two sat with concentration etched across her brow and her hands bound to the older with loops of string. She worried her bottom lip with a row of gapped teeth as she tried to keep the string tight to her thumb.

Elin touched my elbow and invited me to sit. Before I responded, I turned to locate Anna, half expecting to see her still in child's braids. She stood in the wide opening between the dining room and the parlor. The sun poured in and illuminated her eyes, lending them the unearthly blue of the sky. She spoke with Johan, his shoulders hunched in a posture of rapt attention. Anna smiled, without hiding her grin behind her hand, and reached up to tuck an imaginary wisp of hair behind her ear.

She must have felt my gaze and turned to find me while Johan studied the bend of her neck and the strong tendons that ran to disappear under her collar. Turning back, I motioned for Anna to sit in a chair next to Elin and me.

"You decided not to bring your children?" Elin asked as she shuffled between the back of her chair and another and maneuvered herself onto a sturdy wooden seat, worn smooth from years of use.

"Hulda and Hjalmer stayed home with Liona." I hoped she wouldn't press further. I didn't add I hadn't wanted them to come with us. We had discussed it, and Anders assured me there would be other children here; but what I did not ask, and what I did not want to concern myself with, was the kind of other children who would be here. I glanced around the room. Other than the children by Elsa, the families appeared to be respectable.

The chairs were arranged to allow everyone a view of Jakob. The gilded-edged pages of his Bible reflected the light as he stood behind the dining room table. Elin, to my left, I, Anders, Anna, Johan, and a couple I did not know made up the first semicircular row. The benches to the sides of the room pressed against the walls. Grateful mothers took advantage of the support.

Elsa sat on one of those benches next to the woman with the large brood. The third row spilled into the front room and was filled by women with small children in their laps and at their feet. Their husbands stood behind. I shifted, feeling my spine rub against the turned spindles on the back of the chair, and wondered if Jakob would be long-winded and if the standing men would eventually find a place to sit.

Jakob wore a black suit with every button fastened. His white collar contrasted with his sun-darkened skin and belied his true occupation. After a few years of farming, the skin never returned to its light color, even in the dead of winter. He opened with the typical church greeting and prayer. I looked around, the formality feeling foolish without the added ceremony of high beamed ceilings and stained glass windows. His voice was soothing though, and by the end of the ritual, the familiarity had lent a sense of security. I sat back with my legs crossed at the ankles. My stockings were soft, and I wished they traveled the length of my legs, rather than just over my knees.

At the conclusion of the prayer, Jakob nodded in our direction, and for a moment I felt lost. I glanced at Anders and Elin, eventually following Jakob's gaze behind me where I saw Elsa draw the head of a sleeping child off her lap and place it onto the lap of the child's mother. Elsa stood and I wondered what part she would play, until she took a breath, closed her eyes, and opened her mouth to strains of notes we all knew. They were notes my grandmother tied together with words when I was a child, and notes I still sang.

Others joined in the song, and the perplexities of singing in a dining room with a group of strangers gave way to a warmth that traveled up my chest until I took up the familiar melody, adding my weak voice to the solid, vibrato-laced notes emanating from behind.

Hymns without the cover of an organ spoke louder and clearer; somehow they felt cleaner. In church, I would do the same as everyone else—mouth the memorized words until the organist heralded the end of the song with a few measures of particularly grandiose notes. But in this place, people closed their eyes to sing words of praise and dedication and thanksgiving. The notes flowed from their lips in promise, and I felt guilty for staring, but I couldn't stop.

They were loud and seemed sincere. Every individual voice, the treble of the women, the rumbling bass of one of the men who stood behind me, all of the voices settled from the rear of the room into the back of my neck, and I was compelled to push the energy forward. My lungs expanded, and I gave over to a trembling power I had no idea lay dormant in the dusty, ancient words.

When the song finished and the last strains of notes floated away, a hush filled the room. No one moved. No one wanted to break the spell. When we opened our eyes, I realized we were all standing. I didn't remember being told to do so.

"Everyone may be seated."

I was absurdly aware of the sounds I made.

"We will begin with Psalm 91." He paused for a second before continuing. "I will say of the Lord, He is my refuge and my fortress: my God in him I will trust."

My mind flashed to the man waiting in the snow and the way the light fell only to the legs of his horse, how he remained in shadow, and how his horse's breath shone.

"Surely he shall deliver thee from the snare of the fowler, and from noisome pestilence."

From the corner of my eye, Elsa reached over to grasp the nameless woman's hand. Due to her seated position, I could see how threadbare the knees of the woman's skirt were, and I tried to grasp what it would be like to send one's children to bed every night with their needs unmet.

"Thou shalt not be afraid for the terror by night; nor for the arrow that flieth by day."

Anna faced forward; her gaze intent and her fingers worrying the cuticle of her thumb. The sun shone in small, floating circles through the lace curtains. Those circles moved and rested on my lap and on Anders's hands and on the side of Jakob's face.

The timber of his voice changed as he spoke of Jesus's sacrifice, of his mercy, of his love. The rich tones strummed my troubled thoughts and focused my attention on Elsa's hands. A tear fell from the woman who held it in her grip. It landed on one of Elsa's broad fingers and went unnoticed. My own vision blurred with tears for the woman, and I shifted in my chair.

"What doth it profit, my brethren, though a man say he hath faith, and have not works?" Jakob quoted a passage I recognized from the book of James, his pace quickening and his hands moving back and forth, palms toward the congregation as if by his movements alone he might instill our souls with the depth of his meaning.

Anders looked down at his clenched hands. I didn't think he saw his white knuckles and purple nails.

The woman next to Elsa sniffled and released Elsa's hand to wipe the tears that spilled down her cheeks. A nearby man reached into his pocket and pulled out a handkerchief, handing it to her. I was consumed by her hunched shoulders and thin children and guilty because I noticed how the handkerchief was not as white as it could be. I could have reached in to my pocket and offered help, but instead, I waited for someone else. How often I waited for someone else.

Passages about Pharisees weighed down on me, stealing my breath and threatening to overflow my bleary eyes. The moisture made the room brighter and I longed to close the light out, but knew if I did the tears would run down my face.

"...confess with thy mouth the Lord Jesus, and believe in thine heart that God hath raised him from the dead, and thou shalt be saved."

Visions of dusty roads and a crown of thorns flashed before my eyes. I fought back, controlling my breathing and counting the nails in the floorboards until they too were the nails pounded into Jesus's hands. Every blow of the hammer, another of my sins accounted for. Every jeer from the crowd an insult hurled from my lips. My skin burned, my ears rang, and I was blinded by light when I saw Anna drop from her chair onto her knees. I found relief as I did the same.

Jakob's tone droned on; his words were no longer intelligible, but somehow soothing. I gave thanks for the hard floor that bit into my knees and for the uneven wood that I pressed my forehead into. My belly was warm and my shoulders relaxed when Jakob ceased to speak and the room filled with a thick silence.

Everything was damp—my eyes, my cheeks, the air—and although I shaded my view, the white that filled my vision was brighter than any sun. It filled the floor underneath me until no shadows remained, all was exposed, and I was clean. I lay in the new softness. I swallowed it. It wrapped up and around and a peace settled in deeply over me and my baby.

We did not speak on the ride home; the darkness lent itself to reflection. When we found our bed, Anders put his hand over my belly and pulled my back to his chest. The bedclothes smelled like us, and I felt his heat as he wrapped himself around me. Our breathing relaxed into a synchronized pattern. An embrace I doubt my mother ever knew. My mother. Anders's warmth had almost lulled me into forgetting the danger of our new beliefs.

"I saw it," he whispered into my hair. "The light, I saw it cover you."

What I did not say was that I was only lying on the train of the mantle that covered him.

Chapter Six

March 1880

Thursday, soup day—I waited all week for that day.

From where I stood at the children's upstairs windows I watched the house empty. Liona left first, after kissing the top of the children's heads and heaving a nap-heavy Hjalmer into my arms. He moved easily to me, a transition that always made me nervous. It would have been difficult if he'd showed preference for Liona over me, and I knew it was always possible with the amount of time she doted on him. Thus far, I had avoided the hurdle.

"Mama," Hulda tugged at my skirt and squeezed between my thighs and the window sill to look down.

After Liona, a couple of men from the stables walked from the rear of the house around to the front, their coats unbuttoned despite the cold. This was their afternoon off, and everyone was warmed without aid of fireplaces. They passed around the corner, laughing and joking. The sound of their deep voices rumbled through the glass, but not the words they spoke.

Samuel followed behind, kicking stones and taking his time. When he saw Elsa secure the front door behind her, he picked up his pace. Somehow he looked younger, and they shared a youthful smile that made me nostalgic. Karin, in her new coat and hat, lagged behind. The three of them made their way toward the fence line, Samuel with his arm around the ample waist of his wife and Karin watching the trees for signs of the scurrying life she no doubt heard amongst the dead foliage.

Spring could not be far off. The day before, the snow had crunched hard beneath our boots, our feet breaking through and leaving large, round shapes that gave the illusion of giants walking about our yard. At that time of year, the afternoon sun warmed the snow, and on some days the trees would drip down. Then, night froze everything to a hard crust we would crunch through during the morning work and sink into in the afternoons.

Elsa had been the last to leave, and I knew she had soup on the stove and the table set for an early dinner. I felt the tension leave my back by degrees as the silence sank in.

I reached up to tickle Hjalmer's soft belly through his thick sweater. He squealed and kicked and asked me to do it again. Hulda jumped around, drawing my attention, but I pretended not to notice her until her dance brought her within arm's reach. When she glanced away for a second, I reached to trail my fingers along the back of her neck, making her giggle.

The mantle clock in the parlor chimed twice as we descended to the main floor. On most days, I never heard it.

At the base of the stairs, Hulda tugged at her coat while she waited for me to help Hjalmer with his winter clothes. I seated him on the bench near the garden door in the kitchen, and pulled the tangled mess of crocheted hats and mittens and scarves from the bin next to us. His coat hung from an overhead peg, and as I stretched up to pull it off, condemnation from my mother reverberated in my mind. *If you reach above your head, you'll loop the cord around the baby's neck.* I sighed and stood to retrieve the coat. It wasn't worth the risk.

"I…can't…get…my boots on." Every word came out of Hulda with a corresponding grunt.

"Try the other foot." I strained to push Hjalmer's boot over his heel. "Keep your knee straight." I ground out the words through clenched teeth.

By the time I finished and turned to check Hulda's progress, she sat on the floor, waiting for me to button her coat. Everything else was on. The seam of her hat was in the front. I wondered how old she would be before she remembered she could button her own coat if she didn't put her mittens on first.

Hjalmer waited on the bench, sweating, with his arms straight out to his sides. I pulled on my coat and hat and bent over to buckle my boots only to realize the task had become much more difficult in the past week.

Instead, I lowered myself onto the bench next to Hjalmer, bent a little more to my side, and fastened them with one hand. The left was a bit more difficult, but when we opened the back door to a rush of cool damp air, it proved worth the effort.

The blinding sun glimmered through the trees and off the white snow. Hjalmer pushed past me, his legs straining to reach the ground. There was no stair there, just a large step down from the kitchen. Hulda pushed past, calling for me to hurry.

The wet snow swallowed our boots to the ankles. Just last week, it had been halfway to our knees. The front of my skirt did not even come close to touching the thick white blanket. I let it drop out of my habitual grasp and quickened my pace to keep my children in sight.

They headed for the path that led past the first barn and down to the stream. The water ran over our acreage in a narrow trickle. It traveled along the fence line from one corner to the other, dipping under at its most restricted point. It was not so wide in any place that a horse could not easily cross, nor was it impervious to a hard freeze, halting all movement. On that day the warm afternoon had released even the surface ice from the center of the stream, and we heard the gurgling before we reached the line of gnarled oaks that marked the beginning of the woods.

There was very little underbrush in the woods, most of it tramped down or eaten away during the summer by livestock let loose to graze. In the winter, the smooth white stayed largely undisturbed in the expanse between the trees. There was an inherent freedom in walking where there was no path. I called and motioned for the children to move to the left so we could continue off the trail.

The oak bark was wet-black from the melting ice, and the leafless canopy ineffective in blocking the sun. We walked with our eyes squinted to slits. The snow had long since lost its icy sheen, but the overpowering white made every other object stand black in contrast.

We moved to the south end of the woods where I knew a path connected to the road to my parents' house.

"Can we go to Grandmother's?" Hulda struggled back toward me in hindered leaps from one footprint to the next. When she reached a place in the snow where Hjalmer's small prints wove in and out of hers, crushing them, she frowned at him and continued on.

"No," I said.

A simple answer for a simple question, but the pout she leveled at me was too mature not to elicit a twinge of guilt. Months had gone by with

49

no word, and I had no desire to change that. Jakob had spoken about forgiveness that past week while Hulda fidgeted next to me on the bench in his dining room, but I suspected it wasn't the idea of forgiveness that gave me pause. After such a long time, it seemed more a case of indifference.

"Maybe when the snow is gone." Maybe it wasn't a total indifference.

Hjalmer stomped on a patch of ground where the snow had melted away. Dead leaves stuck to his boots, and he bent over to pick at the clinging dirt. His boots were miniatures of his father's, and similar to the ones we'd picked out for the children with whom Hulda and Hjalmer had played at church.

Elsa had spoken with me the morning after that first service. The colors had still been bright, and my breathing fast with a nervous sense of community. Over a simple breakfast of porridge, I asked about the woman who'd cried in her lap.

Six children, Elsa had told me. The woman had six children, and their father—as providence would have it—was the man Anders had fired. The Ankerburg children. My heart sank. The woman's name was Astrid.

Elsa confessed that she had been baking an extra loaf of bread occasionally and taking it over to their farm on her way home in the evening. She spoke the confession into the pot of coffee as she poured. Her hand had trembled when I thanked her.

"What do they need?" I'd asked.

"Food."

"They also need boots that fit." I thought how the money from my allowance had built up during the winter months, when shopping in town was not practical. Guiltily, I realized I could probably clothe the lot of them without even asking Anders for more.

"Boots, clothes, almost everything." Elsa had lowered herself onto the seat across from me and met my eyes with her sharp blue gaze.

Meanwhile, Karin had stood nearby, with one of her stockings hanging low beneath the hem of her dress, exposing her bare leg to the cold air. When I'd looked back to Elsa, her eyes had echoed my concern for the child.

That night I'd spoken with Anders. I had a list prepared with things I thought the children might need. He'd looked at me with a mixture of pride and surprise, but I didn't care. Astrid had no one to turn to. No one knew where her husband was staying, and the parish church certainly wouldn't help, considering she had stopped attending services in favor of Jakob's gatherings.

My own children, warm in their fur-lined coats, played ahead of me in the snow. The sun lent its yellow to their blond hair and pink to their cheeks in a world dominated by hues of black and white.

"Mama." Hulda waved her arms to encourage me to move faster. I tromped with exaggerated effort, a show for her entertainment. She giggled. Hjalmer circled around and tugged at the back of my skirt, adding extra weight.

I was genuinely breathing harder when I reached the edge of the stream. With a stick in hand, Hulda bent and poked under a few rocks. My gaze followed the shallow trickle, then crossed to the other side where the fence ran the length of the shore.

The sun glinted off the surface of the water and sparkled with the first promise of spring life. I ran my palm over my belly, feeling the slow roll of the babe inside. I had been blessed with two children born healthy, head first, not too much bleeding, and I sent up the same prayer, word for word, that I had prayed countless times before. The one I was sure echoed every other expectant mother. I imagined waves of pregnant prayers, heavy and slow, settling at God's feet—at once hopeful and ritualistic, reflexive and superstitious.

My eyes adjusted to the shifting shards of light and traveled along the fence line. Instead of smooth snow punctuated by fence posts, I saw disrupted meadow grass, torn up and lying on the dirty, churned-up snow. There were tracks, left by a shod horse forced to run on uneven, rocky ground.

The trail looked recent. It traveled next to the stream until it dipped under the fence posts. Farther upstream, it disappeared with the fence into the woods.

"Hulda." She looked up from her job of flipping rocks over in the water with a crooked stick. "Hold Hjalmer's hand and follow me."

I led the way next to the water, careful of my footing along the rocky edge. One of Hjalmer's hands was tucked into mine and the other into Hulda's as we picked our way through thick, streamside underbrush. Our feet sank into the hollows of air created by snow piling deeper on top of last year's ferns and bushes. We walked away from the stream when the thorns of berry bushes began to snatch at our scarves and mittens.

"Where are we going, Mama?" Hulda asked.

"You'll see in a minute."

"It's dark in here."

"I know, baby. We'll be out of the woods in a bit."

"I don't like it."

Hulda let go of Hjalmer and walked to my other side. She nestled her hand in mine instead as I looked to see where the horseman cut through our property.

I liked to walk in those woods because of the solitude, because there were no paths and no risk of running into someone. No roads connected to anywhere that would make our woods a convenient shortcut, and none of the servants' homes lay in that direction from our house.

"Where are we going?" Hulda asked again.

Sweat gathered between my shoulder blades and dripped down to my high waistband, where it collected in a cool, tight belt. I was hot and uncomfortable, and I wanted to get back to the house.

"Let's go back." I turned away from the tracks to look at my trailing children.

"Oh, good." Hulda sat down on a rock. "I'm tired."

I searched through the woods to measure how far the tracks stretched into the trees and noted familiar landmarks so I could come back out the next day, without the children. But the tracks veered to the right—in the direction of the house. I considered the waning sun, planned our path back and hoped the horseman chose the same one. "Besides, it's beginning to get colder."

I picked Hjalmer up and slung him onto my hip, which had all but disappeared. He readjusted, trying to find a comfortable position with my belly in the way. I chose my footing carefully.

"My legs are tired." Hulda fell back a couple of paces, and I knew I had kept them out too long.

"Come on, we're almost there."

The light in the woods took on the wintry dim, pre-evening hues of a landscape waiting to hear from the sun. In a few more minutes, the re-crystallizing snow would reflect orange or lavender or pink, but at this time of day, there was nothing but the confusion of shadows. Noise from countless small animals and the limbs of trees cracking with the temperature change combined with our footfalls to make the trudge through the underbrush seem harder than usual. The hoof prints moved to the line of trees surrounding our house and stopped. I stood in the clearing with Hulda holding my hand, pulling me toward home.

"Let's rest a bit, Hulda." I paused to catch my breath.

I moved back to the trees and searched until I found where the horseman made a sharp turn and followed the circle of trees around the house while staying under the cover of the forest.

Something was wrong.

"Go on. Let's get into the house."

The first cramp of a small contraction brought a twinge of guilt. I should not have been carrying so much weight. I should not have been walking through the deep leftover snow drifts by the stream. I put Hjalmer down and let him walk the rest of the way.

There were no strange footprints by the kitchen door, but the ground was so disturbed by our tromping boots, it was impossible to distinguish one print from another.

We stepped in, and I turned to lock the door. I knew Anders would enter through the front when he came home. There was no need to have extra doors unsecured.

Hjalmer plopped to the floor. I tried to walk over him, but my boot glanced his shoulder, knocking him off kilter. Normally the move would have presented no challenge, but Hjalmer's whimper and stuck out bottom lip reminded me of the things I should not attempt, at least for the following few months, including fast, off-trail walks through the woods. I unwound my scarf and dropped it onto the kitchen counter, knowing Anders would be unhappy to hear about our Thursday afternoon strolls and calculating how I could tell him about the horseman while keeping my secret intact.

"Hulda, would you help him get his boots off, please? I'll be right back."

On the stove, the soup bubbled, releasing periodic clouds of steam. The bread rested under a cloth on top of the cabinet. Nothing was out of place in the kitchen.

The dining room table was set for our simple dinner, and the silver was untouched; the front room rested just as we had left it, with the reassuring tick of the mantle clock measuring my steps down the hall toward Anders's study.

The room's long, north-facing windows did little to light the area. It was easier to distinguish the individual trees in the line of woods than the furniture that dotted the room.

My skirt weighed down on my stomach. I fought against my mounting fatigue. Shadows shifted behind the bordering pines, and I stepped closer to the window. Uninterrupted snow in shades of blue filled the expanse between the black trunks of the mature trees to the warm wood ledge that brushed against my skirt. I leaned closer to the glass, looking for a pattern, familiar prints, imagining someone in the forest.

With the metal latch in my hand, I strained against the frosted panes until the ice gave way with grinding protest and the wood ledge bit into my thighs. I scanned first for movement in the woods, and then I noticed the line of footsteps trailing from the pines through the snow to the clearing under the open window. The twilight air scraped against my cheeks and a breath-stealing gust forced my eyes down to where the trampled snow displayed the boot-print evidence.

I leaned farther and studied the stone façade, searching for hints of what the man might have been after. Cold swirled around me. A chill crawled up my spine and I pulled at the window, trying to close it against the prickling sense of intrusion.

Firm hands closed around my waist.

I tensed and choked back a scream.

"What are you looking at?" Anders leaned in over me. His eyes followed the path mine had taken.

I forced my body to relax. His warm breath played with the hair on the top of my head, and I forced my breathing to return to normal. I let go of the tight grip I had on the window ledge and turned, glad for the darkness that covered my flushed face.

"You scared me," I chided as casually as I could.

"What were you looking at?" His eyes still scanned the line of trees. "Where are the children?"

I knew I should tell him, but he would be displeased about our unescorted hike through the woods and the trail I followed, which was likely nothing. A good wife did not burden her husband with domestic matters. Of course, a good wife probably never did anything to cause concern. I took a deep breath.

"We were just getting back from a walk." It was almost the truth. I grasped the front of my skirt and moved to go around him. He stepped in my way.

"But what are you doing in here?"

"I was only trying to see into the woods. I thought something moved in the shadows." I shrugged at my second half-truth while he reached around me to latch the window.

I smiled up at him, only able to make out a dark form without detail. I felt his eyes drop from my face and move down my body to my growing stomach. His hands came up to the hard sides, measuring with a certainty that seemed out of place; as if he knew things he had no right to know.

"I think you are bigger this time," he said as his hands slid around.

I turned to lead the way out of the room, my secret intact.

Chapter Seven

"Stay here, I've got it," Anders rasped out in a sleepy voice as he rolled to the edge of the bed to sit up. I cracked my eyes open to a thick pre-dawn dark, unsure of what he was taking care of but grateful for the warmth of my pillow, and grateful he was taking care of whatever needed attending to.

"Mr. Modig, are you awake?" Samuel called from the hallway in a harsh whisper, followed by urgent, staccato taps at the door. I sat up.

"Lie down. Stay covered. I'll see what he needs."

"But he shouldn't be here yet. What time is it?"

Anders was at the door before my comment reached him. He cracked it open, keeping me concealed. I pulled the quilt to my chin, but remained seated in the middle of the bed.

Candlelight flickered in wavering shadows. They silhouetted my husband and fell to illuminate insignificant objects behind him. The patches of light spread to only one side of the brush resting on my table, one spindle on the leg of a chair, a few folds of the heavy drapes.

"I have to go. I'm not sure when I'll be home." Anders was back at his side of the bed, pulling a still buttoned shirt over his head. He turned to sit on the edge of the bed and searched the floor for his boots. "It's Astrid's family. With Jakob gone, I need to step in and help. Samuel has already been to the bishop, and the bishop said it will all work out on its own without our interference."

"What will work out?" My sleepy brain felt slow to follow, but I remembered that today was Saturday and tomorrow was Sunday, the day Jakob had asked Anders to preach because he and Elin would be gone.

Anders stopped to look at me. I couldn't see his features in the dark. "It's the Ankerburg children. Lars came back home on Thursday. The oldest, their daughter, knocked on Samuel and Elsa's door early this morning. They can't find her brother. He's fourteen. They don't know how long he's been gone."

"How can they not know how long he's been missing?" I pushed the blankets down and shifted to get out of bed.

"That's all the information I have." Anders ignored my last question and made his way to the door. "We're going to pick up Johan, then start looking for the boy. Elsa is on her way to Astrid. I'll send news when I know what is happening. Stay here. There's no reason for you to get up." He took a couple of long strides back to my side, pulled the blankets up, and dropped an absentminded kiss on my forehead before he turned and was gone.

The door latch clicked shut. I threw the covers off and lit the lamp on the bedside table. The clock on the chest read a quarter to five—too early for anyone else to be up, but too late for me to go back to sleep. Sleeping would have been impossible anyway.

I fastened my robe above my stomach and pulled one drapery panel to the side. Things had not gone well for Astrid's family since Anders fired her husband. In truth, things had not gone well long before that. Lars had chosen to live in the barracks with the other men, even though Astrid and their children were not far away from the base. When he stopped coming home on weekends, and began sending less and less money each Friday, things got desperate. Their children had been seen running with some of the other beggar children.

No one expected him to return. At church, Astrid confided she had not seen him in weeks. She feared he had abandoned them completely. From the sound of it, it might have been better if she were right.

Out of the window, below me, I saw Anders and Samuel rush their horses up the drive, the horses' hooves scattering the gravel as the men urged them on. They rounded the corner. I pulled the drape closed again and searched the wardrobe for my riding habit. I had not put it on in a while, but the button still fastened above my waist. It would do for what I had in mind.

Liona was sleeping when I tapped on her door, much as Samuel had tapped on ours. She eased it open a crack.

"Who is it?" she asked in a sleepy whisper.

"It's me."

She opened the door and waved me in, her eyes still half closed. "Is one of the children sick?"

"No, Hulda and Hjalmer are fine. It's Astrid."

"What happened?" Liona tied on her robe and lit the candle on her nightstand. "Are they okay?" She shook the match to extinguish the flame and set it on the candle base.

"We're not sure what is wrong, but one of her boys is missing."

"Missing?" Now fully awake and standing in the weak light of the candle, Liona took in my riding clothes and the gloves I pulled over my fingers. "You're not going out, are you? Where is Anders?"

"He's looking for the boy. I need to help. Elsa should already be there, but who knows what they will need. Can you handle things here while I am gone?"

"Don't worry about us." Liona grabbed some hairpins off her dresser and stuck them into the braids she always slept in. In seconds, her hair was secured atop of her head and she was rifling through her armoire for a dress. "I'll start some breakfast for the stable lads. I imagine they'll be up soon. Do you want me to do anything else?"

"If Hulda can help keep an eye on Hjalmer this morning, it would probably be helpful if you started the baking. I'm sure we will be taking food and other things over there later today."

"I know it isn't my business…" Liona dropped her dress on the bed and glanced at my rounded midsection as her sentence died off.

"I'll be fine. I'll ride slowly." I touched her sleeve with my gloved hand before turning back to the door. "Thank you. You have no idea what it means to me to know you are here."

Liona nodded and waved me away as she stooped to slip on her house shoes.

I eased down the back staircase and out the kitchen garden door.

The path to the barns was dark and quiet. Samuel and Elsa would not be here, and the stable hands most likely had gone back to bed after being woken up to saddle Anders's horse.

The stones under my feet were cleared of the winter snow, and even most of the icepack was gone. I could see my breath in the patches of light that made their way down through the canopy of pine boughs. There was no wind, and I looked ahead for the barn clearing.

After the first service we'd attended, when everyone else had gone and Anna and I stood talking with Elin, she'd explained how they had become involved with Astrid's family. One evening, several months ago, she'd heard something outside her kitchen door. She glanced through her window and had spotted one of the Ankerburg girls, the girl about Hulda's age, searching through their scrap bucket for the edible, discarded pieces of their dinner. When she opened the door, the girl ran off, but she came back the next afternoon. When the girl found the extra barley loaf Elin placed in the bucket, she stuffed the warm bread in her coat and ran off again. The next night she'd stayed. She had told Elin, through mouthfuls of herring, that her mother was ill and they didn't know where their father was.

I followed the path to the barn's side door. It was big enough for me to slip into and back out of the building with my small mare without sliding open the heavy barn doors at the front of the building. The babe inside me turned a slow roll, and I was keenly aware of the directive not to ride after a pregnancy began to show. I prayed for grace and vowed to ride slowly.

My mare whinnied when she saw me, and I hushed her, not wanting her to wake the stable hands. Her bridle hung on a peg just outside her stall. She was not so tall that it was difficult to buckle, so I did so, with memorized movements. With the reins in my hand, I picked my way through the aisle between the stalls. The other horses snorted to get my attention.

When I'd stopped riding, I'd begun to visit only to run a brush down their muscular necks and to ply them with apples until they nuzzled me with their soft noses and hot breath. They had come to expect the attention—a punishment for my spoiling. I hurried past and avoided eye contact. My mare's saddle hung next to the door near the back of the barn, and I was thankful for the straw that muffled my footfalls.

Voices made their way through the quiet as I neared the windows. I considered the saddle, and was faced with the decision to continue saddling my horse myself, or have the stable hands saddle my horse for me. I thought they must have been awake, but decided the possible report to Anders was not worth the risk. The question was forgotten as a female voice floated through the open door. I wrapped the reins around the nearest post and made my way along the wall until I was close enough to make out the conversation.

"You know me," a smooth masculine tone reached me, "I'll be here tomorrow too, and the next day, for as long as you are here."

I knew the voice, but couldn't place it. It was too old to be one of the stable hands, and not familiar enough to be one I heard often, but I knew it, nonetheless.

"I know. I hope I am here forever," Karin, Elsa's niece, answered. Her tone was experimentally sultry. I was embarrassed for her and angered at whatever man was taking advantage of her youth.

"Your new coat is pretty," his voice dropped to a rumble I could not make out.

They spoke for a while as I inched closer to the window in an attempt to discern his identity.

"So, you will be here tomorrow?" he asked in a deceptively hopeful tenor.

"No, I have to go to church, remember?"

"Where is that again?"

"At Mr. and Mrs. Dahlberg's. Tomorrow Mr. Modig is preaching. He's been practicing at night in his study." Her youth seeped through in her voice and words. I rested my hand on the top of my belly and leaned my back against the wall. In a couple of years Karin would be of marriageable age, and I might not have been surprised to walk in on a conversation like this if it were with one of the stable hands. But this was a much older man, and it made me nauseous.

"Ah. What time do they leave in the morning?" he asked, his words colored in a candied hue.

"About nine, so I won't have time to see you. I would rather be here. I think we will be there for most of the afternoon. We'll have communion, and we'll eat dinner together afterward."

It was a careless revelation. I would have to speak with Elsa. If the bishop were to hear this, I knew it would be only the start of many new troubles.

"Communion? Who'll administer the communion?"

I placed his voice. I knew who it was, and with his pointed question, my heart doubled its rhythm. I focused my attention on controlling my breathing. It was the bishop's assistant, and Karin was not safe.

I almost moved to intercept the interaction, when he said good-bye. There were parting murmurs and the sounds of his foot sliding into his stirrup, and then mounting his horse. He ducked into the woods, presumably taking the trails I would depart on. I crouched down under the level of the window so Karin wouldn't see me as she walked back.

There was no sense in confronting the issue now. The damage was done. I no longer had a choice about involving Anders. I chided myself for falling again into the bad habit my mother had instilled in me. There was now so much to tell, it would be almost impossible for me to do so without it looking like I had been hiding information. But I had, and I knew it.

When Karin was out of earshot, I grabbed the saddle, which didn't even feel heavy, strapped it on my mare, located a box to mount from, and headed in the direction of the Ankerburg house under a sky that was already announcing the sunrise.

The sun colored the landscape as I rounded the bend and came into sight of Astrid's house. The gate hung from half a hinge, and I stepped my mare around it carefully so as not to knock it off completely. The front stoop listed to the side at an angle that called all other angles into question. I had seen this house before, but the hopeful pink light of morning made the sight all the more dismal.

There was no foliage in the front of the house and no color; not even the dormant spring brown that dominated that time of year. Here, there was only dirt, and mud, and deep ruts filled with icy water. Rocks dotted the landscape here as they did everywhere else. But unlike the battle waged against the ever-emerging boulders on most farms, this small patch of acreage had surrendered the war long ago.

No firewood was stacked in the lean-to built on the side of the house. Instead, a desperate pair of chickens lay in the mud, and it occurred to me that I had never seen chickens outside and not pecking at something or other. A dirty-faced child peered out of the window, and one of the young boys hauled a heavy bucket to the barn. It swung from his thin arms. He was not wearing the coat we'd brought over earlier in the winter.

I dismounted from my horse carefully and tried to stand up straight. My legs ached from the short ride, but, as if to reassure me, I felt an elbow or knee jab me from the inside.

Nothing in the yard was upright enough to tie my horse to, so I fastened the reins to a nearby, gaunt-looking tree and picked my way up the front steps.

Knocking seemed out of place, but so did walking in without invitation. "Elsa?" I turned the knob and rapped on the door. "Are you here?"

The front door opened with a squeak, and Elsa turned from her place in front of the fire.

"Mrs. Modig? What are you doing? How did you get here?" She set the spoon on the table next to her and hurried to take my coat.

"How is Astrid? What happened? Have you heard about her boy?"

"She's resting."

Elsa's look was meaningful, and I followed her eyes to the curtain that hung in the doorway on one end of the dark room.

The air was thick with the scent of unwashed bodies, overlaid with the yeasty backdrop of a tavern. Elsa didn't seem to notice, and I did my best to hide my reaction. My mouth watered in protest, and I tried not to breathe through my nose. Elsa turned away from me with stiff shoulders to stir the pot hanging over the fire. I knew my reaction was meeting her old expectations of me.

"I planned to return to your house as soon as I made sure Astrid was settled." Elsa jumped to the assumption that I'd come looking for a wayward employee. I resented the need to prove my intentions and sent her a look I could only hope conveyed my annoyance. Instead of explaining, I walked across the small room and lifted the threadbare curtain that separated the two downstairs rooms.

Astrid slept on a rough-framed bed pushed up against the wall. A small uncovered window was only a short distance from the foot of the bed, and I could feel the drafts swirl. Astrid looked like a bruised child under a quilt that was far too nice for the rest of the room.

Elsa pushed past me with a bowl of fragrant broth and lowered her ample body to the edge of Astrid's bed. The ropes under the mattress moaned in protest.

"Astrid, roll over," Elsa commanded in a grandmotherly voice she had never used with me. It was soft, and I imagined Anders as a young boy responding to such subdued inflection. She reached into an apron pocket that always seemed to hold the right thing and pulled out matches to light the lamp.

Astrid responded and turned her face toward the light, and for the second time in only a few minutes I had to try not to embarrass myself by getting sick.

Her right eye, almost swollen closed and surrounded by an angry red welt, cracked open to see me in the room. Her chin was bruised and her forehead misshapen by a large raised bump. She moaned and tried to sit up, but Elsa urged her down and began to spoon broth through her cracked lips. The magnitude of Astrid's plight fell on me, and the only prayer that came to mind as I ducked out of the curtained doorway was *Dear Jesus, find her boy.*

Six children. I needed to start a count.

"Is anyone up there?" I called in a loud whisper up the ladder to the loft. One grimy girl, the same one I'd seen in the window, peered around the corner and disappeared into the dark. I resigned myself to the rungs and began to climb.

I knew that Elsa had brought over a number of things for the children, but there was no evidence of our gifts in the little house. I was almost embarrassed by our paltry attempts at charity, as it was apparent their needs extended so far beyond material goods. We should have been more . involved. We should not have left her in a situation like this. I didn't even know where to start.

The girl who peered around the corner sat against the slope of the roof under one of the quilts Elsa and I had tied. She had the fabric wrapped behind her and over her head. It was gathered in her fingers under her chin. My eyes began to adjust to the dark and I saw two other children huddled on the same dirty straw mattress tucked on planks under the rafters. The oldest must have been about six, the youngest, maybe two.

The room was not large enough for me to stand up straight, so I crawled to the children. An un-emptied chamber pot, filled almost full, reeked in the corner, and damp mold from invading winter frost crept along the cracks between the boards on the wall.

"Come here." I patted the plank floor next to me. The middle child, maybe five years old and the only one who would meet my gaze, pushed back the blanket, ran to me, and sat on the pooled edge of my skirt. Her head lowered until it rested on my thigh, all the time her eyes never leaving mine. I touched the fine skin stretching across her shoulders, and I was surprised by how dry it felt. The three girls wore little more than their shifts, with their thin arms, legs, and bare feet exposed to the winter air. As the room boasted no furniture, I wondered where their clothes were, until I noticed a heap of scraps.

The littlest one stood next to me and wrapped her thin arms around my neck. She left smudges of dirt across my shirt, and for a brief, awful moment, I was glad Astrid was probably too destroyed to recall the last couple of days.

I wiped the tears from my cheeks and pulled the quilt off the mattress. "Let's go downstairs and sit by the fire."

They filed down the ladder and to the warmth of the hearth. I prayed that Anders could find their brother. Only so many tragedies should be allowed in one room, and this tiny room already had its fill.

Chapter Eight

I lifted the last of the three girls from the bottom rung of the ladder and carried the thin bundle of cold limbs to the folded quilt in front of the fire. She weighed nothing—half of what Hjalmer weighed. It was like holding a ghost.

She wiggled into the narrow space between her sisters. They must have slept like that, the youngest in the middle.

The boy who'd carried the bucket to the barn returned, slamming the door closed behind him. He rubbed the bits of mud from his feet onto the bare boards. When he saw the fire, his sharp, tense shoulders hunched under his thin shirt as the unexpected warmth melted the hardness of responsibility, giving way to the needs of a child. It was not an easy thaw. I could not decipher his guarded glance, and I felt the need to win him over, to push him back into childhood. A childish wish of my own, afforded only by my life of little want.

I ladled Elsa's steaming stew into bowls. "There's enough for you too," I reassured him. I knew the question in his posture. My heart ached for the proud character of the boy. He would never have asked, waiting for his sisters to eat. He was a man, seasoned by need, in the body of a child. Why some men exuded character from that tender age, while others—grown men, his father—sacrificed responsibility and embraced treachery was beyond me. I hoped I could unravel the mystery in time to raise sons of mine to be men of honor.

The oldest of the girls moved to make room for her brother, and he shuffled over, finding his place in front of the fire.

"Thank you, ma'am," he said into his lap. I responded with a wooden bowl filled with fish stew.

The children ate in huddled silence. They followed a quiet, rudimentary etiquette, and I was filled with respect for a woman who could have presence of mind to care about teaching manners in that level of desolation. Or was it that the children had learned to be invisible under the fist of their father?

Men's boots on the front step jarred me out of the safe little female world I'd created. I placed myself between the door and the children, knowing not what I would have done if Lars was on the other side. Anders, Samuel, and the missing child stepped in, and my fear gave way to relief. The boy had been found. I quickly closed the door behind them, and my mood settled on a mild distaste for the masculinity that filled and crowded the tiny room, bringing cold drafts and causing the children to huddle closer still.

The oldest son, tense with authority borrowed from the men to his left and right, took in his siblings sitting by the fire and the closed curtain at the bedroom door.

"Would you like some stew?" I asked, as if we had not spent the night worried and searching for him.

He didn't meet my gaze. He shifted his weight from foot to foot. His hair was a dirty blond and his features, angular. His expression revealed no need. The child was hard; he needed guidance beyond the nurturing I could offer.

"Son." Anders placed a hand on his shoulder. "Go check on your mother, then come out and have something to eat."

I filled another bowl for the child and placed it on the table.

"Brianna, the carriage should be here any minute with some supplies. You can go back home with them."

His toneless words reached my bent back as I stirred the largest pieces of fish from the bottom of the steaming kettle. I stood in response, attempting to minimize the obvious strain of my pregnancy, and turned to find him standing over me. For a second I resented his look of concern. Then, I felt guilty. He'd spent the cold morning hours searching for another man's child.

I lifted my eyes to his. "Maybe we could talk outdoors?"

He nodded one curt nod, and I pulled my shawl over my shoulders before I followed him into the bright cold.

There was no wind, so the sun weakly warmed the exposed skin on my face and my hands.

"You should not have come here."

I couldn't help but turn away to look toward the house. Daylight made it no less disheartening.

Anders pressed his point, "It wasn't safe."

"Not safe? Helping children devastated by their father is not safe?"

"Not when you risk another child to do it." He shoved his hands into his pockets and glanced down to where my shawl hung on either side of my swollen stomach.

"I rode slowly. Besides, what would you have me do?"

"We returned the boy. They will be fine. I told Samuel that Elsa may remain here for as long as she is needed, and supplies are coming with the coach."

"How do you expect them to recover? They have nothing. Even the things we gave them—which in retrospect were completely inadequate—everything was taken by that man who calls himself their father. I don't think ten coaches of supplies could fix what has gone on here."

Anders's eyes darkened and the sides of my face tingled.

I could feel the flush creep from my neck to my ears, but pressed my point further. "The children have a beaten-down straw mattress on the floor of the loft and a pile of rags in the corner. I assume the rags are their clothes, but I suspect they have been sleeping under the mass of worn garments rather than wearing them. There is no food, no furniture, and Astrid is beaten beyond recognition. Where is the constable? And where is the bishop? And how can you say they will be fine? It will take Astrid weeks, if not months to heal, not to mention what will happen if he comes back."

"The constable says it is a family matter." A small piece of rotten wood broke off the fence post in Anders's hand. He tossed it to the other side, and then stared at the ground where it landed. "The bishop enjoyed it a little too much when he told me to encourage Astrid's new minister to counsel them." He turned and tested the strength of the fence with his weight. With a dry crack, it threatened to give way. Anders frowned at the house.

With Jakob gone, we were the closest thing this family had to a church leader. I breathed out and realized I couldn't see my breath. It was warmer than it felt. "How can they care so little?"

"She left the church. They feel she is reaping what she has sown."

The sun did little but toss its weak rays onto the rocky soil. I dug my toe into a hoof print in the mud. "Nothing but weeds will grow here this year. These children will not survive. Anders, please, go into that house and look around, really look. If we have to act as their leader, then we need to do right by this family."

A brown bird, perched on a rotten shingle at the peak of the roof, let out a single, high chirp. Anders held out his arm for me, and we picked our way through the mud and back to the house.

The fresh air had cleared my lungs of the dankness, but we plunged back in, Anders stooping under the low door behind me. I nodded toward the loft ladder. He only needed to stand on the bottom rung in order to get enough of a view. He turned to look at the children watching him invade their territory and cleared his throat. The curtain to Astrid's room hung to his left. He knocked on the wall next to the doorway.

"Yes?" Elsa said.

"May I step in?"

There was a rustling of movement from the other side of the faded fabric, and Elsa's red hand pulled the curtain over for Anders to step in. The fabric dropped behind him, and I moved back to the children. Samuel had gone to see to the horses, and the runaway boy sat hunched over his steaming bowl at the table.

Anders walked out from behind the curtain, blinking fast. "Where is Samuel?"

"He stepped outside."

With a nod, he left, the latch clicking softly behind him.

I turned my attention to the newly returned child. "I'm Mrs. Modig. What's your name?"

"Isak, ma'am." He watched his soup until my silence required eye contact. Under thin eyebrows, he glanced up.

"How about your brother and sisters? What are their names?"

"Otto." He nodded toward the boy huddled by his sisters, and then went down the line. "Margit, Molly, and Melena." They continued to eat through the mentioning of their names, but paused when the sound of horses announced the arrival of the coach. The only child not in the home was the one who had gone to Samuel for help. That child was older, and living and working at a nearby estate. I was marginally relieved to have all the younger ones gathered in one place.

From the window, I watched as Anders approached the driver. He was one of our stable hands. Anders ran his hand over the mane and neck of the harnessed horse as he passed by. Its skin twitched under the weight in a welcoming ripple. I was strangely proud of the animal's reaction to my husband.

The driver returned to his seat and waited as Anders and Samuel made their way back to us.

The four on the quilt had settled into a nested huddle, the youngest having worked her way between the next two, under their arms. The boy was turned away from the girls on his side with his knees drawn up and his back against the back of the oldest. I wondered when they'd last had the privilege of sleeping with full stomachs.

Anders ducked into the room again, this time followed by Samuel. "Son."

Isak stood with his back stiff and his stew forgotten on the table.

"I have a business proposition for you."

"Yes, sir." Isak almost stumbled as he rushed toward the men at the door.

"It would seem if you are old enough to leave and make your own way, you are old enough to work and help your mother until she feels better. Can you drive a team?"

"Yes, sir!" Isak's voice escaped with a harsh squeak.

"As chance would have it, we are in need of another stable hand. Do you think you might be interested? You would have to bunk with the other men in the stables. It is not fancy and the work is hard, but it is clean and warm. You would earn your keep and the same money as the other lads earned when they began working."

Standing in front of the men, Isak appeared to be growing by the second as his back straightened with every word. "Yes, sir."

"I already spoke with your mother, and she is in agreement."

Isak's eyes shifted to the curtain, then to his brother and sisters by the fire.

"Let us take care of them." I stepped in. "You are the man of the house right now, and I am sure your mother would be grateful for some of your earnings."

"Go tell your mother and hop onto the carriage next to Aaron," Anders instructed. "He will take you back and introduce you to the other lads."

"Brianna, would you stay here and prepare a list of things we'll need in order to transport them to our home for tonight? Give it to Samuel, and he will bring the supplies when he returns with an extra carriage."

Samuel nodded in my direction, and we exited the house together.

The list in my head was unending, but I settled for blankets, extra coats, shoes, stockings, mittens, hats, and anything else we could use to bundle this family to safety.

Aaron snapped the reins, and I watched as they moved past the trees and around the broken fence with purpose. The sky was turning pink as Anders slipped out of the house and toward the barn. I wondered what he would find there, and if we took this family under our wing, who would care for those wretched-looking chickens.

Astrid's crumbling house had finally warmed completely. The fire crackled in the hearth, every once in a while popping with a wayward spark. I imagined the exhausted children soaking the warmth deep into their bones.

I sat on the only available chair and stretched my legs out in front of me. My boots were dirty and felt two sizes too small after all the activity of this day. I tried to wiggle my toes. There was little room to spare. I knew that when I took my boots off later that night, the lines from my stockings would be imbedded in my ankles.

Leaning back, I let my arms hang down and shifted my bottom to the edge of the chair. My stomach protruded to a degree that surprised even me, but I let my head fall back and tried to relax some of the muscles across my back and shoulders.

"Do you feel well?" Elsa whispered from above me.

I scrambled to preserve some sense of pride, but her hand came down hard on my shoulder. "Stay there. I just came out to get some water. I wish they had milk, but at least their well seems to be one thing on this land that's not trying to make their lives harder."

"I'm fine, just a bit tired."

She walked over to the bucket of water and ladled a cup full. I sat up, trying to discern just how long my eyes had been closed.

"Astrid should be fine to travel the distance to your house." Elsa pushed the curtain aside. "I know I will feel much better without the threat of Lars returning to them here."

The curtain fell behind her, and the thought that had nagged at the back of my mind for most of the day returned.

Anders still didn't know of the horse path through our property, and now it was too late to speak of it. I didn't want to admit to our Thursday afternoon strolls through the snow-drifted woods, nor how I had walked out the next warm afternoon to find the path compressed and packed. The horseman had made more than one visit.

I owed it to Anders to say something. Especially since he had included me in the plans to care for Astrid's family.

It was a deplorable situation, but I couldn't help but find satisfaction in the fact that my opinion counted for something. And if my opinion was important to him, it was only right to show him that his was important to me. Sometimes, there was strength in weakness—it was the reason I never remembered my parents happy; they were both too strong to find strength through each other.

I would not make the same mistake.

Molly, the youngest, sighed and snuggled deeper between her sisters. I could see the rise and fall of her ribs under her shift, and I leaned over and covered the children with my shawl. The cold leaked through the walls of the house. I stood and made my way to the window. Anders was still in the barn.

My thoughts turned again to the path at home that wound through the woods. The day after our Thursday walk, I'd followed it, dipping under branches. It snaked back to the edge of the trees and continued to the north side of the house. There, the path changed as the horseman must have dismounted and continued on foot across the wide expanse of the north lawn to the tall windows of Anders's office.

I should have gone inside then and waited for Anders to get home from work, but I didn't. Instead I followed the path, my skirt dragging next to his tracks. I tried not to step where his boots had crushed.

The footprints paced in front of Anders's windows before ducking under the hedge of bushes surrounding my small courtyard. I traced his path to where he'd tried my door, and then urinated on it. The greasy residue dripped down the glass pane and froze in impotent yellow rivers that melted through the surface of the snow.

I didn't have evidence to say the intruder was Astrid's husband Lars, and if it was, he wasn't able to get into the house anyway. Surely, with such devastation following him he wouldn't show his face again. The temptation to push the experience into the past and let it stay beckoned. But what if it was the bishop's man stirring up trouble again?

Looking through the grimy window, I watched as Anders ducked out of the barn door with a wire mesh cage in one hand. He had either found it or built it out of scrap to carry the pathetic chickens back to our house.

He walked with purpose toward the dirty animals.

As he moved toward the lean-to, the chickens made a terrible noise. Margit stirred and rubbed her eyes. I couldn't wait to see the children settled into proper beds. I stepped outside.

When I rounded the corner, Anders had the last of the pair of chickens by the leg and was forcing it through a hole cut into the wire. The bird was clearly unhappy, with wings askew and feathers bent at odd angles, but not as unhappy as Anders appeared as he slammed the opening closed behind the wretched pile of filthy feathers.

He stood to brush off some of the dirt as he slid the crate onto the porch with a grunt. "I wonder how long it will take Samuel to return," he said as he turned back to the barn after noticing my attempts to hide my grin. Now was not the time to talk.

Back in the house, I was greeted by four pairs of blinking eyes. Yes, we needed to do right by these children, and if the church thought Christianity was found in the kinds of rules that would encourage this squalor, it was no church at all. The youngest opened her mouth in a wide yawn.

In Jakob's absence, and despite the consequences, we were their church family.

Chapter Nine

Sunday dawned bright and clear with almost no sunrise—just night, followed by day. Downstairs, Elsa prepared a quick breakfast of porridge, hardboiled eggs, and bread with lingonberry jam, all while six pairs of blue eyes followed her movements from the edge of the table. I stood at the doorway, and my heart gave a longing lurch at the sight. There were five years between Hulda and Hjalmer. During that empty time, Anders never expressed concern for the lack of a son. But in the space between Hulda and Hjalmer were unsettled, barren years— even if only in my mind. I rested my arm on the curve of my belly and hoped to feel movement. I liked being pregnant because I was never alone.

Astrid's children finally looked like children. Resilient and loving, the shadows were replaced with noisy normalcy.

Anders was in his study, practicing his sermon. He planned to serve communion, as required by the Bible, but I was nervous. It was man's teaching that forbade a layman to serve it, and man's teaching should have been easier to shed in the face of the truth. Truth be told, my concern was two-fold—what if we were wrong, what if it was a sin; and even if we were right, what kind of retribution would we face.

Nearby, Liona's dark hair fell in waves down her back, collected loosely by a ribbon. Before Elsa could ask her to, she took bowls from the cupboard and brought them to the table. I didn't often see her with her hair down, and I couldn't help but stare at the iridescent reflections in the morning sun. She turned and smiled.

"Good morning." Her voice was light and the children listened with rapt attention for the lilt of an accent. They were as charmed as me.

She placed six bowls in a line, reaching around each child from behind. Spoons followed before she went back to the stove to retrieve the bubbling porridge. Liona grasped the ladle, and the contrast from the want of yesterday to the fulfillment of today assured me that our interference was right.

The latch on the door leading to the kitchen garden lifted, and Samuel stepped in, followed by Isak and Aaron. Aaron gave Isak a jovial slap on the shoulder. Isak hid a smile behind his hand.

Elsa had already set the small table under the window with dishes for the men. A loaf of bread sat wrapped in a towel at the center with a jar of jam next to it. A spoon was buried deep in the thick, red abundance of summer. Isak sucked in his bottom lip and seemed to miss the conversation between Aaron and Samuel. I knew it would take longer for Isak to shed his burden—he was older than his siblings—but it would happen in time.

"Sit down, son," Samuel pulled him back into the conversation. I took their coats and hung them from the pegs by the door as they took a seat at the table.

Liona brought the steaming pot of porridge. She held the handle with a green cloth that made the skin on her hands look like cream. The men sat a little taller in their chairs, and Isak, with his mouth open under his freckled nose, stared. Like me, they were captivated, and again I wondered what Liona's future held.

There was a knock on the door, and I rushed out of the kitchen to open it. We expected Anna and Johan. He'd planned to pick her up and bring her over so we could travel together to Jakob's house, where Anders would preach.

Anna had no idea what had transpired at Astrid's home the day before. I was sure she didn't expect a house full of children, and I couldn't keep myself from smiling as I opened the door.

"Good morning!" Anna greeted me with a hug.

Johan stepped in behind her with his hat in his hand. "Good Sunday, ma'am." He bowed with formality and a flourish that exaggerated his lanky height. I took their coats and hung them on the stand near the door.

Anna's clear eyes measured me.

"A lot has happened." I focused my attention on Anna's companion. "Johan, Anders is in his study if you want to see when he will be ready to leave. I think Samuel is getting the horses hitched. He should bring up the carriage shortly."

Johan glanced at Anna and headed down the hallway. I questioned her with my eyes, but before I asked for details, I had to tell her what had happened here. I grabbed my skirt with one hand and her sleeve with the other and pulled her down the hall.

To the sounds of six small children with full stomachs, I explained everything. The intruder, the bishop and the constable, what Lars did to his family, Astrid's injuries, the children's needs, and how they were living with us. Anna took it in quietly.

"But what will you do with them now?"

"Brianna?" Anders and Johan stepped into my morning room. "Are you ready to go?"

Johan didn't take his eyes off Anna, and for the first time, rather than noticing how large her hands were, I noticed her long fingers. Her hair was swept up, but instead of resting on top of her head, the bun sat at the base of her neck, and escaped tendrils framed her high cheekbones and clear forehead. She looked soft, pretty, and Johan and Anna shared a blush.

A large number of the normal attendees were already at Jakob's house when we arrived. Their carriages crowded around the hitching post and every available fence post.

Anders picked his way through the visiting families to the front of the room. His Bible was tucked under his arm. He looked calm and radiated confidence, but when I placed my hand on his chest, I felt the warmth spread through the wilting cotton. Above his collar, his Adam's apple made one bob.

I gave him the careless kind of smile that said I hadn't even thought to be concerned and found my seat in the front row between Hulda and Hjalmer. My own starched shirt was growing damp under my arms, and I shifted my weight on the warm wood. The sun streamed across the hospitably scrubbed, clean floor planks. It illuminated the toes of my shoes, and I tucked my feet under my chair.

The sermon went well. The tenor of Anders's voice rose and fell in a comforting rhythm, but the absence of Elsa's rich tones during the hymn was apparent. She had stayed home with Astrid's children, and I wondered how many people knew why she was missing. Glances from those who surrounded us flicked across our faces.

Johan and Anna shared a bench. Hulda fell asleep with her head on my shoulder while Hjalmer's energy knew no end. Keeping him seated in one chair for any length of time was trying. Those around me bowed their heads in reverence, and I did my best so they wouldn't be disturbed.

We shared communion.

The cup was passed from hand to hand. As it neared, I moved closer to the edge of my seat. I tried to think only of Christ's blood, but my mind wandered to the blood Astrid shed at the fist of her husband. I grabbed the cup out of the hands of the woman next to me, startling her with the abrupt movement.

I shrugged my shoulders and apologized without words, and then I apologized to Jesus, to Anders for the secrets I still held, and to my children for the risk inherent in taking part in this communion. I sipped the bitter-sweet wine and watched the door for the bishop.

It slid down the back of my throat and washed away the bile I hadn't realized had gathered there. A giddy nervousness eased down my spine as well, as we who were gathered found brotherhood in the ritual and—I tried not to think—in our rebellion.

The days were lengthening, and the sky was pink when we left. Many in our church family traveled to get to the home service, and so they brought food to share. We often visited into the night. But spring was nearing, so when we left late that afternoon, we could still make out the fog that gathered in patches around Jakob and Elin's house. It took on the mild color of the evening. The sun had been warm that day, and the melting snow still hung in the atmosphere, low to the ground. What was color now promised to create a black night.

"You spoke a very nice sermon," Anna complimented Anders from her seat across from mine in the carriage. She was traveling home with us to stay for a couple of days. I watched her say good-bye to Johan as he helped her into our carriage. He offered his hand to her, then didn't let go of hers until she blushed. I wanted to ask Anders if Johan had said anything of his intentions.

"Thank you. We're glad you could be here," Anders responded to Anna's compliment as he settled in the seat next to me. His knees touched the opposite bench. I was surprised he hadn't decided to ride separately. He found carriage rides torturous and usually tried to avoid them.

The lanterns swinging on either side of the carriage did little more than illuminate the surrounding, darkening mist. Anders's eyebrows came together, and he reached up to tap on the roof, signaling to Aaron we were ready to leave.

The carriage lurched forward, and we settled into the horses' rhythm. Hulda and Hjalmer began to nod off—Hulda, pressing her face into the hollow between Anna's arm and her ample breast, and Hjalmer resting his cheek on her thigh. Every so often, Hjalmer's thumb snuck its way into his mouth. I leaned over and tugged it out.

Anders rubbed away the condensation forming on the windows with his coat sleeve.

With the sun below the horizon, the lanterns bleached the fog to a milky white and the trees closest to the road flashed by us in an erratic staccato.

"Mr. Modig?" Above us, Aaron tapped on the roof.

"Mr. Modig?" His voice rose in pitch and was accompanied by pounding.

Anders opened the small sliding door that separated us from Aaron, but it was too difficult to make out his words through the noise of creaking axles and crunching gravel.

The fog acquired a hint of a yellow glow, and we all craned our necks to see out of the small, wet windows. The coach slowed.

"Mr. Modig. The road is blocked. There is a crowd of men." The statement was clear above the growing din outside.

"Don't slow down." Anders slid the small door closed and grabbed the door handle.

"What are you doing?" I asked.

"Just cover the children."

Anna placed her skirt over Hjalmer's head and hunched over Hulda. "What's happening?" Her blue eyes were grey in the shadows.

Anders opened the door of the moving carriage, looked forward and shouted not to stop.

"But they are blocking the road!"

"Push the horses faster." Anders's voice jumped an octave and Aaron responded with a shout at the horses and a loud snap of the reigns.

Hulda woke and tried to sit up, but it was impossible with my hand holding her head to Anna's lap. Anna's face was white, and a sheen had spread across her forehead. I wiped the cool, greasy residue from my own face. As the fog grew brighter, and the carriage pushed faster, drops of condensation traveled down the panes of glass.

"Don't slow down!" Anders hung out of the carriage with one hand holding the inside of the roof and the other on the handle of the door. Voices from the crowd became clearer as Anders shouted unintelligible orders directly to the horses.

"Anders!" an unknown voice from the mob bellowed.

"Wait, maybe it's Bishop Modig now," another man called out above the din. Laughter started as the drunken rabble grew in boldness and closed in. Despite Aaron's best attempts, the horses slowed at the nearness of the crowd.

"Want to buy me some boots?" a man shouted. Something hit the top of our carriage.

"Hey, me too, maybe a fancy new hat!"

One voice rose above the others. It didn't have the same mischievous tones.

"It's Lars Ankerburg." Anders ducked in. The hair on the back of my neck stood up.

"Preacher Modig," Ankerburg bellowed, "what wise words do you have for us now?"

Anna's eyes searched mine, and with both hands I tugged the back of Anders's coat, thinking of the disturbed snow outside my window.

The horses lurched forward with another crack of the reigns and stamped a path through the mob. I heard a rending of fabric as I pulled Anders in by his coattails. Hands and debris pounded the sides of the carriage.

Torches and lanterns closed in. Hulda struggled to get up, and for the first time I heard Hjalmer's cries over the noise outside. I held my arms out to him but Anders pushed both of them to the floor. He seized the back of my neck and pushed my head, then Anna's, toward the center of the carriage and covered us with his body.

We were a tangle of arms and legs when a cramp shot from my back to my toes and tightened its fist around my belly. I held in a moan as the light of a torch illuminated the red and yellow on the lap quilt. A ball of sparks struck the window, showering us in shards of glass.

A loud ringing pierced and drowned out the crashing noises from above and the screams from below, and I realized it was my ears. I was dizzy, and I kept my head down as the carriage raced into the welcoming dark under a hail of debris.

Finally, it ended. Anna was the first to sit up, pulling Hulda off the floor with her. Anders pulled me to my seat, his hands hard on the top of my arms. Into my lap he thrust a clinging Hjalmer, who reached around my neck and squeezed until it hurt. I didn't try to loosen his grip.

Anders checked for cuts on the children and me and Anna, and slipped his arms out of his coat in hopes of containing most of the glass that had shattered over his back.

My white hand stood in contrast to Hjalmer's dark coat. I noticed my hand wasn't trembling even as my ears were ringing, but when the carriage stopped and Anders led the children into the house, I grabbed the spokes of the rear wheel and retched. Mercifully, the ringing stopped.

I wiped my face with my handkerchief and followed the rest of the family. When I reached the door, Anders was standing there, and I knew what had to be done.

The inside of the house was quiet. The Ankerburg children were already sleeping, and Liona greeted us at the door. Seeing our expressions, she ushered Hulda and Hjalmer toward the stairs, Hulda a little more reluctant to let go of my hand than usual.

"I'll be up in a minute to say good night." I pressed her hand a bit tighter before letting go. She climbed the stairs with her eyes on me.

We moved to the front room where the fire still offered warmth but little in the way of light. None of us moved to light a lamp.

I was the first to sit. Anders carried the footstool over and placed it under my feet. I let him, even though I didn't deserve the courtesy. Anna sat down next to me and turned her head away as Anders reached under my skirt for my ankles. When I was settled, he sat in his chair and watched the dying embers in the hearth. The orange light played with his profile; it flashed over his cheekbones, his hair, and the stubble on his jaw. I couldn't help but feel that my silence had put us all at risk.

"Who were they?" Anna was the first to speak.

A loud knock interrupted the question that no one dared to answer, and Anders heaved himself out of his chair to open the door.

I dropped my exposed feet off the stool as the bishop's assistant entered.

"The bishop would like to speak with you." He removed his hat and fiddled with the brim. His restless fingers didn't appear to move out of nervousness; instead, they seemed to have no other purpose and almost looked as if they moved independent from thought. In mock humility, he watched the floor. I looked away and toward Anna so my curled lip wouldn't betray my distaste.

"Is there anything I can get you?" Karin entered the room. She halted when she saw the man at the door. An ugly blush turned her ears and the sides of her face a mottled red. I sent her a glance that said I knew of their clandestine meetings.

"No, Karin, we will not need anything at this time."

Elsa must have sent her in when she heard all of us come home. Karin fumbled with her apron, her eyes never leaving our uninvited guest.

"You may go back to the kitchen and tell Elsa," I ordered.

Karin nearly tripped in her haste to leave the room. Anna and Anders didn't know what I'd overheard. Yet another thing I would have to explain.

The bishop's assistant's eyes met mine. They were small and light enough to appear almost translucent. Clearly, he suspected I knew.

Anders stepped into the path of his dead stare. "You may tell the bishop I will call on him tomorrow."

The man backed out of the room and out of the house. Anders didn't move to close the door behind him; instead, he watched as the unwelcome man let himself out.

"What happened?" Anna finally asked no one in particular.

"It was a man from the base I'd fired." Anders dropped into the chair across from mine. "Astrid's husband, Lars."

The fire crackled in the hearth, and the room grew warm.

I shifted forward, facing Anders. My silence, my secrets, had put more at risk than just our relationship. "I have something I need to tell you."

<hr />

"How is she?" I asked Elsa.

It was Monday morning. Anders had left early for the base, and the events of the last night were already taking on the unreal hue of a storm passed. I'd told him everything, including what I had overheard from Karin in the barn. He'd been shocked that I had held so much back. But besides securing a promise from me to be more forthright, he'd said little. He was so unlike my father. Retribution and punishment were not his goals. Instead, he digested the new information, and we made plans to move forward. Anders wanted Karin sent away, as much for her own safety as ours.

"Astrid is doing much better." Elsa flipped the mound of dough she was kneading and sprinkled more flour on the board. It was a rare moment of quiet in our greatly expanded family. That morning, Astrid's children joined in Liona's lessons upstairs. Liona had all of them lined up; older next to younger, with the older holding the slates and the younger copying the letters with chalky hands. The two youngest, Hjalmer and Molly, were stacking blocks in a patch of sunshine streaming from the window.

Elsa flipped the dough again and folded it under, making the top smooth and round.

"She ate a good breakfast this morning and is washing up now."

Elsa placed the dough in a bowl and covered it with a dishcloth. She set it next to the stove to rise and wiped her hands on her apron.

"Good morning." Anna stepped into the kitchen and sat at the small kitchen table, her brightly colored skirt pillowing around her. Elsa gathered the teapot and three cups and carried them over. I found the jam and bread and joined Anna, once again noticing a change, not so much in her appearance as in her posture. She was infused with a new confidence, and I found I couldn't help but sneak glances when I thought she wasn't looking.

"Good morning." From the other side of the kitchen, Astrid took careful steps into the warmth of the room.

"Join us, please." I hurried to stand and pull out a chair.

She crossed to where we sat. We watched her in silence until she settled onto the chair and raised her chin enough to make the most minimal eye contact. A large bruise began at her eye and traveled across her cheek to her yellow and green ear. Angry fingerprints dotted her neck on the other side as if her husband had held her with one hand to keep her in place for a beating with the other.

Anna took in a sharp breath, and Astrid quickly dropped her gaze.

"I'm sorry. I'm so sorry." Anna brought her hand to her face to wipe her own eyes. She took a deep breath. "Let me pour the tea."

Astrid thanked her and accepted the offering with a shaky grip. The cup rattled against the saucer before she placed it on the table. Her fingers were small and skeletal thin, and the knuckles on her right hand had swollen to double their normal size. Her left hand, wrapped to support knitting bones, she held hidden in the folds of her skirt. I hoped Lars was nursing at least a few wounds of his own.

She wore my clothes, and even though they were made for a small woman, they hung on her. She'd pinned the black skirt at the waist, and the shoulder seams on the white shirt rested below where they should. Elsa's eyes gauged my reaction to Astrid's clothing.

We hadn't talked about it, hadn't had the chance to. I nodded my approval. "Elsa, please sit with us for tea."

Astrid relaxed with the inclusion of her protector.

"I peeked in on the children." Anna picked up a spoon and dipped it into her tea. "If you feel well enough, I can show you where they are."

Astrid nodded. "Thank you very much."

I took a slice of bread, covered it with the ruby colored jam and placed in on Astrid's plate as a tear slipped onto her sleeve, leaving a wet spot on the white fabric.

"I don't know what to do," she whispered into her lap.

Anna wiped her eyes again, and Elsa reached her hand across the table, offering it to Astrid.

I looked at the bread on Astrid's plate. I wondered when she was last able to eat without worrying she was stealing from her children's mouths.

"Brianna." Anna broke the silence. "Can we talk?"

We left Astrid and Elsa with their hands joined across the table. They looked as if they were praying, but I knew they had no words. I wondered if God counted wordless prayers.

"Johan asked me to marry him." Anna's hands were gripped together and stuffed into the folds of her skirt. Her knees performed a nervous bounce as she sat in the chair across from mine in my morning room.

A smile flitted and disappeared, only to reappear as she met my eyes.

I thought back over the past couple of months and realized how much I had missed.

Her joy was obvious.

"Why didn't you tell me yesterday?"

"He asked me on the way over to your house, and then it was so busy when we arrived, and with last night, there just wasn't a good time."

"So Mother and Father don't know?"

"No, and I have not yet said yes."

"When will you see him next?"

"He plans on taking me home from here tonight, but I know he and Anders will talk about last evening at work today, and honestly, I don't know if I want to go home so soon. He might not want me to be alone, and I'm not sure I want to be alone, and I don't want to leave you." Anna stood and paced in front of the hearth, then crossed to the window and stared at the line of pines surrounding the property.

I stood and joined her.

Snow fell from one heavy branch. Having lost its burden, the branch swayed up and down until most of the other branches on the tree, disturbed by the movement, had shed some of their own burden as well.

"Do you want to marry him?"

Anna looked down at the sill. "Yes, I do." She sighed before she continued, "Father will be angry, and Mother will be disappointed, but she has never been anything else." Anna picked at invisible crumbs on her shirt.

"He'll treat you well, you know that."

She paused to look at the ceiling and back down to me. "He wants to get married right away."

"Of course he does."

She sent me a dark look, and I smiled, for once playing the role of the more experienced sister.

"We can't get married in the official church."

I hadn't thought of that. "Father and Mother will never recognize it if it is not blessed by the bishop."

We sat back down again and settled into our thoughts.

"Do you love him?" It was an improper question, as it was none of my business, and I regretted it as soon as it left my lips. "I'm sorry, I…"

"Yes. Yes, I do." Anna turned and leaned her back against the window ledge. She crossed her arms over her chest and looked to the ceiling.

She'd changed so much. She'd always been stubborn, but the trait had faded— it had matured to confidence.

"There's something else." Anna fidgeted with the buttons on her shirt before meeting my gaze.

"What else?"

"Johan and I will be moving to Stockholm." She shrugged. "He wants to be involved with a church there."

She didn't say Johan was moving, or they were thinking about moving, or that he wanted her to move, rather she'd used the words Johan and I. Her decision had already been made. And although she'd introduced the idea by telling me that Johan wanted to move, I knew she looked forward to the change as well. She wouldn't be going if it wasn't something she was excited to do. I took a deep breath. I was losing my sister.

"I'm happy for you," I said.

Anna nodded, blinking fast.

"How do you feel about Mother and Father?" I asked. Their poor reaction could be assumed.

She dropped her arms and snorted like she did when we were children. "I don't care. I know it's wrong that I don't care, and of course it would be nice if they suddenly accepted everything, but they won't. We both know that."

I nodded. It was something we both knew well. I glanced back to Anna's face. Her smile had changed, too. She was nervous, but relaxed and free.

She'd abandoned the idea that she could ever please our parents. Right or wrong, she'd found the freedom that comes with that sacrifice, and I envied her.

Chapter Ten

April 1880

The letter sat unopened on Anders's desk.

It was from his parents. The white envelope stood out brighter than the other piled papers. I knew what it would say, or at least its tone, but also knew he should be the one to open it.

The narrow passageway between his office and my morning room was dark. Elsa had already pulled the curtains of my room closed. I returned to stand by his desk again. A chip in the wood top was more discernable in the evening light, and I moved the letter a little to the left to cover it.

The business was doing well. I didn't know why they wanted to interfere.

Under my fingers, the paper felt smooth and expensive. The large dark letters of Anders's name, scribed in thick ink, appeared as if they would burn through the page and down to the wood. For no reason I lifted the letter to check the other side, but I only saw the chip. I covered it again with the letter.

I expected this. The bishop was reporting to Anders's parents. He didn't even have the pride to try to hide it. He openly admitted it. He said he felt it was his duty, out of respect for upstanding citizens like Anders's kin. Anders did not ask how much his parents had contributed to the cause. It was unclear whether it was his parents who first contacted the bishop for help convincing their son to fall into step, or the bishop who contacted his parents looking for another persuasive voice. Either way, no one was satisfied with the outcome. Anders remained firm in his decisions. Our decisions.

"How was your day?" Anders stepped into his office, surprising me a little. I hurried to take his jacket.

"A letter arrived from your parents."

He paused before setting his papers down and shrugged out of his coat, handing it to me.

I folded the shoulders of the jacket together and smoothed the heavy fabric over the back of a nearby chair.

"We knew it was only a matter of time." Anders placed both palms on his desk and lowered himself into the upholstered seat, settling in to read.

The bishop had questioned Anders, but not in the way he'd expected. He congenially inquired about our interference with Astrid's family. He didn't ask about the beer. He didn't interrogate about the communion Karin told his assistant about. Instead, he had questioned our intentions to baptize the child growing inside me. I sat on the edge of the chair, careful not to lean back against Anders's coat and crease it.

Anders broke the seal and held the letter to the light. I dried my hands on my skirt. The paper clasped in his fingers didn't waver. He exhaled and placed the letter face down on the desk. "They are requesting we travel to see them, immediately."

"They know I can't travel right now."

"I know." Anders stood and walked around the desk to the chair next to the one I sat in. He sunk into it. His knees extended far beyond the edge of the chair, and I marveled again at how tall he was. He filled every room he entered, and I was grateful.

"We will be fine if you make the trip by yourself. It will be faster if you go alone."

Anders shook his head. "I'm not leaving you and the children, even if only for a couple of days."

I glanced to the papers on his desk. He had piles of work. "You really need to go. Besides, I'd rather you go now, before the baby arrives."

Anders stood and crossed to the windows. Outside, scattered patches of snow reflected the last of the sun. The trees, their branches now free of the burden of snow and ice, still waited to bud.

"I will speak with Johan. If I leave tonight I will be there by tomorrow, and we can have this behind us." He paused to consider, "Johan will be able to take care of things at the base for a couple of days." He picked up a book he'd been reading and slid it into its space on the bookshelf before sitting in the chair next to mine.

I ran my hand over my ever-expanding belly. It was swollen and hard. I wished the child could remain safe inside forever. The bishop's questions about baptism were unsettling.

"I can ask Samuel and Elsa to stay here while I am away." Anders reached toward me, and I placed my fingers inside his. His hands were rough, harkening back to the days when he worked cutting lumber for his father. Even years of office work had not smoothed them completely.

He tugged at my hand until I stood in front of him.

"I would prefer not to leave you right now." He placed his hand on my belly and ran it down to the underside. His head was bowed, and I couldn't read his expression.

He pulled me down until I was cradled in his lap.

"Everything we've done has been for the right reasons." I offered reassurance I knew he didn't need. He supported my back with one hand; the other traveled to my ankle and up to the back of my leg to my knee where his fingers brushed against the bare skin not covered by my stocking.

"I could send a note back telling them I will visit after you are delivered."

"You know that will only make them angry and delay the inevitable. They need to hear from you directly. It's probably past time anyway."

I sank to rest my forehead against the skin of his neck. The stubble of his beard scratched, and I rubbed my face across it while his hand crept further up my thigh.

"They will not agree. In their eyes, no amount of conversation will provide an excuse for not baptizing this baby."

The decision had been made. I knew we were both in agreement. We had taken the evening hours to scour the Bible, looking for the place it said to baptize infants, and came up empty handed. Anders even asked the bishop where in the Bible it told us to have our infants sprinkled. That was when the conversation ended. We just hadn't said it out loud before now.

It was easier than I had anticipated.

His hand stayed on my thigh, and I couldn't help but squirm. I contoured my body deeper into his and breathed in the winter clinging to his skin. He kissed the top of my head, took in a deep breath and held it.

The early evening sky lent a silvery lavender shade to the darkening room, and I waited until he was ready to continue the conversation.

"From what I hear, Lars Ankerburg is gone." He pulled his hands from underneath my skirts and placed his palm over my belly, where I assumed the baby's head rested.

I touched his face, compelling him to meet my eyes. "We have not heard from him in almost a month. Astrid and the children have been settled back in their home for over two weeks now and haven't seen him either. He's probably run off to America with the rest of the people hiding from their past." I paused before continuing. "We can't hide. We have to live our lives."

I watched his hand trace the shape of the baby through my skirt, and I was embarrassed by the desire to feel his rough fingers rub against the dry skin stretched across my belly without the hindrance of fabric.

"Nonetheless"—Anders moved to sit up—"I'll ask Samuel and Elsa to stay."

I stood and brushed the creases from my skirts.

"Come with me." Anders picked up his coat and folded it over his elbow. "It's still awhile before dinner will be ready, and you can help me pack my bag."

He wove the fingers of his free hand between mine and pulled me to the door.

Once in the hallway, I looked to see if anyone was watching before I followed him up the stairs. I knew he desired much more than my assistance packing.

I pulled the white fabric from the bottom of the embroidery basket. Threads hung in varying shades of blue, and for a moment I considered the compulsion to tug and unravel the tiny flowers, cleaning the white expanse. Instead, I placed the string between my teeth to tighten the weave before I threaded the needle.

I had new inspiration to finish the baby's blanket, as now I needed to begin Anna's wedding quilt. Elin promised squares of her own, along with some from the other women of our small congregation, and Astrid planned to assemble the bulk of the quilt. A few weeks from now, we would gather in what would hopefully be warming weather to tie the finished product.

The bright red and yellow tones in my basket would be combined on a white background. We would present it to her in about a month, after the ceremony.

I still needed to speak with Elsa about the breakfast smorgasbord we planned to host. Mother and Father would not attend, and neither would our siblings. I stabbed the needle into the fabric and pulled until I could hear the thread move against the tight weave. My intense stitch puckered the white background, and I worked it back out with the tip of my needle.

Anna sat across from me, drawing out the stitching that would run along the bottom edge of her skirt. Red and pink flowers would chase around her ankles, echoing the winding pattern on her sleeves and collar. As it was not summer yet, flowers for her hair were not available. Had we still been near Stockholm, we could have procured hot house flowers, but we were not. Instead, we arranged a wreath of ribbons to loop and incorporate into her long braids and gather at the nape of her neck.

"He's been busy at the office," Anna said of Johan. "I haven't seen him much."

"Anders should return this evening." I dropped the fabric into my lap and watched Anna's profile as she stared out the window. "When he returns, Johan's hours shouldn't be so demanding."

The firewood hissed in the hearth, and I stretched the muscles in my neck. Anders had been gone for four restless days.

"I wonder what his parents want." Anna looked back to me.

"I don't. I know exactly what they want. I just don't know why he has to be there to hear it." I rolled the fabric I should be working on and pushed it to the bottom of the basket at my feet, making a mental note to pull the tight stitches later.

"When will you tell Mother and Father that you will not be baptizing the new baby?"

"When they ask, I suppose."

A slow ache worked up my lower back to underneath my shoulder blades, where it settled until I corrected my posture.

"When was the last time you spoke with them?"

"Around Christmastime." I twisted to relieve the tension that had settled into my hips.

"Ma'am?" Elsa knocked lightly and stepped into the room. "If you won't be needing anything else, we'll be turning in."

"Thank you, Elsa." I nodded. "We have everything here. If you would like, I don't see why you should have to stay the night. Anders will be home sometime soon."

"It's fine, ma'am. We'll stay tonight. We assured Mr. Modig we would watch over things until he returned."

Elsa ducked out, and I frowned at the door.

"They're only doing as they promised." Anna stabbed the hem of her skirt with a needle full of bright red thread.

"I know that. It doesn't mean I have to like it."

The noise of horses' hooves on gravel reached us through the closed panes of glass. Anna looked up from her flower.

"Could he be early?"

"It might be Johan to pick you up." It was dark now, and although I didn't relish the idea of Johan escorting her home in the dark, the long hours at the base had dictated the timeline.

A loud pounding at the door interrupted my thoughts, and the hair on my arms rose in response to the insistent noise.

"I'll answer," Liona called from the front hall.

"Liona, no." I scrambled out of the chair in time to see her open the front door to a halo of orange light.

"Well, who have we here?" A man's voice leached through the opening. Liona, realizing her mistake, pushed to close the door, only to be stopped by a muddy boot.

"I came to speak to Anders," Ankerburg's voice slid through the crack in the door, "…but I think I might be happier with you." He took his boot from the threshold and moved as if he would take his hat off and welcome himself into the parlor.

Anna and I reached the front door. We forced it closed and dropped the ancient timber in place to secure it.

"Is Anders not home, ladies?" he yelled through the now closed door.

Elsa ran into the room, tying her robe, with Samuel at her heels.

"It's Ankerburg," I whispered loudly.

He pounded on the door again.

"Get off the property, Ankerburg," Samuel shouted through the door.

Liona stepped over to the window and pulled the lace back before Elsa had a chance to block her. Ankerburg rapped on it in response. "If Anders is not available, maybe you can send the dark-haired one out instead."

Liona paled and stepped behind Elsa, her small form completely hidden from view.

Heavy boots took a few steps away from the front door, and I held my breath. The blood rushed to my legs, and I wanted to run.

"He's going around back," Samuel said, adjusting his grip on a gun I didn't realize he carried. "Everyone to the kitchen."

We willingly followed. A stab of pain jolted between my legs. Low. I caught my breath. Anna watched me as we crowded through the service door. I waved her concern away as the building pressure faded to a blossoming ache. The dying embers were the only light in the kitchen. We were satisfied with the meager assistance, standing in the middle of the room, craning our necks to see out of the small windows.

"Mama?" Hulda stood like a specter in the shadows at the base of the kitchen stairway. Her nightgown, buttoned to her neck and flowing to the floor, was completely motionless. Her blond braids, tied with bows, trailed down her chest. The ribbons stood out blood red in the dim light. I rushed to her.

"You need to go back upstairs, baby," I pleaded, bringing my face to her level. She smelled clean. Her eyes were pale and wide.

A dragging noise began at the front of the house and made a careless journey up and down the siding boards toward the back. Hulda ignored my request and clenched the back of my skirt, pulling tighter as the noise approached.

"Go upstairs now."

"Open the door, ladies." Ankerburg pounded at the garden entrance.

I pushed a struggling Hulda into the stairway, closed the door behind her and stood in front of it. She turned the knob and forced it against my back.

"You can let me in, or I will let myself in." He banged again.

"Mama." Hulda shouldered the door hard, and I adjusted my stance for leverage against the pressure.

Ankerburg began to pound a slow, repetitive tap. It was loud and sharp. He was not using his fist.

"He's not going away." Anna moved next to me and leaned with me against the door.

"What does he think he's doing?" Samuel, his back pressed against the wall, strained to see out of the window. He leaned back again as the outside noise swelled.

"I said, open the door," Ankerburg shouted, abandoning the repetitive knocking for sporadic, muffled banging. He was using his fists now, and I couldn't help but see visions of Astrid's bruised, broken body.

Samuel stepped to the middle of the room, cocked the gun and leveled it at the door. "Go upstairs," he instructed us.

"What are you going to do, shoot him?" Elsa stepped in behind him with the kitchen shotgun in hand and loaded it. I wasn't sure what she thought she would do with a gun either, but two seemed better than one.

The metallic click of the barrel snapping closed resonated deep, and I felt a tug and release. A slow dribble of fluid began to soak my underclothes.

"There's another gun above the fireplace if we need it." Samuel waved Anna away without taking his eyes off the door.

The dragging and banging noises began again. Anna rushed out of the room to find the gun.

Hulda stopped pushing at the door. I relaxed my muscles, tensed from holding back, and turned the knob to see if she'd returned to her room as I'd instructed. She was huddled in the corner where the stairs turned. Her hands were over her ears and her eyes squeezed closed. I wanted to comfort her, but the noise had grown over the sound of my voice.

A cramp ripped across my belly, and I was on my hands and knees. I shouldered the stairwell door closed again and whispered an apology to Hulda as my muscles clenched and more fluid escaped to soak my skirts.

"Brianna?" A gun dropped to the floor near my head. The barrel glinted, and Anna's hand brushed a damp strand of hair that clung to my forehead. My muscles were locked, and I held my breath until they released.

It was happening. Another contraction and my forehead met the cool boards of the kitchen floor.

Anna reached to tug at Elsa's skirt, and then Elsa was on her knees lifting my head off the floor.

The banging grew louder. Ankerburg's unintelligible shouts carried over the hail of stones he threw at the door and window.

I locked my muscles against another pain and held my legs together, willing it to stop.

"Liona, see to Hulda," I gritted out between clenched teeth. Liona maneuvered her slim form behind me and pulled the door open, apologizing. She squeezed into the passageway and the door closed behind her. I struggled to my knees.

"Dear Lord Jesus." Elsa took in the damp wood underneath me. "Get her upstairs." She nodded to Anna and pulled me off the floor by my elbows.

A gunshot rang from outside, and we all dropped to our knees again, expecting a shower of glass and splintered wood.

But silence prevailed. My breathing was shallow and quick and loud. Elsa's forehead shone in a stream of moonlight. A bead of sweat trickled down her temple, following the erratic pattern of tiny hairs.

There was more pounding at the door. "For God's sake," Anders said through the heavy wood, "let me in."

People came in and out of my room, whispering and carrying armfuls of linens, but it was only me in the bed with my shift plastered to my breasts and bulging belly. A thin blanket covered my secrets.

Something was wrong. The pains ripped across my middle, but the pressure between my legs didn't build. The people around me communicated in loud whispers through a crack in the door to people in the hall who would presumably relay messages to others standing farther down the hall. Another pain shot to my core, and I fought the urge to let it take me.

I moaned, and the midwife was at my side telling Elsa to send for the doctor. "It's breach."

"No." I struggled to my knees and turned to hold the head of the bed as another cramp tore through me and down to my toes. Pulling on the wood headboard, I traced the variations in the white wall with my eyes until finally, the pressure built, and I pushed against the bright stars at the edge of my vision.

Elsa supported my back from behind as I bore down. I tasted blood.

"Stop pushing." The midwife knelt on the bed behind me and lifted the back of my shift. The cool air settled onto my thighs and backside as she placed her fingers inside me.

Another contraction stole my breath, and the midwife hissed into my ear to push and keep pushing until the baby was fully out.

I pushed until the ringing in my ears rose in pitch.

"Keep pushing." She pulled her body to mine from behind and wrapped her arms around for more support, angling me correctly.

The baby burned its way out of my body.

"Brianna, push. We can't have the head stuck."

The baby's soft body hung between my legs. I could feel the midwife's hands work as I fought to push through the black relief that beckoned.

"Push!"

The baby fell between my knees into a puddle of blood and fluid. A cat-like mewling escaped from the tiny, thin girl-child, and I reached down to feel the warm, wet life. The heavy cord looped around her arm. It was still attached from her belly to a place hidden inside.

Elsa smoothed a dry sheet to my right and directed me to let go of the headboard and lie on my side. My legs trembled. The sheet was cool on my bare arm, the pillow dry, and the babe next to me squirming and pink.

The midwife tied off the cord while Elsa dried and wrapped the baby. Elsa placed her next to my face, and I looked into her watery blue eyes while the midwife pushed on my softened belly and instructed me to push the rest of the baby's world out of my body.

I felt light and cool. A healthy breeze slid through a crack in the window and caressed us. I pulled the sheet to cover the baby's tiny ear, still white and sticky, and closed my eyes with visions of tiny pink fingers wrapped around mine. She'd come early, and she was so small, but she squirmed and grasped and squeaked. She was alive, and that was all that mattered.

"How do you feel?" His whispered words vibrated the small hairs at the nape of my neck. He molded his long form around my back, and I felt no bigger than the babe asleep at my breast.

"Fine." I yawned wide and smiled at the sleeping baby.

"Lars shouldn't be a problem again. I took him directly to the constable's office. There were so many witnesses. He'll be in jail for some time."

"Thank you."

"For what?"

"For coming home when you did."

"You know that doesn't make any sense, right?"

"I know. But I'm still grateful you were there."

He reached around me and touched the baby's soft check. "So, Esther it is?"

"Esther."

"She looks like an Esther."

I hummed in agreement. Anders's breathing deepened as I inspected Esther's wispy red hair in the morning light. She was perfect.

Chapter Eleven

May 1880

I glared at my reflection in the mirror.

It had been almost a month, and still I was unable to completely fasten the back of my skirt around my waist. Instead, the one hook I could close dug into my flesh, pinching tighter with every breath. My black skirt pulled the fabric so close, every wrinkle in the tucked-in shirt etched lines in my skin. I was buttoned to my neck and my wrists, and once secured, the hook at my waist refused to budge. Finally, it released, and I sucked in a relieved breath and peeled the yards of fabric from my hips.

The wardrobe offered no solutions. Defeated, I carried the offending garment back to the edge of my bed and opened the drawer of the bedside table. I found the well-worn black ribbon, threaded it through the eye, and tied a small loop on the end.

"It won't be too long." Anders watched me through the partially open door.

I hummed a response, a little annoyed at his intrusion.

"How is Esther today?"

The sleepy baby in the cradle by the window took in a shaky breath, as if she knew we were talking about her.

"Quiet now, I suppose."

She was bundled, wrapped with her arms immobilized at her sides. The cold wet spring breeze fell on her cheeks—the only skin exposed—and lent them a chilled, pink tinge. Her lace bonnet was tied around her ears and under her chin. She looked like a porcelain doll.

Last night she had not been so doll-like.

"She cried a lot last night." Anders looked over the sleeping pink and white bundle, examining her as if she were a faulty piece of machinery.

"Babies cry." I shrugged and stood to pull up my now adjusted skirt.

"I don't remember Hulda or Hjalmer crying so much."

"Maybe that's because you were usually sleeping."

The brush sitting at my table was a tarnished silver with yellowed bristles. It was a present from my mother, who likely never had a child who cried enough to make my father take notice.

The brush tangled with the first stroke through my hair. I tugged until it released, leaving a snarled mess in its wake. Anders searched my eyes in the mirror. He knew. We both did.

"I'll speak with the doctor on Monday."

He nodded and changed topics. "We should be on our way. I am sure Anna is waiting for us by now." His words were punctuated with a swift, awkward clap of his hands. He adjusted his posture in the mirror and straightened the lapels of his jacket in a flurry of business-like masculinity.

His glance shifted to the cradle.

"Why don't you take her to Liona? I'll be ready to go in a minute."

Anders crossed to the wooden cradle that held Hulda, then Hjalmer, and now our tiny Esther, and my chest constricted with the hope that there was enough goodness left in the wood of this cradle to see a third infant through her first year.

He reached in and rested the bundle in the crook of his arm. She looked as if she weighed nothing; just a bit of flesh wrapped in a bit of fluff, and I apologized to God for seeing weakness in his creation.

Protesting the interruption, she squeaked until Anders jostled her into a more secure position. A smile tickled the corners of his mouth as he left the room.

There was a box on my dressing table, inlaid with mother of pearl. It had gold hinges. I reached in and found my cameo. I unclasped the gold at the back and wove the sharp pin through my collar, high under my chin. The clasp evaded me, and I pricked my finger before I could fasten it in place. A red bead of blood formed on my fingertip. I wiped it in the folds of my black skirt and pressed my thumb over the pinprick until the blood stopped.

With my fingers pinched together, I found my handbag and closed the bedroom door behind me.

Esther's faint cry reached me from the nursery. I paused before continuing down the stairs with heavy, tingling breasts.

When we returned, my sister would be married.

Anders opened the wooden doors of the city hall, and Anna and I stepped into the smell of paper and ink and records and record keepers. Sunlight streamed from the panes of glass and reflected off floating bits of dust. Anna's typically dull blond hair glowed gold, and a man with ink-stained fingers looked up at us. He was unnervingly bored for someone welcoming a wedding party, no matter how small.

The ribbons wreathed around Anna's head acted at once as both her bridal crown and an admission of guilt. I was embarrassed for her, even though I knew she held none of the same sensibilities. Every virgin bride in the parish had the opportunity to marry in the church, wearing the same bridal crown that adorned generations of brides from upstanding families. The book keeper glanced over our clothes before dropping his eyes to Anna's midsection, trying to discern if this was a marriage of less than ideal circumstances.

"We have an appointment, I believe." Johan, divining the man's unguarded thoughts, stepped in to halt the examination of his bride. The man paused and frowned before tapping his pen on his desk and turning to fetch the official.

I smiled at Anna, but she had no need of the support as she already shared a smile with Johan that made me blush. Her life was beginning, but it would take her away from me. Johan's proposal did not come without a price. Anna looked forward to the move, but she would leave me here.

The official read the necessary words without ceremony. Anna and Johan didn't seem to notice. It was just as well. Mother and Father wanted nothing to do with Johan and his vision for the new church. They wouldn't even be at the wedding celebration to take place later that day.

I still pressed my fingers together, as I had been doing for most of the morning, even though the pinprick had ceased bleeding.

The ceremony ended without flourish and we exited—a smiling, hopeful crowd. Nothing had changed and everything had changed. Once again we had taken a tiny step into a new world that looked and felt exactly like the old one. Six months prior I would not have believed I would ever have been standing with my face in the sun, on the steps of the city hall, a new religion, an un-baptized baby, and a sister who was happily joined in marriage in a ceremony reserved for pregnant peasants. Yet, there I stood.

"Let's go back to the house." Anders brought up the rear of the group and ushered us toward the carriages.

New leaves spilled from the tips of stiff, overwhelmed branches, and the sun fell in pieces through the canopy of young green. The spots of light quivered against my sleeves and skirt and traveled up my body as the carriage heaved ahead. The horses whinnied and huffed and stomped with an irreverence encouraged by the strengthening sun. I rested my head on Anders's shoulder and breathed in the clean scent of his coat. He reached over and covered my hand with his. Johan and Anna followed behind us in Johan's coach. It was hard to believe they would soon be gone to start their own lives away from the pressures of family.

Part of me was envious—envious of their new start, lack of encumbrance, and that they were brave enough not to look back. The cottage Anna cared for, and the meaning of her presence to my parents and the rest of our siblings, released.

Sun-bathed mud fields flew by. Soon they would be dotted with bent people, sewing precious seeds in hopes of a winter-sustaining harvest. The small plots of land bordered by their wide stone fences would be alive with the haze of bright green. Hopefully. I prayed the summer would bring a plentiful harvest, enough for winter stores, enough to feed the farming families of our community. Last year was difficult: the planting late, the harvest meager.

"Next week they'll pull stones from Astrid's plot of land." Anders watched the fields on his side of the carriage. Pulling stones, the harvest of winter, was an annual task for the members of this community.

The horses slowed and we turned up the drive to our front lawn covered with carriages and visitors. Hulda darted around to the side of the house, followed by a gaggle of girls her age and one too young to keep up. The child yelled after the older group, returned to sit on a still winter-barren stone planter, plopped her chin into her hands and pouted.

Aaron led the horses to a smooth stop, and the little girl hopped off her perch to run and see who else had come to the party. Anders reached for the door latch and jumped out, offering his hand to me before Aaron had the chance to secure the reins and scramble down from his perch.

Dark blond braids with sun-borrowed touches of strawberry trailed behind the child that bounced up to greet us.

"Is that Astrid's Molly?" Anders asked. She looked nothing like the child she was just a couple of months ago. I nodded.

"Well, hello, Molly." Anders bent at the waist to greet the now shy girl. "Your dress is very pretty."

"Mama made it," she said with her chin to her chest, suddenly awkward with the attention. She examined the floral print band that ran high above her waist to tie in a neat bow in the back. It was hard to believe she was the same child we pulled, hungry and cold, from a dirty loft.

Things changed fast. She bounded away after the other girls, her happy gait flaunting her success and health to the last vestiges of winter; she was like the spring spectacle of trees we waited for. I felt like whistling.

Johan and Anna's carriage stopped behind ours and the gathering crowd ended their conversations and placed their baskets full of gifts and food down as they rushed to wish blessings for the new couple.

Anders and I made our way to the front door, where we were greeted by Jakob and Elin.

"How have things been for you?" Jakob slapped Anders's back.

"Do you want to see the baby?" I asked Elin as we stepped inside.

"She's sleeping." Liona hovered as Elin and I made our way across the soft nursery rugs. "It took her awhile to settle in." Liona pulled a strand of dark hair and tucked it behind her ear. She was probably fighting the urge to tell me to let the sleeping child alone.

"She should wake to eat soon anyway."

Liona shrugged, abandoning the respite of a few extra quiet minutes. She walked with Elin and me to the side of the cradle.

"Oh, she's so tiny," Elin's voice was edged with desire, and I wished for a way to share my joy with her. They had waited so long, and in weaker moments she'd confessed of the monthly disappointments and the ensuing week of sadness she couldn't shake.

Elin crossed her arms and held her elbows tight to her sides. She would be a wonderful mother. Not for the first time, I wondered at God's favor as he burdened poor farming families with too many mouths to feed, yet withheld the pleasure from those who would be blessed by the presence of a child.

Esther, for once, had found a moment of wakeful peace, and she stared toward our faces with a translucent blue gaze.

"Do you want to hold her?" I asked Elin. She smiled and responded with a barely perceptible nod.

Esther was so light. Picking her up felt like holding a baby bird, and I fought the urge to clasp her to me tightly as if to keep her from flying to perch on the window sill where she might decide not to return to my arms.

Elin took her from me with somewhat awkward movements that made me want to take her back. I pasted a smile on my face and looked up to Liona, who had pasted an equally uncomfortable expression; hers was underscored with a furrowed brow and eyes that darted away from mine when they met.

Esther brought her knees to her chest and her arms tight to her sides, grimaced, and screamed unlike anything I had ever heard.

With numb fingers, I took her from a pale Elin.

"I'll leave you two," Elin said. She escaped to the door while I struggled to unbutton my shirt and feed her. I couldn't help but worry though, even as she fought and suckled, that there was little I could do to satisfy her.

"When do you expect you will be leaving?"

I walked up in the middle of a conversation. Anders, Johan, and Jakob stood in a group just far enough from the center of the party to observe the others in attendance. Anders and Johan, both at least a head taller than Jakob, were shoulder to shoulder with arms crossed over their chests. Jakob carried the conversation with the tips of his fingers from both hands meeting together in front of his chest in a posture that mimicked his preaching posture. I wasn't sure if the stance was a façade or if it was truly who he was.

Anders acknowledged me with a nod that didn't invite me into the conversation, and I turned to find Anna and Elin tending to the tables of food.

Elsa had done a beautiful job of preparing for the smorgasbord. Fresh baked bread and pastries surrounded and highlighted the stews, sausages, cheeses, and jams. Many of the guests contributed to the feast, and the hodgepodge of serving dishes only enhanced the jovial atmosphere. My mother, if she were here, would have been in hysterics over Anna's chosen lowly lifestyle and unmatched tableware.

"In a few weeks," I heard Anna say to Elin. The question of when Anna and Johan would move seemed to be the only question on our guest's minds.

"There's no baptizing church yet in Uppsala. We plan to open our home as soon as we get settled." Anna continued to explain to the group of surrounding women. The women hummed and mumbled things about God's call and ministry and how they thought their move was admirable. I couldn't help but notice how none of them were going.

Faint breezes and the sounds of children floated in through the one open window. I tried to picture Anna in the city, without her garden of herbs, where fashion sailed in from England and women promenaded, corseted and even bustled. Anna rearranged the flowers that adorned one of the tables with business-like efficiency. I hoped she would be at peace in the city.

"Hi."

I turned to see Astrid. Her once hollow cheeks were filling back out and the sleeves of her shirt were crisp and white.

I felt for the pinprick from this morning and pressed until I found the tiny jab of pain. "How have you been?" I settled my gaze on the bridge of her nose. Direct eye contact was an ability I failed to summon.

"He's gone," Astrid said. "I didn't know if you knew or not, but I wanted you to know."

I searched for an appropriate response. Being glad would have been too harsh; he was her husband. Being sad would have been false; he'd attacked our family.

Astrid filled the silence, "He left with the last group to go to America."

Now I was the one looking into Astrid's eyes, trying to correct any sense that in my silence I might have blamed her for her husband's actions. "Anders told me a while ago."

We shared the hesitant smile of those for whom too much has gone unsaid, and I wished Anna would turn from her conversation with Elin, but she was engrossed.

"How have things been for you?" I asked.

"Busy." Astrid's shoulders dropped at the soothing, mundane question. "I have more work than ever. The people have been generous. I seem to get requests for mending daily and even a few orders for new shirts."

When Astrid moved back into her house, we knew she wouldn't be able to farm her small acreage without the help of a husband. Anders and Johan organized our group of friends to fix up her place and arranged for neighboring farmers to lease some of her land in exchange for a percentage of the harvest. They were more than agreeable, as land was hard to come by. The grateful farmers had already begun the task of preparing the neglected fields.

"How are the children? We saw Molly outside. Is everyone healthy?"

"They are all fine. The older girls help with the laundry from the base. I don't see Isak very often, but when he visits, he seems happy." Astrid brushed an imaginary wrinkle from her skirt.

"From what Samuel says, he is doing a fine job in the stables. Anders tells me he is a fast learner and a hard worker."

Astrid blinked a little too quickly, her pride evident.

"You have done a good job with him," I added softly.

She lowered her chin and whispered her thanks before mumbling something about seeing to Molly and turning toward the door.

"What happened?" Anna walked to where I stood alone in the middle of the room.

"I'm not sure."

"It must be hard for her here."

I catalogued the events of the past few months. "I don't know if I could do it."

"Johan says a lot of the men at the base are bringing their laundry to her now. They say she gets it so clean they only have to get it washed every other week."

I shared a smirk with Anna. I wished she were not leaving.

"Is Esther fine?" The abrupt change in topic caught me unprepared.

"Of course," I answered too quickly and with more inflection than necessary. "I mean, I hope so." I took a step closer even though no one was listening. They were all huddled in groups, holding plates of food, engrossed in their own conversations. "She cries all the time. I feed her, and moments later she screams like she has been stuck with a pin. I am beginning to think she doesn't sleep, just passes out between fits."

I looked to see if Anders heard my outburst, but he was still engaged in conversation with Jakob. "I plan to call the doctor on Monday."

A faint wail reached me, and Anna nodded, accepting my apologies before I'd even offered. Monday couldn't come soon enough.

Chapter Twelve

"Mrs. Modig?" Elsa eased my attention away from the feverish babe in my arms. "The doctor is here."

It was later than I'd thought. The sun revealed my disorientation in distorted rectangles on the floor. It was too easy to stand with this month-old child in my arms. I thought the blanket might weigh more than she.

"He's downstairs in the kitchen."

I led the way with Elsa, Liona, Hulda, and Hjalmer trailing behind. Seeing the doctor was not an everyday occurrence.

"Mrs. Modig, what seems to be the trouble?" He juggled Esther out of my hands and laid her on the work table before I had the chance to answer.

"She is thin." He examined her legs. They were still, with knees angled out, the pink skin dry and dull under his scrutiny.

He untied the ribbon at her neck.

"Hulda, take Hjalmer upstairs."

They had been quiet, hoping I would allow them to stay and watch. Hulda's shoulders slumped at being sent away, but she did not complain. I knew the doctor must have questioned my abilities as a mother, and I looked to see if he had taken note of her good behavior.

Instead, he frowned down at Esther as he peeled her blanket back. He lifted her nightgown and took a long slow breath in and out. Her ribs rose and fell in a rapid, staccato rhythm.

"How often does she eat?"

"Constantly. Whenever she is not sleeping."

He didn't glance up with a reaction to my response. Instead, he continued to disrobe Esther until she laid naked, arms and legs stretched out, and still, except for the occasional twitch. He bent to listen to her heart. I stopped breathing.

"Has she had a fever before now?"

"Here and there." The answer seemed insufficient. "Sometimes she feels warm, but usually it only lasts a short time."

She took a shuddering breath, pulled in her arms and legs, and screamed. The doctor flinched. Elsa took a step back, and Liona wiped away a tear. I walked to the table and wrapped her back up, pushing the doctor's hands away.

"How are her bowels?" He allowed me to pull Esther close. He opened his bag and took out a vial with an eye dropper sealed at the top. The sun glinted gold off his collection of glass jars of potions. He opened one, measured out some water and added it to the powder inside.

"She soils her clothes with every feeding, and every time, she cries." Her wailing stopped, and she watched me with huge blue eyes rimmed in strawberry lashes.

"I think she has an infection in her bowels. It is common for babies born early. It can be very serious, so it is important for you to follow my instructions closely." He found a few more vials and lined them up on the counter, large too small. "You need to feed her goat's milk. Add six drops of this"—he held up the medium bottle— "to each bottle. The medicine in the large bottle is to rub on her skin." He picked up the smallest. "This is for pain." He met my eyes and placed it in my outstretched hand. "When she cries in pain, give her one drop. Only one."

I swallowed and pressed the smallest vial deep into my apron pocket. He packed up his instruments.

"I'll send Aaron for goat's milk," Elsa said, and disappeared through the garden door.

"When should she be better?" I spoke the words to my baby.

The doctor paused, and I could feel him watching us. "If the goat's milk agrees with her, she should begin improving with each feeding. Call me if she worsens."

Liona escorted him back to the front door, and Esther and I found the rocker by the fire. I gave her a drop from the smallest vial when she grew uncomfortable, and she slept in my arms while Elsa prepared glass bottles with rubber nipples, full of goat's milk.

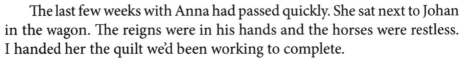

The last few weeks with Anna had passed quickly. She sat next to Johan in the wagon. The reigns were in his hands and the horses were restless. I handed her the quilt we'd been working to complete.

"Thank you."

"Sorry it's late. We wanted to finish it in time for your wedding, but I guess now it's a housewarming gift."

Their furniture was piled high behind them in an open wagon. It was strange to see things I had a connection with, wood tables I had touched, linens I'd folded, chairs I'd sat in, all piled together. History mounded on itself, and as soon as the horses pulled away, their meaning would evolve without my influence.

Anna reached down to take my hand in both hers. "You send word about Esther."

I nodded and blinked, my throat tightening to pain.

Anders put his hand on my shoulder. "And you send word once you are settled. Let us know if you need anything."

I watched their carriage until they turned at the end of the drive. I didn't know the next time I would see her.

"Your mother is here," Elsa announced through the nursery door.

Esther lay limp in my arms. Another turbulent night had relinquished its hold to a sedated sunrise. I was a mess—in the same vomit-stained clothes as the day before. I brushed my skirt, covered with the leavings of tears and feedings and too many diaperings to count.

Liona stepped in to take Esther, but I ignored her wordless offer. If my mother was here, she was here to assess the baby. I was sure the gossip wenches were running rampant at the mouth now that we had a sick, un-baptized child in the home, born after we left the church. If my mother had come to assess God's vengeance, so be it.

"She's sitting in the parlor." Elsa sent a wary look to Liona.

I nodded to Elsa and tucked the end of Esther's blanket closer to my body, wrapping her tightly, folding the stains under.

I saw her before she saw me. Her back was turned; the severe cut of her dress made her look as if she were displaying it at the dressmakers, rather than wearing the garment. She turned.

"You look a wreck," she said as I rounded the banister. "Let me see that baby."

She took Esther from my arms and wrinkled her nose. Her blue-white skin creased in distaste at the sick-bed odor lurking in the folds of the cloth.

Elsa skirted the front room, having followed me down the stairs.

"You"—my mother pointed to her—"ready a bath for this child." My mother's bony finger pointed to the kitchen door. Spittle fell from her mouth and landed on Esther's forehead. Now she seemed dirty, and I itched to scrub her pale body back to pink. I reached for her.

"No. You go wash up and put on a clean dress. Do you want Anders to come home and see you like this?" She looked at me like I had left my senses.

"Mother, please. I'll clean her when you leave."

"Not necessarily." She mumbled to herself and sat with Esther in her lap. She pulled back one corner of the blanket, then the other. Esther lay limp, feet relaxed to the sides, hands unclenched across her chest.

Mother took an audible breath in and covered her back up. Ugly red emotion crept up her neck and rested in purple blotches on her cheeks and nose. "I don't know what's going on here, but I am calling the bishop. This child needs to be baptized."

"No."

"What do you mean, no? How dare you risk the soul of this child?"

"Her soul is not at risk," I said too loudly. I took her back. Her eyes opened, she pulled her legs up and screamed.

My mother stood, indignation dripping from her posture. "You have no right," she spat. "No right to risk the child, no right to risk all your children. Do you know what you are doing? The price you will pay? The price we all pay every day because of this foolishness?"

Her face was red, her fists clenched to white. She stood in my face, trembling. Esther squirmed in my arms. One thin leg slipped from her blankets. My mother's gaze dropped to it. She turned, gathered her things, and carried herself out of my house. No slam. No stomp. No huffing or sighing. Just a silent, brewing protest.

She did not even have to send for her coach. The horses and driver had waited for her in the damp spring air.

Her carriage pulled away with the slow dignified crunch of gravel under hooves and wheels. I reached into my pocket, fingering the dropper bottle given to me by the doctor. It was amber glass, a rich, sticky color. I held it to the sun and watched my hand glow gold. I knew we were right. God would not reject a babe because she was not sprinkled with a bit of water. She was fine.

The medicine would help, and I knew when summer came, she would learn to crawl through the tall grass, and in autumn, she would sit in a pile of scarlet leaves, and I would have to fish bits and pieces of dry leaves out of her mouth and chubby, wet fists. She would learn to sing hymns because she found joy in them, not because she had no choice. She would walk with God, not in spite of him, and my mother would watch the entire time. I would parade my healthy family past her door, on the way to our church. She would have to watch, and know she was wrong.

Jesus, help my baby. She lay in my arms, blinking up at me.

"Ma'am?" Elsa stood in the doorway, her hands grasping her elbows in an insecure posture I never imagined hid in her sturdy frame. "Do you want me to take Esther?"

"No, I'll take her back to the nursery. It's fine." I turned toward the stairs. Elsa hugged herself tighter and turned back to the kitchen.

"Elsa?" She stopped, her back still toward me. "Thank you."

She nodded slowly and walked through the door as I found the stairs. Down the hall was my morning room. I couldn't remember the last time I had been there. I knew newspapers and correspondence piled up in the basket on my desk. Perhaps even news from Anna, but Esther squirmed, and we were close to another attempted feeding.

Everything else could wait.

Liona burst into my bedroom without knocking. "Do you have her?"

Disoriented, I tried to remember what day it was. The days and nights had blended into a mass of hours, slipping by without distinction.

"Do you have her?" Liona pulled back my blankets. Her eyes were wild, her bun loose at the nape of her neck. It flopped back and forth as she rooted through my blankets.

"She's gone. We can't find her, ma'am."

"What are you talking about?"

"Esther, she's gone."

I jumped up, my legs numb and hands cold. I fumbled through my blankets with Liona before I realized I hadn't brought her to bed with me when I lay down to catch a few minutes of rest between feedings.

We stopped and looked at each other across the rumpled bed.

"When did you last see her?"

"I put her in the bassinette in the front room," Liona said.

We pushed each other through the bedroom door and ran to the stairs.

"She was asleep." Exasperation drenched her words, and I felt like I was in one of those dreams where the thing you need rests at the tips of your fingers, but some invisible barrier keeps you from touching it.

"Hulda," I said. "Maybe she has her."

Liona shook her head. "They are in the nursery."

"Elsa?" We both stumbled toward the kitchen.

She stood over the stove. "Do you have Esther?" We asked in unison.

I was already looking on chairs and tables for her basket. I could see the answer.

"No. What do you mean?" Elsa began opening and searching through cabinets, and it did not seem at all absurd. "She's missing? Really missing? You can't find her?"

Liona shook her head.

"Run to the stables and get Samuel. Tell him to send Aaron for Anders." I continued moving through the rest of the house, looking in every cupboard and under every pillow and blanket. I was sweating and running toward the stairs to continue my search when Samuel burst through the front door with Isak at his heels.

"Aaron saw a carriage in front of the house not long ago," Samuel said.

"Did anyone knock on the door?" I turned to Elsa.

"Not that I heard."

We all looked out the windows to the empty drive. I wondered if Lars had not fled to America as we thought he had.

Isak's eyes measured each of us. I could feel them on me, and I wanted to reassure him, but I couldn't summon anything magnanimous. Eventually, he watched his shoes. Samuel placed a hand on Isak's shoulder.

"I don't know what he would want with a baby," Isak said, voicing what we all thought.

"We can't assume," Samuel said to the boy, who truly looked like a boy, not the young man I knew he was. The air was thick, and my hands shook. I had the need to run and search, but no place to look.

"We should have asked Aaron what the coach looked like before he left," Liona added, looking out the window at the empty drive. I folded and unfolded the blanket left in the bassinette, the blue ribbon first on the inside, then out.

"I saw the coach." Isak's eyes locked on Samuel's face, his chin still tucked into his chest.

"What did it look like, boy?"

"Do you think they could have Esther?" His hopeful tone revealed his own tragedy, but mine was still unfolding. I made it to him in one stride and took him by the shoulders.

"What did it look like?"

He hesitated and turned his head again to Samuel, but I took his chin and pulled him up to meet my gaze. "What did it look like?"

Liona touched my arm, and I loosened my grip.

"Black. It was shiny and black with red spokes on the wheels," he said.

"Were the horses a matching pair? Very dark?"

He nodded, and I released his shoulders.

"I'll ride over." Samuel was already out the door as he spoke the last word.

There was only one family in town with such an opulent team—my brother's. I did not relish the idea of seeing him again.

"What would he want with an infant?" Liona asked.

"I am sure it must be some mission of my mother's." I felt the vial in my pocket. "What will they do? They don't even have her medicine?" I walked to the front door and outside. It was unseasonably warm, or maybe not. I didn't know. It had been so long since I had last stepped outside to see the sun.

One foot in front of the other, I walked to the gate and down the drive. Suddenly, I knew what my brother had done. It shouldn't have surprised me.

"No." I tormented the inside of my bottom lip with my teeth until I tasted blood, each step faster until I could see where our road met the main road. He took her to baptize her at my mother's behest. I wiped away angry tears with my sleeves, and the black carriage rounded the corner to begin its stately approach up the drive to where I stood in the way.

"How dare you," I said, knowing he could not yet hear me.

The horses stopped and my brother opened the door to see what had caused the interruption. Faint cries escaped from behind him.

"How dare you." I walked too close to the restless team. They sensed the instability and the driver had to pull on the reigns to keep them under control. *Good*, I thought.

"You look a fright." My brother stepped down and offered a hand to help me into the carriage.

I slapped his hand away when I wanted to slap the smug grin off his face.

My nervous sister-in-law, nothing more than a childless infant herself, handed a stiff, screaming bundle into my shaking arms. I'd always pitied the woman. She wasn't much more than a child when he'd married her. He was almost thirty years her senior, and he was not a kind man. But at the moment I couldn't muster anything more than a glare. She flinched when our hands touched.

"Get in. We'll give you a ride back to the house," my brother offered to my turned back as I swaddled her again in the thin blanket they stole her in. Women who hadn't had children could never wrap a baby right.

"You," I spat at him, "can go to the devil. Don't ever come near us again."

"Well, sister, I guess you can thank me later for insuring your child does not make the trip with me," he said before closing the door and instructing the driver to turn the horses.

I was back to the house in seconds. I passed Elsa and Liona and closed the door to my little room. My shirt opened to the waist, I sat nursing with dried-up breasts. She suckled, and swallowed, occasionally, and I prayed my milk wouldn't poison her. She felt hot, and she had stopped crying, and I hoped maybe the medicine might be helping. I couldn't stop shaking. I knew what was coming.

Anders stepped in through the adjoining door and sat without saying anything. I didn't look up at him. It was dark before he got up again.

"Baptizing her didn't do her any harm," he said as he stood to leave. He touched the skin across her forehead and whispered a prayer I couldn't hear before he returned to his study to stare at the papers on his desk.

I could see him in the lamplight. He was reading, or praying, I didn't know. But that night, in my room, I held Esther to my breast until she grew cold.

The night before the funeral, I couldn't sleep. I had napped in increments for most of the day, lulled by the constant drone of people in and out of the house, and startled awake by the lack of a cry.

But that night refused to end. The moon rose until it was framed in my window, and then it stopped. The charcoal branches of one ancient tree clawed up to the silver orb but couldn't reach. They remained black and solid underneath the reflective light. Occasionally, a breeze stirred the sparse new leaves, and they would tremble and hum and turn silver bellies in response.

The undercurrent of the next day seeped up through the floorboards so much that I expected the planks to be cold to the touch. But they were warm. I knew she lay in a box just downstairs.

Anders had not come to bed. His place remained undisturbed. It was the second night, and also the second night I did not care. I didn't know if that was wrong.

They, I didn't know who, removed the cradle from my bedroom. What they did with it, I never knew. I walked over the empty spot on my way out of the room.

Hulda's door was left open a crack. I could hear her breathing. In and out. So fragile. The only light visible in the hall was a faint glow that echoed up the stairwell walls from the spaces below.

I descended and found Anders slumbering in a chair next to Esther. I turned from the intimacy and made my way to my morning room. It was dark until I pulled the drapes wide. The full moon streamed in to pool at my feet. It illuminated my garden, bright enough to leave shadows on shadows. I opened the doors to the cool, wet air.

My house shoes crunched on the gravel walk. I circled the small space once, touching the newly leafed-out hedges. My disturbance sent tremors through the tiny leaves, and they spilled condensed dew in droplets onto my fingers. Drips ran down my wrists and wet my sleeve. I ignored the stone bench and sat in the wet grass by the place I'd planted Anna's bulb. It had been a gift; a rare specimen, she'd said.

It was Anders who had found me and took her. He'd placed her in the cradle in the parlor, the one my brother had stolen her from. He'd covered her tiny face with a blanket and then fell asleep in the chair next to her.

I saw him that night, there, sleeping, but I couldn't disturb the scene, and I didn't invite him to our bed. Instead, I'd wandered. When the house woke, I retreated to my bedroom to lie on my back with my eyes closed.

Anders had done the job of informing everyone, because soon the house vibrated with the pressure of subdued duties. I imagined how Elsa would wash and dress Esther, and how Anders would call Hulda and Hjalmer into his office to tell them. Possibly he would step into the nursery to give them the news. I heard Hulda cry and Hjalmer play. I was sure the doctor instructed Liona to pack Esther's things away to help me get over the loss, and she had, all while I stared at the ceiling.

I ran my fingers through the leaf rot I'd buried the bulb under last autumn.

In the afternoon, Hulda had shuffled around my door. She didn't say anything, just climbed over the edge of the bed and molded her body to mine. She rested her head on my shoulder. Guiltily, I smoothed her braids. She was so big compared to the missing babe. A bit of stickiness from breakfast still coated her chin. Her nails were grubby. Like us all, she was alone in a house full of grief. I'd kissed the top of her head and wished I wanted to do more.

She'd wiggled, reaching into her apron pocket and pulling out a single white tulip. The head hung limp from the stem, the edge of one white petal creased to brown. She had been in my garden, had found the bloom born of Anna's bulb. She placed the flower on Anders's pillow, took a deep breath, and slid away, back out of my bedroom.

I knew the next day I would watch as they lowered the tiny box filled with white frills, the filmiest of fabrics, and my baby into the ground; into the hole that had already been dug. Then they would blanket the horrible cradle with shovelfuls of dirt. Her thin arms and legs, her impossibly delicate fingers, her tiny, perfect lips would rest in a dark bubble of air that forever would be hers alone. No movement, no sound, no light. I worried if the frost would reach her during our harsh winters.

I dug my fingers deeper into the leaf rot, the potent smell of night and earth filling my senses. I found the bulb root, pumping life into the headless flower, and pulled. It resisted, more than I had anticipated, and I pulled again, yanking the roots from their life-gathering hold on the cool soil. The moon illuminated the ugly brown lump in my hand, root hairs hung from one end, and a wilted, headless stem from the other. I cut the stem off with my fingernail and pulled at the fine roots, rubbing the dirt onto the grass before tucking the bulb into my apron pocket.

My eyes rested on the stone bench. Anders and I used to sit there, touching and talking. I wondered if we would ever be those people again.

I closed the door behind me but did not pull the drapes. Instead, I walked by moonlight to my desk. Piles of correspondence in neat rows waited for my attention. Newspapers—I wondered when Esther's death would be announced—rested on the nearby chair. The church members would say we deserved this. My mother would say she was right. My brother would congratulate himself for his actions.

My embroidery basket, tucked into the corner by my chair next to the fireplace, spilled its neglected contents, most of it for Esther. It was meaningless now. A pair of booties I had almost finished rested on the top, waiting for the final lacy row, crochet hook still attached. I picked them up. The white yarn trailed from my basket to the little sock, and with memorized movements, I pulled one loop into another, until the yarn was sliding through my fingers in a steady, familiar rhythm, and I finished the pair. I made the knot, and bit the end of the yarn off, leaving the tail a little damp. I wove it back into the lacy finish.

Anders still slept in the chair next to Esther when I made my way back through. The fire in the hearth provided only a wavering half circle of light that reflected against the polished floor and colored Esther's veil.

I lifted the veil. She stood out stark and dark against the white-filled casket. Her strawberry lashes dusted her cheeks. Her fingers, tipped with the tiniest of nails, were still. One was cut a bit jagged. I touched it. I lifted her cold hand to my mouth and bit the edge of the nail off so it was even.

I lifted her dress. Elsa had covered her feet with a sensible pair of stockings and booties. I pulled at the ties until they released and slipped the booties from her heels and off her toes. Then I replaced them with the ones I just finished. I smoothed her dress again and took one last look at the way her hands rested, the arch of her transparent eyebrows, her perfectly shaped doll's lips. I tried to memorize everything, but knew I would fail; that, with time, her face would fade.

Deep in my pockets, my hand brushed against the bulb. I tucked it into the folds of fabric at her feet. The bruised flower Hulda had picked and given me, I had pressed in the pages of the family Bible before returning to my bedroom.

I laid there, still awake and thinking what the next day would bring, the moon having slipped from the frame of my window. I listened to Anders stir in the rooms below. Eventually, that morning, he came to bed. He tucked me tight against his body and wrapped his arm around my waist. I felt him breathe in the scent of my hair. Then, I slept.

Chapter Thirteen

June 1880

The sun glinted off store windows as Elin and I passed. I'd planned the trip to town that morning with the intention of finding new ribbons for Hulda and to order a new suit for Anders. He would travel to Stockholm within the next month to begin plans for a match factory—the first project to come his way without the influence of his father.

Men nodded and tipped their hats, women smiled. I avoided eye contact with those who navigated baby carriages through the crowd. To my comfort, so did Elin, but for reasons of her own.

Stores still sold the preserved jellies of the past fall, but the rather empty shelves looked expectant rather than desolate. Thus far, the spring rains had been healthy and the early summer growth met expectations. There was a real hope for a sustaining autumn harvest that year, and the green summer breezes were alleviating the fear of winter poverty.

"How may I help you ladies?" The man behind the counter took a step out. He was short, portly, with eyes that turned down at the outside corners. The crinkles at the edges of his eyes expanded out, wider than the polished, brass-rimmed spectacles balancing on the bridge of his nose.

"I need to order a new suit for my husband."

"Ah, yes. Really, he should come in himself so it can be properly fitted."

I thought he must be new. I was glad our little town was expanding.

"He always orders his suits here. You must have his measurements. Nothing has changed. His name is Anders Modig."

"Mrs. Modig." He fumbled a bit in this haste to get his round form out from behind the counter. "What an honor it is to meet you."

Elin looked at me with a smirk as the man took my hand in both of his and bent at the waist with a sweeping bow.

"Let me show you the newest fabrics…just arrived." He hurried back around the counter. "I'm Vilhelm Dalmon. I've just purchased this shop from Mr. and Mrs. Strand. He told me about your family's long history of doing business here."

He began pulling one bolt of fabric after another off the shelves, lining them up on the counter.

"Where have the Strands gone?" I asked, a little surprised I hadn't heard they'd sold their shop.

Mr. Dalmon measured me over the rim of his spectacles. "Why, haven't you heard? They went with the last group to sail to America." He watched me, probably wondering how I could have missed such important information.

"I've been a bit busy lately," I groped for an excuse, sending a wordless plea to Elin.

"So much to do in the spring," she weakly added for me.

"Yes, yes, there certainly is." Mr. Dalmon was already distracted by the fabrics in front of him, and I breathed a sigh of relief. "Isn't this one simply astounding?"

Astounding, to say the least. Elin covered her mouth with her handkerchief to hide her smile.

"Ah, yes." I ran my hand over the royal blue fabric. It boasted yellow and white pinstripes, and I couldn't help but think of Anders's expression when I would show him the finished suit. "Maybe something more similar to what he already has?"

"Oh." Mr. Dalmon valiantly attempted to curb his disappointment. "What about this?" He rolled up the stripes and pulled out a textured blue. All of Anders's suits were black. Some summer weight, some winter weight, all black, but Mr. Dalmon's enthusiasm was infectious.

"What about that grey?" I pointed to a bolt of fabric waiting for a spot on the shelf.

"Yes! Yes, that just came in from England. They have so many new options," he added, a bit wistfully. He brought the fabric to the counter, making a show of removing the rejected textiles. He smoothed the dark grey in front of us. Elin reached out and ran her hand along the weave.

"It is very fine."

I trailed my fingers down the yardage. There was a slight sheen to the dark grey, not something Anders would choose. He liked things predictable, orchestrated. Mr. Dalmon's round cheeks, previously bunched up under his eyes, descended in degrees down his face as each second ticked by.

"Let's order one," I said.

Elin shot me a look, and Mr. Dalmon's cheeks rose to new heights to almost hide his eyes.

"Oh, yes. Let me make sure I have his measurements. Of course, I would like for him to stop by to pick it up so I may be sure of the fit."

"Of course," I agreed.

We did the necessary paperwork, I said no to some ridiculous accessories, and he closed his ledger book.

"What church do you attend?"

"Pardon me?" I asked.

"I was just wondering what church you attend. I'd like to introduce you to my wife. The ladies all seem so nice, with us being new and all. I wondered if you might have met her at one of the functions."

"No, I don't think so."

"Do you attend Bishop Peterson's services?"

"We don't attend there, but I would be happy to meet your wife sometime . . . ."

He opened his mouth to interject, no doubt to ask where we attended.

But I continued before he could. "Do you know how long it will be before the suit is ready to pick up?"

"Oh." He lifted the fabric off his calendar and checked his schedule. "In two to three weeks." He tapped his pencil and glanced at me over the rim of his spectacles. "Will that be sufficient?"

"Fine, that will be fine. I'll tell Mr. Modig to stop in then." I gathered my things and turned to leave before Mr. Dalmon could open his mouth to ask another question.

"It was nice to meet you." Elin halted any further interrogation.

"Yes it was," I agreed, and we made our way to the door. The tiny bell announced our escape. I called out an extra thank you over my shoulder, and we stepped onto the street.

Karlskrona was a bustling navy town. The new barracks Anders was laying the foundation for were not far away, and we turned to walk toward the port and his offices. Everything about the city was nautical, from the fishy—but not unpleasant—salt-laden sea air, to the heavy ropes strung between timber piers, running the length of the walkway. The city felt almost as if land was not the sailor's first choice, so they brought the ocean and ships inland as far as possible. Karlskrona, the city, felt like an entirely different country from the slow, green surrounding farmland.

A spot of sun found its way through the buildings and shone in an odd rectangle on the street. I stopped and lifted my face to the warmth, the noise and wet air cocooning me so unlike the warm, grief-drenched atmosphere at home. I made a silent vow to bring Hulda and Hjalmer with us the next time we came to town.

The tension left me by degrees. I caught my reflection in a store window. I had lost some of my gauntness. I wondered how long my brow had been furrowed and my cheeks drawn tight to my teeth. I glanced toward Elin's reflection. She looked pale and drawn. "Are you feeling ill?"

She leaned against a post and pressed her handkerchief to her nose and mouth. Her skin was blanched almost to the color of the cloth in her hand. "Maybe it's just the walking?"

I grabbed her arm and dragged her to a nearby bench.

"Or these stays." She twisted her back against the confinement. She hiccupped and pressed the cloth to her mouth again. "Or the fish smell," she gagged out.

"Oh my." There was only one thing I knew of that could turn a stomach so quickly. "Elin, are you expecting?"

It was an improper question, but she answered anyway with a hesitant nod.

"How long?" I sifted through my memory for the signs I should have registered earlier. They had waited so long.

"A few months." She paused. "I didn't know how to tell you." She twisted the handkerchief in her tiny hands.

"Do you think you feel well enough to walk to the restaurant and get some tea? You look like you could use a little something to eat. Besides, it wouldn't hurt to get a bit farther from the docks."

She nodded and watched my face, searching for my reaction while I sorted through the pictures flashing through my mind. My own round, pregnant belly, the funeral, tiny fingers gasping mine. "I am so happy for you." It was the truth. I brushed her clasped hands with the tips of my fingers. Her thin pink lips trembled into a tentative smile. "Let's get you some tea and maybe some toast, and you can tell me all about it."

Later that day we bought the softest of yarns and fabric printed with a smattering of yellow flowers. We talked about babies, smiled into passing carriages, and when Anders came to me that night in bed, it was still with some apprehension but tempered by an ever-present promise.

"When the base work is complete, my father wants us to return to Varmland so I can run the lumber mill." Anders paced once in front of the fireplace, then checked his movements and found his desk chair. I could hear his toe tap against the wood floor. The letter sat in front of him. He picked it up and held it out to me. In language that could not be taken as anything but a demand, they informed Anders they were of the opinion we would all benefit from closer contact with family. His brother would be given the next government contract in Karlskrona, and he would oversee the timber framing of the barracks. They assumed we would be looking for work.

"You haven't told them about Edsvalla?"

"No. I was waiting until the contracts were finalized."

It was still hard to believe we would be moving. I had known the home wasn't permanent, but so much had happened that for the first time a move felt like we were leaving more than a house behind.

"Have the contracts been drawn up? How long until the plans are complete?"

"We'll have everything in place within the next month. Of course we won't be ready to start until September, or maybe later, but the papers will have been signed before then."

He had no intention of returning to work in his father's mill, or raising his children in a city where his family owns the land, the trees, the lumberyard, the cabinet-maker shops, and the furniture store. In short, he didn't want to live where his father owned the town, the people, and the church. Neither did I.

"When will you tell them?"

"I was hoping to put it off for a while, but if he thinks I'm returning, he'll be transitioning my brother out of the mill and readying my position there." He leaned back in his chair, head against the leather cushion. His shoulders, as wide as the back, appeared anything but relaxed. "I'm going to stretch the decision out as far as I can. If he wants to hear from me earlier, he can come here and talk to me." He placed the letter to the side and punctuated his statement with a paperweight.

"Liona's been collecting papers for you in here." He gestured to a pile on the other side of his desk. "I've finished with them if you want to take a turn."

I knew I would never get through them, but at least I could glance through the pictures to see the styles and the advertisements. Reading in English was still a painfully slow process. I balanced the stack and carried them through the adjoining door.

"Oh, here's something else." Anders stood and followed me with another paper. It was a small poster with large block letters, but instead of announcing an upcoming play, or a visiting musician, it was emblazoned with BAPTISMAL SERVICE in large black letters. The date, time, and place were printed underneath, along with the name of a minister I didn't recognize.

"Who is this?" I set the pile of papers down on my desk next to my unanswered correspondence. I took the sheet from him and scanned through the details.

"He's from the Stockholm area, grew up here, but when he was sixteen he went to America. Now he's returned. He said God called him back to Sweden to baptize the believers here."

I read it more closely and felt a corresponding rush in my stomach. From the edge of my vision, I could see Anders's gaze measuring my reaction. We'd spoken at length about being baptized. Jakob had brought it up during sermons, and I knew the rest of our small congregation would be excited by the opportunity. But it was one more step away from our roots. Another chance to disappoint our families.

I handed the paper back to him. "It looks interesting." I tried to keep my voice even, and wondered what it would be like to be called by God, and how one found such a designation.

"Yes."

"We could go; it is on a Sunday morning." I turned my back and waited for him to agree.

"Do you want to go?"

He was going to make me say it. And for as much as had happened, the decisions made, the consequences paid, all that, and still I didn't want to be the first to say yes. Yes, it felt right. Yes, my heart raced from either a spiritual significance or from the sheer rebellion of it all. Yes, I comprehended Jesus's mandate that all should be baptized. Or maybe, yes, we had come this far, why stop now. But the melting in my heart said yes, I wanted to be washed clean, to come out of the river, sun in my hair, shivering with cold, or excitement, or community, or spirit. Yet, I still wanted him to say it first.

"Do you?" I turned away.

He slouched into the chair by the fire. "Yes."

"So do I."

He nodded and glanced back to his office, frowning.

The decisions about church had been easy for him. At least he had made it look that way. His faith had been steadfast, confident. The potential to disappoint our parents, to embarrass our families, to anger our friends with our decisions—while worrisome for me—had been little hindrance for him. This though, this slow burn of responsibility from his family weighed heavily. And there was nothing I could do to help. Except maybe watch for the constable.

The quilting circle day, scheduled a week prior to the baptismal service, dawned perfect. Samuel had Isak bring chairs up from the stables to the front yard. Elsa made tea cakes with jam hidden in the centers, and Liona dressed Hulda and Hjalmer in clothes we would have to constantly remind them to keep clean. Although Hulda needed less and less of a reminder. I knew letting her hems out that fall would not be enough. We would have to make some new dresses—possibly go to town and find some fabric. One of the women's shops in Karlskrona always seemed to have the newest things, and I wondered if they might have some of the striped silk taffeta I had seen on a couple of ladies when Elin and I were last shopping.

"It's been awhile since we've had a group of ladies here," Elsa said as I watched Hulda stoop to run her fingers down the silky black spine of one of the barn cats. It rubbed against her shin, wrapping its tail up and around her calf muscle. The cat was unusually tame, the animal's hunting resolve softened by the unexpectedly warm day. It purred and flopped on the ground at her feet.

"Yes, it has been awhile." I took my sewing basket from Elsa. In truth it had been a long while, a very long while.

When we first came under suspicion, and the bishop scrutinized our every move, our friends quietly disbursed. I didn't immediately realize what had happened. It began with fewer family invitations, and dwindled from there. Mrs. Olsen, the deacon's wife, was one of the first. The others followed suit. Before I knew it, I was left completely unaware of the ladies' gatherings. With those ties severed, the rejection spilled over to our business acquaintances. We were too busy though—too busy defending ourselves and wondering what had gone wrong to notice our own isolation.

"Set the table under the big oak," I instructed Isak. Hulda followed him, skipping just steps behind, asking questions. She had a crush. He was far too old, but I felt far too young to have a daughter old enough to notice boys. I wondered how our isolation might have changed her, if it would influence her interactions with other children, and it had. Her eyes were on Isak, a boy substantially poorer than herself. He had been abandoned by his father, and was working to support his family. Isak was being raised by a mother on the fringes of society. Yes, we had all changed, and I had a hard time believing it was anything but good.

Elsa walked back out of the house again, carrying a blanket to spread across the grass for the smaller children to play on. Her hair curled around her ears and absorbed the sunlight. It glowed yellow. Elsa was a seamstress to envy, that much I knew by the tiny, even stitches and flawless decorations that marked her aprons. She was also a part of our new church family, and she was Elin's friend. She had become much more than a servant.

"Are you going to join us today, Elsa?" I held the other end of the blanket and smoothed it over the grass. She stood to measure me, and I felt a hint of the old insecurity in the moments before she nodded and smiled, transforming her round, severe face into that of the grandmotherly one Anders would recognize.

Elin sat in the empty chair to my right. There were a total of eight of us, nine including Astrid's youngest who sat on her lap. She was snuggled up to the frame with wet fingers stuffed into her mouth. The needles darted in and out, thimbles occasionally coming to the top of the quilt and catching a glimmer of sun.

"I've been looking forward to this," Elin said. The upcoming visit by the missionary gave us all the reason we needed to finish the quilt. It would be a practical gift of gratitude for their service to our small church.

"So have I." I surprised myself by the truth of the statement.

"Well, we finally have a reason to finish it," one of the women facing me said. She was new to our small church, and her husband had some business dealings with Anders. Older than us, their two boys were grown and worked at the naval base, but she was younger than Elsa, who sat next to her tying knots with calloused fingers.

"I hope his wife likes it." Astrid ran her fingers along the even stitching bordering a red square. The child in her lap wiggled down to play in the grass at her feet. "I'm sure she will," she continued, a bit wistful. She had not heard from Lars since he left for America, and that information was only earned through gossip. More gossip said she was entertaining a man who worked at the base after he began bringing his laundry to her.

I knew she wasn't entertaining men in the same sense some of the mean-spirited women in town meant, but I was aware of a building friendship, and I did wonder what she would do if it ever came to that. Married was married, but abandoned was another thing entirely. I wondered what Anders thought on the subject.

But her wistful look, whether warning or blessing, was at least hopeful, and more than what she had six months ago.

"When will they be here?" Elsa directed the questions toward Elin. After all, the missionaries would be staying with Elin and Jakob until they moved on to Stockholm, and eventually to Norway. Karlskrona, being the port town it was, was their first stop.

"We're hoping they make it by this week, as the baptismal service is planned for the next weekend and there are people traveling from all over the area for that service." Elin's needle moved faster with each word until we all stopped and just watched her small hands pushing and pulling on needle and thread with mechanical precision.

"I don't know how you keep your stitches so even and work so fast," Astrid said.

Elin colored a little and one side of her mouth rose in a sheepish smile.

A breeze moved just the upper branches and the sun fluttered across the bright colors in fleshy pieces of light. "I'll be right back." Elsa pushed her chair out.

"Do you know anything about the missionary?"

"Not a lot more than what we have talked about before," Elin said. "He and his wife were born in Sweden and then traveled with their families to America. That's where they met. They married, and he studied theology. They opened a small church in Minnesota but both felt called to bring back to Sweden the news of what God is doing in America."

The ladies nodded in agreement.

"Is he still in contact with any family in Sweden?" I pulled a tiny pair of silver scissors from my pocket and snipped an extra thread.

"No. They left Sweden with their parents when they were in their teen years. His parents, for land, her parents for a place where they could worship as they pleased, without reprisal from the church."

"Isn't it amazing how they were both born here, but traveled all the way to America before finding each other?"

We all looked up to one of the younger women in our group. Barely past a bride herself, her romantic outburst made her blush bright. The older woman next to her patted her hand. "You're right, dear. It is incredible how life unfolds sometimes."

"Speaking of life unfolding, I do have an announcement to make." Elin's fingers stopped and fell to her barely expanding midsection. I had been hoping she would choose today to make her news known. Guarding her secret was becoming more difficult with each gathering.

She never even had to say the words. Suddenly, chairs were pushed back and women were at Elin's side.

"How long?"

"How have you been feeling?"

"When will the baby arrive?"

"Do you think it will be a boy or a girl?"

"Are you too hot sitting outside?"

The circle twittered and hovered like so many mother hens. I backed out of the group to arrange some of the silverware Elsa had brought out for the tea. A spring bouquet graced the center of the table, surrounded by pink linens and my floral tea service.

"Are you okay?" Elin came up behind me when some of the questions had ceased.

"I'm fine." I smiled. Truthfully, it was a relief to feel the spirit of expectation hovering so close to our home again.

Elsa walked by with the tea tray balanced on her arms. "Let me help." I picked up a dropped napkin and followed her back into the house.

We walked in and out, disbursing tea cups and cakes to the mass of fawning women. Elin sat at the center of attention with her hands tucked into her lap. The sun caught the blue of her eyes, and they glowed the color of the sky.

And I began to look toward the future.

Chapter Fourteen

July 1880

"Anders, have you seen Jakob's carriage yet?" I was too busy preparing the house to look out the window for the missionaries. They'd arrived a week before the scheduled service, and we were hosting a welcome smorgasbord.

"I just came up from the barns. No sign so far."

The food, spread throughout the dining and front rooms on a variety of tables, offered the jovial feel of abundance. Some of the other guests had already arrived, but most milled about the front room and the yard, waiting for the guests of honor.

I rushed back to the kitchen to get the last of the pastries from Elsa. She'd outdone herself. Multiple trays of cookies and the tiniest of cakes rested on the counter, ready to be taken out. I grabbed one and backed out of the door in time to turn and greet an empty room. Everyone had moved outside, presumably to welcome the missionaries.

"There you are." Anders took the tray and made a place for it on the wrong table.

"But…" I pointed to the other table.

"It's fine." He grinned and waved away my concern. "They're here."

I untied my apron and slipped it off. Anders stood at the front door with his hand on the latch. I bunched up the apron, stuffed it under one of the floor-length table cloths, and then frowned. Even though no one could see it, I knew it was there.

Anders laughed. It was the first time I'd heard the rumbling comfort since Esther had died. I slid my hand in his, and we walked outside together.

The missionaries were not as I'd expected. They stood, surrounded by our friends, laughing and smiling and looking as if they belonged. Knowing he'd been a student of theology, I'd anticipated a bookish aura. But as we all walked back into the house, I could see much the opposite was true. He was heavily muscled, with a blacksmith's gritty hands. He wasn't tall, but commanding nonetheless.

"Anders and Brianna, please meet Mark and Pia." Jakob introduced us using our given names, but with so much jostling and so many introductions, it seemed efficient rather than rude.

Mark stood next to Anders. His average height surprised me. His face was open, and when we were introduced, his gaze bore into mine as if he were as interested in my world as he was in Anders's. His scarred hands were gentle when he tugged at Pia's elbow to get her attention. She, too, seemed larger than she was; her shoulders, broad and strong and a prominent feature. Elin and I stood across from her, and suddenly, I felt inadequate.

"You have a beautiful home." Pia spoke first. The men shifted their conversation to the side, leaving me to sort my way through a conversation with a stranger.

"Thank you," I said. "How was your journey?"

Pia laughed heartily. "It was fine as far as journeys go."

I couldn't help but like her.

"Let's pray, and then we can eat." Anders called from across the room. He motioned to Jakob, and we all bowed our heads and offered thanks for the food and friendship and for Mark and Pia's safe journey.

After the prayer, it didn't take long for our guests to find their plates and wander around the tables to fill them. A number of conversations turned to America.

One family, already in the process of selling their farm, took the opportunity to pepper Mark with as many questions as he could answer. They'd hoped the sale would raise enough money for their tickets—with some left over to support them until they were established. They were blessed, though, because their brother had already made the trip. The wife of the couple carried a worn letter describing fields as big as the sky, and forests so dense, one step off the path and the traveler found themselves engulfed in near-night darkness. Mark confirmed even the most unbelievable elements.

"They do this in America, too." Pia slid up next to me as I eavesdropped on the men's conversation. Her Swedish was very good. She gestured to the piles of food. "But rather than have tables everywhere, they have one long table where people line up to take what they want, and then they all sit to eat."

"Oh. Would you like to sit down?" I asked. Gathering food just to sit down seemed like poor planning, and it defeated the purpose of a meal intended to promote visiting between new friends, but I wanted her to be comfortable.

"No." Pia smiled again. "I was just noting the differences. Don't worry about me. I think this is a wonderful way to eat." As if to demonstrate her enthusiasm, she stuffed a small bit of cheese in her mouth.

Mark, Jakob, and Anders joined us. Pia stepped to her husband's side and slid her arm into the crook of his. He covered her hand with his and smiled down at her. She returned the smile with one that was openly flirtatious, but absolutely correct.

Her hands, like her husband's, were rough, as if they toiled together—as if they lived lives that were won, rather than accepted.

I offered an excuse and moved down the hall. Her magnetic laugh followed me. She'd stumbled on a Swedish phrase, and I glanced back to the group. They were relaxed and happy.

It seemed the boundaries in America were less strict, yet the way Mark watched Pia, there was no doubt she was still protected. I nodded and smiled to the other guests until I finally reached my morning room. With the door closed behind me, I breathed a sigh of relief.

I liked Pia. More than that, I envied her a little. I wanted to stand with the confidence she stood with and touch my husband so boldly. When she'd slid her arm into her husband's, the muscles in his neck twitched. It made me want to touch Anders, to see if I might hold that latent power under my own skin.

And people were drawn to her. Elin watched her, and the other guests seemed unable to look away when she spoke. It might have been her American accent, or the way she laughed so openly, but they watched as if entranced.

Unfortunately, so did the constable.

We all knew he was reporting to the bishop, but even the upcoming baptismal service broke no laws. The church could shun us, but they couldn't force the constable to arrest us. At least we hoped they couldn't.

The evening before the baptismal service, Anders left to meet with Jakob and the missionary to work out the details of the next day's service and pray for God's blessing and protection. I stood in the briefly empty foyer and took stock of the house. By then we had rooms full of people, and I spent my free moments trying to make light of the constable's men lurking behind lanterns at the edges of our property.

It wasn't a new experience for our guests. The occasional monitoring, the bit of trouble when credit was needed for an extension at the bank, or when record requests from the city went unanswered, all were expected and tolerated. Some had experienced worse. One man in our group spent some time in the town jail before the constable's superiors stepped in and ordered him released.

But that night the constable's men made no move to cause any trouble, so we did our best to ignore them. With Elsa darting in and out of the room, Samuel taking coats and welcoming our guests, and countless children carrying blankets up the stairs to the nursery, I didn't have time to reflect on the increased monitoring.

As more people arrived, Liona entertained and settled the children, herding them up the stairs while their parents shrugged off the journey. Elsa, in the kitchen, bustled from one steaming pot to another, wiping her brow with the back of her sleeve. Her face shone.

"Do you need anything? Any help?" I marveled at how smoothly it all seemed to be going. A couple of girls I didn't recognize were already helping, one chopping potatoes, the other folding napkins. They didn't even look up.

"No, I think everything is fine." Elsa wiped her reddened hands on the front of her apron. "Dinner will be simple, but there will be enough."

We had discussed whether or not to have a formal dinner the night before the baptismal service, but chose instead to serve hearty, simple fare—potatoes, fish, bread, jam—due to the fact so many of our guests would be exhausted from the journey and ready to retire for the evening.

"Good. Let me know when you are ready." I turned and almost ran into a woman I barely knew as she stepped through the kitchen door. A baby girl rested on her hip. Probably less than a year old, the baby had strawberry hair and the fairest of complexions. She sucked heartily on her fist.

"I'm sorry to be a bother, but is there a place where I could wash her up?" The young mother shrugged, her hands full.

I caught my breath and turned away before she could see my tears that threatened to spill.

Elsa intervened. "Right here." She gestured to a basin near the empty laundry tub and moved around the counter to help. "Everything you need should be here."

I closed the door quietly behind me and took a deep breath. The surprise moments of mourning were less frequent than they had been, but occasionally they still took me unaware. I reminded myself of the blessings I did have and made my way back to the front door where I could hear another family had arrived.

Anders's voice rose above the noise. I was glad he had returned safely, and a little resentful that I was forced to feel uneasy about the constable and his intentions. Anders entered behind a woman I hadn't yet met and began the introductions.

"Have you met them yet?" the woman asked about Mark and Pia after we were introduced to her, breathless from walking up the stairs, holding a child who seemed too large to carry. "You have a beautiful home."

"Thank you, and yes, I have." My eyes dropped to the child's legs. One foot was twisted, with toes turned in and angled almost straight down. "Please, have a seat. Is there anything I can get for you?"

The girl, I guessed about five, watched my eyes as they moved from her foot to her mother's face. I made an effort to look the girl in the eyes when I told her there were many children present, and she was sure to have fun with them. She looked to her mother to gauge her reaction. Her mother smiled and nodded, and for a second I worried how I would make sure she was included.

"Who have we here?" Liona's voice came from behind me.

"This is Sarah," the child's mother introduced her to Liona.

"Hi, Sarah." Liona adopted the girl's quiet manner. "Do you like to play with dolls?"

Sarah nodded.

"Do you want to come upstairs with the other children? The girls are playing with the dolls right now."

Sarah tucked her chin down.

"I'm going to read a story in a few minutes. Do you like stories?" Liona pressed.

She nodded, Liona held her arms out to take her, and in the space of a few seconds, they were gone. Liona whispered something that made the girl smile and wave to her mother who had already joined the group gathered in conversation around Anders. I was left to wonder where I had lost my abilities as a hostess.

The previous year I'd opened my house almost weekly to one group or another: church activities, dinners for Anders's colleagues, and gatherings of families and friends. Never did I need to rely on my cook to keep me from collapsing into tears in front of some unsuspecting young mother, nor did I need to be rescued from awkward silence by my children's nanny. I used to navigate from one group to the next with simplicity and ease. But as I looked up to the sound of genuine laughter, I realized our group had changed.

Anders always stood in the center of any group of people, and I was envious. People gravitated toward him. It had always been that way, but in this new group of friends, he'd found his purpose, his calling. If one could use the word calling. It was a heavy word.

The first day we had attended Jakob's service I knew something had changed. I saw it, I felt it, and I was not at the center of it. It didn't depend on my abilities. It didn't require my understanding, and for the first time I bucked against my lack of abilities in this new crowd of friends and my own lack of importance.

Where was my call? I had given up what I was good at and traded my identity for one with no direction, all while watching Anders grow into his. People counted on him, talked to him, asked his advice. He preached and they listened, he encouraged and they walked away with a smile. The next day he had promised to assist Mark and Jakob in baptizing any who asked, and our house was full of expectant, excited, hopeful people. People responded to him because he had the ability and he responded to God.

But why didn't God ask anything of me? The abilities I had were gone along with the group of people who appreciated them, people who shared my parents' sensibilities, and I had nothing left to fill the space.

I walked the full halls of my home and smiled at the strangers, hoping they didn't see the gaping hole in my abilities.

The service had been planned for the morning so those who needed to travel could reach home before nightfall. We woke before dawn to the smells of an early breakfast. Samuel, Isak, and Aaron were occupied bringing horses and wagons up from the stable to the waiting men. The women in the group were gathering breakfasts for their families from what was set out by Elsa. They tied biscuits and eggs in colorful napkins as their children clung to their skirts. We would all eat on the way to the river.

When the sun came pink over the horizon, we were on our way. Anders was the last out of the house. Liona rode with us. Samuel and Elsa sat in the driver's seat of a wagon full of people. Before Anders turned away from the door, he pulled a key out and turned it in the lock. He tucked it into the breast pocket of his jacket. I had never seen him lock the door before.

The caravan lurched with a celebratory tug, the sounds of the forest and of wheels on gravel interrupted by an occasional eruption of song. The bishop and a few other men, apparently chosen for brute size rather than intellectual prowess, weaved in and out of buildings and trees, watching our progress. We were all aware of them but chose to ignore any possible interruptions.

I could smell the river before I could see it. The air grew damp and the animal sounds changed. A hush fell over us as the horses slowed, and we strained to hear the hollow melody of Pia's nyckelharpa. The wagon with Mark and Pia had gone on ahead of the rest of the group, so as we approached, the music of bow on strings, at first one with the sound of wind through the trees, diverged as separate instruments, with the wind accompanying the echoing notes. The song was a familiar hymn, calling us to come to the river that was Jesus. At the clearing, the horses and wagons split off, running east and west and spilling their inhabitants in a quiet stumbling to the edge of the water.

Pia sat on a large stone. Her right hand glided with artful precision up and down the humming strings; one note sustained to the next. Her left hand cradled the keys, hidden under the polished wood, almost motionless as they attended to the instrument. She loved the instrument as a mother loved the child whose hair she softly ran a brush through. The sun glimmered off the water, sending vibrations up to strings, through the bow and the bend of Pia's arm. It was a pulsing, familiar cadence that surged with my blood to my fingertips, leaving a tingling expectation.

Patches of lavender flowers spilled to the river's edge. They competed for dominance with the golden foliage that interrupted the living carpet in irregular patterns. We stood amongst the flowers. Some of the children sat.

Pia played on, the sound reverberating in the cathedral of leafed-out trees. Birds flit from branch to branch, spots of brilliance amidst an impossible number of greens. The canopy fractured by the movement of white sun in an evolving ceiling of stained glass. Jakob stood with Mark, waist deep in the water. It rippled around their bodies, plastering their shirts to their chests. Jakob motioned for Anders to come forward. He was to be first.

He handed Hjalmer to me and bent to unlace his shoes. He pulled them off, walked to the water's edge and stepped down. There was no shoreline, no sandy surface for him to sink into gradually and let the water inch up over the arches of his feet, then ankles, caressing calf and the sensitive area behind his knee. No, the carpet of tiny flowers ended where the water eroded their foothold, leaving those who chose to enter the water standing knee-deep in patches of yellow or lavender, and then with their first step over the edge, knee deep in the water. Fish scattered at the intrusion and crawfish scuttled under rocks and decaying branches.

It was quiet, except for the melodies floating from Pia's fingers and the mumbled prayers of those who surrounded me. The words Mark and Jakob spoke over Anders before he covered his nose and was plunged under were words and prayers that remained a mystery to those of us on shore.

Elsa stood behind us with her eyes closed, and Liona sat amidst the flowers. Hjalmer had crawled into her lap. I had no idea if she would choose to be baptized today. As close as we were, she was always very quiet about anything that carried emotional weight. I said a quick, silent prayer for her and turned back to watch Anders be plunged down and come back up.

I could hear the water fall in sun-laden drops from his hair and elbows and hands; the pieces of prism in a rush to return to their stream home, interrupting the glassy surface in ever-expanding rings of light. Anders climbed back to dry land, back to his family, back to me, washed of his sins. I imagined them left crawling into the mud, dissolving at his feet and disappearing, hopeless, destined to fertilize the nutrient rich banks along the river. Our sins diminished to the duty of enhancing the beautiful things at the water's edge; God's creation, once again, fulfilling its purpose.

No one spoke. I wasn't sure what I had expected, but Anders motioned for me to follow his path to the edge of the water. Suddenly, I was aware of the sounds I made: the small twigs snapping under my feet, the rustle of my skirts, my breathing. Astrid and another woman stood at the water's edge and took my hands to support my first step into the cool water.

I wanted to shed my clothes, to feel the water rush up to my skin, unhindered by the trappings, but I took the next step and was submerged to knee, then thigh. Waist deep, the cool mud worked around my feet and rose in a cloud until the weight of the blessed water pressed it down again. The birds above were quiet, and I stilled to feel the fingers of water playing with my ribs and hear the old oak at the stream's edge moan sweetly, the breeze rubbing one limb against the next, all to the time of the bow drawn across the instrument in Pia's lap.

They prayed over me. Mark took my elbow, Jakob stood at my back, and I was not pushed or pulled into the water. Rather, I was drawn in, my nature losing the willful battle. Finally submerged, I understood.

My eyes flickered open to see the world turned upside down, the slow floating streams of light, the creatures swimming toward the yellow beams, and those hiding. The branches, once alive on a tree, were still alive underwater, but in a way they could have never imagined, and needed no less than when they were beautiful, pushing new foliage from their tips.

I saw my hand. For a second the warm light fell into my palm and danced there with a disturbed bit of leaf, and I knew. I knew my purpose, even if unseen, was not diminished by my ignorance.

Soft hands pulled me up. The sun, full, having a body of its own, shone on Mark's hair and on the freckles spattered across his nose and on the backs of his hands. We stood together as one, gathered, as God gathered the waters. I climbed out, hands and knees on the bank, water dripping down my face, knowing it was not my duty to make my abilities an acceptable offering.

I only needed to surrender. God made me. He wanted me as I was. What I had to offer was irrelevant. As I climbed onto the shore, Astrid laid a warm blanket across my shoulders, and I turned to see Liona step into the river.

Everything was brighter. An iridescent beetle scurried up the stalk of a weed, rushing to a place of protection under a leaf. I walked to Anders's side and stood as witness to our friends, our new family, as one by one they went under and crawled back to a new life on the shore.

The afternoon meal was at our house. People laughed and talked. I laughed and talked. Mark and Pia were surrounded and peppered with questions about America, because there was not one in the room who had not, in their quietest moments, let their minds wander to that place.

When it was time, we stood together in the front room and prayed for safe travels, for struggling loved ones, for the child with the turned foot. I touched her arm and knew, someday, she would walk.

I was not the only one with hopes for the child. That night Anders and Jakob sat up in Anders's office, drawing and planning.

Weeks later, the girl was back, standing next to her mother, balancing on a contraption unlike any of us had ever seen and leaning on a crutch for extra support. It fit to her foot and climbed up to her knee with straps and buckles holding it in place. The plan was for her to eventually walk without the crutch, and I knew then that sometimes the miracle we seek has more to do with the work we are willing to do than anything else. Sometimes, I learned, waiting for God was an excuse to put off the simple work a miracle might take. And I knew we had a lot of that simple work to accomplish.

Chapter Fifteen

"What did you think of Pia?" Elin leaned over her dinner table and whispered. Anders and I had come to visit and talk about our little church.

"I liked her," I said.

"Can you imagine, traveling to live in a different country?"

We both left the question unanswered and listened to the drone of the male voices on the other side of the table. They were in a heated discussion over some recent incidents of vandalism at the base. Of course, the constable wouldn't step in, said it was probably just kids having fun. *Sure*, I had told Anders when he relayed that, *probably his kids*. But the events were growing more serious, and the emerging question was how one could protect oneself from the law when necessary.

"How are you feeling lately?" I pushed a potato to the side of my plate while Elin speared another lump of fish. I knew her answer. She was eating like she had never seen food before, and her cheeks had lost the early pregnancy pallor for two rose-colored spots at the front of her cheekbones. She still didn't show—much anyway—but she looked satisfied, whole.

"Great." She smiled. "You know, this past week I went walking and made it all the way up the bluff before I thought I should go home because I might tire, and it wouldn't due to tire on a bluff by myself, so I walked home, but when I got home I still felt like I could keep going so I baked a pie."

I liked this new, chatty Elin.

"What do you think, Brianna?" Anders asked from across the table. He was handsome, even in his old suit. I looked forward to seeing him in his new one. He would wear it when he traveled to Edsvalla the next day. We had received word the contracts were prepared and waiting.

"I'm sorry. I didn't hear what you were talking about."

"Do you think every other week we should hold service at our house? That way Jakob and Elin would be able to travel and hold other services."

I nodded, understanding it would mean Anders would share in the preaching; a fire I knew had been burning ever since the Sunday Jakob had been absent.

"Besides," Jakob said. "Then we will be able to see how our contraption for the little girl is working and make any adjustments if necessary."

"That would be good," Anders addressed him with his fork in hand. "You know, I thought of another way we could attach the device so her foot could move more freely." Anders took a pen and a scrap of paper out of his pocket and drew out his idea. Jakob gestured and pointed, asking questions, and I looked at Elin, realizing with that conversation I had become a preacher's wife.

Anders drove home slowly, allowing the horses to set their own pace. "Are you sure you're fine with that?" he asked.

I looked up to the stars and breathed in the damp night air. Animals scurried across the road to safety, and I wondered why they would choose such a path. There was forest to the left, and forest to the right, yet instead of hunting and nesting deep in the safety of one or the other, they chose the danger of hooves and wheels and were satisfied with the risk.

"Yes, I know it's what we should do." Peace accompanied the statement, along with a prayer that, unlike the animals that watched us pass by from under the leaves, we might avoid being crushed by the path we were choosing.

"Yes." I scooted across the bench so my leg ran the length of his. "It's fine. It will all be fine." Anders's lips turned up at the corners, and he put his arm around me to draw me in for a kiss he planted on the top of my head. I reached to run my fingers down his thigh and felt a corresponding twitch in his arm. I hid my smile in his coat and kissed him in the hollow between his jaw and neck, the stubble of his beard rough against my lips.

He smelled like salt and soap, and I felt younger than I had any right to feel.

<hr>

The letters hadn't stopped arriving only because he left for Edsvalla. Quite the opposite; it almost felt as if a new one was delivered daily. Elsa placed them on his desk, and there they waited—a collection of thinly veiled directives, first from his father, then his brother. They were attempting to complete the plans for him managing the Varmland plant and the Karlskrona base once the stonework was complete.

I had finally found the stomach to see to my own pile of correspondence a few weeks ago, including the stacks of letters from Anna after Esther died. First, the ones before she knew, then the ones after Anders's message had reached them. Those dripped with empathy, her round letters perfectly slanted, the tails at the end of the words long and curved. I read one and tucked the rest away, unread, with Esther's things. I wrote back of the local news, of what our brother did, of benign gossip. I told her about the new tailor in town, about the baptismal service, and about Elin's news. I had told her Anders would be preaching in our home every other week.

She had written back. It had not taken long to make connections with the new church around Stockholm. Johan was preaching, and they were to host Mark and Pia in the upcoming months.

A light tap at my door interrupted my sorting through some of the accumulated newspapers. It was Saturday, the morning I went through the household accounts.

"Come in," I called without looking up.

"I wanted to drop these off for Mr. Modig, but there's an article I thought you might want to see first." Liona walked in with another pile of newspapers in her arms. I rose to take them from her.

"The one on top."

A headline burned black across the front of the page: Lumberjacks Move to Demand Rights. I nodded to Liona, not taking my eyes off the page. She left me to read. The article told of an incident that had taken place prior in the week. Harvested logs, improperly secured, had rolled off a train car, crushing one man and injuring others. The workers had cited long hours and working into the dusk with inadequate light as the reasons. The company, I read further down to confirm it was indeed Anders's father's company, had yet to respond. It was the lumberyard his brother managed. The one his father was planning for us to oversee when the stonework phase of the base was complete.

I opened the door between our studies and walked to Anders's desk to rifle through the letters and look for the overly-bold, black strokes of his father's pen. Separating them out, the number of letters was alarming. The smooth, expensive paper slid through my fingers. It was cool to the touch. I slipped my nail under the edge of the envelope and broke the seal.

His father demanded his return. In a single line, near the end of the explanation of what had taken place, was the out-of-character postscript ". . . we are unsure of our next move." The world shifted. Anders's father was asking him to come home. The letter included a demand, but those small words admitted a skill in negotiations that father saw in son, an acknowledgement of abilities. Suddenly, our upcoming move to Edsvalla went from a risk of rebellion to a risk of betrayal. I checked the time, wondering when Anders would arrive.

The next day we were to host the communion service with Anders preaching. If we moved back to his parents, we would be expected to take up where we left off, in the church his parents attend, in the same social circle. Back at my desk, Anna's letters sat next to my ledgers. My accounting was filled with transactions placed with local merchants who shared our convictions, charities and anonymous gifts to people in need. The substantial offerings we made to the bishop's flock had been transferred to investments in our own community. I thought of Astrid and Elin, how they wouldn't have been close to sharing our circle of acquaintances in the north.

Not to mention Samuel and Elsa. Over the past year, they had become indispensable. Hulda and Hjalmer considered them more as grandparents than servants. In Anders's parents' world, the relationships we had built with them, the dependence, even the respect, was completely impossible.

Anders's mother demanded proper service: the flatware always polished to mirror quality, tea served in silence, never a clink of spoon on saucer. I couldn't imagine what she would say of a dinner conversation between host and servant, let alone the occasional meal together.

We had come too far. I closed my ledger book and sat back in my chair. There was no possibility I could muster the necessary distain for the lower classes needed to demand perfection in service. How could I look at a mother in poverty and not see her children huddled in the loft, thin arms seeking comfort around one another's necks.

We were not the same people, and Anders's parents would not understand. Our priorities had shifted, and although we still went to work every day and did all the things one did to get by, we were no longer the center of our world. Instead, it was what we could do, what we could accomplish in our short time. The letters and receipts pointed to a new truth: we were too different to slip into our old lives. And I was glad.

People arrived on time for the service, but I was focused elsewhere. The next day we were to travel, first by carriage, then by train to visit Anders's family. The contracts for the Edsvalla bridge were signed, our housing secured, the decisions made.

I knew he had gone to Edsvalla for that purpose, but when he returned and told me of his success, I realized I hadn't expected it to go so quickly. That, and the pile of his father's letters, fairly humming with urgency, had me packing trunks like a squirrel preparing for winter. Hjalmer sat at my feet, pushing a wooden horse across the floor. He crashed it repeatedly into the bottom of the trunk, and I hoped that the banged-up toy wasn't an omen for how the journey would transpire.

The noise downstairs swelled to the point where my continued absence would be noticed, so I left the trunk open, picked up Hjalmer, and headed down.

We would sleep in the train the next night, and I was making lists in my head: Elsa's, a list of provisions; and Liona's, a list of things for the children. Liona's list included a number of items meant to entertain. It was difficult to imagine children ever existed in Anders's childhood home, and I never could decide if that impression was intentional. But from the moment the huge oak doors would open, I knew it would be a test of endurance—mine, my children's, and Liona's.

I would not be pretty enough, or smart enough, or severe enough. Hulda and Hjalmer would be expected to be quiet and adult-like. Liona would have to manage the children's façade while maintaining the demeanor of an unruffled, invisible servant. Anders's mother would not like Liona—too exotic, too pretty with her dark looks. My mother-in-law chose her servants out of a stock that was lower than her in every way. Every way except love, or joy, or peace—the Bible verse about the fruit of the Spirit came to mind—and self-control.

That day, however, we were surrounded by our friends, the ones who had stepped into the water with us. As my foot hit the last stair, and Hjalmer pulled his hand from mine, I was greeted by our new family, and knew when we left for good it would feel like severing a limb.

The service flew by, and before long, the communion cup was passed. The wine was a red pool in the bottom of the glass. The liquid quivered in the cup as I took it from the woman next to me while watching the faces I had grown to care for. This time was silent, each of us lost in our own introspections. Communion had ceased to be a ritual presided over by a minister. Instead it was a time of reflection, commitment, awareness.

I passed the cup to the next person seconds before the sound of shattered glass tore through the room. We all watched a red brick thump and roll to rest on its side in the middle of the floor. No one rose to look out the window to see who had thrown it into our house. It didn't matter. We passed the bread, and when the final prayer was complete, Elsa rose to get a broom. Anders left with a few of the men to go to the barn for boards and a hammer.

"We'll order new glass tomorrow," Anders said as he nailed up the wood.

In some ways, I was not sad to move on.

Chapter Sixteen

August 1880

Hjalmer had never ridden in a train, so the first half hour of the trip to Varmland we spent in blissful silence as he stood, nose to glass, watching the countryside speed from window to window and finally out of sight. Hulda sat straight. She was too old to wear her enchantment on her sleeve, but interested, nonetheless. Her braids swayed ever so slightly from left to right, mimicking the slight waver of the train on the tracks.

The half hour passed quickly though, and the remainder of the trip was spent trying to keep Hjalmer quiet. Anders, like the other men on the train, feigned intense interest in the newspaper—open as far as it would open—while Liona and I kept Hjalmer busy and Hulda entertained.

By two hours into the trip, Liona had lost numerous hair pins and her dark strands were sticking to the blue velvet stretched across the train car's seats and walls. Anders had not moved a muscle, and I was sweating. The sleeves of my traveling suit were tight on my arms. I had the intense compulsion to take a pencil from Hulda and poke Anders with it. Not that I didn't appreciate how he provided for us—I had seen the lives of women who did not have that—but sometimes I wondered what it would be like to be a man, to have two different worlds, work and home, to never experience the draw on your body when a child was conceived, as

I suspected another had taken root in my own.

Leaving the rocky coast, the landscape changed from one town to the next until at last we spilled out into the land of tall pines and black-green bluffs. Anders stood on the platform with Hjalmer's hand in his own. His chest moved with a deep breath in, and he smiled down at me. I turned to watch as a sternly thin man in a well-cut black suit fought his way through the crowd of passengers to stand in front of us.

"Your father sent me for you." The man didn't offer his name or a smile. He waved for a porter to take our trunks, clearly setting himself above the task. A pair of young men scurried to the job while we were shown to the waiting carriage where we would close one more door.

Anders's family estate was impressive to the degree that each time we visited, the drive up the tree-lined road inspired gaping jaws and silence in the coach. When the house came into view, Liona looked at Anders as if she had never seen him before. Anders stared straight ahead with the muscle on the side of his jaw clenching and his hand gripping the edge of the seat. I put my hand over his. It didn't ease his tension. I knew this visit would be difficult.

"Hulda, Hjalmer, you both need to be your very best," I whispered in their ears while licking my thumb and rubbing away non-existent smudges of dirt. Hulda brushed my hand to the side and sent me a withering glance I hadn't realized she'd mastered.

The coach slowed, and we stepped down onto compacted gravel bordered by bleak, searching grass, cut tightly to the edge of the drive. There were no flowers, or even manicured hedges. No climbing vines to protest the huge stone behemoth that rose out of the ground. The house, the estate, simply interrupted nature in one jarring, smooth wall of rock. Like its owners, there was no buffer, no whimsical, apologizing nods to nature, no planters full of seasonal offerings—just God's creation, with man's creation plopped directly, crushingly, on top.

Anders's mother stood thin and severe on the top stair. She was dressed in the choking fashion of the decade prior, with a black fitted jacket buttoned to her neck. The heavy fabric and her rod-straight posture gave the impression that the only animate parts of her body were her darting eyes and long thin fingers, stark white against her black skirt.

A leaf blew to land near her foot. She scowled at it and caught the gaze of a diminutive maid standing exactly two paces behind and one pace to her left. The maid scurried to find someone with a broom. I avoided Liona's gaze as she ushered Hulda and Hjalmer to line up in front of us. We stood as if we were posed for a photograph for my mother-in-law to study. And she did, as if she held us in her hand, testing the weight of the tin, scrutinizing flaws from the shine of the exposure.

"Hello, Mother." Anders picked Hjalmer up and made his way to the stairs. We filed behind him and into a wood-paneled, towering entryway. A forbidding staircase ascended straight up from the front door and disappeared into the depths of the estate. A chandelier, dripping with perfectly polished pieces of cut glass, burned bright overhead but failed to illuminate the room.

"Your father is in his study." Anders's mother gestured to Anders. His eyes narrowed at her cool demeanor. She was always what on a good day I would have described as stoic, but that day she bordered on hostile. I stopped myself from chewing the inside of my cheek and stood, waiting for directions. She turned to the girl at her side.

"Stand up straight, girl," she said through gritted teeth. "Take Mrs. Modig and the rest upstairs so they can change for dinner." She met my eyes for the first time. "John will be here with his family for dinner tonight. I'm sure you will all want to change out of your traveling clothes." She turned and disappeared into the lounge to the right.

Our bags and trunks had already vanished, I hoped to our rooms, and I turned to the girl who was instructed to see us to where we were to stay. I had the itching temptation to arrive to dinner in our traveling clothes, only because Anders's mother had felt the need to suggest otherwise. Instead I sighed, asked forgiveness for my rebellion—she was, after all, my elder—and opened my mouth to ask the girl whether the windows in our rooms faced the southern border of the property. Anders's mother had not used her name, though, and I hesitated.

"I'm sorry. I didn't catch your name." I took a step closer. Her chin was still turned down, but she slowly lifted her gaze to meet mine.

"Karin?" I asked. The girl who had made the unwise alliance with the bishop's assistant stood in front of me. She was dressed in the proper clothes of a housemaid: a floor-length black skirt, a small white bonnet bulging over a tight bun, and a pristine, starched white apron tied tight around her waist.

"Yes, ma'am."

"How are you?"

She glanced toward the door to which Anders's mother had exited and lifted her chin. "You may follow me, ma'am. First I will show you to the children's rooms. There is an adjoining room for Liona. Then I will show you to your room." She turned, and we followed her up the stairs.

I marveled at how Anders's mother had taken an unruly child and, in the span of a few months, turned her into a servant with whom even a royal household could not have found fault. The light was gone, though. The curious, troublemaking child had been tamped down, paved over and built up to be a proper servant. I thought about the cost, and not for the first time wondered at the class system that required vibrant children either to allow themselves to be molded into what those in the upper classes wanted, or face life as one long struggle.

I looked over to Liona as she watched Karin ascend the stairs and wondered at the thoughts snapping behind her dark eyes. If Liona had been hired here, would she have succumbed, or would she have brushed the dust from her feet and moved on? It is said that in America birth was not a predetermination for the rest of one's life. I wondered if many rose to the occasion, or if eventually those who emigrated there would settle on a system like our own. When the land was gone, would sons be satisfied to work the farms? Would they move into industry? Would they group themselves in classes like we had done?

The children's room was down a long paneled hallway. Our traveling shoes hit the polished wood floor in an uneven staccato. Karin's uniform must have included house slippers because her footfalls were a trained study in silent invisibility.

The walls of their room were white. Gold drapes hung heavily on either side of the windows. A child-sized table and chairs sat on one end of the room next to a small shelf neatly arranged with a pyramid of worn wooden blocks, an assortment of picture books, a wooden horse, and a stiff doll with yellow braids sticking straight out of either side of her head. It was, at best, a nod toward childhood.

Karin motioned to a door off the main room, and Liona opened it to a small white space with attic-slanted ceilings. Across from a sagging mattress stood a diminutive chest of drawers, over which hung a chipped mirror. Its framing was too fine for the room, and it was quite obvious the defect in the glass was what earned its place over that chest. A nightstand with a sensible lamp was pushed into the corner next to the bed. One picture hung over the head, a faded needlepoint on stretched canvas that read FOR ME AND MY HOUSE, WE WILL SERVE THE LORD. I stepped back out of the room, collectively embarrassed for our entitled beginnings, and praying I had never been so myopic.

Liona peeled Hjalmer off my skirt and nodded for me to go while she distracted them with unpacking the trunks.

Down the hall, farther away from the children than I was comfortable with, Karin opened the door to our room, and I made my way into a cavernous space. The only light shone through a crack in the red drapes until Karin slid them wide open to a blast of southern sun. Finally, some light. I felt my shoulders inch down by degrees.

"Your things have been unpacked already." She motioned to the armoire. My brushes were neatly lined up on the dressing table. Karin stood in the sun, particles of dust floating around her and never quite landing.

"If you don't need anything else?" It wasn't a question. She wanted me to dismiss her.

"Thank you," I acquiesced, and she turned away.

"Karin, are you happy here?" I asked as her fingers reached the door knob. She paused and turned it.

"Dinner is at seven, ma'am," she said facing the hallway, then with a soft click, closed the door behind her.

The evening meal was semi-formal, with the children to be brought in just before the first course was served and be removed immediately after the last. Hjalmer squirmed in the chair next to mine while Hulda did her best to mimic the ultra-straight posture of my beautiful sister-in-law.

The table was arranged with Anders's parents anchoring the ends. Anders and his brother sat to the right and left of their father—both tall, both dark, but John, a shallower, softer version of his brother. My sister-in-law and I sat on either side of Anders's mother, with the children spanning the distance down the middle of the table. We were, in essence, family versus family.

Anders's brother and his wife had only two daughters. My sister-in-law's eyes deadened when she saw Hjalmer brought to the table. Of course she would want a boy of her own.

Their daughters, one favoring the father, and the other, the mother, measured Hulda from head to toe. The look that passed between them made me want to hide Hulda. Although similar in age, she was not a match for the pair seated across from her in manners or appearance.

My mother-in-law's ice blue gaze fell to the children. She raised a brow as an orchestra conductor might raise his baton, and picked up her spoon.

For all the sparkling dinnerware and impeccable service, the food was Spartan. The first course of fish soup was seasoned with salt. I couldn't make out any other flavors, and at once I remembered how she stayed so frighteningly thin.

"How are things at the lumberyard?" Anders was the first to speak. His father studied him as if he were daft.

"They've been better," his brother said with a clipped, annoyed tone.

"Father wrote to me about the accident. What are you finding to be the biggest difficulty? Have you made any changes in production methods or timeframes?"

"There's still talk of the workers organizing," Anders's father interjected as if that would answer Anders's question.

After a pause to smooth his napkin over his lap, Anders continued. "But have you made any changes? It was my understanding the men blamed fatigue for the accident."

John's face grew red and his lips tightened as the first course was cleared and the second placed in front of him. "I won't talk about changes while they threaten organization. Whatever we do will cost us, and if it's not going to satisfy them anyway, we'll wait to see what they demand and work from there. There are enough men looking for work. If they continue to give us trouble, they can be replaced."

Anders's father nodded his agreement.

"We pay fairly enough, and if they work long hours, they're paid extra for those too. They have little to complain about."

"Except dead friends," Anders said without emotion.

"If they make mistakes, how can I be held accountable? They're responsible for following protocol." Anders's father dropped his fist to the table. The glassware shuddered. "If they feel too tired or too drunk to do their jobs, then they need to move over for a man who can."

"Don't worry, brother," John continued his father's thought. "You'll get your chance soon enough to fix all the problems."

The courses appeared and disappeared in succession by the almost non-existent servants, likely hired for their deafness, because their expressions never wavered. The girls across the table stared at Hulda. Her long braids running down either side of her chest labeled her as rural—as easy prey. Even more worrisome was her enamored returning stare. Liona and I would have to discuss how to keep Hulda safe, and Hjalmer. Their cousins looked like they could quite happily push him down a flight of stairs.

"Well, we will need to discuss some of the plans," Anders interrupted my thoughts. All of the children looked at him.

"Discuss what?" His father sputtered out around cheeks full of pulverized food.

"It's a topic maybe best saved for later." Anders rested his fork on the edge of his plate, indicating he was finished. The plate was immediately whisked away.

"You do plan on relinquishing the base project?" A touch of anxiety shaded John's words. "We've already sold our house. We need to be out within the next month."

My sister-in-law stared, expressionless, down the length of the table. Her daughters, on cue, followed suit.

"No, we're prepared to move, and the stonework at the base is wrapping up. The timber framing should be ready to begin on schedule. It's just that another opportunity has opened up for us."

"No. You will be running the lumberyard," Anders's father dictated. "There are no other contracts in the planning stages right now. You will return home." His voice remained calm, just as if we were having a conversation about a favorite fabric color. Choosing a path outside his expectations was not a possibility for him.

"Do you mean not to come back?" His mother's rising pitch said she understood the implication.

"I'm sure that's not what he means, Gretta," Anders's father muttered into his dinner.

"Are you?" she spat, and then addressed his father. "How do you know what's going on in his head?"

"Gretta—"

"Maybe," she added sarcastically, "he'll come back as a traveling preacher."

There it was. I set down my silverware. My sister-in-law snickered into her napkin, and John leveled a superior gaze at Anders.

"We hear you've become quite the savior of souls." Small bits of food were stuck to Gretta's teeth; her dry lips failed to keep them contained. I was already feeling nauseous when a piece of something landed and stuck to the side of my glass.

"I know," she said, refusing to stop, "we can lead those revival services right here in our own home." She stood and threw her crumpled napkin next to her unfinished dinner. "We can invite all our friends, and with your newfound wisdom, you can preach to us all." She paused for a minute to correct her posture and brush away any wrinkles that dared crease her skirt. "I believe I will retire early tonight." She turned and left.

Anders cleared his throat. "Like I said, it might be a conversation best saved for later."

Dessert plates were placed in front of us.

"This is very good," Anders's father announced between giant mouthfuls. "Really, very good."

I looked at the gelatinous mound in front of me, and my stomach flopped over. In my mind, there was little doubt about the impending pregnancy. Hulda poked at the pudding with her fork while Hjalmer looked on. She took a small taste and went back for more. Apparently convinced, Hjalmer filled his mouth with the ooze. A satisfied smile crossed his features, and he followed one bite with another until it was gone.

I didn't indulge, and neither did my sister-in-law. A small battle had somehow formed between the two of us for reasons I failed to understand, yet I knew without a doubt, the first to wrap her lips around that sweet fork would be the loser. Little did she know there was not a possibility I could have even considered placing the pudding anywhere near my mouth.

"Well, yes." Anders's father pushed up from his chair. "Let's finish this conversation in my study."

The three men vacated the room, and Liona and another servant came to collect the children. The cousins pushed out of the room first. Liona took the opportunity to meet my gaze and communicate she knew the dangers. I smiled, thinking again how blessed I was.

"Poor thing," my sister-in-law said when we were finally alone in the room. The grandfather clock in the hallway ticked distractingly loud.

"Excuse me?"

"I said poor thing. Your maid. She'll never get along with the others. Too pretty."

I nodded a fake agreement.

"Don't know why you would want a servant that pretty anyway. The less temptation the better, I would think."

I felt hot, and an ugly blush threatened to creep up my neck. I backed up a couple of steps. "We did make a very long trip to get here. I'm sorry, but really, I'm exhausted. You'll excuse me if I retire to my room rather than the sitting room?"

Her eyebrows dropped along with her tone. "Of course. I'll be sure to tell Anders you retired early." She turned, accompanied by the deep rustle of silk taffeta as it covered her agitated stride down the hall.

I climbed the stairs, but instead of retreating to my room, I found the children with Liona. I didn't actually think anything bad would happen to them, but I knew there was little opportunity for good in that house.

"What did he say?" I sat up in the bed when Anders entered the room. "How much did you tell him?"

He loosened his tie, undid the top buttons of his shirt, and sat on the side of the bed. He kicked one boot off, then the other, and shrugged his jacket from his shoulders. He pulled his still buttoned shirt over his head. I touched the bare skin of his back to remind him of my question, and he released a breath that sounded like he had been holding it ever since we arrived that afternoon.

"He just would not have any of it."

"What?"

"He refused to accept it. We talked about the plans for John when he moves to Karlskrona. Oh, and John wants to know if Samuel and Elsa will stay…"

"What did you say?"

"I told them I would talk to Samuel." Anders turned and looked at me. "Then the strangest thing. My father said it would be nice to have them back here as Elsa makes the best sweets."

"But didn't you tell them we were not planning to move here?"

"That's what's so strange. The more I insisted, the more he ignored it. I looked at John, and John didn't give any indication that he noticed the disconnection. I told them everything—about the new contracts in Edsvalla, about our home there—he just didn't acknowledge any of it. He expects we will be here within the month, and he's not preparing for anything after my brother leaves. You should see his desk. There are piles of what looks like unanswered correspondence, and I don't know if my brother doesn't see it, or if he is working on it, but I've got to do something. I can't leave them like this."

My life under my mother-in-law's fist hovered in my imagination, and I didn't want any of it.

"The contracts are signed. What's your plan?" I asked.

He paused and looked up at nothing. "Do you think Johan and your sister would consider working up here for a while, since he grew up near here? At least until the timber work in Karlskrona is through and John can come back?"

The pieces began falling into place. The last letter I had had from Anna said they were still traveling to home churches on the weekends. They had met Mark and Pia, had been baptized, and were baptizing others. During the week, Johan filled positions for a number of businesses. He processed paperwork and worked on their accounting, but he had yet to find a permanent position. I knew Anders was considering him for a new project in Stockholm, a match factory, but that was at least a year out.

"They might. It's worth asking." I reached over and turned down the lamp. Anders leaned back on top of the blankets with his hands tucked behind his head. "We'll deal with it tomorrow."

Neither of us slept much that night.

"Good morning," Anders's father addressed each of us as we entered the dining room. Steaming platters of food that I knew looked better than it tasted lined the buffet on one wall. Breakfast was casual. We all took pieces of what we wanted and carried our plates to the table. Hulda and Hjalmer were finishing their breakfasts as I sat down. They jumped up as soon as Anders's mother entered, talking about something in the barns they wanted to see. I handed them off to Liona, plastered a relaxed smile on my face, and resumed my duties at the table.

"I suppose Anders left early?" Anders's mother started the conversation, her lips pursed into a dry, cracked line.

"That's how we always did it." Father shook his head for emphasis. "That's how it needs to be done." His voice rang with pride for his son.

"They're not coming back," Mother said with a tired, bitter overtone. "They want to preach, or build a bridge, or baptize the poor, or commit heresy." The last comment she said with a sneer into her plate.

"Preach, ha!" Anders's father laughed. "When he's here he will start work every day before it's light. We'll increase production and get things back on track. Those men will see who pays them, and they will work." He pounded his fist on the table. "He won't have time to preach!"

My mother-in-law met my gaze, and I understood what was at stake. For once, her proud posture turned defeated, and I looked down at my plate.

"If you'll excuse me, ladies, I have work to do." He exited, leaning heavily on his cane, leaving just the two of us and a table full of cooling food.

"You can see what has happened here, right?" she asked me with a glare.

"Yes, I can, as well as Anders."

"And you still plan on abandoning him?" She nodded to the exit her husband had just shuffled through.

"Anders is working on it. Abandon, no. I'm sure he wouldn't just leave, but he does have another contract—other obligations. We had no way of knowing," I tried to explain.

"No way of knowing? Possibly you could have started by not ignoring the letters?" Her voice rose in pitch. The room was growing stuffy. I picked up my fork and set it back down, lining it up perfectly with the pattern on the table linen. I took a deep breath before continuing.

"We didn't ignore your letters. We were occupied with a dying child." I surprised myself with the residual bitterness that throbbed out between the words. I dropped my shaking hands to my lap.

"Children die every day. I've lost my own. It's no excuse for abandoning your family."

I clasped my hands tighter, not wanting to expose the trembling weakness her words had unearthed.

"The child was baptized, right?" She looked directly at me, expecting an answer. I didn't meet her eyes. From the corner of my vision I could see her hands come up to cover her mouth. "The child wasn't baptized," she said through her fingers. I let her erroneous assumption stand.

"Her name was Esther," I said.

"Are you saying that in the grips of your new religious obsession, you abandoned even the soul of your child?" Her voice rose to a screech. "We already know you have no pride, no sense of preserving your own standing, or even our standing, in the community. What am I to tell our friends? Our oldest son has chosen a radical religion over family responsibility? Where is God in that?"

I stood. "If you'll excuse me, I must go check on the children." I left her berating Anders under her breath and made my way to our room to begin packing. There was no reason for the children, Liona, or me to stay there. I knew Anders had no intention of bringing us back to live under his parents' rule, and I also knew he wouldn't leave without securing things. That was bound to take at least a couple of weeks. There was no sense in torturing us all.

I scraped the biggest trunk across the floor to the armoire and began pulling dresses off hangers.

"Mrs. Modig?" Liona knocked on the partially open door and stepped in. "What are you doing?"

"Packing." I glanced up in time to see the smile Liona tried, without success, to erase. "There is no need for us to be here. Would you please start gathering the children's things? I'll be there to help as soon as I'm finished."

"I only unpacked for immediate needs. We'll be ready to go when you are."

"Are we going, Mama?" Hulda peeked around the corner of the door. She held a struggling Hjalmer back from bounding into the room.

"Yes. We have a lot of packing to do at home, and your daddy is going to need to be here for a while to get things settled. I thought it best if we started soon."

"I'll get our toys ready," she said and dragged Hjalmer down the hall behind her.

"I guess I better go supervise." Liona chuckled. "Send word when you are ready."

"I would imagine we will leave after the noon meal. It should be delightful; you might want to feed the children in the nursery. Anders plans to be back late morning. I need to tell him our plans."

Liona nodded and left, closing the door behind her. I folded one more dress and pulled my traveling clothes from the closet. They had already been pressed by the servants who took up far less than their fair share of space in the household. Laying the clothes flat on the bed, I sat at the desk and opened the top drawer. Of course, paper and pen awaited me. My first duty was to write directions for a maid to carry to the stable lads. I reached in my purse and added some money for train fare to the note. They still had time to buy tickets for us for an afternoon stop.

Secondly, I wanted to write to Anna. I knew Anders would be sending a request to them, and while I needed to be honest about the challenges they would face, I had to stress to her how important Johan's presence would be at the lumber mill. Not only was he capable of getting through the paperwork, which I knew would be a daunting task, but also he was equipped to do so in a diplomatic manner, preserving Anders's father's status in the town. For as wretched as his mother was, I couldn't help but think some of it, most of it, was due to the need to keep up appearances.

Johan would be essential in organizing the inner workings of the mill. He had charisma enough to gather and inspire the men around him. Hopefully he could help stave off some of the talks of the laborers organizing—at least until everything was put back to right.

John was not the man to do that job. But with him taking our place in Karlskrona, I hoped even if he wasn't the kind of leader who could solve problems and grow a business, at least he might be the kind who could take a well-running job and see it through to completion.

Religion would be a challenge for Anna and Johan. Although I would have had a difficult time thinking of someone better equipped to deal with Anders's mother, I wanted at least to purge my guilt for sending them into the flames by seconding the warning I was confident Anders would provide. It wouldn't hurt for Anna to arm herself with a few extra prayers should she ever need to face Anders's mother.

"You do realize I'll have to stay for a while?" Anders said from the doorway of the room. He scanned the trunks and bags and approached me carefully.

"I'm fine." I waved him away as I added a postscript to the bottom of Anna's letter. "Our presence is not going to smooth any negotiations between you and your family, and this trip is going to require more than the few days we had planned. If we leave, I can continue to pack and finish planning for the move. It will give you more time to get things settled."

"Breakfast was that bad?"

"Oh, worse. But truly, I'm fine. It's just time to move on." I handed him the letter for Anna. "You can place this in with one you will be sending, I would guess, soon."

Anders took the letter and tucked it into his jacket pocket. He measured me, looking down as if to divine some hidden hurt. I was as relieved as I think he was when I realized there truly was no pain left unexamined. It was simply time to keep moving in the direction our steps had already dictated. We were not at a fork in the road, that fork was a Swedish mile behind us. We were just pausing, breathing for a minute, taking time to understand how our lives had changed.

He reached for my hand and kissed the backs of my fingers. "I'll send someone ahead to buy your tickets and make sure your travel arrangements are made."

"No need. I already have."

I met his eyes, and they held for a moment. Long enough for me to notice a smile at the corners of his mouth and the look of pride that flashed across his face before he turned and took long, purposeful strides out of the room.

Chapter Seventeen

October 1880 – Karlstad, Sweden

"It seems to get dark earlier here," Liona said. She looked up from the paper folded neatly in her lap and out the dark window. "I know our latitude hasn't changed so much to be noticeable, but look out there, it's completely black."

I nodded, too busy examining the tiny knots in my embroidery to look up. "I thought the city would make it feel lighter later, because of all the lamps in the windows, but maybe the buildings block the last bit of sun, and the city has the opposite effect."

I had used the vibrant green thread that dangled from my needle to create the tree in the summer scene that spread across the fabric. There was no questioning the similarity to the country views we enjoyed in Karlskrona. Our new home felt vastly different from our quiet country existence. Packing and moving had been uneventful.

Liona, of course, came with us to Karlstad, a city near the Edsvalla bridge work. Samuel and Elsa stayed on. They didn't want to leave their home and the friends they had made, and although I knew we would miss them terribly, I was glad they were still in Karlskrona as a support to Astrid. I was also relieved Elsa would be available to assist Elin if any difficulties arose when it was her time to be delivered. John and his wife moved in as we were moving out, and as most of the furniture stayed, the transition was relatively simple.

"I miss Elsa." Liona tucked her paper under another book on the table next to her. She smoothed her skirt. "I know they chose to stay, but I feel bad for them." She glanced back toward the black window. "Their new mistress is not a kind woman."

"That, she is not." I set my own project down and stood to stoke the fire. It was a cold night, and we didn't expect Anders home for at least another couple of days. I didn't want to involve Liona in Samuel and Elsa's affairs, but Anders had made sure they had enough of a pension to leave their new employers if they felt it was necessary. Part of me wanted to tell her—the part of me that considered her more friend than servant. I wandered over to the window and looked at other lamps in other people's windows. Our new home was small, nice, but offered little in the way of distractions.

The most difficult of the changes was what to do after all the crates and trunks had been unpacked. I missed my sitting room with its high windows looking out over my garden. Our landscape of pine trees interrupted by clusters of birch had been exchanged for a view of a wide paved boulevard and women dressed in unfamiliar fashions.

Karlstad, a good deal west of Stockholm, although distanced, had well-traveled roads that led directly from one city to the other. Hence, fashions traveled faster to Karlstad than they did to the seaport town of Karlskrona, and most of my clothes, if not out of date, lacked some of the more modern touches that were paraded back and forth in front of my window.

"How is your reading going?" Liona interrupted my thoughts. She motioned to the stack of English papers on the table next to my chair.

"Slow. Confusing. Especially the articles about America. It seems the stories speak of either wonders or horrors. There's nothing about everyday, typical lives. Yet, I suppose that wouldn't be newsworthy, would it?"

"I suspect not. Have you ever thought about it?"

"About what?" I sat back down but didn't take up my needlepoint again.

"About going to America. Have you ever thought about starting over, completely new?"

"I suppose. I know Anders has."

"You would be giving up a lot."

"Not as much as it would have been a year ago." I let the truth roam around in my thoughts. Our business was no longer as heavily linked to the family. We left our church in Karlskrona. Even if it wasn't a formal church, we still left our friends. I looked at the black window, framing nothing but my own reflection. Our current lack of connections found me where I sat, next to a new hearth, settled in a strange city, with unfamiliar sounds and scents and people moving in the dark, somewhere, on the other side of the glass. I stood and made my way back to the window to pull the drapes closed.

Liona leaned over to dig out her crocheting. She looked beautiful with her dark hair down for the night. Her dress, a heavy blue, stood in contrast with her warm skin, and I realized how much she didn't need us. I could see her on a ship, at the rail, the wet wind teasing her hair from under her cap; sun and salt and life, the ship moving and moaning with the heave of the waves. Someday, she would be on a ship to America.

"I guess there's always something to give up. Everything has a price. Even America."

"The land of the free," she said in English. "That's what they call it."

I tested the words. They were soft. They stood at a contrast to the ice that gripped the city. I ran my hand along the silky stitches in my lap and knew then where our path led—to the land of the free.

I didn't know how it would happen. Anders and I certainly never discussed it at first. But in small degrees, I began to live it.

Fabrics were chosen based on how sturdy the weave. I squirreled away the household money. We ate simply, and I chose not to hire a cook. We shared a maid with the neighbor. We paid a young girl to help with the laundry. Without family, restrictions and expectations eased, and we learned to go without what we previously considered necessary. On a particularly dark winter night, I packed away the unused china. Liona helped. She didn't ask why.

Anders was gone more and more as he divided his time between Edsvalla, plans for the match factory in Stockholm, and the occasional trip to his father's land. I suspected he, too, was working to build our savings.

Johan and Anna were adjusting well to the lumber business. More importantly, to the unique needs the presence of Anders's father placed on the already stressed factory. Anna wrote how every morning Johan would arrive at the lumberyard to begin work; often times, she accompanied him. Anna, as I heard from Anders, became extraordinarily valuable as a distraction to Anders's father. In truth, they became fast friends during their daily walks through the production areas. He would point to lumber stacked unevenly, or a missing tooth on one of the gigantic saw blades, and Anna, his dutiful sidekick, would follow, pencil to paper, noting all he said, then deftly refocusing him when he would waylay a busy employee with tales of his past.

It was obvious his condition, whatever the cause, was worsening, but Johan kept things running smoothly and people paid on time. When Anders's father suddenly passed away in the night, just before the spring thaw, he was remembered by his employees as a fair and honest man.

Anders's mother, however, was not a happy woman. In the spring, Johan and Anna moved back to Stockholm, and John and his family returned to work at the lumberyard.

The timing worked well. Johan was able to see to the setting of the foundation at the match factory while we were delayed with some of the more complex stonework in Edsvalla. Winter had been unusually bitter, and the stonemason's work, slow.

Liona and I continued to pack until spring, until the new baby would no longer allow his presence to be denied. On an April Sunday morning, Victor joined our family. He was a dark, fierce boy, with intense night-blue eyes; the opposite of my Esther. I knew from the first sight of him, as the midwife laid him on my stomach, that God would let me keep him. He demanded our attention, and we were happy to give it to him.

Chapter Eighteen

May 1881 – Stockholm, Sweden

One late spring evening, we walked to Anna and Johan's, accompanied by the city sounds of wheels on cobblestones and the smells of various dinners as we passed by open kitchen windows.

When the weather had warmed and the bridge work in Edsvalla had been completed, we moved to a small wooden home in Stockholm. The downstairs consisted of a kitchen, dining room, a front room, and an office I shared with Anders. There were four bedrooms upstairs. Like the other houses on the street, ours, with its white walls and red painted trim, was tucked neatly to the edge of the sidewalk. The neighborhood was known for its window box flowers that cascaded down and hung over, occasionally brushing the arm of a passerby.

Stockholm was both white and beautiful and new on some streets, and dirty almost to the point of wretchedness on others. A fire had swept the city in the decade prior. An aura of expectation glossed over the desolation of those who had never recovered, and a sense of inequality permeated the experience of living there. That, and being so close to the sea, the city was defined by a climate of constant change. Tiny home churches met on Sundays, and for the first time since leaving Karlskrona, we attended services led by Johan, in their house only a few blocks from our own. It felt like coming home.

Anna had been to visit us earlier that day. She invited us to dinner with Mark and Pia. They had just returned to town and were due to sail back to America in only a month's time.

"Can you imagine what it would be like?" Anders watched the carriages pass one another on the wide street. Liona walked ahead of us, holding Hulda's and Hjalmer's hands. Both Hulda and Hjalmer, now eight and three, had grown so much in the past year. I carried Victor. He was sucking on two fingers with ardent intensity. Anders reached over and touched his back. "How do you think he would do on a trip like that?"

"He's healthy. If the ship was a good ship, and we were prepared to eat well, I think we would all fare admirably."

Anders nodded, and we stepped into Anna's home.

The smells and the feel of the little kitchen were so similar to her cottage back in Karlskrona, I knew without a doubt she was where she belonged. If we would leave, we would be leaving her. I committed to memory the scene of my sister, hunched over the sink, heaving with the soapy water. I memorized the spicy smell of the lavender and garlic hung in the corner of the kitchen. I closed my eyes to feel the humidity of boiling kettles and let the warmth spread to every inch of my body. I opened them to see her set a red pottery bowl in the center of the table, her large hand deftly and quietly placing it within our reach.

Our eyes met and her ageless gaze said she knew our time would be brief. Johan watched her movements. He watched with envy the attention she paid to the wooden ladle resting in her palm, and I knew she would be happy for a very long time.

"Would you like to pray for us?" Johan asked Anders.

The prayer was one of gratefulness and hope and loss. I found I had to concentrate on how my fingers looked with my hands folded in my lap in order to keep any stray tears from making their presence known.

"How do you expect the trip to go?" Anders asked Mark.

"It's long, and it depends on the weather. The steam ships are faster, but the trip still can take more than two weeks." He looked down at his plate. "In all honesty, it would probably have been better had we waited a year or so to return. There seems to be so much to do here. Weekly, I am turning down congregations who have asked for baptismal services, only because we will be leaving in another month." He glanced at Pia. "We've also recently become aware that our little family of two will be expanding to three."

Pia blushed hard and couldn't hide her smile. "I think I'll be fine," she said, her eyebrows arching in hope. "The ill feeling usually goes away, right?" She looked at me.

I nodded, not having the heart to tell her how sick I was with Hulda. The thought of being on a ship, pregnant, day and night, made my stomach roll in sympathy.

"If you sincerely don't want to leave now, why are you going?" Johan asked Mark, his fork halfway to his mouth. It was apparent Anna's food agreed with him.

"We purchased the tickets almost six months ago. The ship isn't typically a passenger ship, but they've changed it over, and there was room. The captain was willing to reserve a space for us. We wanted to take advantage of a new ship. The last trip here was overcrowded and difficult."

"What do you mean by difficult?" Anders questioned.

"One woman was sick the entire trip, and from the onset, there seemed to be one pest after another, from lice, to the occasional rat, to just plain filth. Families were separated, the men and boys in one room, and the women in another. It was an unpleasant experience. But then, one doesn't expect a trip across an ocean to be exactly pleasant."

"But you have reason to believe it will be easier this time?"

"With the new ship and fewer people, yes, it should be an easier passage, as far as passages go. They will allow families to room together. That's a big improvement."

"If you hadn't purchased the space, would you still be going?" Anders set his fork down and sat back with his arms crossed over his chest.

Mark glanced at Pia. "Probably not."

"What would have to happen to keep you here for another year? Or at least until things settled?"

Mark shifted in his chair. "A place to live, and the money from the tickets."

Anders cleared his throat and Anna studied the food on her plate. We all knew what was coming next.

"What if you have a place to live at no cost—a nice place with furniture that would be yours for the next year? Would you stay then?"

"Absolutely, Anders." All eyes were now on Mark, and Liona began to clear the dishes away—some full of cold, untouched food.

"Don't bother, Liona." Anna motioned for her to sit down. "We'll see to those later."

Hulda sat with her hands in her lap, eyes alert to the changing tension in the room. Liona sat across from her, appearing trapped.

Anders touched my arm, and I nodded, avoiding Anna's gaze. I would have never thought it would be so simple—just a gesture—to change the course of our lives. "What if we offered to exchange our house for your tickets," Anders asked Mark. "The lease is paid through next year."

Pia covered her mouth with her hand, nodding to Mark, relief flooding her face.

"Yes, without question we would do that."

"Johan," Anders asked. "Would you mind if we used your office to discuss some details?"

Johan agreed, and the men left the women at the table to work through our own details. Anna began clearing the dishes, dropping one bowl loudly into another.

"I'm sorry." Pia moved to help.

"Oh no, Pia," Anna said, pausing with the bowls in hand. "I'm delighted we have the opportunity to keep you for a while. It will just be hard to say good-bye. I know, if not now, they would be leaving soon anyway."

It was a conviction I shared.

Liona resumed stacking the dishes left on the table. She carried them to the basin. I followed her with my own pile.

"You will be welcome to come with us. I'll talk to Anders, and he'll find a way. That is, if you want…" I set the dishes on the table. "You don't have to make a decision right away."

She nodded without turning to look at me.

I couldn't imagine the trip without her.

I rolled over in bed and tucked my shoulder under Anders's arm. He wrapped it around me, and we listened to each other breathe.

It had happened faster than we'd thought possible. Anders had sold his share of his father's business to his brother. In the negotiations, we gained what we'd expected financially but lost more than anticipated. He'd come home without our name. It was a concession to his mother. She didn't want the family name diluted in America.

Finally, I interrupted the silence. "Did we make the right decision?"

I felt his chest expand, and he held his breath for a moment. He exhaled. "I hope so."

"Can you give up your name?" I whispered.

"Can you give up yours?"

We had both been stunned by the necessary sacrifice.

I raised my head and looked at him in the dim light. His glance shifted from the ceiling to me. He lifted a hand and pressed it to my cheek. "I never thought I'd have to ask you to change your name."

I blinked back the tears that threatened and sat up to face him. Reaching through the dark, I found both of his hands and raised them to my chest. "Listen to me. We've left our church, our families, our jobs, and our lives. And we've done it because we want something better. We know there's something better. I have you. You have me. We have Hulda and Hjalmer and now Victor. I don't know about you, but that's all I need."

He tugged at my hands and pulled me back to rest on his chest. "You can't possibly know how much I love you."

Before bed, after the children had been tucked in, we'd practiced alternative names. We let the choices roll off our tongues. We'd laughed as we practiced them the way we thought an American would say the syllables. Finally, we'd settled on combining "Blom" for his grandmother's name, and "berg" for the rolling, pine-covered landscape where Esther was buried.

When he'd left the room, I practiced writing it like a new bride. I drew it first, with a proper looking "B," but the weight of the "B" could not balance the rest of the eight-letter, oversized body. I tried again, but "Anders" appeared buried under the new, bigger "B." And no matter what I did, the "g" at the end always came out like the Modig "g."

I tucked the quilt tighter around us both and whispered how much I loved him back, and we slept until the sun burned bright.

Chapter Nineteen

June 1881

Anders stood in his study, in front of his bookshelf. He picked up volume after volume, only to return them to the exact spot on the shelf. Even with all the things we had let go, from Karlskrona, to Karlstad, to Stockholm, deciding what could travel with us was not an easy feat.

The lists were endless. I had begun with the things we would need—clothes and food—and continued on to the things we would want. I think some part of my mind clung to the idea we would someday return, even though I knew it was not likely. I found myself asking Anna to keep things for me, and, similarly minded, she agreed.

Liona and I had made lists of everything we could find, and then crossed off the things we didn't want. When the list was still too long, we put a line through the things we wouldn't need, the things we probably couldn't use, the things we wished we had room for, and finally the things we wanted to keep, but knew wouldn't fit. Anders flipped the book over in his hand yet again, clearly deliberating its fate.

"Have you decided?" I was carrying yet another pile of linens down the hall and to the waiting boxes in the dining room.

"Decided on what?"

"What you're going to take."

"None of this." He didn't take his eyes from the shelves but crossed his arms over his chest.

"You don't think we can take even a few?"

"But which few? Do I take a favorite novel? A storybook for Hulda maybe? A volume for studying the Bible?" He turned and picked up the empty crate at his side and set it down again a couple of feet closer to the wall. He lined it up evenly across the lines of the wood planks.

I crossed to his desk and set the linens down with other brightly colored and embroidered table napkins and runners with a pattern for each season—a pile we would not be taking. The summer set was my favorite, with daisies sprinkled across a light green fabric. I had planned on keeping it, but soon realized even one of the four was extravagant, so they were all going to my sister.

His desk was nearly empty. He sat in the chair as if he were preparing for an evening of work, but there was little work to be done.

It had happened so easily, had fallen into place with such simplicity that the resulting decisions of what to give up and what to take, the guessing of who we would become when we arrived, and what those people would need to be successful in their new lives, seemed churlish to worry about. But it was practical.

"I'll be glad to get on the ship." Anders took a pen from the inkwell and examined the tip for imperfections. "This pen is still good."

"What are your plans for tomorrow?" I walked to Anders's side of the desk and leaned against the arm of his chair.

He put the pen down and leaned back. "The ship is in port now. I thought I would go and speak to the captain, see how much space we can reserve for storage. Then I will tend to some financial matters; sign some papers at the bank."

"Everything is fine, right?"

"Yes. My brother transferred the last of the money he'd promised."

I nodded and shifted my weight to leave.

He pulled the fabric of my skirt back down so that I leaned on the arm of his chair. "Are you happy?" he whispered, pulling me closer.

It was an interesting question. I wasn't unhappy. I was busy.

"Yes."

He watched my face, his eyes traveling to mine.

"Are you worried?"

"About what?"

"About anything. Traveling, leaving..."

Lines crossed his forehead, and for the first time I could remember, there was a hint of uncertainty in his voice, a tremor of something I couldn't place. I bit the inside of my cheek and raised my hand to cover his. His fingers felt hard under mine—the skin so different from my own. The roughness and scars earned from a lifetime of burdens of which I knew little.

"No. I know we will be fine." I laced my fingers through his.

"What about Victor? He's still so young."

An echoing, demanding wail erupted from the kitchen. "He'll outlive us all." I chuckled and rose to leave the room. "I have to see to Victor. He's hungry again."

Anders stood and crossed back over to the shelves.

I paused at the door. "I'm sure we can make room for a few books. Maybe you could pick out one we can read while on the ship, and one for Hulda to take in her things?" Anders hummed his agreement, and I left him in the same place he was in when I entered the room.

"I think I have everything." Liona exhaled loudly as she dropped another bag at the bottom of the stairs.

"I'm sure that will change in a few minutes." It had become almost tradition to reach the bottom of the stairs proclaiming victory over the packing, only to realize yet another important item was almost left behind. Liona was packing a bag with a few things to keep Hulda and Hjalmer busy on the ship. I suspected even if the bag were bottomless, it would not hold enough for that task.

Anders had visited the ship, and he'd come home less than reassured. By sailing standards, it was a fine vessel, but by landlubber standards it was small and cramped even for a man of average height. For Anders, it would be uncomfortable.

We were blessed. Most immigrant ships were filled to overflowing. So much so the men bunked in one room, and the women and children in the other; sometimes separated by only a curtain and often requiring the passengers to sleep in the same bed with strangers. Our situation was not like that. The ship was new and intended to carry livestock and cargo. Although at first this sounded like a negative, we later realized it meant the rooms were sectioned off like horse stalls, allowing each family at least a bit of privacy. Anders and I would sleep on a pallet with a straw mattress with the children in the bunk above. Hulda was excited about the bunks. Liona, being single, would room with the other single women in one large, shared area. She was not looking forward to her bunk.

"How is everything?" Anna walked through the front door and looked at the organized chaos. It was the day before we were to embark, and things were stacked and scattered throughout the downstairs rooms. Anna squeezed between two crates and into the dining room, where there was even less space to walk. "I see you are almost ready."

"Let's go into the kitchen. I still have some packing to do in there."

Anders had purchased a barrel for food storage. The captain vowed there would be more than enough food and water on board, but after hearing numerous tales of woe from almost everyone, he thought we should plan to bring at least some of our own food. Hard cheese, dry meat, hardtack, and honey were layered into the barrel a little at a time so we would be able to pull them out as needed. I picked up a small jar of lingonberry jam and worked it into an empty space between the cheese and meat—a luxury I knew, but one I was sure we would appreciate. Anna smiled; she knew my passion for the tangy berry.

"We have room," I rationalized.

"I know. I'll miss you."

I looked up and said nothing. There was nothing left to say.

"I brought this for you. Maybe you can tuck it into a little space?"

It was a bulb. Clean and dry and ready to be planted when we found our new home.

"White?"

Anna nodded. I didn't tell her where her last bulb hid.

"Thank you." I wrapped it in a clean cloth and placed it on the table.

"You have to write as soon as you get there." Anna turned, and I saw her hand come to her face to wipe a tear that dared escape.

"I will."

"Good." Anna took a step toward me and grabbed my shoulders in a crushing hug. I could feel the catch in her breath. Her strong arms held me still, as if she could will time to stop by strength alone. "I'll wait for your letter." She dropped her arms and took a step back. "What do you have left to get done? Tomorrow will be here before you know it."

I wiped my face with my apron. "Hulda might like some help. She is going through some of the toys she no longer plays with and making a list of the children she wants to give them to."

"I can get them to the families later this week." Anna pushed a chair out of her way and headed down the hall. "Is she in her room?" she asked, too far away to hear my answer.

"What still needs to be done in here?" Anders entered through the garden door in the kitchen. I continued to layer the barrel with preserved food.

"I wish there was some way to bring some fresh food aboard. And if food is in short supply, what good is this really going to do us? Are we going to fight off the hungry people so we can feed ourselves?"

"I think most families bring some supplies of their own. We can't go wrong bringing extra." Anders shrugged his shoulders. "I sold the jewelry."

"Good. Did you get what you were hoping to get for it?"

"Yes."

I looked up, and he looked away.

"What's wrong then?" I asked.

"I didn't want to sell some of it—some of your pieces. We don't need the money. I would rather you have kept some of it."

"It's not going to do me any good if we end up short. I would rather know we had a little extra in case of an emergency."

"I know. I'm going to start moving some things around, getting ready for tomorrow."

"Did you get the name of the minister from Mark? He said he already sent a letter so he will be expecting us."

Anders patted his breast pocket. "Name and address," he said, and met my eyes.

There was little else to say.

Anders started the day earlier than the rest of us.

The crates and bags were packed. I wandered from room to room, bewildered by the number of things we intended to leave behind. To Hulda, it was an adventure, to Hjalmer a curiosity, to Victor, a reason to squeal, as we were all too busy to stop him. For me, it was a curiosity. I waited to feel something, but there was nothing there—only tasks to be completed, papers to gather, children to attend amidst the chaos.

In the end, Anders loaded five crates onto the wagon and took them to the ship. When I ran out of things to double and triple-check, we waited in the house for him to return to us. We sat on our bags instead of the furniture and took turns watching out the window. Johan went with him, planning to stay at the docks to see our things safely loaded.

"How long will we be on the ship?" Hulda asked again.

"A long time."

"Will we sleep there?" Hjalmer said.

I looked at Liona. We had discussed this with him before; he just couldn't seem to understand the concept of sleeping on a ship.

Neither could I for that matter.

"Yes, we will." I reached down to smooth his hair. Liona straightened his shirt and lifted him to her lap. I looked in the bag next to me to check for nothing in particular.

"Hello?" Pia squeezed through the partially blocked front door.

"Come in," I said.

"How is everything?"

"Going well. Are you ready to move in?"

Pia looked around the room, took in the furniture and the high ceilings—the china left in the glass front cabinets. "We really can't thank you enough." She ran her hand over her slightly expanded middle.

"Pia, this is what we wanted too."

"Is everyone ready?" Anders stepped in through the door, brushing the front of his jacket off as he reached for the first bag. "Johan is waiting for us at the docks. We should get moving." He ducked back out of the house.

"Nothing left in any of the cabinets," Anna called from the top of the stairs. She had been doing another look through to make sure I hadn't forgotten anything. She walked down, trailed by a summer weight, blue skirt.

"It's a long way," Hulda announced to Anna.

"I know." Anna stepped off the bottom stair and reached to tug one of Hulda's braids.

"Will you come and visit?"

"I will write a lot of letters."

"That's not the same."

"I know."

"We'll come back and visit," Hulda turned and informed me, nodding once for emphasis.

"You never know." I picked up a small bag of dried fruit and stuffed it in the larger bag that we would use until we reached Liverpool. There we would buy a few more things before crossing the Atlantic. "Would you take this outside to your father?"

Hulda grabbed it, tilting under the weight. "I got it." She struggled through the door.

"She'll always remember," Anna said from behind me. Her tone struck a corresponding cord somewhere in my spine—a shiver of familiarity. I turned to hug her again before we both picked up bags and set them outside in the sun for Anders to load into the wagon.

I could hear the docks before I could see them. Not individual noises, not shouts or the sound of things dropping. All of those noises were there, but in such vast quantity they swelled to a consistent roar. A few blocks from the water's edge, fishmongers yelled to the fishermen, arguing about the weight of the fish. Store owners shouted back, demanding a better price, throwing fish appearing too old or too small back on the table. Hulda and Hjalmer watched with large eyes. Victor slept, even while being jostled around in my arms. I had just fed him before we left, making up for what was going to be a long day.

Once at the water's edge, Anders spotted Johan through the crowd, waving his arms high over his head.

"There it is," he leaned over to me, shouting above the noise. He pointed to a ship tied to the docks behind Johan.

Four masts stood at a slight angle. There were two to the front of the ship, and two to the rear—fore and aft masts I would later learn. A heavy steam stack jutted up from the center of the ship, and passengers already lined the docks.

Anders slowed the wagon and hopped out. I handed Victor to him and climbed down. The tangy smell of fish and fishermen thickened the air. Johan made his way toward us and began pulling bags off the wagon. I took Victor from Anders and settled his warm forehead into the bend of my neck.

"At least this time of year you should expect good sailing," he shouted above the din. I nodded, knowing my voice would likely never make it through the noise.

"Liona, you grab Hjalmer," Anders said, lifting Hulda from the back of the wagon. "Hulda, you stay right by me. Hold on to my jacket, and don't let go." Hulda reached for the edge of his jacket and held on tight.

"You have to write as soon as you're settled." Anna shouldered one of the bags and started walking us toward the end of the line.

I hadn't realized we were at that point. It happened so fast. And with whispered prayers for safe travels, and a few last minute tearful smiles, we were alone, standing in line, waiting to sign our names for the last time.

Anna waved from the dock, and I didn't know when I should turn away. Pulling out to sea, in a ship measuring over 100 meters, holding countless passengers and crew members, was not a fast process.

I watched until her blue skirt and white shirt blended in with those moving around the dock, until the only sounds were water and sailors, until expressions faded. I watched long past the time we ceased to wave.

Anders looked a decade younger, holding his hat as it threatened to be swept off his head and laughing at Hjalmer's fascination with the waves as they slapped the hull of the ship.

I had signed my name for the last time as we lined up to board. Between balancing Victor on my hip, watching Liona's grip on Hjalmer, and counting our trunks and bags as the sailors carried them up the gang plank, I hadn't pause to reflect.

They handed me a carbon. They gave me the papers identifying us with our old names scratched across in a scribbled rush, our identity, one last time, making itself known to the world. When we would dock in Philadelphia, "Philly" I heard the sailors say, we would shuffle off and sign new names on new papers.

They handed me the paper, and I folded it and tucked it deep into my pocket where it rested, a weight against my hip, crinkling as I rubbed against the rail, the last of who we were, now my burden to hold. I wondered if Lars had changed his name, and how many men like Lars would be sharing a ship with us. Would they be as intent as we were to start a new life, or were they simply running? Were we running? Were we so used to fighting the church, and then our families, that moving, running, had become a habit? Or were we meant to be here?

I glanced to the brown waters that lapped against the hull. I closed my eyes, remembering the feel of the water around me, the peace, the understanding that it was not my job to divine my purpose. Trying to be where we were meant to be was a slow seduction away from God's peace. I opened my eyes and took a deep breath of the salty air. We would do our best no matter where our path led us, and once in Philly, I would sign my third name.

Blomberg still fell off my tongue with a slight halt, slow at first, with a pause, then tumbling out. I blushed at the thought of the impending deception of offering a name I had never known as mine, but I would offer it. I would start new. We would start new, and like Lars, or any of the others leaving Sweden as an escape, or for hope, it didn't matter. We would arrive at a place of opportunity, and hopefully a place of peace, no matter where we landed and no matter what our names might be.

The crowd on the deck thinned as people left the rail to find their bunks. Some were only on board for the short sail to Liverpool. Others, like us, were staying on board until America.

"Do you think we should get settled?" I asked Anders, finally turning from my watch at the rail. Anna was gone.

"I suppose so."

I glanced around the deck. We were near the center of the ship. A stairway led down to the mid-deck, where we would be sleeping. Some of our things were already there, but we needed to make beds and arrange our things in some sensible order for the rest of the voyage.

"Liona, will you help us carry everything to where our bunks are?" I leaned over and picked up one of the bags and slung it over my shoulder. "Then you can find your own bunk and get yourself settled before dinner."

"That sounds fine," Liona quickly replied. "It will be nice to see where we'll be spending most of the next couple of weeks."

The middle deck where the passengers stayed was the space between the open air deck outside, and the cargo hold at the very bottom of the ship.

We descended the steep staircase, which was something more akin to a ladder, and entered a long room. Anders's head almost touched the ceiling, and in some places where beams encroached on the head space, I could tell his height would be a challenge. Bunks lined each wall, side to side, front to back of the ship. In the family area, where we stood, the beds were wide, meant to hold more than one person each.

The place teemed with a variety of people from different places. Some were dark, some light, and others somewhere in between. They crowded into the center aisle, juggling bags over their heads. One woman hunched over the bottom bunk, untying the knot on a bundle of bedding with her teeth. Children were relegated to the top bunks so the mothers could see to the tasks without worrying about them wandering off.

"We're over here somewhere." Anders pulled his ticket from his breast pocket and read the numbers aloud. "Two hundred seventy-two."

"I think it's this way." Liona gestured behind the stairs. "There's two thirty-seven, and that's two thirty-eight. It must be farther down here."

I hefted my bag higher on my shoulder and followed Anders as he weaved through the mass of people. Hulda held on to his jacket, and one of his hands kept a grip on the shoulder of hers. Liona held Hjalmer, although he was a little too large to carry, and I followed, trying not to lose sight of them in the mass and noise of the other passengers. I couldn't imagine what a crowded ship must have been like for this to be considered spacious.

Anders ducked into one of the sections, and I moved with the crowd until I reached the same space. The number written on paper and nailed to the end of the wall read 272.

"Hulda." I bent over to meet her gaze. "Remember this number. Don't forget. If you ever get separated from us, just come here and wait so we can find you."

"I will," she said, her eyes big with the significance of the statement.

I dropped the bag I carried on the floor next to the bunk, sat down, and started untying our own bundle of bedding while I assessed the situation.

The place was smaller than I had expected with only one wide bunk to the left of the little "room" that was the cattle stall. It had no doors, and, like a typical horse barn, the wood walls stopped at chest level. Metal bars spanned the distance from the top of the wooden walls to the ceiling. I was glad I had purchased so much canvas. Pia said I would want to, and she had been right.

"I'm going to need some rope," I said to Anders.

He stood hunched over under a beam. "Where did we put it?"

"It should be in that box, although I hope I brought enough."

"So do I." Anders looked around the room. I could see he was calculating how much rope we would need if we wanted to partition ourselves off entirely. He took a key out of his pocket and unlocked the biggest of the trunks. "Where is the canvas?"

"It's tied in the bundle of bedding over there."

"How are you going to keep Hjalmer on the bed?" Liona asked, examining the top bunk. "He's going to fall off the first night."

"We'll have to use more of the rope to make a barrier of sorts." Anders stood up, pulling a coil of rope from the top of the trunk.

I stood up next to him and tried to shrug out of my outer jacket. The air was sticky. It smelled like fish, unfamiliar spices, and spoiled milk. Liona looked equally uncomfortable. Her hair had escaped from under her small bonnet, and was sticking to her forehead. Her cheeks, forehead, and chin were flushed pink. "You have your number, right?"

"Yes. I'll be number three hundred eleven, 'A.'"

"Why don't you find your bunk and get settled in? You can meet us back here before the dinner hour if you want."

She looked around. With so little room, and until things were stowed under beds, or shoved into corners, there was little space to stand, let alone try to entertain children. She nodded in agreement.

"I'll put my things away and then be back."

"Liona?"

She turned back to me.

"Thank you for coming with us."

"I wanted to."

As the hours dragged by, things did not get easier or quieter as I had expected they might. By the time Liona fought her way back to our bunks, we had successfully strung up rope across the opening and hung the canvas curtain I had prepared. Instead of using rope through the bars that ran down both walls, we cut the top of the fabric in strips and tied knots around each bar to make the curtain. It was marginally successful, with only a few places where a very interested party could have peeked through. Anders was busying himself tying all the gaps together when Liona knocked on the wall next to our curtain.

"How is everything settling here?" She scanned the cramped space. Hulda and Hjalmer were entertaining Victor on the top bunk while Anders and I crowded into the two feet of space between the beds and the wall.

"As well as can be expected." I closed one of the bags and slid it under the bottom bunk just as the German mother in the next room erupted with a fit of deep-toned demands. Her tiny husband scurried to do her bidding, and I was glad I didn't speak German.

"I'll start working on this curtain." Anders smothered a smile as he held up the canvas to block out our view of the woman. She stood and frowned directly at me. Liona noticed, and we turned away together to stifle our laughs. He couldn't get that curtain up fast enough.

When all was settled, the straw mattresses pulled down and made up with our linens, the curtains hung, and our things secured in case of rough seas, we headed up to the main deck for a briefing with Captain

A.A. Saunders.

———✦———

Mr. Saunders stood no more than five feet two inches tall, and I suspected even that stature was due to his highly decorated shoes.

His portly face was stained dark by the sun, and I had difficulty making out his home port from either his color or his accent. His English wasn't difficult to understand, when he spoke in words I knew, but his expressions were foreign and never appeared to match the content of what he said.

He began with the rules, placing emphasis on all the wrong words. "There will"—he said this meaningfully, as if the words *there* or *will* were especially difficult to comprehend—"be no seaman on the passenger deck, nor shall there be passengers found in the sailors' quarters." The rest of the sentence spilled out, taking no more time than the first two words were given. I looked questioningly toward Anders, and he shrugged.

The rules were endless, full of common courtesies and expectations, punctuated occasionally by an important informational tidbit. Eventually, the men separated off to discuss and divide the daily tasks and the women were left to mull in the open. Land was no longer visible. I held on to the rail with one hand and Victor with the other. The paper was still in my pocket, and I stood at the rail, pressing it hard into my hip.

———✦———

Our first night out was heralded by an almost full moon. It hung heavy and gold on the horizon. The rippling reflections danced along the surface of an almost still ocean as the ship steamed toward Liverpool. The passengers huddled close and whispered to one another. The air was damp and cool on the deck, and I didn't look forward to returning to our tiny space after the stifling dinner we had shared.

There were two kitchens mid-deck, one for the passengers to use, and another, larger one, for the ship's cook—a frighteningly thin man with a pock-scarred face and one thin patch of hair molded to the crown of his head. Hulda took one look at him and backed in behind my skirts. His responding, high-pitched laugh did nothing to ease the tension but reassured me I didn't need to worry about apologizing for Hulda's rudeness. He seemed to enjoy her response.

We stood in line, waiting to fill our plates and sit down at the long tables that lined the perimeter of the room. The galley was in the front of the ship, near the men's quarters. Anders did not like the arrangement. He would have preferred for us not to have to stand amidst the men's bunks in order to wait for dinner. The single women's bunks were opposite, at the rear of the ship, as far away from the single men as possible. The families, the largest group, took up the center bunks. For this, I did not complain, as there was less rocking in the center of the ship than on the fore or aft areas; I noticed as people pushed their salted pork away untouched, some of our numbers had already turned a fair shade of green.

On the ocean at night, the stars stretched from the heavens to the water, and if I watched for long enough, they swam in, so it felt like I could reach and collect a handful of the twinkling lights just like I might have gathered sun-soaked blackberries while listening to the river go by in the woods near our home in Karlskrona. The air cooled, but with Victor in my arms I stayed warm. I had nursed him on deck, under a blanket, turned away as best as possible. Other women in my condition gathered around. We used our numbers for privacy.

Anders sat on a bench not far away with Hulda and Hjalmer. He was pointing to the stars and answering questions about the ship. For the distance to Liverpool, the captain didn't plan to use the sails, but even I was excited to see how fast we could move through the water under both steam and sail. If our parents had undergone this journey, the trip would have taken more than a month to complete. As I thought about the way we would sleep that night, a month seemed unimaginable. The ten days we'd planned on didn't even seem possible. But there was no going back.

"Are you ready to go below decks?" Anders stood next to me, averting his eyes from the women who had not yet finished nursing their infants.

"No, but we should get them to bed."

Anders responded with a grunt. If I was uncomfortable in the cramped space, I knew sleeping in that tiny bunk was not something he would enjoy.

We stood in line, waiting for the people in front of us to work their families down the stairs. At least it was a clear night, so I knew the hatches would stay open. They did little to clean the air though, and as we stepped under the beams, our senses were once again assaulted by dinner and people and the unmistakable odor of those who had lost their dinner. I covered my mouth with my shawl. Hulda mimicked me. Anders closed his eyes for a moment, before stooping under the beam to take the last step down.

"What's that smell?" Hjalmer said loud enough for heads to turn our way.

I ignored the question and found our curtained-off room.

Hulda and Hjalmer slept on the top bunk, with room to spare. Anders and I tried to fit on the bottom bunk with Victor between us. That didn't work. Eventually, I fell asleep, pressed against the wooden wall with him in my arms.

The space was dark and thick. The canvas blocked what little light and air might have reached us. Anders rolled onto the floor and stood up to tie back the curtain, but doing so didn't help, and it just meant every person walking by looked into our space. He secured the curtain closed again.

"How will we ever sleep?" Anders eventually whispered into the dark.

"I'm not sure. It sounds like Hulda and Hjalmer fell asleep though."

"I wonder if the snoring next to us is coming from that woman or her husband."

I giggled and poked Anders with my elbow.

"This isn't going to work, with Victor sleeping on you the entire trip." Anders returned to the very real problem.

"I know."

"You could sleep up top with Hulda and Victor, and I could sleep down here with Hjalmer."

I had thought of the idea myself but didn't want to suggest it. I didn't want to sleep in a different bed than my husband. "That would probably be the best arrangement."

"We would have more room."

I hummed in agreement. Victor squirmed in my arms. A loud thump made me jump as the person in the next bunk must have rolled and hit the thin wall between us with their knee or elbow.

"This is not going to be easy." Anders tried to sit up, but laid back down when he remembered there wasn't room between the bunks to sit upright. "Besides, I don't like the kids up on the top bunk with only a curtain and bars separating them from the next family. They have four kids on that top bunk, and one of them doesn't look very healthy."

Sickness did concern me. Although the trip had shortened with steam-powered engines, people still suffered illness. Some died, some gave birth. I counted a few very pregnant women on board and found myself wondering who would deliver the babies if the time came and there was no midwife around. I hoped there was a midwife on board. I couldn't imagine giving birth hunched in one of the bunks and in pain, trying to clean the baby and yourself with rationed water.

There was a pregnant woman in the single women's bunks. Liona told me about her, told me how the other women turned away when the pregnant woman entered the room. Like Liona, I worried the woman might have no one. I prayed for her and the family next to us, and somehow, I fell asleep.

Chapter Twenty

"The men say we won't actually dock in Liverpool." Anders returned from his morning duties of handing out the water ration. He ducked under the curtain and sat on the closed trunk near the head of the bunk. "There aren't enough people getting off or on to make it worth the delay, so the ship will anchor for a day and the sailors will run small boats to and from the port." He looked up at me. "How are we for supplies? Did we plan on buying anything in Liverpool that we won't be able to do without?"

"I can't think of anything. It might have been nice to walk on dry land again before we start out for the next two weeks, but I wouldn't want to leave our things on the ship unattended anyway. What about you? Anything you can think we might need?"

"Other than some fresh air, a long enough bed, and a lamp? No, nothing."

The night had been endless. We woke to the gentle rocking of the ship, and the sounds and smells of sickness. Hulda kept her dress buttoned over her nose. When I asked her to straighten the bedclothes, I could see her calculating how she would accomplish the task while maintaining her pocket of clean air. Eventually, she let the fabric fall, coughed a couple of times, and got to work.

"Are you ready to go to the kitchen?" Liona called from outside the curtain. People were beginning to walk back and forth down the aisle.

Sometimes they would brush against our fabric border. It irritated me, although I knew it shouldn't—there was nothing we could do about it. Everything was just so close.

"I will be in a bit," I called back through the curtain. "How does the line look for the toilets?"

"Long."

"Do you think it will go down any?"

"No, I would expect there will be a line for most of the trip since they only have the two toilets."

"The children used the chamber pot already this morning." I lifted the curtain and stepped out with our metal coffeepot and small bag of grounds. "I suppose there's no use standing in line if we don't have to. Anders, I'll be back with the coffee. I don't suspect it will take too long."

"How did your night go? Did you sleep well?" I asked Liona. Her dark hair was pulled up in a tight knot, and her face scrubbed clean. I wished I was closer to her so I could smell her soap rather than the other aromas coming from the bunk spaces that were now opening up to the center aisle. Each family had their own scent. None were what I would call pleasant, but some were infinitely worse than others.

The German family to the right of our space smelled of meat and spices. The family to the left, with four children, smelled of cheese. The elderly couple next to them smelled of old people.

The line outside the kitchen was at least twenty deep.

"This might take a while," I said.

"Yes, it might. What do you think most people are making? They serve breakfast in only an hour or so."

"Coffee, like us."

"Do you think it's worth it?"

The thought of facing the morning without coffee or tea made me want to sit down right there on the floor. "Yes, we'll try it today and see how fast the line moves. How is your section? Are the women nice?"

"Some of them are. They're all pretty quiet."

"Did you speak with the one next to you?" The pregnant woman, although I didn't mention that part.

"No. She slept the entire night. I think she has to have made a trip like this one before, she's so calm. She doesn't wear a ring."

"Have any of the other women mentioned anything about her?"

"Nothing."

"Do you think she is healthy?"

"She sleeps a lot. I hope she is healthy. She rolled onto her back in the middle of the night, and she is very big. She looks uncomfortable."

"Maybe we should go to her and offer her some coffee when we are done here."

"That might be a nice idea. If anything, she is alone."

A woman shoved us from behind, offering no apology. The line was getting longer.

We moved over so a woman with a steaming pot could get out the door. She wiped her forehead on her sleeve and nodded a thank you. I smiled in return.

"I suspect Anders would prefer to have no coffee than to be cooped up with the children for this long."

Liona nodded her agreement.

"I wouldn't doubt we will get back with the coffee and find them nowhere in sight."

"I think you're right."

It was our turn.

The room was smaller than I expected, much like everything on the ship. Three stoves lined one wall. Each iron stove was covered with as many kettles as would fit. The women crowded around the stoves in a mass of multi-colored skirts, moving their kettles over to the warmest places as soon as someone vacated her post. The rude woman from behind me pushed into the crowd, elbowing her way to an empty few inches on the stove. I looked at Liona, and she shrugged.

"Excuse me," I said. No one even turned around.

"Excuse me," I said louder. This time a sweaty woman turned and looked, only to turn back to face the stove.

I looked at Liona again, and she shrugged again. If we wanted coffee, I was going to have to force my way into the pile of people. I stepped in and reached toward the stove. The woman who had looked at me grabbed my elbow roughly and pulled me in toward her.

"You're going to have to get serious about it if you want your coffee," she instructed in Swedish.

"Oh, thank you," I answered, more grateful for the Swedish than any assistance she could have offered.

"Give me your kettle."

I handed it to her. She set it down with a bang on a few empty inches of stove surface, and then pushed. The other pots trembled at the intrusion, and one threatened to spill off the other end. A cloud of steam burst from the disturbed kettles. A cacophony of voices erupted in different languages, berating the woman for her actions.

"Go to the devil," she shouted back in Swedish, giving a hard poke with her elbow. She turned to me and smiled wide, without the benefit of teeth.

I quickly smiled back, lest the elbow next be aimed in my direction, and I heard Liona's snort of laughter from behind me.

"Thank you," I shouted and tried to move away. It was useless. I was pushed in tighter than ever.

"Where you from?" she shouted in my face. Her breath reeked of morning and rot, and I tried not to take in any air.

"We lived in Stockholm," I yelled back, our conversation now as loud as it could be and still drowned out by the other women.

"Mine's done." She found the corner of her apron, edged her way closer to the stove and grabbed her kettle by the handle. Lifting it high over the heads of all the women circled around the stoves, she fought her way to the door. She exited and two more entered.

"Do you suppose it's hot yet?" Liona shouted in my ear.

"Do you suppose I care anymore?" I shouted back. I reached in with my potholder and found the handle to my kettle.

We made our way out of the smoky, steamy kitchen, anticipating a breath of fresh air, only to be met with the stench and humidity of the middle decks. The sweat gathered under my arms and dripped down my ribs. Even my thighs were sweaty. My skirts wrapped around my legs, bunching up with every step. We returned to the room, if one could call it a room, and pulled the curtain back. No one was there. Anders had taken all three children above decks.

I pulled a key by its chain from out of my bodice and unlocked the food barrel. Hardtack and lingonberry jam were on top. Liona held her apron out to make a basket, and I piled them in. I found a chunk of cheese before slamming the lid shut and locking it.

On our way out, I pulled a few metal cups off of their nail hangers. I secured the curtain, and we pushed our way back into the group now gathered outside our room. People were beginning to stand in line for breakfast. The line already wove from the front of the ship, through the men's quarters, and back through the family bunks.

"Excuse me!" I heard Liona shout into the ear of a man who was not about to be moved. The accompanying expression she leveled at him did the trick, and we broke free toward the stairs. The air cooled as we approached, and once at the top, I took in a breath for what seemed like the first time that morning.

My clothes were drenched, I was exhausted, thirsty, not a bit hungry, and my breasts ached to feed Victor.

"Over here!" Anders shouted from the rail, not far away. He had Victor in his arms, red-faced and crying. Hulda held on to a rope tied to Hjalmer's waist. Hjalmer strained at the confinement, attempting to get to me.

We reached them. I looked at the rope, and then at Anders.

"It was the only thing I could think to do! I didn't want to risk him disappearing."

Victor thrust himself at me. Anders didn't look much better off than Liona or I. He had already removed his jacket, had a day's worth of stubble, and the posture of a sulking bear.

"I guess that's fine," I conceded, wondering if I was a terrible mother. I knelt next to Hjalmer and retied the knot in a bow. At least it looked more planned that way.

I glanced to where the nursing mothers had gathered the night before to feed their babies, and saw a few of them already feeding there again. Liona was coating the hardtack with jam and handing pieces to the children.

"We're going to have to plan for something different in the mornings. I either have to get up earlier, or we'll have to do without coffee."

Anders nodded in agreement. I must have looked a wreck for him to even consider a morning without coffee as an option.

"This morning, I thought instead of waiting in line on the mid-deck for breakfast, we could just eat some of our provisions here, out in the air." I looked at Anders for approval.

He glanced back to the stairs that led below decks. "Agreed. Maybe I'll take one of the boats into Liverpool and stock up on more provisions. The less time we have to spend down there, the better."

Liona nodded.

"It stinks down there," Hulda added to the conversation.

"You are absolutely right, Hulda," Anders said. "It does stink down there."

No one added to the horrifying thought, because we all knew that sometime soon we would all have to go back down.

The boat brought Anders back to the side of the ship, and I breathed a sigh of relief. He climbed the nearly vertical ramp to us.

I'd watched him leave. He had walked down to the boat, and it had taken him away to shore with the people who intended to stay in Liverpool. When we decided he would go and stock up on more provisions, I'd not anticipated the way Hulda would grip the fabric of my skirt, nor the way I would hold Victor even when he struggled to climb out of my arms.

But he was back, and Hulda jumped up and down in place at my side.

He carried a sack, tied closed and slung over his shoulder. It swayed with each step, until he reached up and dropped it next to me on the deck. Hulda hugged him around the waist while Hjalmer peppered him with questions. His hand brushed the small of my back. I lifted my chin to see an expression of relief on his face that mirrored my own.

"What did you do while I was gone?" he asked the kind of mundane question one asked without thinking.

I didn't answer right away.

"What did you get?" Hjalmer was on his knees next to the bag, unsuccessfully pulling at the ends of the cord.

"I guess you'll just have to wait and see," Anders said.

We walked together toward the rear of the ship, to a place where less people mulled around.

"Liona and I visited that young woman—the pregnant one," I said after sitting on a metal bench. Anders lowered himself next to me.

His brows furrowed as he lifted Victor off my lap to settle on his. "I'm not sure we should get involved."

An elderly couple walked past. I wondered if they were traveling to meet family in America, or if they hoped for a new start for themselves. I faced Anders.

"I mean, she probably has family. Maybe we shouldn't bother her," he said.

I dropped my gaze to my folded hands.

"I know." He exhaled loudly. "What did she have to say?"

I understood his hesitation. After all, we had more than enough to concern ourselves with. But that didn't make it right not to show concern for another person.

"She didn't say anything." I studied my nails, not wanting to meet Anders's gaze. "We left her some bread and poured some of her water ration into a cup, but she just stared straight ahead, as if we weren't there. I hope she doesn't give birth before we land. She's quite large."

"You don't think she's sick, do you?"

"No. No fever. From what I can see, her coloring seems fine—pale but fine. She walked onto the ship without assistance. I think she hears us, she just chooses not to respond."

"Well, she's on the ship for the duration now." Anders pointed to the men hefting the ramp back up on the deck. We'll just have to look in on her occasionally."

We listened to the water splash against the hull as the last boat moved away from the side of the ship.

"We'll be pulling up anchor shortly." Anders craned his neck to watch the sailors scurry across the ship. "I know this will not be fun, but I'm looking forward to seeing this ship cut through the ocean under full steam and sail." He tapped his long fingers on the bench.

I couldn't help but be consumed by the thought of two weeks without bathing, but I kept it to myself. Instead, I smiled at a young, scrawny sailor as he half-saluted us while running toward the back of the ship.

"Please bow your heads," the ship's captain instructed all of us who had chosen to join the Sunday services on the deck. There were more people than I had expected, especially after hearing many of their conversations below deck for the past several days. I did not think our numbers included so many with faithful tendencies. I attributed the impressive attendance to boredom, and probably searching for a reason not to be near the bunks. Tomorrow was deemed cleaning day, and it was a good thing, because spending any amount of time down there currently was next to unbearable.

We sat near the back with the other families with children. It was not a quiet service. The older passengers and the single passengers sat nearest to the captain. In truth, I could hear very little of what he said, and I understood only a portion of that, but Anders understood and found the appropriate passages for me in our Bible. It was nice to have a distraction. I worried about the old woman who roomed close to us who had coughed all night long. I prayed—half for her, half for the rest of us. No one needed to see a sickness sweep the ship.

At least one family was sick already. Hulda noticed they had not opened their curtain in the morning and pointed it out to me. Anders looked in on them and alerted the captain. The unconcerned man gave us permission to bring food for them out of the dining room. The cook kept a vat of soup broth hot during meal times. There were no lines there, so Anders took broth to the family, and I sent over some flatbread. The wife was doing the best of the three. She thanked us in a language I didn't understand. I planned to check on them again that evening. I hoped it was only a severe case of seasickness.

As the captain continued his sermon, the cool breeze coming off the water provided relief from the sun and the decks below. He ordered the sails unfurled. They billowed and filled, snapping open and giving the sense that the air had a body all its own. One we could feel and appreciate. Our prayers of thanksgiving were honest. We were healthy, for now.

We didn't anticipate the storm. It blew in during the night.

The gentle rocking of the ship, the rhythm we had grown accustomed to, altered. My dreams shifted from meandering dreams of discovery, to dreams of riding in a carriage to nowhere, to those of being pursued. I woke to complete blackness, unsure of where I was and where I was headed. The ship shuddered beneath me. I licked my lips and tasted salt.

Our bedclothes were wet from seawater that had somehow made it into our bunk. Someone had closed the hatches, but left open the vents, and there were no lamps lit. Something fell in the room next to ours, and I heard a scream, then the sounds of someone being sick.

The smell permeated the lower decks as more people joined the ranks of those ill. My own stomach turned as I listened to the splatter, and I scrambled out of the bed to try to get to the chamber pot.

I splashed to the deck and could only imagine what I stepped in. The stench of spilled chamber pots and vomit rolled up from the floor. I held tight to the bunk rail. Hulda screamed. I added my dinner to the others on the floor.

"Mama?" Hulda said. "Papa? Where are you?"

"I'm here," I yelled back against intense noise; children crying and parents shouting directions to tie things down. Someone banged on the hatch above the stairs and demanded to be let out. Sailors above us shouted over the storm.

"Where's Victor?" Hulda asked. Victor, Hulda, and I had been sleeping together in the top bunk. Anders jumped from his place and slid in the mess on the floor that sloshed from room to room. I clambered to get back on top of my bunk, but kept slipping. Anders pushed me the rest of the way up.

"Is he up there?" Anders said above the noise.

I scrambled around the bed, pushing Hulda out of the way.

"He's not over here," she said.

My heart sank as I started pulling blankets from the straw mattress in the pitch black. "See if you can find him on the floor," I shouted to Anders as I continued to look. He was only a baby.

I heard Anders hit his knees on the floor as my hands hit warm flesh at the bottom of the mattress. "I found him," I said, pulling him from the bedclothes.

Putting my lips into the crook of his neck, I found the beat of his tiny heart. His breath puffed against my cheek.

"He's fine. Anders, he's fine."

Hulda felt for where I sat at the end of the bed and snuggled against my thigh. We pushed ourselves into the corner against the hull of the ship and the bars on the wall. Anders lifted a crying Hjalmer to share our corner. Hjalmer sat on Hulda's lap, and she held him tight. Anders ran his hand down my shoulder and to Victor's head. There he paused, and then continued down my arm to clasp my hand. He stood, holding my hand until daylight broke in through the cracks in the vents and the seas settled.

It had been the longest few days of my life. And we weren't even halfway there.

People spilled out into the sunlight, coughing and blinking, as soon as the sailors opened the hatch. They rubbed their eyes and gulped in the fresh air. The storm had lasted past the breakfast hour. No one complained of hunger.

I assessed our clothes and found our situation impossible. Captain Saunders quickly ordered additional rations of water for everyone. The sailors were put in charge of collecting teams of male passengers for repairs and cleaning. I sat on the deck and nursed Victor—the only passenger who slept soundly through the whole ordeal. It felt as if he should have been nursing us.

"How is everything?" Liona found me where I sat with my back to the rail and my legs extended straight out in front of me. My legs were exposed to the knees, and I didn't care.

"We're all here. During the storm we thought we lost Victor for a few minutes, but he was only sleeping. We couldn't see him in the dark."

"It was very dark." Liona nodded. "Have you seen the family that's sick yet?"

I looked around. "No, actually, I haven't. Have you?"

"No, I haven't either."

My stomach turned again, and this time I knew it had nothing to do with the gentle rocking of the ship. "I hope we didn't lose anyone last night."

Liona's eyes met mine.

"When we go back down, I will look in on them," I said.

"I never want to go down there again."

"Neither do I." I rested my head back against the metal and let the salt air fill my lungs. After that first breakfast, I'd relinquished my stays in favor of common sense and unrestricted movement. At least my ribcage could expand freely.

"Mrs. Modig," Liona began, ". . . I—"

"I'm not Mrs. Modig anymore," I reminded.

"Sorry, I forget. Mrs. Blomberg—"

"Please call me Brianna." I sighed. "After this journey, doesn't the formality seem a bit nonsensical?"

Liona smiled a crooked smile and chuckled. "I suppose it does."

She moved over to lean against the wall next to me and stretched out her legs. Her feet were still tiny, but her vomit encrusted shoes matched mine perfectly. Victor reached up and tugged at her dark hair.

The whistle blew. The captain called us to gather in the place we met for the church service for an announcement. Anders found Liona and me at the rail with the children, and we walked together and stood near the rear of the crowd. Despite the monumental cleanup waiting for us on the deck below, the sun improved everyone's mood and the passengers were exchanging their stunned expressions for determined ones. The men had all formed groups and were ready to get to work.

"I have some unfortunate news." The captain stood on a crate and lifted his thick arms, earning everyone's rapt attention. "Last night we lost a young passenger to illness. It does not appear contagious, but I would like to remind everyone to let a member of the crew know if anyone else falls ill."

I reached to feel Hulda's neck, then Hjalmer's. I slid my hand under Victor's shirt to check for a fever.

The captain continued. "We will need a couple of volunteers to make a coffin. We have wood and tools available."

Anders looked at me, and I nodded. He, along with a couple other men, lifted their hands above the crowd.

"Thank you," the captain said. "Please find the first mate after this meeting is concluded. He will show you where everything is."

I held Victor tighter to my chest.

"Now, before the men can start scraping the deck below, we'll need the individual families to gather all of the linens, including any canvas curtains that have been soiled, and bring them up to be laundered. If anything was stored under beds, the items should be gathered and checked to be sure there was no fabric soaking in the water that got in last night."

People shuffled and began whispering plans to one another.

"One more thing before we begin," the captain said, raising his voice over the growing noise. "Sailors will be posted throughout the mid-deck. They are not there to help clean. They are there to make sure one family's belongings do not end up in another family's space. Thievery will not be tolerated, and anyone caught stealing will spend the rest of the trip in the cargo hold."

Everyone nodded their agreement. Previously, I had overheard a few of the women discussing things that had gone missing, but nothing of ours had yet disappeared. I hoped that would continue to be true. It was hard to imagine the people next to me might be thieves, but again, I reminded myself that Lars also went to America. Not everyone who made the trip did so to create a new life. I looked to the men standing on the sun-drenched deck. Some people, I was sure, made the trip in search of new victims.

"The funeral service will take place this evening, after dinner."

The crowd was silent.

"If there are no questions, I think we are ready to begin cleaning." The captain turned and stepped down from the makeshift podium.

"Are you ready?" Anders asked me.

"How do you think they bury someone at sea?"

"I'm not sure."

"I'm glad they make a coffin."

"Yes," Anders agreed. "Let's get down there and start removing things so I can begin helping the men clean."

I turned to Liona. "What do you need to do on your own?"

"My things are fine. When the ship started rocking, I gathered everything up off the floor and tied them on my bunk with me. I'll want to wash my bedding, but I can bring that up when we bring up the rest."

"Would you mind sitting with the children while Anders and I gather things to bring up to wash?"

"Not at all."

"I could pull the linens from your bunk and bring those with," I offered.

"That would be fine. I'll take the children and stand in line for the water."

I nodded, and Anders and I headed into the hot stench.

It was so much worse than I had imagined.

When they'd first opened the hatches and the vents, no one took the time to look around. We just abandoned the mid-deck in hopes of fresh air. But on returning, the odors that escaped the hatch were unlike anything I had ever encountered, and for a brief second I thought of my small morning room back in Karlskrona and the high ceilings and doors that opened to the fresh breezes from my garden. I almost laughed at the situation I now faced. Instead I tied a scarf around my face and descended.

Standing water covered the floor, but it was not water. I took my first step, and I almost slipped. Anders caught me by the elbow. The captain's orders to "scrape the floors" began to make sense. No broom or mop could come close to cleaning the mass off the floor. It would have to be scraped and removed, one bucket at a time, out the hatches.

We found two seventy-two. Our curtain hung in the muck, partially torn down. Anders began untying ropes as I pulled bedding from the bunks and piled it on the mattresses. Thankfully, Anders had had the foresight to seal the crates and trunks we had packed with tar. I opened the trunk with our clothes and things appeared undamaged. I felt sorry for the women I had seen who had packed most of their family's belongings in tied bundles.

Surveying our small space, I realized we had come away relatively unscathed.

"I think I will go to the single women's bunks and collect Liona's bedding before we take these things up."

"Do you need any help?"

"No, I'll get her things and bring them back here, and then we can carry everything up together."

I tiptoed out of our room and out into what served as a hall. It seemed that for passengers on a ship, anticipating what horror next awaited was a luxury no one had time for.

Chapter Twenty-one

The crowd swarming through the mid-deck spaces moved efficiently, and for the first time, there was little arguing and shuffling. The passengers, now with a common goal, were prepared to work. The death during the night provided an additional motivator, as suddenly even those with questionable hygienic standards were intent on cleaning.

The women's quarters were smaller than the family bunks. The beds were narrower, and as they did not have the benefit of cattle stalls, were pushed so close together even I had to turn sideways in order to walk to the head of the bed. Fumbling about, I managed to find Liona's bunk as she said it would be, with her things secured by a rope, strung around from post to post. I stumbled over a number of items strewn about the floor, wicking up the muck. I stepped around them, hoping they were not prized possessions, but knowing they were. Everything on the ship was chosen because it was something the owner couldn't do without.

I squinted into the darkness, feeling around the bed for the folds in Liona's linens. I tugged and heard a moan.

Standing still, I listened in the dark. From the bunk next to me came whispered words I couldn't understand. Another moan had me feeling my way around the bunk.

My hands landed on a clothed arm. Fingers covered mine. I reached up and felt the young woman's face for signs of fever, and there were none.

I trailed my hands down her body and felt the hard swell of pregnancy. A contraction lifted the muscles under my hand, and the woman moaned again, this time on the whisper of a breath. I had no way of knowing how long she had been laboring.

"Anders!" I yelled toward the family quarters, knowing he couldn't hear me. "Is there anyone out there?"

No one answered. They were all too busy.

"She's been like that for a while," a voice said from the dark.

"Who's there?"

"She seemed fine last night, but she didn't go up after the storm."

I hadn't even looked for her. I had been so busy with our own troubles.

"Is anyone helping her?" I asked.

"We don't even know why she is in the single women's bunks. She obviously shouldn't be here."

"Can you come down and sit with her while I get some help?"

"I can watch from here."

I could have argued with her, but thought it pointless.

"I'll be right back." I couldn't tell if the pregnant woman could hear me. "Is there anyone I can get for you?"

She didn't answer.

"Anders, that girl is in labor." I was out of breath when I reached his side.

He was helping the neighbor take down their curtains. "What girl?"

"The girl in Liona's section."

"Did we find out if she has anyone?"

"I don't know. I don't even know what language she speaks, but I need Liona down here, and a lamp, and a midwife."

Anders handed the armful of fabric he had collected to the woman standing next to him and pulled our lamp from the hook at the foot of our bed. He reached into his pocket for a match and lit it.

"Let's go," he said.

I was busy collecting the cleanest blankets I could find, along with our ration of water. I tucked my sewing kit into my apron pocket and followed Anders down the hall.

He handed me the lamp. I swung it out in front of me and found the foot of the woman's bed. She wore shoes with thin soles; the right foot had a hole. Her dress was pulled to her knees and her legs were limp.

"There is something wrong here. I have no idea how long she's been like this." I looked for the woman who had spoken from the dark. She had left, and the room was empty.

Anders pulled my arm up toward the head of the bed. Her face was white, her hair hung in dripping ringlets. Her eyes stayed closed.

"I'll see if I can find a midwife," he said. "There's a doctor on board, although I know he is tending to some others right now."

Her breath grew shallow, and she moaned again.

"Get Liona first. I'm going to need some help."

I set the meager supplies I had brought on the bed next to hers. Water was needed first. I pushed my knee under her head and tipped the jar to her dry, pale lips. She swallowed a bit. Most dribbled to wet my skirt.

"I'm going to look under your skirts," I said aloud. More for myself than for her, as she still had yet to respond to anything I had said.

I walked to the end of the bed and lifted the hem of her dress. Her petticoats were soiled and bloody. I turned away as a stench rose from her bed. It was soiled and wet. She moaned again.

I lifted her knees and let her thighs spread wide, hoping to see no evidence of an impending birth, but knowing better. In the flickering lamplight, her exposed body revealed the knot of a baby's head. Before I knew what I was doing, I reached and touched the wet, hair-covered head mushrooming between her thighs.

"Jesus, help us," Liona's whisper came from behind.

"I'm sorry you have to see this, Liona, but I'm going to need your help."

"What should I do?"

"We have to get her off this bed. It's filthy."

Liona looked around. "Where do you want to move her?"

"The next bed is fine."

I took out my sewing kit and pulled my scissors from the case. Snipping the sewn edge of her hem, I started a tear in the fabric, and then I ripped it up to the waistband. I handed the scissors to Liona.

"Cut it the rest of the way off of her."

I spread the clean linen out on the bed next to her.

She lay naked from the waist down and uncomplaining.

"What's wrong with her?" Even Liona, unexperienced in the birth room, knew something was amiss.

"I'm not sure. Lace your arms under her shoulders and help me lift her to the bed."

Liona nodded and we lifted. She was far lighter than I had expected. The baby's position hadn't changed.

"No," I heard her say, grunting. Her knees came up as if on their own. Her stomach stood up from her body, her muscles doing their work. At least I knew she was English. The *no* was unmistakable.

"Grab her knee and push it up," I instructed Liona.

The baby's head inched further down. The woman opened her eyes for a second, and then turned her head away.

"You're going to have to push," I said to her. Her head turned back toward me, and with the next contraction, she did as I said, and pushed.

The head came out completely. I tugged gently, and the body followed. The baby girl lay limp between her legs. Blood gushed out behind her.

"Is that normal?" Liona watched the red seep into the straw mattress.

"No, it's not."

I picked up the lifeless body from the pool of blood. She flopped over in my arms, her tiny hand lying open against my skirt. Long and delicate, her fingers jerked in the smallest of spasms. I looked at Liona. She had seen it too.

A blanket rested next to me. I grabbed it and started rubbing the baby, turning her over and working on her back, rubbing her hard. Slowly, little by little, she came to life. Eventually, she let out a gusty wail.

Liona's hand rested on the forehead of the child's mother. She shook her head. In that brief time, the woman had died.

"What do you want us to do now?" she whispered to the dead woman.

I wrapped the baby as best I could and looked up. A small crowd had gathered at the entrance to the women's bunks. The women either watched in horror at the bloody scene, or turned away in disgust. The men averted their eyes. Liona took a blanket and covered the dead woman.

The captain pushed his way through. "She assured me she was nowhere near to givin' birth." Disgust laced his tone. "Single girl like that has no business being in that condition anyway."

"What was her name?" I asked, holding the squirming baby in my arms. It let out a mewling sound that drew the attention of the women in the room.

"I'm not sure. I'll have to look through the records. Anders, would you be willing to make another coffin? It looks like tonight we will have two burials. Probably three, but the baby can go in with the mother." He looked at the baby in my arms before he huffed and turned to leave the room. The crowd parted, and then slowly drifted after him.

Anders, Liona, and I stood in the room alone with the baby.

"Does he think the babe is dead?" I asked Anders.

"No. He's leaving it up to us."

I stood, planted to the dirty floor. The captain expected me to let the babe go with the mother. The thoughts of how that might be accomplished filled my mind. I felt the bile rise to my throat.

"No," I said, holding the babe tighter to my chest. She moved against me in protest.

"I know," Anders said.

I had sat under the captain's sermon the day before, listened to his prayers, prayed with him. I kicked a soaked pile of soiled linen out of the way and left the room, babe in my arms.

The mid-deck still reeked. The people still worked. They paused to watch me stalk up the stairs into the open air. I dragged my wet, blood-stained skirts to the area where the nursing mothers gathered and sat. I opened my bodice and put the babe to my breast. She pushed her tiny face toward me and took my nipple in her mouth. The strength of her suckle tugged all the way to my spine. The thought of placing such a life in the ocean, closing her up in the box with her mother, letting her take the sea into her lungs, was incomprehensible. I would have gladly consigned the captain to the box in her place.

How he blamed the mother for her condition without even knowing her made me want to spit in his face. I watched him walk around deck, giving orders, glancing occasionally in my direction.

"Brianna," Liona's hesitant voice interrupted my thoughts.

I looked up. She held Victor in her arms. He was anxious to get to me too. Liona placed him in my lap. I handed her the babe and Victor took off where the babe had left. It was a ritual we would practice again and again.

The babe settled into the crook of Liona's arm.

"How could he say such a thing?" She sat next to me on the deck. I just shook my head.

For the first time I looked up. The women surrounding me averted their gazes so not to meet my eyes. These were women I had talked to when language didn't hinder, women who had shared stories of their homes and plans for their futures. Apparently, even holding a bastard child indicted me in the crime. I looked back to Victor. Did he matter so much more because his parents had been married?

Liona placed her hand on my leg and leaned in to whisper. "I don't think they hate the babe so much as they are worried you might ask them to help." She had read the disgust in my expression. I closed my eyes and forced my face to relax.

I took a deep breath and addressed the women seated nearest to me. "I won't ask you to take a turn nursing," I reassured them. "I understand fearing for your own children. I think I will have enough milk for both of them."

It was their turn to look down.

"I'm sorry," one of them mumbled in English. Whether sorry for the situation, or her reaction, I couldn't tell.

"Is it a girl or a boy?" another woman asked.

"A girl."

Hulda and Hjalmer walked over, holding hands, to sit at our feet.

"Did you watch Hjalmer and Victor by yourself for a while?" I asked Hulda. My mind was finally putting things in order.

"Yes." She studied the pattern on her dress.

"You did a good job. That was very grown-up."

Hulda looked up to examine the baby in Liona's arms. Hjalmer reached out and touched the baby's fingers. The baby's fingers curled around Hjalmer's, and held.

Two coffins waited at the edge of the deck. They were well made. One the size of an adult, the other, smaller, for the child who had died during the storm. The child's parents, still ill themselves, held each other up.

The captain said a few words, and they lowered the small coffin into the water. Holes were drilled in the sides and the top to let the water in. Weights were added inside to make it sink. The parents watched it disappear under the still water.

"Lower the other coffin," the captain ordered the sailors standing by. It was clear the woman was to be buried without the honor of a few words.

"Would you mind if I prayed?" Anders stepped nearer to the coffin.

"Do as you please," the captain mumbled to Anders, keeping his eyes on me.

A few families stayed. They bowed their heads out of duty. Anders prayed. She was lowered into the water while her baby slept in my arms.

"How are we going to do this?" Anders considered the two bunks as he held Victor. "He's not going to sleep with me."

"I'll have to take the top with Hulda and Victor like before. Only now I will have the baby too."

"Is that even possible?"

"It's not going to be comfortable, but is anything comfortable on this ship?"

Anders lifted Victor to the top bunk, and I handed him the baby. I climbed up after, and he handed her to me. Hulda followed. It would be a long night, but we were already past the halfway point of the trip. One thing was sure. I would never attempt it again. If everything were to go wrong in America, I would still be glad to stay if it meant I wouldn't have to step a foot on a ship ever again.

"I want to go up," Hjalmer whined to Anders, tugging on his jacket. I heard Anders's voice answering him, but not the words he said. They were effective though, because Hjalmer settled right in to sleep.

Liona had not been looking forward to the women's quarters. After the body was removed, and the evidence of the worst of the horrors erased, the women had counted their own cost. Two less bunks—they didn't want to sleep on the cursed places the dead woman had occupied—and their illusions of the beauty of pregnancy shattered. Of course, they rationalized the turn of events as the unmarried woman's just due. Liona told me she planned to go to bed after everyone else was sleeping, and get up before they woke.

I laid the baby between my knees and lifted Victor to my lap. He knew it was time to feed, and he was growing restless.

"Can I hold her?" Hulda asked quietly.

She was getting older. She would remember this trip. Part of me was glad. She would be stronger than I ever was, but the part of me that wanted to shield her from the awful truths that played out in the lives of the people sharing this small space with us bucked against the part that was proud of what we had accomplished.

She held out her hands. They were the hands of a girl who was almost ready to understand. I nodded, and she picked up the baby, supporting her head just right.

I touched her cheek and her eyes met mine. I wanted to apologize to her that I wasn't tucking her into bed in our beautiful home in Karlskrona, and I wanted to say I was sorry she would never know the comforts that belonging to our family should have provided. But I wasn't. I wasn't sorry, because if we had not been here, the little girl Hulda held would be on the bottom of the ocean with her mother. Even the Christians on the ship refused to help. They prayed on Sunday and would have let the captain smother the baby on Monday. I prayed we had the strength to raise our children to see the value in taking the more difficult path, and I prayed they would never seek comfort over integrity.

"She's so pretty," Hulda whispered, touching her soft, pink skin. The baby breathed easily. I could hardly believe she survived the birth, let alone the horrendous conditions of the ship.

"You need to lay down now and sleep too." I laid a sleeping Victor on the bed near Hulda's feet and took the baby from her.

Hulda nodded and yawned. She rested her head against the straw mattress, and fell asleep to the gentle rocking of the ship.

Anders snored quietly from below. The people to the left and right whispered and snored and coughed. It didn't disturb me anymore. I rested my head against my bunched up jacket and turned on my side to fit the baby between Hulda and myself.

The baby woke every couple of hours as one might expect. She fed and fell back asleep, and I was thankful I had been the person to find her mother. I was grateful God had chosen me to save her.

The whistle blew again, which meant the captain wanted to speak to the passengers.

We left what had become our typical post at the rail near the back of the ship and shuffled toward the front.

The captain stood on the deck area outside of the bridge. We all craned our necks to see him. We were flying through the water under full sails and steam, and we all felt the end approaching. It was amazing what a single seagull sighting could do for the mood of an entire ship.

"We will see land tomorrow," the captain announced. The man next to Anders slapped Anders's back, and they exchanged an enthusiastic handshake.

"Just because we see land, it does not mean we will dock right away. It is common to have to spend some time anchored out until a dock opens up, or until they are ready for us."

He could have said we had to wait a month, and people would have still felt like cheering. We wanted to see land. I wanted to see green. I wanted grass under my feet, and my fingernails full of honest dirt, not the filth that caked them now. I curled my fist closed to hide the grime.

"When you disembark, there will be long lines to stand in. Be prepared to wait. Everyone must be processed. You will all be inspected for health, and you will all be required to register. After—and only after—all the requirements are met, will you be allowed into America."

The people around us cheered. The babe in my arms gave a soft cry. I whispered in her ear. Victor, in Liona's arms, clapped with the rest of the passengers.

"When you first step into the streets of Philadelphia, there will be people waiting to assist you. They will offer you everything you expected and dreamed of. Do not talk to these people. They are thieves, and they know you come off the ship with everything of value you own. If something sounds too good to be true, it is, and don't let your plans change. If you were going to live with your family in New York until you get on your feet, then go to New York. Don't let a stranger sell you land that doesn't exist. Contrary to what you may have heard, there are evil people in America, just like in every other nation. Be on your guard."

I watched the faces of the people surrounding us. I knew they only heard half of what was said. I wanted to warn them that Lars was probably there—that he had beaten his wife, that he'd abandoned his family, and that now he was probably living in America, enjoying a new start, and finding new victims.

The captain completed his instructions, and we returned to our place at the rail.

Anders had asked the captain for the deceased woman's name. She was Flora Daniel. At least that was the name she gave to the captain when she signed on.

Our own, old names were still tucked in my pocket. With my back against the rail, I pulled the paper from my pocket and rubbed out the sweat-creased folds. They had faded from the journey, but it was of no consequence. We had signed names we would never again use. Anders held our new identification.

I stood and studied the water. We were still too far away to see land. Liona sat nearby with the children. I counted them, something I had done countless times in the past couple of weeks. Again, I came up one short. We left her in Sweden, resting under a tree.

In my daydreams she was always about seven. Perhaps it was different for other mothers who had lost babies, but for me she was always a child, able to run with her brothers and sisters, laughing and playing in the tall grass, trailed by strawberry braids and waving to me from the distance as I hung laundry or washed dishes.

I took the new babe in my arms, and she nuzzled closer. She wanted to be fed again. I made my way toward the other women and sat in their circle. As far as they were concerned, the babe was mine. I thought the captain was likely of the same opinion. He hadn't even asked what we would do with the child. I wasn't even sure what we were supposed to do.

I nursed her and visited the women with halting English sentences. Sometimes someone would utter a Swedish phrase, and for a minute I would feel like I was at home. The women didn't know my name. They never asked, and neither did I ask theirs. Names, I had learned, were of no consequence.

We knew one another by our actions, our smiles, our arguments. When all was stripped away, and we were equal, labels became useless. We all had tasks to complete, and, in this instance, they were all the same. Keep the children healthy, stay as clean as possible, check for lice, find food when the children were hungry, and try to sleep when it was time to sleep.

That night I knew some of the passengers were planning on dancing. Those who had brought instruments would take them out, and they would celebrate. I found myself anticipating the distraction with some excitement. I might put on a clean dress. Anders might ask me to dance. Much time had passed since we had shared a bed.

I finished nursing and walked to the rear of the ship where there were fewer people. The water churned from underneath us, and I thought back to Sweden, to my sister standing on the docks. The paper with our names was still in my hand. Reaching over the rail, I dropped it. It fluttered to the blue and white surface of the ocean. I was surprised how quickly the water took it away.

"What are you doing back here?" Anders's voice came from behind me.

"Thinking."

"About what?"

"Nothing important." I turned to face him and looked up.

His eyes rested on my face and traveled down across my jaw line and down my neck. "I'm looking forward to reaching dry land." He took a step nearer.

I hummed and rested my head on his chest. "I'm looking forward to a bath."

I could feel his smile against my hair. "Yes, that too. Should we go back to the children? It's just about time to wait in line for dinner."

We lingered for a moment. One last night. Only one.

Chapter Twenty-two

We woke up the next morning to a lavender line of dry land in the distance. It was so far away, it could have been mistaken for a bank of clouds.

"I think I can smell the land," Liona said. She stood next to me at the rail holding the new baby. Victor wrapped his arms around my neck.

"I don't even want to go back down there to get our things. I would almost be just as happy to get on shore and leave everything here if I never had to choke on a smell like the one in the rooms ever again."

"I agree completely." Liona glanced back to the stairs that led to the mid-deck. "You would think they would put in more ventilation or something to help—at least more toilet facilities."

"Is that Philadelphia?" Hulda leaned over the rail, pointing to the line that expanded across the horizon.

"Part of it must be."

"When will we be able to get off the boat?"

"It will be awhile yet," Liona answered. She made a move to trade Victor for the baby, who wanted to be fed again. I had forgotten what feeding every couple of hours really meant. Primarily, it meant I was hungry. I had taken to walking around with a pocket full of food. The decision to bring extra had been a good one.

Hulda held Hjalmer's hand and followed Liona through the crowd in hopes of finding an unoccupied bench. I took the baby back to the circle of nursing women.

They stopped talking as I approached, so I kept walking to the back of the ship.

As most of the passengers were excited to see the line of land, the back of the ship, pointed in the direction of our past, was largely unoccupied. I found a metal bench in a quiet corner and sat to nurse the baby.

The ship, we were told, would not be docking. Instead, we would be loaded onto barges and taken into port. Why this was, they did not see reason to explain, but we did as we were told, packed our things and stood ready.

And stood ready some more.

I held the baby, Anders held Hulda's and Hjalmer's hands, and Liona followed with Victor.

We were first loaded onto large, flat barges with our things and standing room only. The few crates we had packed would follow later. Anders was not pleased about trusting they would reach the shore, but as a whole, the group of us anticipated the feel of land under our feet too much to see fit to complain. The captain watched us walk off with the baby.

The smell of the docks filled our senses first. We leaned over the side rail to watch the brown water slosh against the side of the boat. Fishermen pulled in their rigging and wound it around huge iron piers while the small boat captains jumped onto the docks to negotiate prices with buyers. Primarily, men walked the docks, but there were some women, dressed in foreign styles and walking with their heads high. They walked like the men, with confident steps and swinging arms. Everyone was in a rush to get to somewhere important. I looked forward to having something to do besides try to keep my family clean with limited resources.

The barge slipped toward the dock. Soon the sailors leaned over the railing, measuring the distance to the heavy wooden piers, until they finally threw the thick rope to a waiting man. Land, at last!

The people behind us surged forward. We were pushed and pulled up the ramp, organized into lines, three deep, and ushered into a large room with green walls and long benches before we could even take a moment to relish the feel of the dry ground under our feet.

Where the building started and where it ended was difficult to discern.

Surrounded by so many people, it felt as if we moved from barge to building without so much as a glimpse of the cloud-covered sky.

People shouted directions in English so fast I couldn't make out their words. I looked at Anders, and he pointed to a short staircase. The steps and railings were painted the same color green as the walls. At the top was a door with a glass window. The blind was drawn. All eyes were on the door.

"This is the medical check. When they open the door, we will go through there to be examined before we are allowed to register," Anders leaned in close to explain in Swedish.

I nodded.

"What do you think happens if someone is not healthy enough? Do you think they send them back?" Liona asked from behind.

I hoped not.

The door opened and a matronly woman with a long thin nose stepped out. She spoke loudly and slowly, nodding her head with each shouted point. Again, the crowd moved forward around us, and we found ourselves pushed toward the stairs.

The baby was getting ready to feed. I had seen a number of women give up the struggle for privacy and feed their children while standing in line. I looked at Liona. She maneuvered the bag off her back and pulled out a blanket. We draped it over my shoulder so I could join the ranks of women who had lost all modesty.

Once through the door, we followed one another in a line. Anders was first, and I watched as they opened his mouth and looked in. They pulled up his shirt and examined his skin. He buttoned back up as the matronly woman squeezed my checks with her fingers, forcing my mouth open. She lifted my chin, then pushed it down and checked the skin on the back of my neck.

"No." Hulda pursed her lips closed when the nurse reached her.

"Hulda," Anders chastised.

She stiffened her back but complied.

Hjalmer gladly held his mouth open.

When we had passed the medical screening, we were herded into another room. Opposite the dingy, ocean-facing windows, a row of stone-faced clerks stood behind a counter. Ledger books open, and pens in hand, they took down the names of each person. We followed roped-off lines until someone asked us, "Name?"

"Blomberg," Anders responded. "Anders Blomberg."

I wasn't prepared for how strange the names sounded when put together.

"Birthdate? Country of birth?"

Anders answered. He gestured to me. The baby squirmed, and Hjalmer pulled on my skirt.

"I'm hungry," Hjalmer said.

"Brianna," I answered the man.

He adjusted his glasses. "Spell that please." He didn't look up from his paper.

Anders answered, adding the Blomberg surname.

"The baby? Birthdate?"

I gave the date. He looked up from his papers.

"Born on the ship?" The corners of his mouth turned down.

"Yes." I stepped closer to the counter. Anders put a hand on my shoulder.

The man met my gaze long enough to make sure I understood his contempt.

He sighed and looked back down at his ledger. "Name?" he asked, resigned once again to his powerless position.

"Esther," I said. "Esther Blomberg."

We stepped out of the registration building and onto the streets of Philadelphia. Storefronts lined the wide boulevard on one side, warehouses on the other. Shadows from the buildings spread long and thin toward us. Anders walked over to a small window that had Exchange Money Here on a sign in several different languages. Liona and I rearranged a few of the things in our bags and discussed plans for dinner.

Anders made his way back to us. "We need to find a place for the night." He looked over our heads to gauge the traffic. "Hopefully somewhere for the next week or two."

A number of carriages lined the side of the road. A dark haired Irish-looking man jumped from the seat down to the street near us.

"Take you somewhere, sir?" He nodded and took a couple steps in our direction.

Anders looked at us and turned back to him. "Yes. We need to find a place to stay the night."

"Say no more." He held one hand up to communicate he understood us. With the other, he picked up one of the bags and lifted it to the back of the carriage. Anders began helping him load the rest of the things on as we climbed in.

"I'm going to ride with the driver," Anders poked his head into the carriage.

I nodded, settling Victor on my lap.

Liona leaned back against the cushions. "Do you realize it has been over two weeks since we last sat on a cushioned chair?"

I leaned my head back and the horses lurched forward.

As we moved, the streets changed. The docks were grimy, but hopeful. I was sure at night the atmosphere changed, but at least I was not fearful. But as the streets we drove down narrowed, so did the apparent affluence of the city. People shouted from the windows of upper apartments that hung over storefronts like an afterthought. An overabundance of unattended children darted between moving vehicles on the streets. Butchers hung fly-covered meat out in the open. Women paraded with their breasts pushed up to impossible heights. They waved and winked at my husband seated above us. Hulda turned big eyes toward me, attempting to read my face. I looked straight ahead as if nothing was amiss.

The streets continued to narrow, until laundry hung overhead, strung from one building to the opposite. It surprised me, but I found I glanced down each alley to see if Lars lurked in the shadows. The fact that we'd traveled to the same place he'd run away to didn't ease my mind. I imagined this place, a place where people's less-than-white undergarments flapped above us in a festival of harsh reality, was the kind of place where he'd be. The carriage slowed in front of a dingy grey building.

Liona read the uneven letters painted in the window. "That's a hotel," she whispered, placing her hand over Hulda's ears.

I heard Anders jump from the top of the carriage. He opened our door.

"This is a cheap place to stay. We are going to go down the street farther. I already explained to the driver that we don't need someplace this inexpensive."

I nodded, emphatically. He smiled and reached in to touch my cheek before closing the door and lifting himself back up to his seat.

The carriage lurched forward again, and we were driving fast. I sat back to watch the greys and browns slowly lose dominance to red and tan brick, black iron, and the occasional green patch of grass, or even tree.

Liona smiled out the window at no one.

The rooms we found we rented for two weeks. Long enough to make sure we had reclaimed everything we had brought over and make plans for our trip to Minnesota. We would go by rail through Chicago. We wanted to rest a bit first, especially with a new baby.

"I didn't expect that," Anders whispered while lying in bed that first night. The sheets were fresh and the pillows stuffed with feathers. I rolled onto my side and faced him. Moonlight streamed in through the window, illuminating his features.

"Neither did I." It was the first time we had a chance to talk since we disembarked. He was talking about the baby's name, Esther.

"He was so angry about the baby," I said of the clerk who asked her name, "and for some reason, I never thought to think of a name for her before then. To be honest, I thought the captain would stop us, or at least maybe there would be some official we could speak with, but we were pushed through the line so fast, it was the only thing that came to mind."

Anders nodded.

"And then, when he looked at the baby like she didn't even have a right to be there, I could only think that if we still had our Esther, she would have been with us anyway. So I just said her name."

"Well, it's her official name now. I'm more concerned with finding her family, if she has any."

"Do you think the captain will report us?"

"I can't see that happening. It wouldn't surprise me if he wrote in his journal that both mother and baby were lost in childbirth." Anders stared at my face. He reached up and ran his index finger across my bottom lip. "I miss you," he said, leaning in to whisper against the curve of my ear. The children slept in a bed next to ours, and Liona was nearby, in a small room of her own.

"Me too."

"We will have to post the mother's name wherever we can down by the docks. That way if someone is looking for her, they will at least know where to find us. I will also contact the churches in the area. I can always check the records at the city hall for anyone who lived here under that name. We don't know, she might have lived here before and was returning home."

There was one last thing to talk about.

"What if we don't find anyone?" I met his gaze, trying to read his expression.

"Then I guess God saw fit to return our Esther."

Hulda sighed and rolled over in the bed next to ours. We had all had baths and eaten a hot supper in the dining room of the hotel. I brushed everyone's hair with a lice comb in hopes of removing any pests that may have hitched a ride. Hulda's hair I had braided in tight wet braids that ran down her back and dripped onto her nightgown. I had never appreciated water, let alone hot water, so much.

I rolled over to face the children's bed. For Esther, we pushed one of the trunks tight between the two beds, made a cushion out of a blanket, and placed her between us. It would be nice to sleep without her on my chest, but I missed the closeness. I reached out and touched her cool cheek with the back of my fingers and worried. I hoped if we would have to return her to her family that they would love her as much as I did.

Chapter Twenty-three

July 1881 – Philadelphia, America

We woke the first morning in America to the city sounds of passing vehicles, people talking, doves calling, and slight headaches all around. Finding one's land legs, we learned, was surprisingly similar to the experience of acclimating to life at sea.

A very green Liona greeted us and was promptly sent back to bed.

Anders rolled over and rubbed his eyes. "I didn't expect to feel like this."

"Neither did I." I pushed my pillow to the head of the bed and picked up Esther. "Good morning, baby." I brushed Esther's cheek. "Hulda, would you wet that rag and bring it to me?"

Hulda yawned and staggered to the wash basin. "I feel sick." She handed me the wet rag.

"It's getting used to the dry land." I unpinned Esther's diaper and cleaned her bottom. I pinned a fresh diaper on and lifted her to the sunlight. She had blue eyes like the rest of us.

"She has strawberry hair, just like our other Esther," Hulda said. "Are we going to keep her?"

"We have to see if we can find her family first," Anders said. "If we can't, then we will raise her. It will be better than the life she would live in an orphanage."

"What's an orphanage?" Hulda asked.

"It's where children without parents go to live."

"Oh. Is it nice?"

I looked at Anders.

"Hulda," he said, "would you like breakfast in the dining room this morning, or would you rather go for a walk with me to find that bakery we drove by yesterday?"

Hulda jumped up. She shrugged on her dress and then wiggled her sleeping clothes out from underneath. We'd all learned to live a little closer while on the ship, and that included becoming efficient at dressing in a room full of people while maintaining a sense of modesty.

I shrugged. For as hated as the voyage was, we had all learned a few things.

We knew anyone expecting to find Esther's mother would likely be looking for her at the docks. That was where Anders started the search.

Liona and I, noticing a park across the street, decided we would rather spend the day here sitting in the grass than in a carriage, searching for someone we had never known. We followed Anders out of the hotel. People darted back and forth on the sidewalk. The women, dressed in bright colors and carrying handbags that matched their dresses, paid us no heed. They marched to the steady click of heels on cobbles as if they were headed somewhere important and could not be late. Passing men nodded to Anders.

He climbed into a waiting carriage. It pulled away from us and down the boulevard. Liona held Victor, I held Esther, and Hulda and Hjalmer held hands between the two of us as we crossed the street.

Giant trees dominated the sky over the park. Glimpses of blue and white slid by behind the leaves as the breeze carried the clouds from where we were, maybe to where Anna sat in Sweden.

"How is this?" Liona was already spreading a blanket under the leafy canopy. I picked up a corner and smoothed it, then placed Esther in the center. She was so small. Hulda sat cross-legged next to her, letting Esther's fingers wrap around her own. Hjalmer stretched out in the grass, breaking pieces off and throwing them into the web of a harassed spider.

I sat on the blanket and raised my face to the sky. The sun warmed my skin, and the breeze cooled it. How anyone could feel a life at sea was in God's plan was beyond my understanding. I stretched my legs out in front of me and leaned back on my hands.

"Do you know what your plans are?" I asked Liona. She was educated and pretty, and I knew she wouldn't be with us forever.

She paused before she responded, listening to a passing couple's casual conversation.

The woman wore a lavender dress, buttoned to her neck, with lace adorning the wrists and collar. He wore a striped suit. Our clothes were shabby in comparison. My own sturdy shawl was stained with baby mess, and the buttons of my shirt strained against the pressure of milk for two babies. I folded the stain under.

With so much opportunity, Liona could have any life she wanted.

"With the new baby, won't you need extra help?"

"Of course we will. I just don't want you to think you have to stay with us." I gestured to the lovely couple who had just strolled by. "It's not like it is in Sweden. You won't have to always be a servant in someone else's home. Not that that's how we think of you, but someday you might have your own home and family."

"I understand. Truly. For now, I want to travel with you. I might eventually find a husband and a home, but I will stay on, at least until you reach where you will settle."

"Good." I smiled, relieved. "I really don't know what I would do without you. Besides, I would miss you terribly if you were to leave."

Liona smiled in return and reached to open the bag with our lunch. Hjalmer moved closer to the food. Esther had fallen asleep.

"Would you mind if I walked over there for a few minutes?" I pointed to the edge of the park, where a stone cathedral towered over the trees. Stained glass shone in shards of color.

"Not at all." Liona waved me away.

I stood and tried to brush the dust from my skirts. I remembered the days when I would have spent hours choosing what to wear before walking around the town.

The gravel path that cut through the park took a meandering route through a stand of pine trees that smelled like home before emptying onto the street. I crossed, climbed the stairs, and stepped up through the heavy oak doors held open with large bricks. There was no service taking place. I heard a coin drop behind me. An old woman had placed it in a box near a stand of candles. She reached for a match and lit one, then folded her hands in prayer. I tried to muffle my echoing footfalls.

Statues of the saints lined the walls in curved alcoves. They looked down on the empty rows of pews, some of them sad, some disapproving.

It had been so long since I had set foot in an actual church building. I ran my hand over a wood railing, where countless others had probably done the same. There was a sense of belonging, of security. I found a place to sit in the last row.

A man walked in. He couldn't see me in the shadows, but he was dressed shabbily, his shoes worn to almost nothing. A priest I hadn't seen drifted over to stand next to him. I heard the rumbles of a conversation but could not make out the words. The man turned to leave, shoulders as slumped as when he entered.

The old woman watched. If life were fair, he would have been the son she probably prayed for, but he was not. She turned back to the candles, and back to her prayer.

The smell of burning wax drifted over me.

"Can I help you with anything?" The priest stood at the end of the row.

I just nodded, knowing my own halting English would be insufficient for a conversation. His eyes traveled down my dress and rested on my practical, but worn shoes. He nodded and turned away.

A statue of Jesus hanging on a cross towered at the front of the sanctuary. His eyes were closed, and his thorn-pierced face, gaunt. Painted blood dripped from his feet and down the carved cross, but stopped a respectable distance from the stone floor. Even Christ knew where his blood was welcome and where it was not.

I stood to leave. Even in America, where people had the freedom to worship as they pleased, they still chose religion over the cross. Then again, it was different. There was no one telling anyone they had no choice. I knew there must be others out there like us.

Outside the building, the sun blinded me momentarily. People rushed by, carriages rattled down the cobbles and the trees in the park whispered over it all. The man who had stepped into the cathedral sat to one side of the stone steps. He didn't look up as I passed, until I reached into my pocket and pulled out an apple. I placed it on the stair next to him. Then he looked up. He was dirty but had eyes as blue as the ocean. He thanked me in a language I didn't understand. I nodded and crossed the street, knowing I had been to church.

Anders secured the tickets west, and on a Tuesday morning we set out to meet the train.

It heaved its way to the platform, steam escaping from the stack at the front, and from somewhere beneath the huge engine. The bored operator chewed on an unlit cigar while we climbed the metal stairs into the passenger car near the front of the train.

We knew of a number of people from Sweden who had settled in the Minnesota area, so we decided to head that way as soon as we could make the travel arrangements. Anders still carried the address of Mark and Pia's minister, living near Minneapolis.

After two weeks of looking for Esther's family, she was ours. Anders had left a message with the police in case anyone ever looked for her mother. Unsure exactly where we would settle, I spent the last few days in Philadelphia purchasing things a baby would need. I had not packed most of our baby supplies before we left Sweden, so Liona and I had headed out while Anders stayed with the children. He gave us specific instructions where to go and where to avoid. We came back weighted down with practical items: blankets, diapers, and tiny clothes. I bought stockings and a bonnet to keep the wind from her ears, as we were not going to unpack the crate with my crocheting until we settled.

And now we were ready. Anders stooped under the door behind us and handed our tickets to the steward, who promptly pointed to a door at the end of the car. He squeezed to the side to let us by. We pushed our way through, bags catching on the backs of seats. The already seated passengers grumbled at the intrusion. Our family never seemed big to me until it was time again to travel.

At the back of the car, we stepped through the door, outside, and then entered another car—identical to the first. Another steward, seemingly identical to the first, pointed us to the rear in the same manner. We did this three more times before we reached the cars with separate berths. I looked up at Anders. The corner of his mouth kicked up in half a smile.

"I thought this might be a nice way to travel since we will be on the train for a while."

"Can we afford it though?" The seats were cushioned and soft. A bunk folded down on each side overhead, and the seats doubled as narrow beds. There were three curtained windows and a door that slid closed. It had a lock.

"There are toilet facilities at the end of this car," Anders said with pride.

"I thought we would be sitting in the passengers seats day after day, and trying to sleep there at night. I wasn't looking forward to it at all. This will be nice, especially with a baby."

Liona stepped in the room and clapped her hand over her mouth. "Will we ride here?"

I nodded in response. Hulda jumped up on to the upholstered bench and stretched out.

"You won't have that much room." Anders pushed her legs off and sat next to her. "I figure I will sleep on one of the bottom bunks. Hulda and Hjalmer can sleep on the bench across from me. That leaves the pull down bunks for you and Liona. Esther will sleep with you, I'm sure, and Victor can sleep where he is most comfortable. With Liona or me, or he might even fit on the bench with Hulda and Hjalmer."

"That sounds fine." I pulled open a small closet and stowed away one of the bags.

"The dining car is only a few cars away. They will also bring food around for us to purchase if we would like."

"We probably have close to enough right here." I patted one of the larger bags. It held the remainder of the provisions that had traveled and sustained us for the entire trip, along with a few things we bought before heading out.

The whistle blew.

"It won't be long now until we are on our way." Anders watched the people outside, rushing to board before the train pulled out of the station.

"Did you ever think there could be so much land with no homes, or farms, or anything?" Liona watched out the window as the landscape sped by.

We'd made our way through the mountains, and over flat, open spaces that begged to be tilled. "I'd bet they don't even have to pick rocks out of these fields," Anders said what I had been thinking.

"Who do you think owns all this land?" Liona asked.

No one answered, as neither of us had an answer.

Hjalmer slept with his head on my lap, and my leg was falling asleep. I tried to shift without waking him.

"Once we find our place, I will never leave to go any farther than a horse and carriage can take me," I said, trying to stretch the cramp that had tightened in my back.

"You'll have no complaint from me." Anders still stared out the window. "The conductor said we should reach Chicago by tomorrow morning. We'll have the day there to spend in the city after we switch trains for the one that continues on to Minnesota." He stretched his long legs as far as the narrow space between the seats would allow. "What do you think, should we go to the dining car for dinner tonight?"

Hulda looked up and smiled. For her, it was an adventure.

Me, on the other hand—I couldn't wait to get settled.

I opened my eyes to the predawn grey and slid the curtain over to see the still moving landscape. It had taken me no time at all to adjust to the rocking of the train, and I had slept well, with Esther next to me. That way she could nurse on and off throughout the night. She squirmed and blinked awake, and the realization that she was mine seeped in. I touched her soft cheek and wondered if I would ever tell her the truth.

Anders had arranged for her mother's trunk to come with us. We had opened it to see if there were names of any relatives in any of her things, but we found nothing. When we settled, I planned to open them again and try to make out what kind of person she was.

The view outside had changed. Buildings loomed dark against the horizon and filled the sky with a veil of soot that held the sun at bay for longer than it should have. I pulled the curtain open further and looked down. Additional tracks ran along ours, and I knew we must be getting close.

"Anders?" I whispered into the dark of the compartment.

"I'm awake," he whispered back.

"Have you looked at it out there?"

"Yes."

"What do you think?" I glanced again out the window. We rushed through industry after industry. The outlines of individual workers standing in line, holding their lunch pails, and waiting for factories to open, stood out against the monstrous brick buildings.

The smells of city life seeped into the train.

"I think we'll want land in the country. That's a must."

"I agree." I dropped the heavy fabric and picked up Esther so she could nurse on the other side. We hadn't spent too much time discussing exactly what we would look for in land to purchase. We didn't know what would be available for sale. While we both knew purchasing a house in the city was a possibility, the contrast between the rich landscape filled with grass and trees, and the one of the city, solidified our need for space.

"I want trees," he whispered up to me through the bunk.

"And water, maybe land with a small stream running through?"

"Yes."

I pulled the curtain open again. The sky was turning a hazy shade of red and the train whistle blew.

"It's amazing how we traveled from fields and forests to buildings and people overnight," Liona said, watching the view out the windows with the rest of us.

Hjalmer sat up, and Hulda, next to him, stretched and yawned. "Are we there?" She sat up and pulled the curtain open. "Chicago isn't very pretty."

"No it isn't. We're only stopping here. We're not staying."

Hulda took a deep breath, and I marveled again at how fast she was growing, and how aware she was of the risks we took. I prayed our lives would be good enough here in America for her to be grateful for the sacrifices we'd all had to make.

Chapter Twenty-four

We spilled out of the train and stood on the platform blinking. Philadelphia had felt nothing like the bustling, pressing city that brushed by. Loud conversations were yelled from one end of the station to the next. I was constantly turning around to try to make out who was shouting, and if they were trying to win our attention. Of course they were not, we knew no one. Chicago was the first place that fact was truly evident.

"Will they transfer our trunks, or do we need to do something with them?" What we could possibly do was beyond me, as I wasn't even sure what car of the train stowed our belongings.

"They should do that. They gave me a ticket to claim them when we get to Minnesota." Anders patted his breast pocket. "The next train won't be here for a couple of hours, so we can take a walk before it arrives."

"Let's get away from the trains." I gestured toward the glass station doors and Anders picked up as many bags as he could. We took the rest, and moved through the packed crowd.

Once through the station and out onto the street on the other side, we stopped to take a breath. There were still a lot of people, but it was quieter. Anders pointed to a restaurant down the street. "Let's walk that way."

We all agreed. It was near lunchtime.

The bored waitress met us at the door and seated us near the front windows. I would have rather sat near the rear of the restaurant, as none of us were looking our best, but I reasoned it was a restaurant near a train station—they likely didn't have the highest of standards for attire.

The café curtains were pulled to one side, and we watched people cross in front of the window—women pulling lagging children by their forearms, and children dragging tired mothers by their skirts. Suddenly, I longed for some sense of normalcy. I remembered the days where I would wake up and know not only what I would do that day, but what I would be doing for the next week or month.

Tiny storefronts lined the other side of the street. There was a jeweler and a small grocer. Directly across from where we sat was an office with a wooden shingle hanging out. It read LAND AGENT.

"Maybe I should go see what he has for sale?" Anders had read it too. He was already standing.

"We'll wait here." I was looking over the menu, attempting to decipher the options as well as calculate the costs.

"I wonder if he has land available all the way in Minnesota," Liona said.

I hummed in agreement, trying to count out how much the food would cost if we were still in Sweden. It made no difference; we were already seated, watching steaming platters travel from the kitchen to the tables of waiting patrons. Not one of us intended to move.

Anders stood on the sidewalk, waiting for a carriage to pass before jogging across the street. Dirty puddles covered the road. He avoided them and reached the land agent's door.

"Where's daddy going?" Hulda asked.

"He's going to talk to a man about buying land."

We ordered, and the food arrived. It was good, with moderately familiar touches—noodles and meat, but with a bit of German flavor. Anders returned just as we were finishing. He walked between the crowded tables, the other patrons leaning out of his way.

"I know we talked about going to Minnesota, but what would you think about Wisconsin?" He sat down next to me and pulled his chair in with a loud scrape. The people near our table glanced over, then turned back to their food, making comments I couldn't understand.

"Did the land agent have something interesting?" I leaned in, trying to encourage a more intimate discussion.

"There are forty-acre parcels near a place called Ogema. They are wooded, and one of the parcels has a modest cabin we could live in until we can build something proper to get us through the winter."

"Where did the people go who lived there?"

"They were homesteaders who decided to move on."

I took a bite of the food in front of me, tasting nothing but giving me time to think. "Did you ask why they decided to abandon their homestead?"

"He said they decided to return to Sweden."

"There are other Swedish families there?"

"Oh yes, and a couple of names I recognize from the Karlskrona area."

Liona looked up. "Who from Karlskrona?"

Anders recited a couple of names that were familiar—people I had forgotten had come to America.

It was a relief to know there would be familiar families, but the feeling that I'd hoped for when we decided where we wanted to live—the peace that came along when all was right—evaded me.

"I wish we had time to ask them if they are happy there before we make a decision," I said. "It doesn't seem right that someone would abandon a forty-acre farm."

"That's the thing," Anders said. "The train for Ogema leaves tomorrow morning. The next one is in two weeks."

"Can we get our luggage transferred off the train in time?"

"The land agent assures me he can."

"Do you want to do this?"

Anders paused before continuing. "Yes. We talked about living in the country. I know we have a few acquaintances in Minnesota, and I can get a job there, but it is the city. It's a different set of opportunities."

I nodded and glanced toward Liona. She smiled.

"If you feel good about this, then I think we should go," I said.

Anders smiled the same smile he had when we first pulled away from Sweden, and stood up without touching the food on his plate.

"What do you think?" I turned to Liona.

"I think it's nice that other Swedish families have settled there."

"I want to learn to speak English better, but I must admit it will be nice to be able to speak Swedish and be understood."

Liona tapped her finger on the table and leaned in. "I have noticed the people here talk fast."

"I thought it was just my own slow understanding."

"It looks like Anders is on his way back."

He was crossing the street again, headed back to the restaurant. Hulda craned her neck to see. She didn't like it when anyone was gone for any length of time.

I gestured to the waitress we were ready to go. I took the meat Anders had left cooling on his plate and put it between two slices of bread. I wrapped it in a handkerchief and put it in my bag for him to eat later on the train, remembering how the captain had told us not to change our minds on where we were going.

We stayed in a nearby hotel, listening to the train whistles blow. The one that should have taken us to Minnesota left without us or our luggage, and early the next morning we boarded the train for Ogema.

The others on the train were headed elsewhere. They traveled with us for one of the multiple stops between Chicago and ours. I was glad to leave the city.

Once beyond the industry and the disturbing odor of the slaughterhouses, the grass began to turn green and trees sprouted. The farther we traveled from the city, the larger and more natural the landscape. I sat back and watched out the window, knowing that afternoon I would see my home.

The land agent assured us the land had everything we were looking for, including grassy areas perfect for tilling into fields, woods that would supply enough lumber to build our cabin for the winter, and even a stream. I hadn't thought Anders was paying attention to my mention of a stream, but when he told us about it the night before we got on the train to Ogema, he did so watching my face.

The first task once we reached the homesteader's house would be to build a cradle. I glanced down at Esther. She watched my every movement. My arms ached from holding her constantly, but we were almost home. I balanced her on my lap and rolled the stiffness from my shoulders.

"Do you want me to take her for a while?" Anders asked. He hadn't offered like that before. I nodded and lifted her to his arms.

She nestled in, tiny and pink. He stroked her cheek with one of his fingers and she turned her head for it, searching for something to suckle. He smiled down and tucked her in more securely.

Liona sat next to me, I turned my face to hers, and we both blinked back tears before we satisfied ourselves with watching the landmarks fly by the windows, occasionally glancing back to Esther when we couldn't help it. Liona reached over and took my hand in hers. We held hands until Hjalmer crawled up in my lap and announced it was time to find lunch.

It was late afternoon when they announced the Ogema stop and the train screeched to a standstill. From the windows, there was little to see. We were the only people getting off at the stop, and we stepped down to a wooden platform with no station. There was a tiny office centered in the middle where a man stood behind a counter, waiting to sell tickets.

Attendants dropped our trunks and crates on the platform next to us and the train whistle blew. As no one appeared to want to buy a ticket, the man at the counter slowly slid the window in front of him closed, then pulled the shade by the hanging string, watching us until the green fabric blocked his view.

"The land agent was supposed to wire ahead to his partner who lives here, and he was going to meet us at the station."

I wondered if maybe we'd missed the station somewhere. The platform with a small shingled hut—where an attendant hid—did not meet my expectations for a station.

"Mr. Blomberg." a voice called from the entrance to a small general goods store on the other side of the dirt street, separating the railway from the rest of the town. "How good to meet you." He climbed the three stairs and reached to shake Anders's hand.

"Nice to meet you too."

"First things first." He tucked his thumbs into his suspenders. "We need to get you out to your land with as many of your things as possible. I'll have my boys pick up the bigger crates and bring them out to you later tonight. My wagon is just over there."

He gestured with his elbow to a plain box wagon with an unmatched pair of tired horses. Hulda stared at him, and he cleared his throat before bending to take one of the bags and leading the way to the wagon. We picked up as much as we could and followed. I considered how wasteful it would have been to drag the things we brought all the way from Sweden, only to have the crates and trunks disappear at the last leg of the journey.

"Don't worry," he said to me in Swedish. "My boys will be along shortly. You will have your things before nightfall."

I was embarrassed for doubting, but more for the relief I felt at the Swedish tones in his voice.

We piled into the wagon—one last leg of the journey—and the horses lurched forward. Hulda pointed out things of interest to Liona, while I tried to decipher what Anders and the man talked about in the front seat.

We passed a nice home, two stories with an attic. It was surrounded by apple trees and tilled land. The man pointed to it, and Anders looked back to me. I nodded. It was a fine house, indeed. We drove past.

The road narrowed until it was only two ruts snaking through a field. Eventually, as I watched out the back of the wagon, the path continued to disappear until the only sign of anyone having been there were our own tracks in the tall grass.

"Here we are," he announced.

Confused, I craned my neck, searching for where "here" was.

"The house is down that way," he explained in Swedish. "The homesteaders never did cut a road, so this is a far as I can go." He watched us until we grew uncomfortable and unwillingly moved to get out of his wagon.

"Where will our things be dropped?" Anders asked, standing next to the wagon, looking up at the man who remained in the driver's seat.

"They will bring them as far as here, and then you are responsible for getting them the rest of the way to your house."

"And where is the house?"

He pointed toward a line of trees. "See that post with the yellow marking on it? That marks the path. Those posts also mark the borders of your forty acres, so you know where your land stops and the next starts."

He coughed. "I need to go and make sure your things are on the way. Let my boys know when they get here if you have any questions." He tipped his hat and his wagon rattled off down the road.

I sat on a nearby burned-out stump, held Esther to my chest, and cried. We'd traded everything. Absolutely everything. And for what?

The cabin was a shack. Rather than proper logs, hewn to fit, it was mainly constructed of planks nailed to upright timbers with a sod roof. The door hung on one wooden hinge. At least the floor was planked rather than dirt. It was a small miracle. The room boasted a window opening with no glass and a bedframe with rotted ropes and no mattress. It also contained a crumbling fireplace.

"It appears we will need to build immediately," Anders said in a hopeful tenor. I knew it was for my sake, and it wasn't deluding me. A straw broom leaned on one side of the fireplace. I handed Esther to Liona and picked it up. My first brush across the floor brought what seemed to be decades-worth of dust from the cracks. Liona picked up the bag I had just carried in and took it back outside. I continued.

"Maybe I'll go and wait for our things," Anders said.

I hummed a response and gave the floor one mighty sweep, filling the room with a cloud of swirling dust. He slipped out the door.

I picked up the pace. For only one room, there was an amazing amount of dirt. It had to be removed if we were even to sleep in the shack that night. From the window I could see Liona spreading a blanket for the children to sit on while they waited. Of course, Hjalmer began exploring immediately. Hulda sat quietly next to Liona. Victor crawled into her lap.

The man who dropped us off called Anders "Mr. Blomberg." It was still unexpected, and I found myself holding my breath when it happened.

I would have never thought I would be a woman who had had three names. The one I was born with, my married name, and the one to replace the one we lost when we sailed. Hulda was old enough to remember. She would be a woman of three names too. I watched her reach for a nearby wildflower and pluck it from its home. She handed it to Victor, and then took it away again when he tried to shove it in his mouth. I wondered if she thought of her bed back in Karlskrona with the white linens and the armoire full of dresses made for everything but practicality. I wondered if she would miss the comforts her other name afforded her and regret the loss.

I thought of my room back in Karlskrona, with its ceramic-tiled fireplace and walls of books. I gave the floor one more sweep and set the boom back in its place.

A rough wood table sat to one side of the room. It would be inadequate for us all to eat at, but it was a start.

"Liona?" I called out the pane-less window. "Would you start bringing in a few of the bags we will need for the night? Hulda? Keep an eye on your brothers and sister, please."

She stood straighter with the responsibility and didn't flinch at Esther being referred to as her sister. For all her life in Sweden offered, that kind of resilience wasn't on the list. It was something that had to be earned, and she was earning it. I plopped a bag onto the table, unbuckled it, and pulled out the travel-weary items. I had washing to do and dinner to cook, somehow. I had a fire to start and beds to make. And I had a daughter who would be stronger, more independent, and more effective than I ever was. But I could learn.

"He's coming!" Liona shouted through the open door. "Some others are following too."

I wiped my hands on the apron I'd found and walked to the open door. The floor was swept and clean, and I'd cleared out one corner of the cabin to make room for the crates. While we waited, Liona had also helped me string rope from one end of the one-room cabin to the other, essentially creating two rooms. We were only missing the blankets to hang from the ropes. Those were in the crates.

"He's back!" Hulda jumped up and ran through the field to meet him. Shades of lavender were spreading through the horizon. We were running out of time. I surveyed the fire I successfully lit in the hearth. I was watching it closely, as the stonework on the chimney appeared to be crumbling at the corners. The timber mantle was pitched forward, so nothing I set there wanted to stay put.

"It's all here." Anders ducked through the doorway. "A couple of neighbors came by with a cart when they heard we were here. They're unloading it now."

"They can bring the things right in here." I pointed to the empty corner. Anders walked out to help. Seconds later, he was backing into the room with a large trunk in his hands. A thin man with blond hair that stuck straight out from his scalp carried the other side. He smiled a semi-toothless grin and dipped his head in my direction.

"Nice to meet you, ma'am," he said in Swedish. "Name's Sebastian. My wife is Nora. She's at home now. We live right close. The next farm over."

"Nice to meet you too." I had a hard time keeping the relief out of my voice. To have someone so close. After all the traveling. I had to blink away the tears.

"We can set them down here." Anders heaved out and bent over to put the heavy trunk on the floor.

The men both stood up and wiped their foreheads, Anders with his handkerchief, and Sebastian with his sleeve.

"I would offer you something, but I have no idea where anything is." I shrugged.

"Don't worry about it, ma'am. We know what it's like. We just moved here last year."

"How has it been for you?"

"Hard. The winter was cold. Last year's crops were difficult. This year things are looking better. So far the weather has been perfect for growing, and we were able to clear a bigger patch of land, so we have more in the ground." He looked at Anders. "Maybe we should get the rest in here. I'd like to get on my way before it gets too dark." They walked out together.

I took a key out of my pocket and opened the first trunk. In it were two kettles full of kitchen utensils wrapped in dishcloths. I handed them to Hulda and she carried them to the table. The first of many blankets lined the bottom of the crate, and I was beyond grateful for my reluctance to give up most of our quilts. We were going to need them while we slept on the floor. Anders would have to spend the daylight building the house, not constructing furniture. The cradle could wait. First, the house. We could not stay in this shack for long.

Anders carried in a crowbar. "I found my chest of tools." He began to pry one of the crates open. Liona, busy folding a blanket into a cushion for Victor to nestle into, motioned for Anders to be as quiet as possible. Victor had taken to crying after all the things had been brought in, and hadn't stopped. He needed to sleep.

"Here,"—Anders slid one of the chests over toward Liona—"put the blanket in here. It will be a bit like a crib."

"That cover has to come off though," I called across the room. "I won't even sleep if I think there is the smallest possibility that could close while we aren't watching."

Anders hummed in agreement, digging out a hammer and small spike from the chest of tools. He removed the hinges and the top of the trunk fell to the floor.

"We can use this one for Esther." He held up the rounded top as if he'd won a prize. "It will even rock."

Liona lined up the two makeshift cribs along one wall, filling each with its own blanket. Victor snuggled down right away, tucking his thumb into his mouth and rolling his eyes closed. I laid Esther in the other and touched the side with my toe. It rolled a slow rock from side to side.

"Here it is!" Hulda yelled out.

"Hush," Anders, Liona and I scolded at the same time.

"Oh, I found my doll." Hulda held up the treasure, and then stifled a yawn.

"Liona, would you help me get this blanket hung?" I knew soon we would all be too exhausted to do much more.

We split the room into two sleeping spaces. Anders, I, and the babies slept on the side with the door, and Hulda, Hjalmer, and Liona slept on the other side. I shook out a blanket, folded it over, and spread it on the ground. Liona did the same on her side of the curtain.

Once Anders and I had found our makeshift bed, and Hulda and Hjalmer were sleeping, Anders rolled over to face me. "I'll start tomorrow by going to town to get a few tools. Sebastian offered to pick me up with his cart to get supplies. If you want, you could make a list of anything you need now, and I can get that too." He paused to think. "At least there's enough timber on the property."

Moonlight streamed through the open window. Anders had muscled the door into place, but there was little we could do about the window, short of covering it with another sheet, and I wanted to feel the fresh air settling around us as we slept. After a month of travel, my lungs needed room to clear.

Anders rolled to his back and put his hands behind his head. "I'm sorry," he said to the rotting ceiling.

I watched his profile in the moonlight. His mouth turned down at the corners, and he closed his eyes before he continued. "If I had known, I never would have tried it. At the very least, we would have gone on to Minnesota."

"I'm not."

He hitched up on one elbow and studied my face.

"I'm not sorry." I studied his shadowed face. "We came here to find freedom from the people who wanted to keep us as we were—stable, settled, and ignorant of the lives of those around us." I sat up and looked at the empty window. "We thought we wanted to be free to worship as we pleased, but that wasn't it at all. What we wanted was to be free to learn to worship, and learn to live."

Anders nodded, but his eyebrows knotted in question.

"It isn't about finding the right church, or the right people to sing with. It's about learning to be like Jesus. In Sweden, we were wealthy. We were comfortable. We weren't exposed to need—either our own, or anyone else's. We were bound in our ability to grow closer to God due to our ignorance of the needs of others. But we found out, and we had to leave, not because the bishop followed us when we took communion in our home, but because he was part of everything that wanted to keep us ignorant of the needs of the community, and ignorant of the possibilities of the church."

"And what do you see that legacy as?"

A gentle breeze flowed in. It was cool. Anders sat up and pulled the blanket up around my shoulders. I looked across to Esther, sleeping in the top of the trunk, inhaling and exhaling easily.

"Her. It's her. It was the opportunity to care more about life than who her mother was. But more than that, it's the decision we made to do the right thing." I ran my hand over my arms. The muscles were sore from carrying Victor and Esther.

"We made the first step," I continued. "We brought our children to a place where we have the ability to act as we should, not how our families or our church dictates. We brought them to a place of hope. The real freedom is for them, but they will still have to earn it on their own. Freedom is only the tool, and it's just the first step."

I wrung my hands together. I rarely spoke my mind so boldly, but this was a new moment, a new country. "When we stopped on this land, I cried not because I realized the cost, but because I knew that coming here in search of freedom was barely the beginning—there is so much work to be done. I cried because all that we went through was only the preparation for what is to come. I cried because I now understand our path, and that there is no such thing as arriving. I cried because I was hoping to find who I was supposed to be in this new life, and now I understand that with freedom, I will never know who I am supposed to be, because who I am will always change."

Anders studied me with rapt attention, and so I pressed on.

"The only people who know who they should be are those who are told who they will be. I know now that I didn't come here to find a new life—I came here to live it. Arriving is what we will do when we die."

Anders reached for me and pulled me against his chest. "I love you," he whispered in my hair. "We'll do fine here. I'm still sorry this isn't what we hoped for, and I'm sorry we have to sleep on the floor, but I thank God for you, and that we all made it here safely."

He put his fingers under my chin and kissed me on the cheek, next to my lips. "I miss you." He moved his lips to brush against my ear. "I thought we might at least share a bed on our first night on our land." Disappointment rumbled in his tone.

I quickly brought my hand to my mouth to silence my laugh.

He pulled me down to lie next to him and rest on his shoulder, and we slept that first night in Ogema.

A mourning dove woke me with her soft, low song. The sun shone through the leaves of the trees outside the window. I opened my eyes to light scattered across the floor as if it had been spilled from a bucket.

Esther began her mewling, and I picked her up out of the trunk to feed and change her. The ring of axe on tree met my ears. Anders was already chopping. He'd said he would start right away, and he'd brought an axe from Sweden, so he was already working.

After Esther was settled, it was Victor's turn. He crawled over to our nest of blankets on the floor, and I fed him.

Hulda, rubbing her eyes, stepped from behind the curtained-off room she'd slept in. We'd all stayed in our clothes from the day before, and we all looked a wreck, but I imagined it would be like that for quite some time.

"Why don't you take an apple from the barrel and go outside with it?"

She walked over to the barrel that still held some of our provisions and took an apple from the bag we'd bought in Chicago before we'd boarded the train.

"Stay away from where your father is working," I said as she stepped outside. "He's cutting trees. Wherever he is, stay on the other side of the house. And don't go anywhere you can't see the house."

"I will," she called back over her shoulder, her braids bouncing behind her.

"How is everything this morning?" Liona asked in a tired voice from her side of the curtain.

"I think it's all fine. How are you?"

She moaned in response. "You would think with all the noise of the ship, then the cities we've stayed in, that a few crickets wouldn't keep me from sleeping. But there were so many last night, I'm not sure I even want to go outside. Where do you suppose they all go in the morning?"

"Probably under this house."

"That's not really funny."

I'd been joking, but when no one else watched, I planned to check, just in case I'd been right.

Chapter Twenty-five

September 1881, Ogema, Wisconsin

The day we lifted the logs to make walls for our home dawned bright and cool. I stepped outside into the grass. The heavy dew clung to the blades. My skirt brushed the tall stalks. They trembled and dropped their burden of water onto the toes of my shoes. I picked up the hot coffeepot with the edge of my apron and stood to see Sebastian and Nora walking toward us, followed by a mule and their daughter Lena, whom Hulda had already befriended.

Autumn was a busy time, even without trying to build a house, and with everything we were trying to complete before the first snow fell, we'd not had an opportunity to meet Sebastian's wife. We watched them take the long walk through the field. She was a tiny woman, obviously pregnant but unquestionably strong.

"Hi!" She waved, still a bit of a distance away.

"She's Irish," Liona said from behind me, picking up her accent in only the one short word.

Because Sebastian was Swedish, I'd expected Nora would be as well. My heart sank as I realized conversing with her would be difficult.

Lena scooted out from behind her parents and ran to meet Hulda. I poured a couple extra cups of coffee and set them on the table we had moved from inside the house to the outside. We had learned quickly that living outside was easier than living in the tiny shack. We only slept inside and stored our things there.

We had settled into a pattern over the past weeks.

Anders had woken each morning and started chopping early. In the afternoons, he would strip branches and bark, and pile up the logs. It was only a couple of weeks before there were enough to cut the notches in and set up walls.

He had drawn out the plan for the cabin. It was to be two rooms with a loft. One room for Anders and me and the babies, and the loft for Liona, Hulda and Hjalmer. The second room would be for cooking and eating. He enlisted Hulda and Hjalmer to collect rocks for the fireplace chimney. Their pile was growing by the day.

Hulda had found a friend in Sebastian's daughter, Lena, who was of similar age. They ran through the fields. Hulda sometimes followed Lena home and helped with chores there. In return, Lena spent time down at the stream collecting rocks with Hulda.

Liona and I developed a system to get through the days. It began with Liona collecting water from the well that was already on the property while I started a fire in the pit outside. Anders had dug the pit for me after he examined the fireplace in the house more closely. His assessment resulted in a directive to never light a fire in it again, unless, of course, we were ready to burn the shack to the ground. He also built a frame over the fire that allowed me to hang a kettle and placed a stone near the edge to set the coffeepot on. Once the stone was hot, it would keep a pot of coffee warm for most of the day.

We did laundry every day. The barrel that held provisions was emptied and sawn in half. We filled one half with hot water for washing, and the other with water for rinsing. Once rung out, we hung the laundry over lines strung from tree to tree. Eventually we were able to wash everything that had traveled with us on the ship. And finally, today, we would put up the walls with the help of Sebastian and his family.

"I bet you are excited to be moving out of here," Nora said, gesturing to the pile of wood we had called home. She spoke slowly and met my eyes.

To my surprise, I could understand her just fine. "Yes," I answered.

"I know a little Swedish," she said in Swedish. "Sebastian wants the children to be able to speak both languages, so he speaks Swedish to them at home." She smiled at my obvious relief.

"I need to learn to speak better English," I said in halting syllables, the words falling off my tongue like rocks.

"You speak lovely." She took the cup of coffee I held out to her.

Anders had already had the first few courses of logs laid out and the rooms were taking shape. He needed help continuing, however, and he enthusiastically shook Sebastian's hand in greeting. We watched them talk and gesture and nod their understanding. Anders pointed to where the front door would be cut into the logs. Sebastian began tying the mule to the middle of a long log.

"I'll go over and help," Nora said.

"No." I pointed to her stomach, my lack of language skills covering for a host of social sins.

"It's okay," she said. "Watch."

She walked over to the men, and gestured for Anders to give her the reins he had been holding for Sebastian. He shot a surprised look toward Sebastian and pulled the reins away from Nora.

"Don't worry." Sebastian laughed. "She knows what she's doing."

Anders hesitated before relinquishing the reins to her tiny grasp. She took them and slapped the backside of the mule until he tightened the slack on the rope. Sebastian had laid two other logs at angles against the wall, creating a ramp for the next log. He motioned for Anders to go to the other end of the log. With the mule pulling the center, and the men guiding the ends, they walked the log into place. It dropped into the grooves. A perfect fit. Nora clapped her small hands, turning to smile at Liona and me.

The rest of the logs were up by evening, and Sebastian and Nora walked back home in the remaining light. I wished I could have offered them dinner, or at least something for the journey back, but we had nothing appropriate to bring to a table—and no table to speak of either.

"How long of a walk is it to their house?" I asked Anders.

"It takes about twenty minutes." He stirred the pot of venison stew I had bubbling over the fire. "They'll be back tomorrow morning to help with the roof."

The next morning a team of the biggest horses I had ever seen pulled a wagon stacked with lumber to the new house. The wheels left heavy ruts in the tall grass and Hulda and Hjalmer raced back and forth down the paths.

The wagon slowed and the men jumped from their high seats and started loosening the ropes that secured the stacks of lumber.

A familiar form worked quickly to pull the lumber from the wagon, and I couldn't look away. My stomach twisted. I prayed I was not seeing who I knew was there. He stopped and turned and looked right at me.

We'd come across the ocean, crossed half a continent, and Lars Ankerburg stood in our field.

Anders looked up. His posture tensed and he took a step toward the man who had tortured his wife, abandoned his children, and then tormented us. But Anders stopped. Instead, he turned, looking for me. I ducked behind the shack we lived in before he knew I'd seen Lars. My husband didn't need to worry about me. He needed to deal with the evil that had followed us.

But what could we do? A hysterical laugh bubbled up from somewhere deep within. I covered my mouth to smother the impulse and headed into the woods. We'd come to the other side of the earth. And now we'd spent all we had on a plot of land only to be near the man who I couldn't help but blame for my baby's death.

I'd forgotten to tie on my shoes. The long grass between the trees cut into my ankles. I walked faster, punishing my skin with the sharp edges. I wandered until my legs ached, ignoring Anders calling, until I couldn't pace another step. Then I sat on a rock near the stream and dangled my feet in the cool running water.

I heard Anders before I saw him. He didn't speak. Instead he picked me up and sat with me in his lap like a child. I didn't protest. I was too tired to fight.

"He wants to speak with us," Anders whispered into my hair. My head rested on his chest, and I couldn't stop the silent tears from wetting his rough work shirt. We'd given up so much.

"Will you listen?"

"What?" I sat up and wiped my tears on my shirt sleeves, ignoring the handkerchief he held out. "Why would I even sit in the same room?" I struggled to climb off of his lap. "Why would you even think to ask me that? How could you even ask me that?"

Anders stood and looked down at me. "What choice do we have? I don't want to live constantly wondering if he'll be around the next corner. If he wants to talk to us, shouldn't we let him?"

The stream rushed by. It bubbled over the rocks and roots and eroded the soil at the water's edge. "I just don't think I can do it right now. We have to get the walls up. There's so much to be done."

"He already left. He wants to stop by later tonight. I told him we'll keep the cook fire going outside if you are ready to talk to him. If not, he'll not bother us."

Chapter Twenty-six

"They did a nice job." Anders ran his hand down the edge of a board. Back at the building site, I stood nearby, still debating my decision.

"That's the one thing this little town has—a good lumber mill," Sebastian said as he approached.

Anders reached out to shake his hand. "I wasn't sure what to expect when they first took the logs away. To be honest, I just hoped they brought something back to me. Where is Nora?"

"She said she wasn't feeling that well this morning. She decided to stay home. If she needs anything, Lena will come and get me. Should we get started?"

They stacked the lumber in two piles, the longest pieces for the roof, and the shorter ones for the floor inside the cabin. Liona and I walked back to the old cabin closer to the river, where we would begin the process of collecting mud, sand, and dry grass to pack between the new logs. This time I tied my skirts up around my knees and took the winding, sandy path to the edge of the water. Liona stayed with the children. I was grateful for the time to think.

The soil by the stream was rich in thick red clay. I carried a spade and a bucket. When I reached the edge, I untied my shoes, pulled them off, and waded in. It was only ankle deep in the little corner where the water swirled. At my intrusion, the fish darted away into the current.

"May I go see Lena?" Hulda's voice startled me. She must have followed.

"Are you sure you know the way?"

"Yes, we walked together lots of times."

"But you'll be by yourself this time." I knew she was old enough, and I knew I shouldn't be worried, but I couldn't help it.

"I know. So can I?"

She was growing. "I suppose. Take some cloth scraps with you, that way if you think you might be getting lost, you can tie pieces along your path, and we will find you faster."

"I won't get lost."

"Do you want to go or not?"

"I do."

"Then take the scraps."

She looked at my bare feet, and then turned to skip up the path.

I followed her with my bucket full of clay. At the house, Liona was collecting the dried grass we'd gathered the day before and bundling it so it wouldn't blow away. I dumped the clay in the pile I had already started, and headed back down the path. Thoughts of Lars lingered in my mind.

When I had collected enough clay, I moved to another area of the stream for sand. The buckets of sand were easier to fill. The work was hard, but there was healing in work.

By the afternoon, I had finished the project.

"Have you seen Hulda and Lena?" I asked Liona as I brought the last bucket of sand and dumped it on the pile. I had strung my shoes over my shoulder for the walk back, so I turned the bucket over and sat on it to tie them back on. If Liona noticed the scratches on my feet, she chose to remain silent.

"No, although I did expect to see them by now," she answered.

Hjalmer sat in the nearby grass, chasing any number of insects. Victor was tied to Liona's back in a sling of sorts and Esther was rocking in the trunk lid, just inside the door.

"Do you think we should walk over and make sure they are there? At least we can check to see how Nora is feeling."

"I could use a break." Liona stood and tucked a dark strand of hair behind her ear.

"I was thinking, I could bring a jar of our lingonberry jam. I'm sure it's been a long time since Sebastian has had any of that."

"That would be nice," Liona agreed.

Anything would be nice, I thought, if it took my mind off Lars and his impending visit.

Their house was over a hill and around a thick patch of trees. We took our time walking, letting Hjalmer discover things along the way. Esther stayed content in my arms. Soon, however, we were in waist deep grass, and Hjalmer held on tightly to my skirt.

"Have you ever seen grass so tall?" Liona slid her hand along the blades, careful to avoid the sometimes sharp edges.

"No, I haven't."

We reached the top of the hill and looked down at Nora's house. It was quaint, with a small barn running alongside. Her garden was a patch of green against the yellow-green of the long grass. Hulda ran toward us.

"What's wrong?" We picked up our pace to meet her halfway down the hill.

"She had the baby!"

I stopped short. "What?"

"She had the baby," Hulda repeated before she turned and ran back toward the house.

"I think she was alone." Liona's horrified expression matched mine. She grabbed Esther out of my arms. "You'd better run."

I reached the door, out of breath, and burst into her kitchen ready for the worst.

Nora stood next to the stove. "Hi," she said. She appeared fine.

"I'm sorry, Hulda said you just had the baby, I thought you might need help." I grasped my side. It ached from the run.

"I did." She turned, and I looked down at her relaxed stomach. "She's right here." Nora slowly crossed to the bedroom door and pointed at a cradle filled with white frills.

"Oh." I didn't know what to say. Liona burst in behind me, and I stopped her from coming farther into the room.

"She had the baby," I explained.

Liona looked at Nora with wide eyes as Nora moved to sit on the side of the bed next to the cradle.

"It happened so fast," she explained slowly. "I wasn't feeling well, and then I felt the baby's head. I called in Lena and Hulda. They helped."

I started mentally listing the things I would have to explain to Hulda that night. Liona looked fairly traumatized. The only birth she'd seen was the one on the ship.

"Why didn't you send for a midwife, or for us? We would have helped," I said in the best English I could muster.

"There wasn't time, Mama," Hulda said from behind. "She started feeling the pains, and the baby was here." Hulda walked to the edge of the bed and looked down at the baby with pride. Lena carried in a tray with tea and a few crackers.

"It really was a very easy birth," Nora reassured me. "I had just sent Hulda to tell you when you started down the hill. I'm sorry if the news startled you."

"Isn't she pretty?" Hulda said. She reached out and touched the baby's pink fingers. The baby opened its eyes and looked up at her.

I felt the jar of jam, heavy and inadequate, in my apron pocket. I didn't want to give it to her. Here she was, standing, going on with life, after just giving birth. She was relaxed, satisfied, and happy. I could offer her little.

"Is there anything we can do?" Liona asked.

"I don't think so. The girls took care of everything; they heated up water to wash the baby, they took the dirty linens to the basin, and they even took care of my chores in the barn. They were really very grown-up." She assessed them with a critical eye.

Hulda's cheeks turned pink at the compliments, but she stood taller, and rigid with a new determination. I wanted to have something to give. I glanced back to Hulda, seeing hints of the woman she would become. One who was so bold and confident that she could change her own life. I felt the jar again in my pocket.

"I know it's not much, but I wanted to give this to you." I held the jam out to Nora.

"Is this lingonberry jam? Oh, Sebastian will be in heaven. He talks about it all the time." Nora took the jar and set in on the table next to her. "You didn't have to bring me anything." She smiled.

"I know, but we really appreciate what you have done for us."

"You've already done more than you know. You've raised a girl who can handle an emergency like it was a streamside walk. And you came here. To us."

And I understood. I understood the value of being surrounded by people who were determined to overlook differences, even if it was because there was simply too much work to dwell on anything that didn't make the day a productive one. And I understood what it meant to be strong, to choose to be strong. I looked at the humble jar of jam on the table. It glowed rich and red, and I understood that trying to determine value was a fool's errand.

I straightened and gestured to Hulda to join us. "If you are sure you don't need anything then, I suppose we will be on our way, and we'll let Sebastian know."

Nora reached inside the bassinette. She pulled the tiny baby from the blankets and laid her on the bed between her knees. "Hulda, thank you so much for all your help," she said while staring at the new life in front of her.

We backed out of the room. "Why don't you run up ahead and tell the men," I said to Hulda.

Liona and I walked in silence most of the way home. For some of life's surprises, there was little to talk about.

But others required conversation. I knew our cook fire would be burning late into the night.

We heard his footsteps coming out of the dark, and I couldn't force the tension from my spine. Anders reached over and took my hand.

The fire outside the cabin burned bright. Warmth and light radiated, but the chill crept in. I waited for Lars to come into the light.

Eventually, he did. "Ma'am," he said with a slight bow.

His clothes were inexpensive, but clean and nicely pressed. His weathered face looked older than he was. Deep lines etched his cheeks. His nose was crooked to one side. His smile flashed, faded and flashed again.

I nodded my greeting, not trusting my voice. Anders stood and shook his outstretched hand.

Lars settled on a stump on the other side of the fire. I could see he didn't know where to start, and something inside me wanted to help him. He took his hat off and twisted it in his hands. "Ma'am." He nodded to me. "Mr. Modig." He shook his head. "I mean Mr. Blomberg." He took out a handkerchief, wiped his forehead and then stuffed it back into his jacket pocket. "I know it's not worth much, but I wanted to say I'm sorry."

I couldn't look away. He was sincere.

"I'll start at the beginning, I guess." His hands shook.

"I left Sweden. You knew that, I suppose. I was running. I guess you knew that too." He unbuttoned the top button of his jacket and dropped his hands into his lap. "I got on the ship, and the captain found my booze. He took it." He wiped his forehead with his sleeve this time. "I did some pretty bad things before I left. Bad things to your family, bad things to you. Things I will always regret."

I tried not to, but I couldn't stop thinking about Astrid, about my baby, about his children.

"I know I don't deserve it, but I hope someday you will be able to forgive me." He paused and took a deep breath before continuing.

The buttons on his jacket caught a glimmer of fire. They shone. He was no longer poor. "Even before I got on the ship, I knew your baby died. I visited her grave. It was my fault. If I hadn't done what I'd done, maybe you wouldn't have had her so early, and maybe she would have been healthier. And the things I did to Astrid"—even in the firelight, he paled—". . . I don't even remember all of it. I can't even tell you what happened. I just knew I couldn't go back. But on the ship—I wasn't in control—the captain took the booze I'd hidden, and I had to face what I'd done." He looked at Anders, and Anders nodded his encouragement.

I couldn't look away.

He took in a shuddering breath before continuing. "Not drinking was killing me. I thought my insides were turning out, and my head felt like it was on fire. I had nightmares; I relived what I had done to you and to Astrid. It felt like pins pushed into me over and over. Then someone put a cool cloth on my head, and for all the raving, he stayed with me. He was a minister, traveling from England to America."

"He held me when I was sick and fed me from his own stores of food. During the darkest nights, I thought he was an angel." His voice broke, and he took an intense interest in his own rough hands. "He brought me back, and when I realized all I'd done, and wanted to jump from the back of the ship, he stopped me with scripture. *"For sin shall not have dominion over you: for ye are not under the law, but under grace."*

We sat in silence, listening to the fire sparks crack.

"What are you doing now?" I let myself ask. A glimmer of hope flashed across his features.

"I work at the lumber mill. It's a decent place. And when I can, I send money to Astrid. I know she could never be with me again, but at least it's something." He shrugged. "What I did to you, I knew it was wrong. When your baby died I thought even God wouldn't have me."

Lars left with my stunned forgiveness and a handshake from Anders.

We watched him make his way down the road as far as the firelight allowed.

And then we sat alone, watching the glowing embers.

"We're all running from something, aren't we?" I reached for Anders's hand.

He nodded and looked up to the stars.

No one left a life when all was well. And we could fool ourselves into thinking that we left for opportunity, or to worship God as we chose, but we really left because we hoped it would be better in America. We really left because we were not happy where we were. Our dissatisfaction might be born of our own decisions, or might be the result of the actions of another, but once we arrived, we were all the same. We all had the same decision to either make this new life better, or to live in a way that encouraged history to repeat itself.

Anders took my arm, and we walked back to the cabin. We had more in common with Lars than I had wanted to realize. We had more in common with everyone than I had thought possible. Every day we had decisions to make; I had decisions to make. We could be strong or weak, and we could choose to see others in the same light.

I didn't know if Lars would be able to cling to his newfound faith, but that wasn't for me to ponder. I was only responsible for my actions, and in a new place, on the other side of the world, we would move forward, not back.

Chapter Twenty-seven

The first night in the new house would have been a night to celebrate, if we had not been too tired. We'd moved the rest of the trunks and crates in, unpacking what we could, and storing the rest at the perimeter of the room. Near the end of the day, Anders carried in Esther's mother's belongings.

"Where should I put this?" He held up the small, plain trunk.

"You can set it over there with the others." I pointed to the growing stack at the end of the room.

"Dinner is just about ready." I placed bowls around the table Anders had built. He'd also made long benches, and Hjalmer was already crawling across to sit in his place near the end of the table.

We ate together, sitting in our tiny but sturdy cabin with the shutters open to the late summer evening breeze. Later, after we ate, we brought the benches outside and sat leaning against the house. Hulda and Hjalmer chased each other in the fading light. When they would get too far away, Anders would call them back to the house. He repeated this until the stars appeared and it grew too dark to watch them play.

"Go climb in bed now," he told them.

They complied with twin yawns.

"What will you do tomorrow?" I asked.

Now that the cabin was done, the pressure was off to get things completed. I had already tilled a small garden and put in some late plantings, hoping for a warm autumn and at least a few vegetables to put up for winter. I'd also planted Anna's bulb in the ground. I knew it wouldn't bloom until the next spring, but I'd found the perfect hiding place for it. It was near the stream, where the sunlight fell through the overhead leaves—where I imagined my Esther, the baby I left, would play if she were with us.

"Did you know there's a church in town?"

"I heard Sebastian talking about it when he was here."

"Hulda told me that Lena goes there," Liona said from her place on the other bench.

"I thought I might go and speak with the minister tomorrow," Anders said. "The church is called the First Swedish Baptist Church."

"They have services in Swedish?" I stood and brushed a few pieces of grass off my skirt. "The day after tomorrow is Sunday. I'll have to find some clothes that would be suitable. They'll likely need washing and pressing. Liona, have you seen the iron? I know we brought one."

"I take it you'd like to attend." Anders laughed.

"I thought there wouldn't be a service for us—at least not in Swedish. I thought we would have to hold our own services again." I sat back down next to Anders and looked up at the stars. "Do they hold baptismal services?"

"They are a Baptist congregation."

"And no one bothers them?"

"No." Anders reached over and covered my hand with his. I thought of the summer day when we had gone under the water and come up new. I had wanted to breathe deeply, lie in the grass, and watch the clouds move past, leaving shadows on the fields.

"I'm going to go in to sleep." Liona walked through the door. I heard her climb the ladder to the top loft. Hulda murmured something to her. I couldn't understand what she said, but I knew it was a plan for the next day.

That was something we would all learn to do.

We would plan our days, because how we spent each one of them mattered.

Author's Note

I grew up listening to my grandmother's stories about her grandfather, Hjalmer and her Aunt Hulda. Later, as an adult, when looking through old photos and family documents, I found a transcript of her Aunt Hulda's childhood memories.

I was, to put it simply, astounded by the richness and depth of her story. The tale of the persecution her family faced, the trials that brought them to Wisconsin, and the grace and maturity she possessed regarding the things they gave up in pursuit of religious freedom reminded me of how much I take for granted every day. It also reminded me our own potential for strength.

My grandmother's family was determined and faithful, and I knew their story should be told. So I sat down to start working on my first novel.

But writing it was not as easy as I had planned.

Before stumbling across Hulda's words, I had never even considered becoming a writer. I knew nothing about craft or about the industry, but I began playing with the story anyway. First I tried to tell it from Hulda's perspective. I quickly found that her childhood voice was too young. Next I worked on her mother's story. It was there where the main character found her voice.

It also became apparent that I would have to change a number of events recorded in the transcript. Entire storylines had to be created just to give my characters motivation. I wrote and rewrote. It took me years to do justice to the simple truth in Hulda's words. The result is this novel, inspired by a true story.

When I look back now, I can see how that heritage of hard work and faith—communicated through a nine page transcript—was enough to inspire me, over one hundred years later.

It is my hope that this story inspires you to do what you thought was impossible. And it is my hope that you have the assurance that what you put effort into today will not return void. In fact, it might give someone, a hundred years from now, the inspiration they need to accomplish something they never thought they could.

From the transcript of the historical Hulda Blomberg Wickland's Journal

Childhood Recollections

It is with a heart filled to overflowing with praise and thanksgiving to my Heavenly Father that I pen some very weird childhood memories, and I can join with Psalmist in saying, for the Lord is good, His mercy is everlasting and His truth endureth to all generations.

My very first memory of childhood brings me back to a scene which often flashes before me and it has blessed my entire life. Seated in the comfort of my mother's lap, I was taught to sing a hundred songs which, in effect, tells of Jesus on the cross, wounded and bleeding for my sins and that I might someday live with Him. The message of that song and the loving words of my mother in a simple manner, she explained the blessed gospel story that made an impact upon my young life and implanted a seed which has grown throughout the years. I was only three years old then.

My father had the contract to build an army base at Karlskilna [sic], Sweden. He was a stone cutter by trade and had three hundred men employed in blasting rocks and cutting stone. Karlskilna [sic] was a very wicked and ungodly city with no Christian witnesses. There was a religious group called Sjatuaner [sic], but they had no knowledge of salvation. Mother was raised in a very pious home. Her father was religious and lived an upright life but had never experienced true conversion or the new birth. When my parents were married they went to Smaland, Sweden, where father had his contract, but both were grieved by the ungodly life down there and there was no one to whom they could turn, or who could point them to the lamb of God, which taketh away the sins of the world. In their despair they called on the Sjatuaner [sic] priest and he advised them to live a good life and that gradually, step by step, they would attain salvation. This, praise the Lord, they found to be false teachings, and they only became more and more unhappy as time went on. They had nothing to cling to, it was all so empty and barren and they felt themselves drifting farther and father away from God.

Finding no help among the people, they turned in anguish to God and cried unto Him that He might send some good Samaritan to show them His way. The God, who promised that if we call upon Him and He will answer, heard their cry.

One day there came a man to our home seeking work. He was from Varmland, Sweden. When father promised him work he asked if he could room with them. Father said no, but he was persistent, and father finally sent him to inquire of mother, and she could not turn him away. God was working in His own mysterious way and it wasn't long before it became clear to them why he had come. God sent him in answer to their hearts' cry. He began to speak to my parents of spiritual matters, and while mother warned him to be careful of false prophets, father said, "I believe this young man has the real thing." It was through his faithful witness that the precious Holy Spirit worked upon my precious parents' hearts, and they were gloriously saved. Father could not keep quiet but witnessed wherever he went of the saving grace of Christ Jesus and of His transforming power and many were saved through his testimony.

One young man who roomed in our building and who played the violin at dances was also saved and later became a preacher of the gospel and shepherded a church in Omal [sic], Sweden.

When God works, Satan becomes busy. The most ungodly blacksmith was the one Satan used to stir up trouble and to oppose the work of God in their midst, and he got all the others to join him. Father had a meeting one night in a little place about a mile from home (one Swedish mile equivalent to seven English miles). We were all along and as we drove over the crest of the hill we heard unearthly noises, the intoxicated blacksmith cried with a loud voice, "Now we will stone the preacher Blomberg." I began to cry with fear and Aunt Augusta held me tight while mother clung to little brother Hjalmer. Mother cried out to God Almighty to intervene and father commanded the chauffeur to drive on. We couldn't tell what happened but we knew that God had answered our prayer for not a stone touched us and we later learned the first stone had hit one of their members and they began to fight among themselves. As God opened the Red Sea for the Israelites, so had He opened a way for us and stayed the enemy.

Father continued having services and many souls were saved, but Satan again made an attempt to hinder the gospel. One day the enemy decided to kill my father. The instigator was one Oscar Ankerburg. They had learned that a meeting was planned at one of the workers' homes and the way to that home was through a dense forest and it was there they planned to seize my father and stone him to death. On the way to their hideout they came to our home to frighten mother so they rushed up to the door and demanded that our hired girl come out and dance with them. Mother locked the door but then they came around to the window and looked in, stuck out their tongues and cried, "You will die before my very eyes for this." It was an experience I shall never forget. Mother trembled as a leaf and was as white as snow. Then they rushed to the spot where they would lay for father. They lined the road and with a handful of stones they would bombard him as he came along. When father saw them he lifted his heart to God and cried for help and walked through their lines. As he looked back he saw them again fighting each other, bedlam reigned among them. When he reached home to find all well. Then was there another praise and thanks service.

A short time after this experience my little sister, Esther was born. She lived but four months and though I was but five years old I can never forget her moans of pain. "The same moans" I had heard from my mother that frightful night when she was threatened. Little Esther moaned and cried until one day God plucked her from earth and planted her in his garden. Mother's sorrow was so deep that she longed to go back to her home and loved ones in Varmland. Father knew she needed the change, and then he left his business with his brother Alfred and returned to Varmland with his family.

Uncle Alfred stayed with that work and became a well-to-do man. He married, raised TWELVE children and built himself a little villa outside of Sundsvall. His children were all well-educated and became rich in earth's goods, but as far as I know none of them HAD ANY KNOWELDGE OF THE LORD and were poor in matters that counted most.

God had chosen another faith for father—how carefully God does lead His dear children when they permit Him to lead and are willing to follow. We came home to Varmland and bought a little home a short way from Fryklands [sic] Stations. A Swedish mile from Karlstad, just across the bridge lived grandfather in mother's childhood home, her mother was dead. Her oldest sister and her husband took over the mill because grandfather was quite aged. Mother began to get stranger daily and father began once again to witness of all that God had done for them. Then he came in contact with some Baptists and was shown the need of Baptism as an outward symbol of what had already taken place in the heart and to follow the Lord all the way.

It was a chilly day when they traveled the Swedish mile to a place in northern Frykrud [sic] where a little chapel had been built. In a little lake there, mother and father were baptized by a visiting Colporteur. There were no Baptists where we lived so now father began to preach Baptism following conversion and among those baptized was a young man named C. J. Angstrand, who later became a well-known preacher in America.

Father baptized many there but now opposition began to arise among preachers and Bishops and then there was much confusion. Three of the leading men in the state church led the opposition and became very hostile toward us. They forbade us to hold services in the home. It grieved the saved and they gathered in our home for prayer. I can still see the large kitchen where they were all on their knees in prayer and they cried to God that He would stop the men from hindering the work and persecuting us. It wasn't long before all three were gone. One had gone up into his hayloft when the roof caved in and he was killed. Then we began to meet in the homes again but we dared not have Baptism during the day so we had them at night.

One night my father came home down to the lake with some people who had recently been saved and now desired to be baptized. A young man nearby heard them and began to mock and cry that they must baptize him too right away. Father was startled but remained calm and said, "Another will come and baptize you." A few days later he drowned in that very same spot. Be not deceived, God is not mocked for whatsoever a man soweth that shall he also reap. "Galatians 6-7" It caused real revival in the community and many were saved, but mother's sisters and brothers turned against her, all but the youngest, Augusta. She was saved and father baptized her also. Mother's oldest sister and brother became so angry when little brother Victor was born that mother did not allow him to be sprinkled, that one Sunday morning they came to our home, picked up Victor out of his cradle and ran to the church and preacher that he might be sprinkled. Mother cried but father consoled her with the thought that it could not hurt the child for he knew nothing of it.

Now father received word from Stockholm and we went up there and built a match factory and when that was completed he came home and built the Edsvalla Bridge. That was his last piece of work in Sweden. Now he yearned to go to America and he had no peace for there was a power that drove him on. We had been in Varmland five years and Esther was born there also. She took the place of the other little sister that we had lost in Karlskrone [sic]. Father went and worried how he would arrange things so he could make ready to go to America. He had to sell his home and furniture and all. While he went about worrying, God sent a Lutheran preacher who had once been in America. Anyway he and his family came down to the station at Frykrud en [sic] route back to America. They had to stay overnight to await the next train and upon inquiring as to hotel accommodations he was informed that Blomberg had plenty of room and they should ask to stay there. Father became enthused and he pleaded with the Lutheran minister to stay in Sweden and buy his home and let father, who was much younger, go to America instead. No sooner said than done. They began to unpack their trunks and we began to pack and were ready to leave in a few days. Can we doubt the Lord leading in it all?

We were now four children who crossed the Atlantic with mother and father. All went well over the Northern Sea and we arrived safely in Liverpool in England. When we boarded the ship to take us across the Atlantic father began to doubt a little if we had done the right thing for we were placed aboard a cattle ship where even the stalls were in plain sight. We had a young lady with us to help care for the children of the trip.

We could not eat, the food was terrible. Fortunately we had taken food along so we didn't starve, but fared well on dried leg of lamb, hardtack, lingonberry jams, cheese and butter. The weeks were long on the boat and all went well with only one day of storm, when the waves beat high and lashed the boat and we were warned to stay off the deck. Night came on and I slept but we awakened by the cried of people and found that water was pouring in so my hammock was wet. Someone had left the porthole open and it caused panic but soon several of the crew restored order and opened the hatch to allow the water to escape. For awhile I was sure we would never see America, but would go down in a watery grave. Mother with a quivering voice said, "If we come safely across I will never again want to try it." That she never did either. The young lady we had along to help care for the children had forgotten to watch my brother Hjalmer and he slipped away from her and had gone on the deck. When we found him he was sitting on the edge of the boat with one leg over the ledge and he explained to mother, "See I am riding horse back." Mother became so frightened she dared hardly to go over to him and when she did get him he was never allowed out of her sight for the rest of the trip.

I shall never forget the day when we saw land in the far horizon a cry of joy as we realized that soon we would be ashore in the new country. When we landed we were directed to a place where we would await the train that would take the immigrants to their destination. We landed in Philadelphia and while we waited we sat on long benches. Father went down to see that our belongings were claimed and while there a police officer approached him with a gentleman at his side and the officer asked father if he knew the man. Father said he did not and then he introduced himself as Oscar Ankerburg from Karlskroana [sic]. My father did not recognize him for he was so well dressed and dignified. When father returned with a stranger at his side we were startled and then we asked mother if she knew him, and when she learned that it was Ankerburg she became frightened but he had come to ask forgiveness of my parents. Then he related he had been saved shortly after they had left Karlskrona, and he had prayed that he might not die until he could ask my parents' forgiveness. God's spirit had moved him for weeks, he had had no peace and then he was led to go to Philadelphia, and voices told him to go to meet a boat there. Strange as it seems he obeyed the voice and when we stepped ashore he saw us and knew the reason for it all. God once again led in His mysterious way and his prayers had been wonderfully answered. He told of how he had often gone to my little sister's grace with flowers for after he was saved he learned that he had been the cause of her untimely death and mother began to rejoice that her little daughter's death had been the means of saving a soul.

Arriving in Chicago we decided to remain there a week and go on to St. Paul where some of father's fellow workers from Sweden were employed and they had informed him that there would also be work for him and the same kind of work as that which he had done in Sweden. Just as we were arranging our trunks to make ready for father's trip to St. Paul, a man sent by Ostergran, a land agent in Ogema, Wisconsin came and tried to interest us in going to Ogema, Wisconsin. We had some acquaintances there and the agent informed us that the state would make parks out of it and make it wonderful for the immigrants. It was of course a lie to fool poor immigrants but my father believed him and went along to Ogema. Had they known the trials that awaited them there they would never have gone, but it is a good thing that God veils the future and allows us but to see one day at a time. All the jealousy and hatred and persecution was hidden from his view, but father often thanked God for that too.

When the train stopped in Ogema and the man who traveled with us announced that we were there it seemed that all at once we were standing beside the train and mother leaned on an old black stump and wept, "Is this Ogema?" How the castled toppled about her. There was no depot, just a little store and some shanties. The land agent had quite a nice home for himself. The thought often comes to be that if we had but gone on to St. Paul when we saw how we had been deceived how different out paths would have been and how much heartache we might have been spared. The Lord knew best and we belonged to Him. With hardly time to think we found ourselves having purchased a forty of railroad land there stood a shanty which one of the immigrants had built. Several of the other immigrants with no money with to buy had taken homestead. To the little shanty on our forty we started a home. There was no road and we were directed to it by little marks cut in the bark of the trees. We carried our belongings in sacks on our backs. It was but a mile out there and that was far enough. Mother was not strong from the long journey and in another couple months brother Carl was to join the family circle.

Finally we arrived in the little home, it had two rooms, no beds so we slept on the floor on some quilts we had along from Sweden. At the little store we could buy what we needed but we had plenty in the oak chests we had brought along with us. Father got some of the immigrants who had come here the year previous to our arrival to help him, and in six weeks we had a large home built and into it we moved. Those whom he employed were all so poor and were so happy to have work. Father paid them every Saturday night as he was accustomed to doing in Sweden. We were all so happy to move into our new home and mother was the happiest of all.

After the home was built father was advised to peel the bark off the large hemlock because they were paying well for bark in Milwaukee. Many of the immigrants were employed to peel bark which they laid into piles to dry. They worked at it all winter, in the spring they loaded the bark on railroad cars and had it shipped to Milwaukee, only to be informed it wasn't well enough dried and was worthless, so it was a total loss and father even had to pay the freight himself. Had he been able to speak the English language he might have gone to Milwaukee to discuss it, but he was unable to speak and had to suffer the loss in silence.

When a company moved into Ogema and put up a sawmill we were very happy. They cut down a whole forty of large pine for us and hauled them to the mill but never paid us a cent because they had done us a favor in taking them off our land. The large pine stumps that were left were a big nuisance and we worked early and late to clean them away. Father would put a crowbar under the roots and then we children would hang on to the crowbar to loosen the roots. When potato planting time came we could not find the soil for the roots. Finally we purchased a horse from the boss of the mill. That eased the burden a little but one day a freight train went through and when they saw the horse they blasted their whistle and frightened him so that he ran up on the tracks and fell and broke his leg. The strain stood there and they demanded that father remove the horse, but father refused for they had caused it all. The railroad company would not pay for the loss of the horse so my father hired a lawyer and we won the case, but after witness and lawyer were paid there was little left. Then father bought a big ox and brought him home. He named him Bright. Once, the ox staged a run away and father became frantic for fear he would lose him also. He was unable to stop him but the ox was a faithful worker.

There is so much that could be told of the experiences we had in those years, and in every turn we felt the hand of the Lord. Like Job of old we would be tested and tried until we would come forth as gold. Father became very ill with rheumatism and aches in his muscles and for two years he was unable to work. He sought help in different places but nothing seemed to take effect. We were then seven children and there was much work to be done. We had to let the young lady we had along from Sweden go out to earn a living elsewhere. The money we had along from Sweden was almost gone and we all had to eat. Just then all seven of we children became sick with the whooping cough. Mother had a trying time when for weeks she did not get much sleep. God gave her sufficient strength to endure and she leaned heavily upon Him. I would hear her talk aloud at night when she sat and sewed our garments and she always had one of us on her knee as she sewed with the machine.

"Dear children," she would say, "I am talking to God." She seemed so happy after these times of communion with Him. During the years of my life I have learned that I can take the heavenly resources and be filled and happy.

My father became worse for each day and then one day we saw in the Swedish paper, "Vecko Poston" [sic] that a doctor had come from Sweden and he was what they called a "Water Doctor." Father remembered him by name for he had been a doctor in Karlskrona. He became so happy and wrote to him at once about his illness. Then he wrote back to father that he would not help him nor anyone else but he could himself if he had the patience. Father wrote to him and told him that he did have patience and then he sent a long list of what we should do; such as steam baths twice a week using an electric machine cupping. When father's good friend, A. P. Morner heard this he said, "No, don't do it." That frightened mother and she did not dare try it. But after three weeks father's leg was so swollen and he was so weak that he could not move. I had to help mother turn him in bed. Then father said to mother that he knew he would die anyway and she may as well try what the doctor had advised. She called all the children to her and asked us to kneel at father's bedside and pray as we had never prayed before and then mother took the cupping machine and started to work on father's thigh until she had cupped the whole hip. The blood was black as tar. After she had done it father arose and walked across the floor with no pain at all and in six weeks he was out splitting wood. It was then plain to us when we had done all we could that God intervened and did what He did. Praise His name.

God's blessing seemed to rest upon us and we were so happy in Him. That fall he bought another forty and the two oldest boys could help and then he bought more land. Later he built a two story frame home. Two little sons and two daughters were the joy of his later years and they were home to work the farm and help.

Just twenty years later after he had become so ill the Lord called him home. He was so happy to go home to the Lord. He left us with a good home and all we children had our separate tasks, I went to Chicago and took Nurses Training, Esther became a milliner, two sisters were school teachers, one a seamstress and the youngest daughter, Ruth, studied singing and music. My oldest brother became a blacksmith and also a policeman in his town. He worked in a large ammunition factory in World War One. The youngest son was in World War One and came home safely. As I pick out bits of memory here and there and know that they slip into the timeless sea I would cry out in joy. Thank the Lord with all my soul and all that was within me. Bless His name.

As told by Hulda Blomberg – Omega, Wisconsin U.S.A. 1871-1970

Soul Painter

Miriam paints the future...but can she change it?

CPSIA information can be obtained at www.ICGtesting.com
Printed in the USA
LVOW07s1855050515

437311LV00007B/960/P